WHAT THE DAY

Yasmina Khadra is the nom de plume of the Algerian army officer, Mohammed Moulessehoul, who took a female pseudonym to avoid submitting his manuscripts for approval by the army. He is the author of five other books published in English, including the acclaimed bestseller *The Swallows of Kabul*. He lives in France.

ALSO BY YASMINA KHADRA

In the Name of God
Wolf Dreams
The Swallows of Kabul
The Attack
The Sirens of Bagdad

YASMINA KHADRA

What the Day Owes the Night

TRANSLATED FROM THE FRENCH BY
Frank Wynne

VINTAGE BOOKS
London

Published by Vintage 2011

2 4 6 8 10 9 7 5 3 1

Copyright © Yasmina Khadra 2008
Translation copyright © Frank Wynne 2010

Yasmina Khadra has asserted her right under the Copyright, Designs
and Patents Act 1988 to be identified as the author of this work

What the Day Owes the Night was first published in 2008 under the
title *Ce que le jour doit à la nuit* in France by Julliard, an imprint of
Éditions Robert Laffont, Paris

First published in Great Britain in 2010 by William Heinemann

Vintage
Random House, 20 Vauxhall Bridge Road,
London SW1V 2SA

www.vintage-books.co.uk

Addresses for companies within The Random House Group Limited
can be found at: www.randomhouse.co.uk/offices.htm

The Random House Group Limited Reg. No. 954009

A CIP catalogue record for this book
is available from the British Library

ISBN 9780099540458

The Random House Group Limited supports The Forest Stewardship
Council (FSC), the leading international forest certification
organisation. All our titles that are printed on Greenpeace approved
FSC certified paper carry the FSC logo. Our paper procurement
policy can be found at www.rbooks.co.uk/environment

Mixed Sources
Product group from well-managed
forests and other controlled sources
www.fsc.org Cert no. TT-COC-2139
© 1996 Forest Stewardship Council

Printed and bound in Great Britain by
CPI Cox & Wyman, Reading, RG1 8EX

In Oran, as elsewhere, for lack of time and thinking, people are forced to love each other without realising it.
Albert Camus, *The Plague*

I love Algeria, because I have truly been affected by it.
Gabriel García Márquez

1. Jenane Jato

1

MY FATHER was happy.

It had never occurred to me that he was capable of such an emotion.

Sometimes, the sight of his serene face disturbed me.

Hunkered on a pile of loose stones, knees clasped to his chin, he watched the breeze caress the slender stalks of wheat, breathe over them, scurry feverishly through them. The wheat fields billowed over the plains like the manes of thousands of horses galloping. It was like watching the sea as it rises and falls. And my father was smiling. I could not remember ever seeing him smile; it was not in his nature to show happiness – if he could be said to have ever felt such a thing. Moulded by adversity, his eyes usually bore a permanent look of desperation. His life had been an endless series of disappointments; he mistrusted the future, realising it to be traitorous and unknowable.

I had never known him to have friends.

We lived in isolation like ghosts on our patch of land, in the sidereal silence of those who have little to say to one another: my mother in the shadow of our shack, bent over her cooking pot, stirring a broth of root vegetables of questionable flavour; Zahra, my sister, three years my junior, crouched forgotten in some dark corner, so self-effacing that at times we did not even notice her; and me, a sickly, solitary boy, who had barely blossomed before I wilted, carrying my ten years like a burden.

This was not life; we merely existed.

The simple fact of waking in the morning was a miracle, and at night, as we readied ourselves for bed, we wondered whether it might not be better to close our eyes once and for all, convinced that we had seen all there was to see in life and that life itself did not warrant further examination. The days were desolate in their sameness; not a single one brought with it anything new, and each day died taking with it the few remaining illusions that dangled before us like the carrots used to urge on a donkey.

In the 1930s, poverty and disease swept the country, wiping out families and livestock with astonishing perversity, forcing those who survived into exile or vagrancy. We no longer received any news of those few relatives we had left. As for the ragged creatures we sometimes saw in the distance, we knew that they were merely passing through. The dirt track that led past our shack was gradually disappearing.

My father cared little.

He liked to be alone, hunched over his plough, lips flecked white with foam. Sometimes I saw in him some god, fashioning the world and would sit for hours watching him, fascinated by his strength, his determination.

When my mother asked me to take his meals out to him, I had to be prompt. My father ate punctually, frugally, eager to get back to work. I would have liked him to say a kind word, take some interest in me for a moment, but he had

4

eyes only for his land. Only here, in the midst of this tawny universe, was he truly in his element. Nothing and no one, not even those dearest to him, could distract him from it.

In the evening, when we came back to our shack, the spark in his eyes would fade with the setting sun. He would become someone else, someone ordinary, someone dreary and uninteresting; I almost felt disappointed in him.

But for some weeks now, he had been unaccountably happy. The coming harvest promised to be glorious, exceeding his wildest expectations. Crippled with debts, he had mortgaged the lands that had belonged to his forefathers, and this harvest, he knew, was to be his last battle. He did the work of ten men, toiling relentlessly, a fire in his belly; a cloudless sky could terrify him, the smallest cloud electrify him. Never had I seen him pray and pour himself into his work as he did then. And when summer came, and the wheat scattered its glittering sequins across the plains, my father sat hunkered on a mound of loose stones, motionless. Hunched under his straw hat, he would spend most of the day staring at his crops, which, after years of thankless work, of lean cows, seemed finally to promise a sunny spell.

The harvest would come soon, and as the day drew closer my father became more excited. He could already see himself, arms outstretched, gathering in sheaves, trussing hundreds of bales, harvesting hopes so great he did not know what to do with them.

A week earlier, sitting me next to him on our little cart, we had gone to the village some miles beyond the hill. Usually he did not take me anywhere with him. Perhaps he thought that now that things were looking up, it was time to change, to learn new habits, new ways of thinking. On the way, he hummed a Bedouin tune. It was the first time in my life I had ever heard him sing. His voice dipped and soared, so out of tune it would scare the horses, but to me, no singer in the world could compare: it was glorious. Then he suddenly regained his composure, surprised to find he had been so carried away; embarrassed that he had shamed himself in front of his son.

The village was a depressing, godforsaken place, its cob-walled huts cracking beneath the weight of misery, its narrow streets desperately twisting and turning, not knowing where to hide their squalor. A few skeletal trees, gnawed away by goats, stood withered and dying like gibbets. Crouched beneath the trees, the unemployed sat like ruined scarecrows waiting for a storm to come to carry them off.

My father stopped the cart in front of a squalid little shack surrounded by a group of barefoot boys with crudely patched tunics of jute sacking instead of *gandurahs* and shaven heads pocked with oozing sores that looked like some mark of damnation. They crowded round us, curious as a pack of fox cubs whose territory has been invaded. With a wave, my father sent them scurrying, then pushed me towards the grocer's shop, where a man sat dozing amid the empty shelves. He did not bother to get to his feet to greet us.

'I'm going to need men and tools for the harvest,' my father said to him.

'Is that all?' said the grocer wearily. 'I sell sugar and salt too, you know, oil, cornmeal.'

'All that will come later. Can I depend on you?'

'When do you want them, the men and the tools?'

'Friday week?'

'You're the boss. You whistle, we'll be there.'

'Right, well let's say Friday of next week.'

'It's a deal,' groaned the grocer, pulling his turban down over his face. 'Glad to hear you've saved the season.'

'What I've saved is my soul,' my father said as he turned to go.

'To do that, my friend, you have to have a soul in the first place.'

Standing in the doorway, my father stopped and shuddered, detecting some slight in what the grocer had said. He scratched his head, climbed on to the cart and we headed home. The grocer had touched a raw nerve. My father's face, so radiant when we first set out, was serious now. The grocer's remark, he thought, was some dire omen. This was how my father was; at the slightest problem he immediately feared the worst. To boast about the harvest before it was gathered in was to tempt the evil eye. I knew he was bitterly regretting boasting of his success when not a grain had yet been harvested.

He drove home, his body coiled like a snake, flogging the mule with his whip, every lash bearing the mark of his fury.

As he waited for Friday, he dug out old billhooks and rusty sickles and set about cleaning and sharpening them. With my dog, I watched him from a distance, waiting for some word, some chance to make myself useful. But my father needed no help. He knew exactly what had to be done.

Then, without warning, disaster struck. I woke one night to hear the dog howling. When I looked out, I thought the sun had tumbled from the sky and landed in our fields. Though it was three a.m., it was so bright it seemed like noon. My mother stood wordlessly by the door, her head buried in her hands. The flickering light outside sent her several shadows scurrying along the walls behind me. My sister sat crouched in her corner, fingers stuffed into her mouth, eyes vacant.

I dashed outside and saw a sea of fire surging and rolling across the fields, the flames so high they seemed to light the heavens, from which not a single star looked down.

Dripping with sweat, his bare chest slashed with streaks of soot, my father had gone mad. Over and over he filled a tiny bucket from the trough and rushed towards the blaze, disappearing into the flames, then reappeared, filled his bucket again and stumbled back into the inferno. Though his efforts were absurd, he could not face the thought that there was nothing he could do, that no prayer, no miracle could prevent his dreams from going up in smoke. My mother, knowing all was lost, watched her husband tear around, terrified that there would come a moment when he did not re-emerge from the flames. My father was capable of trying to gather in sheaves of the blazing wheat and burning with them. For it was only among his crops that he truly felt at home.

At dawn, he was still trying to douse the wisps of smoke that rose from the charred stubble. Nothing remained of the crops and yet he refused to see it. Out of spite.

It was a terrible injustice.

Three days before harvest.

Two inches from salvation.

One breath from redemption.

Later that morning, my father was finally compelled to face facts. His bucket dangling from one hand, he looked up to survey the extent of the disaster. For a long time he stood, legs trembling, eyes bloodshot, face distorted; then he fell to his knees, collapsed on his belly, and before our incredulous eyes did something a *man* should never do in public – he wept . . . He wept until he had no tears left to cry.

It was then that I realised that our guardian angels had abandoned us, that we would be cursed until the day of judgement.

For us, time stood still. True, the day still bowed before the night, darkness still gave way to dawn, vultures still wheeled in the sky, but to us it was as though all things had ended. History had turned a page and we no longer figured in what happened next. For days my father paced his razed fields, wandering among the shadows and the stubble from sunrise to sundown like a ghost trapped among ruins. My mother watched him through the hole in the wall that served us as a window. Every time he slapped his thighs, his cheeks, she made a hurried sign, called out to every marabout – every holy man – in the region to intercede; she was convinced that her husband had lost his mind.

A week later, a man came to visit our shack. Wearing a ceremonial uniform, his beard carefully trimmed, chest bedecked with medals, he looked like a sultan. This was the *kaid*, escorted by his praetorian guard. Without troubling to get down from his barouche, he instructed my father to append his fingerprints to some documents that a Frenchman, pale, gaunt and dressed all in black, had pulled from his briefcase. My father did not protest. He rolled his fingertips on the ink-soaked sponge and pressed them to the papers. As soon as the documents were 'signed', the *kaid* drove off leaving my father standing in the yard, staring from his ink-stained fingers to the barouche as it moved away up the hill. Neither my mother nor I dared speak to him.

The next day, my mother gathered our few belongings into bundles and packed them into the cart.

It was over.

For the rest of my life I will remember that day, the day my father stepped through the looking glass. It was overcast, the sun hung crucified above the mountain, the horizon was a blur. Even at noon it felt as though we were enveloped in some endless, silent twilight, as though the universe itself had fled leaving us to our misery.

My father took the reins, his shoulders hunched, eyes fixed on the floor, and urged the mule on, taking us I knew not where. My mother huddled against the slatted sides of the cart, hidden behind her veil, barely distinguishable from the sacks and bundles. My little sister, her eyes vacant, kept her fingers pressed into her mouth. My parents had not noticed that their daughter had stopped eating, that something in her spirit had broken on that night when hell itself had rained down on our farm.

The dog followed the cart at a distance, careful not to be seen. From time to time it stopped on the brow of a hill and sat on its haunches as though determined to hold out until we disappeared from view, then leapt up and bounded after us, muzzle trailing along the ground, desperately trying to catch up. When it drew closer, it would slow and then wander off the road and sit, miserable, distraught. The dog knew that wherever we were headed, there was no place for it. My father had made this clear by hurling stones at it as the cart pulled away from the farm.

I loved my dog. He was my one friend, my only confidant. I wondered what would become of him, what would become of both of us now that our paths had parted.

We travelled for miles without encountering a solitary soul, as though fate had cleared the landscape of every other creature so it might have us to itself. The dirt road rushed along ahead of us, bare and mournful. It looked like our fortune.

Late in the afternoon, in the haze of the sweltering sun, a small black speck appeared in the distance. My father jerked the bridle of the mule towards this makeshift tent, a rickety construction of posts and hessian that stood in the deserted landscape as though it had appeared out of a dream. He instructed my mother to get down and wait beside a large boulder. In our world, when men meet, women are expected to withdraw; there is no greater sacrilege than to see one's wife stared at by a stranger. My mother did as she was asked, taking Zahra in her arms, and went and crouched in the shadow of the rock.

The merchant was a small, wizened man with ferret-like eyes sunk in a face mottled with blackish pustules. He wore tattered Arab trousers over mouldering shoes with gaping holes through which poked his misshapen toes. His threadbare waistcoat did little to hide his scrawny chest. He peered at us from beneath his makeshift tent, one hand on his club. When he realised we were not thieves, he dropped the stick and stepped out into the sunlight.

'People are wicked, Issa,' he greeted my father. 'It is in their nature. It is little use to hate them for it.'

My father drew to a halt. He knew all too well what the man was referring to, but he did not answer.

'When I saw the fire in the distance that night,' the man said, 'I knew that some poor soul was heading straight for hell, but not for a moment did I think that it was you.'

'It is the Lord's will,' my father said.

'That is not true, and you know it. If men are evil, the Lord cannot be blamed. It is unjust to burden Him with crimes that we alone make possible. Issa, my friend, who could hate you so that they would burn your crops?'

'It is God who decides our fate,' said my father.

The merchant shrugged. 'Men invented God to distract them from their demons.'

As my father stepped down from the cart, the tail of his *gandurah* snagged on the seat. This, he decided, was another evil omen. His face flushed with anger.

'Are you going to Oran?' the merchant asked.

'Who told you that?'

'When a man has lost everything, he goes to the city . . . Be careful, Issa. The city is no place for people like us. Oran is teeming with villains more deadly than cobras, more cunning than the Devil, who fear neither God nor man.'

'Why do you talk such nonsense?' said my father angrily.

'Because you don't know what you're getting yourself into. The city is a wicked place. *Barakah* – the breath of life, the wisdom of our ancestors – has no power there. Those who go there never return.'

My father raised one hand, imploring him to keep his wild imaginings to himself.

'I've come to sell you my cart. The wheels and the cart

12

are solid and the mule is barely four years old. I'll take whatever you can offer.'

'I'm afraid I cannot offer much, Issa.' The merchant looked at the mule and the trap. 'Please do not think I would profit from your misfortune. Few travellers pass this way now and I am left with melons I cannot sell.'

'Anything you can offer will be enough for me.'

'To tell the truth, I have no need of a cart or a mule . . . But I have a little money, which I will happily share with you. You have helped me many times. As for the mule and cart, you can leave them here with me; I'll find a buyer for you. You can come back and collect the money whenever you like. I won't take a penny of it.'

My father did not hesitate; he had no choice. He held out his hand to shake on the deal.

'You are a good man, Miloud. I know you would not cheat me.'

'A man who cheats, cheats only himself.'

My father handed me two bundles, shouldered the others himself and, pocketing the few coins the merchant gave him, went to find my mother, never once looking back at what he was leaving behind.

We walked until we could no longer feel our legs. The sun was unbearable; its dazzling glare off the arid, desolate terrain stung our eyes. Swathed in her shroud, my mother stumbled like a ghost behind us, stopping only to shift my sister from one hip to the other. My father paid her no mind. He walked on, resolute, forcing us to run to keep up. There could be no question of us asking him to slow down. My heels were rubbed raw by my sandals, my throat burned, but I kept going. To stave off my hunger, my thirst,

I focused on the steam rising from my father's shoulders, on the way he carried his burden, his brutal, unvarying pace determined to trample any evil spirit in his path. Not once did he turn to see whether we were still following.

The sun was beginning to set by the time we reached the *roumi* track – by which he meant the tarmac road. My father chose a lone olive tree behind a small hill, safe from prying eyes, and began to lash the branches together to make a shelter for the night. Then, checking to ensure that he could still see the road, he told us we could set down our burdens. My mother laid the sleeping Zahra at the foot of the tree and covered her with a *pagne*, then took a crock pot and a wooden spoon from one of the bundles.

'No fire,' my father said, stopping her. 'We can eat cured meat tonight.'

'There is no meat. I have a few fresh eggs left.'

'No fire, I said. I want no one to know that we are here. We will make do with tomatoes and onions.'

The oppressive heat died away and a cool breeze rustled the leaves and the branches of the olive tree. We could hear lizards darting through the dry grass. The sun spilled out across the horizon like a broken egg.

My father lay on his back in the shade of a boulder, one knee raised, his turban covering his face. He had eaten nothing. It was almost as though he was sulking.

Just before nightfall, a man appeared on a high ridge and waved at us. Out of modesty, he dared not come any closer while my mother was present. My father sent me to ask what he wanted. He was a shepherd, dressed in tattered rags, his face was wizened, his hands calloused. He offered us his shelter for the night. My father declined this hospitality. The shepherd insisted – his neighbours would not forgive him if he left a family to sleep outside when his little shack was nearby. My father categorically refused. 'I will not be beholden to any man,' he muttered to himself. The shepherd, annoyed, went back to his meagre flock of goats, grumbling and stamping his feet.

We spent the night beneath the stars. My mother and Zahra at the foot of the olive tree, me under my *gandurah*, my father sitting in the shadow of the rock, a cutlass between his feet, keeping watch.

When I woke in the morning, my father was a different man. He had shaved and washed his face in a nearby stream and put on clean clothes: a waistcoat over a faded shirt and a neatly pressed *sarouel* – a pair of loose-fitting trousers – I had never seen him wear before, and leather shoes, which, though shabby, had been freshly buffed.

The bus arrived just as the sun began to rise. My father packed our belongings on to the roof and sat us on a long bench at the back. This was the first time I had ever seen a bus. When it moved off, I clung to the seat, thrilled and terrified. The few other travellers dozed here and there, mostly *roumis* – Westerners – looking cramped in their shabby suits. I stared out of the windows at the landscape as it streamed past on either side. I was in awe of the bus driver. I could only see his back, which was broad as a rampart, and his broad, sinewy arms, which twisted the steering wheel with considerable authority. On my right sat a toothless old man with a tattered basket at his feet, who lurched from side to side with every hairpin bend. After each corner he would plunge his hand into the basket to make sure that everything was still as it should be.

The pungent petrol fumes and the closed windows finally got the better of me and, stomach churning, head feeling bloated as a rubber ball, I dozed off.

The bus stopped on a little square flanked by trees opposite a vast red-brick building. The travellers rushed for their bags. In their haste, some of them trod on my feet; I didn't even notice. I was so dumbstruck by what I saw that I forgot to help my father take down our bundles.

The city.

I had never imagined that such a sprawling place could exist. It was extraordinary. For a moment I wondered if the heat and fumes were playing tricks on me. On the far side of the square, rows and rows of houses stretched as far as the eye could see, with tall windows and balconies filled with flowers. The streets were paved and there were footpaths on either side. I couldn't believe my eyes; I did not even have names for many of the things that flashed before them. Beautiful houses rose up on every side, elegant and impressive, set back behind high black railings. Families relaxed on verandas around white tables on which stood tall decanters of orangeade, while rosy children with hair of gold played in the gardens, their high-pitched laughter bursting through the greenery like jets of water. These privileged residences exuded a sense of tranquillity and wealth that I could hardly believe possible, so different were they from life out in the *bled*, where crops withered to dust, where stables and barns were less pathetic than the shack we had called home.

This was a different planet.

I shambled along behind my father, dazzled by the parks bounded by low stone walls or wrought-iron railings, by the broad, sunlit avenues with their street lamps, majestic and aloof, like glowing sentinels. And the cars . . . ! I had seen at least a dozen cars. They appeared out of nowhere, sputtering like shooting stars, only to disappear around a corner before I had time to make a wish.

'What's the name of this country?' I asked my father.

'Shut up and walk,' he snapped. 'And keep your eyes on the road if you don't want to fall into a hole.'

This was Oran.

My father walked straight ahead, sure-footed, undaunted by the grid of streets and their dizzying buildings that branched out all around us, each so like the others that it felt as though we were marking time. Curiously, I saw, the women in the city did not wear the veil. They walked around with their faces bare; the old women wore strange head-gear, but the younger ones went bare-headed, their hair on show for all to see, seemingly unperturbed by the men all around them.

As we walked farther, the hubbub died away and we wandered through peaceful, shady areas, the silence barely broken by a passing barouche or the clatter of a metal shutter. A few elderly European men with crimson faces lingered outside their front doors. They wore baggy shorts, shirts open to reveal their paunches, and broad-brimmed hats to protect their pale necks. Exhausted by the heat, they chatted over a glass of *anisette* set down on the pavement, distractedly waving fans to cool themselves. My father strode past without greeting them, without even looking at them, trying to act as though they were not even there, but his pace slackened now and lost something of its assurance.

We emerged on to a broad avenue where pedestrians

stood window-shopping. My father stopped to watch a tram pass before crossing the road. He signalled to my mother, indicating a spot where she should wait for him, then, leaving her to look after the baskets and bundles, he ordered me to follow him to a chemist's shop at the far end of a lane. He glanced through the front window first to make sure this was the right address, then straightened his turban, smoothed down his waistcoat and stepped inside. A tall, thin man behind the counter was scribbling in a ledger. He was wearing a three-piece suit and a red fez over his blonde hair. He had blue eyes and a delicate face; a narrow strip of moustache accentuated the thin-lipped slit that served him as a mouth. When he saw my father come in, he frowned, then he lifted a section at the side of the counter and stepped from behind it to greet us.

The two men threw their arms around each other. The embrace was brief but forceful.

'Is this my nephew?' asked the stranger, coming up to me.

'Yes.' My father nodded.

'My God, he's handsome!'

This man was my uncle. I was not aware that I had an uncle. My father had never spoken to us about his family. Or about anyone. He barely spoke to us at all.

My uncle crouched down and hugged me.

'You have a fine young man there, Issa,' he said.

My father said nothing. I saw his lips move and knew he was silently reciting verses from the Qur'an to ward off the evil eye.

The man got to his feet again and turned to my father. After a moment, he went back behind the counter but continued to stare at him.

'You're not an easy man to flush out, Issa. I have to assume that something serious has happened. It's been years since you came to visit your big brother.'

My father did not beat about the bush. In a single, breathless sentence he recounted what had happened out in the *bled*, how our crops had gone up in flames, about the visit of the *kaid* . . . My uncle listened carefully and did not interrupt. I watched as his hands alternately gripped the counter and balled into fists. When my father had finished, he pushed his fez back and dabbed at his brow with a handkerchief. He was devastated, but he held up as best he could.

'You should have asked me for money, Issa, instead of mortgaging our lands. You know what happens with that kind of loan. You've seen many people take the bait, and you've seen what has happened to them. How could you let yourself be swindled too?'

There was no reproach in my uncle's tone, just an overwhelming disappointment.

'What's done is done,' said my father, who could think of nothing else to say. 'God has decided.'

'The Lord did not command that your crops be burned . . . God cannot be blamed for the wickedness of man. Nor the Devil either.'

My father raised his hand to stop the conversation.

'I've come to settle in the city,' he said. 'My wife and my daughter are waiting for me on the corner.'

'Let's go back to my house first. You can stay there for a few days and I will see what I can do—'

'No.' My father cut him off. 'If a man is to get back on his feet, he must do it straight away. I need a home of my own, and I need it today.'

My uncle did not insist. He knew his brother's stubbornness too well to contradict him. He took us to the far side of the city.

There is nothing cruder than the inequalities of a city. Walk around a block and day becomes night, life becomes death. Even now, years later, I still shudder whenever I remember that devastating experience.

The 'suburb' where we ended up broke the spell the city had cast only a few hours earlier. This was still Oran, but now we were behind the scenes, where the beautiful houses and the leafy avenues gave way to a sprawling chaos peppered with squalid shacks, disgusting shops, the tents nomads call *kheimas*, which are open to the four winds, and pens filled with livestock.

'This is Jenane Jato,' my uncle said. 'Today is the day the *souk*, the market, is held. It's usually quieter than this,' he added, to reassure us.

Jenane Jato: a slum of scrubland and shacks teeming with squeaking carts, beggars, hawkers, donkey-drivers struggling with their beasts, water-carriers, charlatans and ragged children; a stifling clay-red wasteland of dust and filth that clung to the walls of the city like a malignant tumour. The abject poverty was unbelievable, and the people – piteous wretches – dissolved into the shadows. It was as though the damned had been driven out of hell without judgement or warning and washed up here; they were the personification of life's futility.

My uncle introduced us to a puny little man with a short neck and shifty eyes. Bliss was a broker, a vulture waiting to grow rich on other people's misery. At the time, with disease-ridden waves of migrants flooding into the city, such predators were unavoidable. Ours was no exception to the rule. Bliss knew that we were ruined, he knew we were at his mercy. I remember he had a goatee beard that made his chin seem abnormally long and wore a filthy fez perched on his huge, bald, misshapen head. I hated him the moment I set eyes on him, his snakelike smile, the way he rubbed his hands together as though about to eat us alive.

He greeted my father with a nod and listened as my uncle explained our situation.

'I think I may have something for your brother, Doctor,' said the broker, who seemed to know my uncle well. 'If it's something temporary you're looking for, you won't find anything better. It's not a palace, but it's comfortable and the neighbours are honest.'

He led us to a yard in front of what looked like a stable, near a stinking stream. He asked us to wait in the street, then cleared his throat loudly to let the women know to disappear – as was the custom if a man was about to walk into a room. When the coast was clear, he signalled for us to follow him.

The house was built around a central courtyard flanked by rooms each crammed with families fleeing the famine and the typhus that raged in the countryside.

'Here it is,' the broker said, pulling aside a curtain to reveal an empty room. It smelled of piss and cats, of dead chickens and vomit. The walls, still standing through some miracle, were black and oozed damp; the floor was covered in a carpet of rats' droppings. 'You won't find a more afford-able rent,' he assured us.

My father stared at the cockroaches that teemed around a drain choked with filth, looked up at the cobwebs spotted with dead flies; the broker watched out of the corner of his eye, like a reptile eyeing its prey.

'I'll take it,' my father said to the man's relief.

Immediately he began to pile our belongings into a corner of the room.

'The communal toilets are at the other end of the court-yard,' the broker said enthusiastically. 'There's a well, too, though it's dry right now. You'll need to watch that the kids don't get too close to the edge. We lost a little girl last year when some fool forgot to put back the cover. Apart from that, there's nothing else you need to know. The neighbours are good people. They've all come in from the *bled* to work, and they never complain. If you need anything at all, come and ask me,' he insisted eagerly. 'I know people, I can lay my hands on anything, day or night, if you've got the money. If you didn't already know, I rent out mats, blankets, oil lamps and paraffin stoves. You only have to ask. I'll bring you the moon itself if you've got the money.'

My father wasn't listening; he already despised the man. As he set about tidying our new home, I saw my uncle take the broker aside and slip something into his hand.

'That should cover the rent for a while.'

The broker held the banknote up against the sunlight and looked at my uncle with malicious joy. He pressed the money to his forehead, then to his lips and yelped.

'Money might have no smell, but my God, it smells good to me.'

2

MY FATHER wasted no time. He was determined to get back on his feet as soon as possible. At dawn next day, he took me with him and we went looking for any work that might bring in a few pennies. Unfortunately, he knew nothing about the city and didn't know where to start. At nightfall we came back empty-handed and exhausted. Meanwhile, my mother had cleaned our hovel and organised our things. We ate like animals and fell asleep immediately.

The following day, before daybreak, my father and I set out again to look for work. We had been walking for hours when we saw a crowd of men milling around a truck.

'What's going on?' my father asked a beggar in tattered rags.

'They're looking for labourers to unload cargo on the port.'

Convinced this was his lucky break, my father told me to wait on the terrace of an ancient ramshackle café and piled into the crowd. I watched him elbow his way through and disappear into the throng. When the truck pulled away, there was no sign of him; he had obviously managed to get aboard.

I waited for him for hours under the blazing sun. All

around me, people in rags and tatters clustered around shacks, squatting on their haunches, perfectly motionless in the shade of their makeshift shelters. Every one of them had vacant eyes and something of the night in their faces. They seemed to be waiting, with unfathomable patience, for something that would never happen. In the evening, weary of waiting, they drifted away in silence, leaving only a few tramps, two or three gibbering madmen and sinister men with reptilian eyes. Suddenly I heard someone shout, 'Stop, thief!' and it was as though Pandora's box had been opened. Heads jerked, bodies uncoiled like springs and I watched a handful of hirsute men swoop on a young lad in rags trying to escape. This was the thief. In the blink of an eye, they had lynched him. His screams would haunt my sleep for weeks to come. When they had finished, all that remained was the broken body of a teenage boy lying in a pool of blood. I was so shocked that when a man leaned down to speak to me, I almost jumped out of my skin.

'I didn't mean to scare you, lad,' the man said, holding his hands up to reassure me, 'but you've been here since morning. You need to be heading home now. This is no place for the likes of you.'

'I'm waiting for my father,' I said. 'He went on the truck.'

'Where is he then, this fool of a father of yours? What is he thinking, leaving a little lad like you in a place like this? Do you live far?'

'I don't know.'

The man seemed embarrassed. He was big, strapping, with hairy arms, a face weathered by the sun and one black eye. He glanced around him, then, reluctantly, he pushed a seat towards me and invited me to sit with him at his table, which was black with dirt.

'It'll be dark soon, and I have to close up. You can't hang around here, got it? It's not safe. The place is crawling with lunatics . . . Have you eaten?'

I shook my head.

'I didn't think so.'

He stepped inside his café and brought out a tin plate with some cold congealed soup at the bottom.

'I've no bread left . . .'

He sat down next to me and watched as I lapped at the plate like a dog with his bowl.

'Your father is a fool,' he sighed.

It grew dark. The café owner closed up but he didn't leave. He hung a lantern from a beam and, scowling, kept me company. Shadows flitted here and there across the murky square. A throng of homeless people gradually took over the area; some clustered around a wood fire, others simply stretched out on the ground and slept. Hours went by, the sounds faded; my father had still not returned. As time passed, the café owner's fury mounted. He wanted to head home but was convinced that if he left me, even for a moment, I would be dead. When my father finally appeared, ashen with worry, the café owner laid into him in no uncertain terms.

'Where the hell do you think you are? Mecca? What on earth possessed you to leave your kid in a place like this? Even criminals aren't safe around here.'

My father was so relieved to find me safe that he drank down the café owner's rebuke like a blessed elixir. He realised that he had made a grave mistake and that had the café owner left me to my fate, he might not have found me at all.

'I went in the truck,' he stammered, distraught. 'I thought they were going to bring us back here, but I was wrong. I'm not from the city and the port is farther than I thought. I didn't know where I was or how to get back here. I've been going round and round in circles for hours.'

'You're not right in the head is what it is,' roared the café owner, unhooking the lantern. 'If you're out looking for work, you leave your kid at home . . . Now follow me, the pair of you. We're about to cross the most vicious viper pit the good Lord ever put on this earth.'

'Thank you, my brother,' said my father.

'Nothing to thank me for. I just don't like to see a kid hurt is all. I'd have stayed here with him till morning if I had to or he'd never have made it out of this hole alive, and I wouldn't have that on my conscience.'

He led us through the cut-throat alleys without a hitch, explaining as we walked how to avoid the worst areas and make it home in one piece, then disappeared into the shadows.

My father followed the café owner's advice to the letter. After that day, he was gone by the time I woke up every morning, and I was asleep before he got home at night.

I no longer saw him.

I missed him.

There was nothing for me to do in Jenane Jato. I was bored. Having been brought up a solitary boy with only an old dog for company, I did not know how to join in the games of the horde of children who constantly squabbled in the courtyard. They were like poltergeists. They were younger than I was – some barely came up to my knees – yet they made more noise than a pack of demons. Sitting on the step of our room, I would watch them, keeping a safe distance from their savage games that invariably ended with a head split open or a knee grazed.

We shared our courtyard with five other families, all of whom had come from the hinterland: bankrupt landowners or *khammès* – tenant farmers – who had defaulted on their lease. The men would leave at daybreak to find work and the women, indifferent to their children's vicious brawls, would spend their days attempting to make a filthy hovel into a home. They seemed to believe this was a lesson in the nasty, brutish ways of life, one their children should learn as soon as possible. They seemed almost happy to watch as, again and again, the children lashed out at one another, then, after a good cry, made up again only to hurl themselves back into the fray with astonishing ferocity. The women stuck together, they supported each another: if one was ill, the others would make sure there was food in her pot, look after her baby, take turns sitting by her bedside. From time to time they would share something sweet, and with touching simplicity, they seemed inured to their hardship. For this, I admired them.

There was Badra, a hefty, strapping woman who loved to tell dirty stories. She was a breath of fresh air. Her crude language made my mother uncomfortable, but the other women loved it. Badra was mother to five little brats and two awkward teenagers. She had been married, to a shepherd thick as two short planks, who, she liked to say, had a dick like a donkey and no idea how to use it . . . There was Batoul, slight and skinny with hair as black as cloves, who, barely forty, seemed like an old woman; she would squirm with laughter before Badra even opened her mouth. As a girl, Batoul had been forced to marry a man old enough to be her grandfather. She claimed to have supernatural powers – she would read palms and interpret dreams. The women in the neighbourhood regularly came to her for advice. For a handful of potatoes, a franc or a sliver of soap, she would tell their future. For the people who lived around the courtyard, she did it for free . . . There was Yezza, a plump, red-haired woman with a magnificent bosom whose alcoholic husband regularly hit her. Her ruined face bore the marks of his constant beatings and she had barely a tooth left in her head. Her 'crime' was her failure to bear him children, something that made him particularly loathsome . . . There was Mama, who, though she had enough to worry about with her brood of children, had the energy of a dozen men and was prepared to do anything to keep a roof over their heads . . . And then there was Hadda, beautiful as a *houri*, who already had two children, though she was barely in her teens. Her husband had set off to look for work one morning and never come back. Left to herself, with no means of support, she owed her continued survival to the solidarity of the women who shared the courtyard.

Every day these women would gather around the well and spend most of their time turning over the past as you might turn a knife in an old wound. They talked about the orange groves that had been repossessed, of blue hills lost for ever, of kinfolk left behind, of a land of misfortune that they might never see again. And as they talked, their faces sagged with heartache, their voices cracked, but just when sorrow seemed about to overwhelm them, Badra would interrupt with some new outrageous tale of her first husband's sexual disasters and, like a magic potion, the painful memories would loosen their grip, the women would fall about with laughter and the courtyard regained a small part of its soul.

The jokes and stories would go on until nightfall. Sometimes, emboldened by the absence of the men, Bliss, the broker, would come and strut about. As soon as they heard him loudly clear his throat, the women would disappear, then he would stride into the courtyard, shout at the children, look for any rubbish and call us vermin if he found the slightest scratch on the walls. He would stand in the middle of the courtyard staring pointedly at the room where the beautiful Hadda lived and, loathsome as a one-eyed flea, threaten to turn us all out on to the street. After he had gone, the women would reappear, giggling, more amused than intimidated by the man's bluster. And Bliss could certainly brag, though he was not up to his boasts. He would not have dared show his face in the courtyard if there were a man present – even if it were only a man on his deathbed. Badra was convinced that Bliss had designs on Hadda. Destitute and vulnerable, the girl would be easy prey, her position made more precarious by the fact that she was in arrears on her rent. Bliss constantly bullied her hoping she would break.

To protect me from Badra's vulgar tongue, my mother allowed me to go out and play in the street – if it could be called a street. It was a dirt road lined on either side with hovels made of corrugated iron and squalid little shacks.

There were only two houses built of bricks and mortar: the courtyard house where we lived, and a sort of stable where a number of families lived cramped together. On the corner of the street was a barber, a small man of indeterminate age, barely taller than a stick of asparagus and so timorous that some refused to pay for their haircuts. Inside his tiny roofless cabin were a munitions case salvaged from a military dump, a sliver of mirror rescued from a wardrobe and a rickety counter on which sat a large jug, a tattered shaving brush, a bent pair of scissors and an assortment of blunt razor blades. When he was not shaving old men, he squatted on the ground outside his shack and sang. His voice was hoarse and gravelly, he could barely remember the words to the songs, yet there was something thrilling in the way he poured out his pain. I never tired of listening to him.

Next to the barber's was a ramshackle lean-to that served as a grocer's shop. The shopkeeper was known as Peg-Leg — a Moroccan veteran who had lost his leg in a minefield. This was the first time I had ever seen a wooden leg. It made a strange impression on me. The ex-soldier seemed proud of it; he would pull it off and brandish it like a weapon at any boy he found trying to pilfer from his jars.

Peg-Leg was not happy in his little shop. He missed the reek of battle and the noise of the barracks. He dreamed of re-enlisting, of going into battle again and tearing the enemy to shreds. As he waited for his mutilated leg to grow back, he ran a thriving black market in jam, sugar loaves and rancid cooking oil. In his spare time he was a backstreet dentist; many times I watched him pull rotten, bloody stumps from children's mouths with a pair of rusty pliers; it was as though he was ripping their hearts out.

Beyond Peg-Leg's shack was a patch of waste ground that opened on to scrubland. I wandered out there one morning and witnessed a battle between two rival armies of children, one led by Daho – a savage child, his head shaven but for a lock of hair that fell over his forehead – the other by a young man who seemed to be mentally retarded and thought he was a warrior king. It was as if the earth had opened up beneath my feet. In a split second I was seized by a forest of arms, and before I knew what was happening they had stripped me of my shoes, my *gandurah* and my fez. They even tried to drag me into the bushes and dishonour me. Shocked and traumatised, I'm not sure how I escaped the pack, but I never set foot in the waste ground again.

My father spent every hour of the day looking for a job, but still the situation was bleak. Every day at dawn, thousands of men went out looking for work. As wretches lay dying on the rubbish tips, their bellies so emaciated you could almost see their spines, the living seemed only too ready to tear each other to pieces over a stale crust of bread. Times were hard. The dreams the city seemed to promise from afar had proved illusory. My father was lucky if he managed to get one day's labour in every ten, and the money he earned was barely enough to buy the sliver of soap to wash himself with. Some nights he would stagger home, his face haggard, his back stooped from a day spent loading and unloading, in so much pain that he had to sleep on his stomach. He was exhausted, but most of all he was desperate. His resolve began to crack under the weight of his doubts.

Weeks passed. My father was visibly losing weight. He was increasingly short-tempered and at the slightest excuse would take out his frustration on my mother. He never hit her, but he would scream at her and she would guiltily bow her head and say nothing. The days slipped away from us, the nights loomed large. My father no longer slept. He spent his nights sighing, clapping his hands, I would hear him pacing the room in the dark; sometimes he would go out into the courtyard and sit, chin on his knees, arms clasped around his legs, and wait for sun-up.

One morning he told me to put on my best *gandurah* and together we walked to his brother's chemist's shop, where we found my uncle setting out his boxes and vials on the shelves.

My father hesitated before stepping into the shop. Proud and tongue-tied, he dithered for a long time before admitting why we had come. He needed money. My uncle, as though he had been expecting this, immediately opened the cash register and took out a large banknote. My father stared at the money in anguish. Realising he would not take the money, my uncle stepped from behind the counter and slipped it into his pocket. My father stood, frozen, hanging his head, and his voice when he finally spoke was faint, muffled, barely audible: 'Thank you.'

My uncle went back behind his counter. It was obvious that there was something he wanted to say, but he dared not burst the blister. His eyes flickered from my father's face to his own scrubbed white fingers drumming on the countertop. Having weighed the situation with infinite care, he took his courage in both hands and said:

'I know it's hard, Issa, but you'll get through this. If you'd only let me help you a little.'

'I'll pay you back every last penny,' my father promised.

'I'm not worried about the money, Issa, pay me back whenever you can. As far as I am concerned, you don't need to pay me back at all. I can give you more. It's no problem. I'm your brother, and I'm here for you, whenever you need me. I don't know how to say this to you . . .' He cleared his throat. 'I've always found it difficult to talk to you. I'm afraid I will offend you, though all I want to do is be a brother to you. But it's time you learned to listen, Issa. There's nothing wrong in listening. Life is a constant learning process: the more you think you know, the less you actually know; things change so quickly, attitudes change . . .'

'I'll get by.'

'I don't doubt it, Issa, not for a second. But good intentions require means. No matter how hard you believe, belief isn't enough.'

'What are you insinuating, Mahi?'

My uncle wrung his hands nervously, searching for words, turning them over in his mind, then he took a deep breath and said:

'You have a wife and two children. It's a heavy burden for a man with no work. It ties your hands, it clips your wings . . .'

'They're my *family*.'

'I am your family too.'

'It's not the same thing.'

'It is the same thing, Issa. Your son is my nephew, flesh of my flesh. Leave him with me. What can he do if he follows in your footsteps? What were you hoping he might be – a labourer, a shoeshine boy, a donkey driver? You need to face facts. If he stays with you he will never amount to much. The boy needs to go to school, to learn to read and write, to grow up properly. I know — Arab boys aren't supposed to go to school, they're supposed to work in the fields, look after the livestock. But I can send him to school, I can turn him into an educated man . . . Please, don't take this the wrong way. Think for a minute. The boy has no future with you.'

My father thought for a long while about what his brother had said, eyes down, teeth clenched. When at last he looked up, his own face had disappeared, replaced by a mask of ashen impassiveness, and with a heavy heart he said:

'Clearly, you will never understand anything, my brother.'

'Don't take it like that, Issa.'

'Shut up. Don't say another word. Perhaps I am not educated like you, but if being educated means belittling others, I want nothing to do with it.'

My uncle tried to say something; my father stopped him with a wave. He took the banknote from his pocket and set it on the counter.

'And I want nothing to do with your money, either.'

With that, he grabbed me by the arm so roughly that he almost tore it from its socket, and pushed me out into the street. My uncle wanted to come after us, but didn't dare. He stood outside his shop, knowing this mistake would never be forgiven.

My father did not walk, he thundered down the hill like a boulder. I had never seen him so angry. He seemed about to implode. His lips quivered, his eyes stared fiercely at the world as though wishing the ground would open up and swallow everything. He said nothing, but his seething silence made me fear the worst.

When we had gone some distance, he grabbed me and slammed me against a wall, staring hard into my terrified eyes; a blast of buckshot could not have terrified me more.

'Do you think I'm a failure?' he asked, choking out the words. 'Do you think I brought a child into the world to watch him die slowly? Well, you're wrong, and your sneering uncle is wrong, and destiny itself is wrong if it thinks I will allow myself be humiliated. Do you know why? Because though I was forced to abandon my lands, I still have my soul. I'm still alive, I'm strong, I've got my health. I have the power enough to move mountains. Because I have pride.'

His fingers digging into my shoulders were hurting me. He didn't realise it. His eyes rolled in his head like white-hot ball bearings.

'I wasn't able to save our land, I know that, but I got it to produce a harvest, don't forget that . . . What happened afterwards was not my fault. Sometime hard work and prayer come to grief in the face of man's greed. I was naïve. I'm not naïve now. I won't be stabbed in the back again . . . I may be starting from scratch, but I'm starting off a wiser man. I'll work harder than any man has ever worked, I'll face down the evil eye and I'll prove to you that your father is a worthy man. I'll drag us out of this pit that's swallowed us up, I swear it. You do believe me, son, don't you?'

'Yes, Papa.'

'Look me in the eye and tell me you believe me.'

He had no eyes now, only two gaping chasms of tears and blood that threatened to engulf us both.

'Look at me!'

He grabbed my chin and jerked my head up.

'You don't believe me, do you?'

I felt a lump in my throat. I couldn't speak, I couldn't meet his eyes. The hand gripping my chin was the only thing that held me up.

Suddenly I felt his other hand lash my cheek.

'You think I'm crazy, that's why you won't say anything. You little shit. What right have you to doubt me? No one has the right to doubt me. If that bastard of an uncle of yours thinks I'm washed up, then he's no better.'

This was the first time my father had ever raised his hand to me. I didn't understand what was going on, what I had done wrong, why he was so angry with me. I felt ashamed that I had made him angry, terrified that he might disown me, this man who mattered more to me than anything in the world.

My father raised his hand again and it hovered in the air, fingers trembling. His face was swollen and distorted. Then he howled like a wounded animal and hugged me to his chest, sobbing, crushing me against him so hard, for so long, I thought I might die.

3

THE WOMEN were sitting around a low table in a corner of the courtyard, drinking tea and basking in the sun. My mother, sitting with them, slightly aloof, held Zahra in her arms. She had finally joined the group but she took no part in their conversations. She was shy, and often, when Badra started in on one of her dirty stories, she would flush and choke on her tea with embarrassment. As usual, the conversation shifted from one subject to another, anything to take their minds off the stifling heat of the courtyard. Yezza, the redhead, had a black eye; her husband had come home drunk again the night before. Out of a sense of propriety, the other women pretended not to notice. Yezza was proud of her black eye; she endured her husband's cowardly attacks with dignity.

'The past few nights, I've had a strange dream,' Mama said to Batoul, the clairvoyant. 'It's always the same: it's dark, I'm lying on my belly and someone sticks a knife in my back.'

The women all turned towards Batoul, waiting for her interpretation. The psychic looked hesitant and scratched her head; she had no vision.

'It's always the same?'

'Exactly the same.'

'You're lying on your belly in the dark and someone stabs you in the back?' asked Badra.

'Exactly.'

'Are you sure it's a knife?' Badra quipped, rolling her eyes lewdly.

It took the women a moment to realise what she was hinting at, then they burst out laughing. Mama clearly had no idea what the joke was, so Badra nudged her. 'You should tell your husband to be more gentle!'

'Badra! Don't you ever think about anything else?' Mama was angry, 'Can't you see I'm being serious?'

'Well, so am I . . .'

The women fell about, mouths hanging open as they brayed with laughter. Mama sat sullenly for a minute, shocked by their lack of restraint, but then she too began to smile and then to giggle.

Only Hadda did not join in the laughter. Her small, slender frame was drawn up. She was extraordinarily beautiful, with high cheekbones and great dark eyes, but she looked distraught. She had not said a word since she sat down. Suddenly she reached across the table and offered her palm for Batoul to read.

'Tell me what you can see . . .'

Batoul hesitated, but seeing the distress in the girl's face, she gently took the small hand in her own, her fingernail tracing the lines that criss-crossed the palm.

'You have the hands of a princess, Hadda.'

'Tell me what you see, Batoul. I need to know. I can't go on like this.'

Batoul studied the girl's palm in silence for a long time.

'Can you see my husband?' Hadda asked anxiously. 'Where

is he? What is he doing? Has he taken another wife? Is he dead? I'm begging you, Batoul, tell me. I need to know the truth, no matter what it is.'

Batoul sighed, her shoulders slumped.

'I do not see your husband, my poor Hadda. Nowhere. I sense no presence, not the least trace of him. Either he has gone far away, so far that he has forgotten you, or he is no longer of this world. One thing is certain, he will not return.'

Hadda swallowed hard, but she carried on, her eyes boring into the psychic's face. 'Tell, me, Batoul, what does my future hold? What will become of me? I am a single woman with two small children, I have no family, no husband . . .'

'We will not abandon you,' Badra promised.

'If my husband has abandoned me, there are no shoulders broad enough to hold me up,' said Hadda. 'Tell me, Batoul, what is to become of me? I need to know. When you are prepared for the worst, it is easier to bear.'

Batoul pored over her neighbour's palm, tracing and retracing the lines with her fingernail.

'I see you surrounded by many men, Hadda, but I see little happiness. You were not made for happiness. I can see brief moments of joy swallowed up by years of bitterness, years of shadows and sorrow, yet you never surrender.'

'Many men? Am I to be widowed, or will my husbands constantly abandon me?'

'The image is unclear. There are too many people around you, too much noise. It seems like a dream, but it is not a dream. It is . . . it is very strange. Perhaps I am getting old . . . I feel tired today. Excuse me . . .'

Batoul got to her feet and stumbled back to her room.

My mother made the most of the clairvoyant's departure to slip away herself.

'Aren't you ashamed of yourself, coming and sitting with the women?' she scolded me in a low voice behind the curtain that screened our room. 'How many times have I told you that a boy has no business listening to women's chatter? Go and play in the street, and try not to go too far.'

'There's nothing for me to do in the street.'

'There's nothing for you to do in here with grown women either.'

'The other boys pick on me.'

'You need to learn to stand up for yourself. You're not a girl. Sooner or later you have to learn to get by on your own, and you won't do that sitting around listening to women gossip!'

I didn't like leaving the courtyard. What had happened to me on the scrubland had made me fearful. I did not set foot outside the house without carefully scanning the streets and alleys all around, constantly alert for anything suspicious. I was terrified of the local thugs, of Daho in particular, a squat, stocky lad who was ugly and evil as a *djinn*. He terrified me. Whenever I saw him, I felt myself crumble into a thousand pieces; I would have walked through walls to get away from him. He was a surly boy, as impulsive as a lightning bolt. He prowled the streets with a gang of young hyenas as vicious and cruel as himself. No one knew where he came from, who his parents were, but everyone knew he would wind up dangling on the end of a rope or with his head on a spike.

And then there was the Moor – El Moro – an ex-con

who had spent seventeen years in prison. He was a giant of a man, broad and strapping, with arms like Hercules, tattoos all over his body and a leather eye patch that covered a gaping socket. The gash of a scar cut across his face from eyebrow to chin, slashing his mouth into a harelip. His very name spelled terror. Whenever he appeared, everyone suddenly fell silent and quietly slipped away, hugging the walls. Only once had I seen him close up. There were a gang of us clustered around Peg-Leg's stall. The ex-soldier was telling us about his exploits in the Rif Valley in Morocco – he had fought with the French against the Berber rebel Abd el-Krim. We were hanging on his every word, then suddenly our hero turned deathly pale. We thought he was having a heart attack. But he wasn't: El Moro was standing behind us, his legs like tree trunks, hands on his hips. He looked the grocer up and down with a sneer.

'You want to send these lads off to get slaughtered, bone-head? Is that why you're always filling their heads with your tall tales? Why don't you tell them how, after years of loyal service, the same officers threw you to the dogs when you had one paw missing?'

Peg-Leg had suddenly lost the power of speech, his lips moving silently like a fish out of water.

El Moro went on, his fury mounting.

'You smoke out villages, slaughter the livestock, shoot poor unarmed souls, then come and lay out your trophies on the public square. You call that war? You want to know what I think? You're a coward; you disgust me. I'd like to take that wooden club you use for a leg and skewer you with it until your eyes pop out of your ears . . . "Heroes" like you don't deserve a monument; they don't deserve so much as a headstone over the mass grave they should be buried in. You're scum, you're a mercenary traitor trying to hide his crimes by blowing his nose in the flag.'

Peg-Leg was green now, and shaking, his Adam's apple bobbing in his throat. Suddenly there was a terrible smell – Peg-Leg had soiled himself.

But there were others in Jenane Jato besides street urchins and loud-mouthed thugs. Most of those who lived there were good people. Poverty had not eaten away their souls, misery had not dampened their kindness. They knew they had little chance in life, but still they waited for manna from Heaven, still they convinced themselves that the misfortune that dogged them would run its term and hope rise again from the ashes. They were decent people, some of them were charming or funny, and all of them kept the faith and, with extraordinary patience, carried on.

The day of the souk in Jenane Jato was like carnival, and everyone did what they could to maintain the illusion. Soup vendors set up stalls and, wielding their ladles like cudgels to beat off the beggars, sold bowls of broth made of chickpeas, water and cumin for half a *doro*. There were several cafés where groups of starving wretches stood outside simply to inhale the smell of cooking. On market day, con artists were out in force – they would come from the four corners of the city hoping for some blunder, some misunderstanding they could turn to their advantage, but the people of Jenane Jato ignored them: they knew these twisted souls could not be healed. Instead they listened to the travelling musicians and thrilled at the acrobats. The biggest draws at the souk were the *gouals*. Hundreds of people would crowd around them to listen. It was difficult to take in everything they said – their stories were as threadbare as their clothes – but they had the gift of bluffing their audience, of keeping them breathless from start to finish. The *gouals* were a beggar's opera of sorts, a form of open-air theatre. It was from them, for example, that I learned that once the sea had been fresh water, until the tears of sailors' widows turned it to salt . . .

After the *gouals* came the snake charmers. They would try to scare us, tossing snakes at our feet. I watched charmers half swallow quivering vipers only to conjure them away into the sleeves of their *gandurahs* – a sight so thrilling yet so revolting, I had nightmares about it. The cleverest of all were the charlatans, who stood babbling and gesticulating next to stalls filled with phials and potions, *gris-gris*, amulets, and the dried corpses of animals famous for their aphrodisiacal powers. They claimed they could cure deafness, toothache, gout, paralysis, terror, barrenness, ringworm, insomnia, evil spells and frigidity, and the credulous crowds fell for it. Some would swallow one of these potions, and three seconds later would be rolling in the dirt, claiming to have been miraculously cured. It was astounding.

There were prophets who came to harangue the crowd. Their gestures solemn, their voices sepulchral, they would stand on their makeshift platforms and hold forth, denouncing the corruption of the spirit, heralding the coming of the Judgement Day. They ranted about the Apocalypse, about the rage of men, the fate reserved for impure women; they foamed at the mouth, railing at innocent passers-by, or launched into esoteric ideas that were seemingly unending. 'How many slaves have risen up against empires only to die on a cross?' one of them thundered, shaking his shaggy beard. 'How many kings have thought they could change history only to end up rotting in a dungeon? How many prophets have sought to expand our minds only to leave us more deluded than before?' 'How many times have we told you you're boring?' someone in the crowd roared back. 'Why don't you put a hood over that ugly mug of yours and show us some belly-dancing and stop this lunatic raving?'

Slimane was among the sideshows. With a barrel organ slung across his chest and his marmoset perched on his shoulder, he strutted around the market cranking the handle while the monkey held out a peaked cap to anyone who came near. Whenever someone tossed a coin in, the monkey would pull faces for them. Away from the main attractions were the livestock enclosures and the donkey sellers, wily horse-traders so persuasive they could pass off a mule as a pureblood stallion. I loved to listen to them sing the praises of their animals; being hoodwinked by them was almost a pleasure, since they treated you with the courtesy and deference reserved for an aga.

Sometimes, into this mayhem, the Karcabo would arrive – a troop of black men bedecked with amulets, who danced like demons, rolling their milk-white eyes. We would hear them coming from the devilish racket of their metal castanets, the roll of their drums. The Karcabo came only for the feast day of the marabout Sidi Blal, their patron. They would come into town leading a sacrificial bull calf draped in the colours of the brotherhood and go from door to door to collect money for the sacrifice. In Jenane Jato, women would rush to the doors to watch – even though it was forbidden – children would pop up out of nowhere like gerbils, eager to join the throng, and as the procession moved on, the noise and the clamour grew.

Of all of the extraordinary sites at the festival, Slimane took the prize. His music was sweet and sad as water flowing, and the marmoset was charmingly mischievous. People said Slimane had been born a Christian to a wealthy, educated French family but fell in love with a Bedouin girl and converted to Islam. He could have lived like a king, they said, since his family had never disowned him, but instead he chose to stay with his adoptive people and share their joys and their pains. We all thought this was touching. No one, Arab or Berber, even the most hard-hearted, had anything but respect for him, and no one would raise a hand against him. I was very fond of Slimane. As far back as I can remember, deep in my heart – the heart of the old man I am now – no one that I ever met better embodied what I believe to be the greatest of virtues: discernment, a quality that is all but lost today, but one which did much for the reputation of my people at a time when few had any respect for us.

Meanwhile, I had befriended Ouari, a boy a few years older than me, who was thin, almost emaciated, with reddish-blonde hair, bushy eyebrows and a hook nose like a sickle. He was not really a friend, but he didn't seem to mind me hanging around, and since I needed him, I did everything I could to win his friendship. Ouari was probably an orphan – or a runaway; I never once saw him go in or come out of a house. He spent his time behind a vast pile of scrap metal in something that looked like a henhouse carpeted with dung, and spent his time hunting goldfinches so he could sell them at market.

Ouari never spoke. I would talk to him for hours; he paid me no mind. He was a mysterious, solitary boy, the only one in the neighbourhood who wore trousers and a beret. All the other boys wore long *gandurahs* and a fez. In the evenings he made traps with olive branches dipped in birdlime. In the mornings I would follow him into the scrub-land and help him set the traps. When a bird landed on one of the traps and began to flap its wings frantically, we'd rush over and put it in a cage while we waited to catch some more. In the afternoon we would stroll through the streets offering our hunting trophies to novice bird-catchers.

The first few pennies I ever earned, I made with Ouari. Ouari never cheated me. At the end of our first hunting expedition – which lasted several days – he asked me to follow him to a quiet corner, where he spilled the contents of the game bag he used as a purse. He divided up the coins, one penny for him, one for me, and so on until there were none left. He walked me home, then he vanished. The next morning I went looking for him at the chicken coop. I don't think he would ever have come looking for me. He seemed perfectly capable of getting by without my help or anyone else's.

I felt good being around Ouari, confident and relaxed. Even the little savage Daho left us in peace. Ouari had a dark, steely, mysterious look about him that kept people at bay. He didn't say much, but he had only to scowl and the street kids disappeared so fast it took their shadows a moment to catch up. I think I was happy around Ouari. I got a taste for hunting goldfinches and learned a lot about traps and camouflage.

Then, one evening, hoping to make my father proud of

me, it all collapsed. I waited until after supper before taking my purse from its hiding place. Hands trembling with excitement, I held out the fruits of my labours.

'What's this?' my father asked suspiciously.

'I don't know how much is there, I don't know how to count . . . but it's the money I made selling birds.'

'What birds?'

'Goldfinches. You catch them with twigs dipped in birdlime—'

My father grabbed my hand. His eyes were like white-hot ball bearings, and his voice shook as he said:

'Listen carefully, son, I don't need your money, and I don't need an imam nipping at my heels.'

As my face distorted with pain, his grip tightened.

'I know I'm hurting you, son, I can feel your pain like it was my own. I'm not trying to break your hand, I'm trying to get it into that thick skull of yours that I'm not a ghost. I'm flesh and blood and I'm very much alive.'

I felt my fingers crushed by his fist, hot tears blurred my vision. I was choking with the pain, but there could be no question of whingeing or crying. Everything was a matter of honour between my father and me; and honour was measured by our ability to endure pain.

'What can you see right there in front of you?' He nodded to the low table, the leftover food.

'Supper, Papa.'

'I'm not saying it's a feast, but you get enough to eat, don't you?'

'Yes, Papa.'

'Have you ever gone to bed hungry since we came to the city?'

47

'No, Papa.'

'And that table there, the one you're eating off, did we have it when we got here?'

'No, Papa.'

'What about the paraffin stove? Did someone give it to us? Did we find it in the street?'

'You bought it, Papa.'

'When we got here, the only light we had was a *marepoza* – a miserable bit of wick floating in a puddle of oil, remember? What have we got now?'

'An oil lamp.'

'What about the sleeping mats, the blankets, the pillows, the buckets, the broom?'

'You bought them, Papa.'

'Then why can't you get it into your head, son? I told you the other day, I might have lost my lands, but I haven't lost my soul. I couldn't save the damned farm, and I'm sorry. You can't imagine how sorry I am. There's not a minute of the day I don't think about it. But I'm not about to give up. I work every hour God sends, I break my back to get us back on our feet. And it's up to me – *and only me* – to make that happen. Do you understand, son? I don't want you feeling guilty about what happened. It's not your fault. You don't have to give me money. I wouldn't send you out to work to make ends meet, I wouldn't stoop to that. If I fall, I pick myself up again; that's the price I have to pay and I don't blame anyone. And I will do it, I swear to you. Like I told you, I have the power to move mountains. So in the name of our dead and those of us still living, if you want to make my life easier, just promise me you'll never again do what you've just done to me, because every penny you bring into this house just makes my shame worse.'

He opened his fist. My hand and my purse felt as though they were welded together. I couldn't move my fingers; my arm was numb up to the elbow.

The following morning, I gave Ouari the money back.

Ouari frowned slightly as he saw me slip my purse into his game bag, but his surprise faded immediately and he went back to his traps as though it had never happened.

My father's reaction unsettled me. How could he have so misinterpreted my modest contribution? I was his son, flesh of his flesh. By what twisted logic could my well-meant gesture be taken as an insult? I would have been so proud for him to accept my money, but instead, I had hurt him.

This was the night, I think, when I first began to doubt the soundness of my good intentions, a doubt that would plague my every thought.

I no longer understood anything.

I was no longer certain of anything.

My father was determined to get back on his feet, determined to prove to me that my uncle had been wrong. He worked tirelessly, worked every hour of the day, and now made no attempt to hide how hard he worked. My father, who until now had always kept his plans to himself so as not to tempt the evil eye, now told my mother every detail of his plans to find more work, earn more money – ensuring his voice was loud enough so that I would overhear. He promised us the moon. Every night when he came home, a twinkle in his eye, jingling the change in his pocket, he would talk about the house we were going to live in – a proper house with shutters on the windows, a front door of solid wood, maybe even a little vegetable garden where he could plant coriander and mint, tomatoes and vegetables that would melt in our mouths. My mother listened, happy to see her husband planning and dreaming again. Though she did not entirely have faith in these plans, she pretended to believe him, and when he held her hand – something he had never done before – she positively glowed.

My father worked morning, noon and night, taking any job he could find, determined to be back on his feet as soon as possible. He spent his mornings helping out a herbalist, in the afternoons he did a shift for a ambulant greengrocer and in the evenings he worked as a masseur in a Turkish bath. He was even planning to start his own business.

As for me, I wandered the streets, alone and worried.

One morning, while I was far from home, Daho crept up on me. He had an ugly green snake wrapped round his arm. He backed me into a corner, rolling his eyes, waving the reptile's gaping maw in my face. I had always hated snakes; they scared me to death. Daho taunted me, laughing at my panic, calling me a sissy . . . I was about to pass out when suddenly Ouari appeared from nowhere. Daho immediately stopped and stood, ready to run if my friend came to help me. But Ouari did not come to my rescue. He stared at us for a moment, and then walked on as though he hadn't seen anything. Daho breathed a sigh of relief and, laughing maniacally, went back to torturing me with the snake. But it didn't matter now, he could laugh all he wanted. I didn't care. Sadness had driven out fear: I no longer had a friend.

PEG-LEG was dozing behind his counter, his turban pushed down over his face, his makeshift limb in easy reach lest he need it to fend off some light-fingered child who came too close to his sweets. His humiliation at the hands of El Moro was a distant memory. His time in the army had taught him forbearance. After years of suffering brutal NCOs with obtuse submissiveness, I suppose he considered the fleeting outbursts of Jenane Jato's thugs just another abuse of power. Peg-Leg knew that life was a series of ups and downs, moments of bravery and moments of cowardice. What mattered was to pick yourself up when you fell, keep your dignity when you had been beaten. The fact that no one in Jenane Jato made fun of him after El Moro's 'humiliation' was proof that no one could have stood up to the man. El Moro was no ordinary adversary; he was death incarnate, he was a firing squad. To face him head on and escape with only cuts and bruises was a triumph; to come through unscathed but for a pair of soiled pants was a miracle.

Next door, the barber was shaving the head of a bald man who sat on the ground like a fakir, his open mouth revealing a single stump of tooth. The rasp of the razor on the strop seemed to give the old man great pleasure. The barber told him all his troubles, but the old man paid him no heed; he simply sat, eyes closed, enjoying the feel of the razor as it scraped across his head, which was as bald as a polished marble.

'There you go!' the barber said as he finished. 'That head of yours is so clear now a man could read your mind.'

'I'm sure you missed a bit,' the old man said. 'I can feel a five o'clock shadow clouding my thoughts.'

'What thoughts, you old fool? Don't tell me that that brain of yours still works . . .'

'I might be old, but I'm not senile. Look again. I'm sure you missed a hair or two.'

'There's nothing, I promise you. It's smooth as an egg.'

'Please,' the old man insisted, 'look again.'

The barber was no fool; he knew the old man was simply enjoying the shave. He considered his work, meticulously checking that he had not missed a single hair on the old man's wizened neck, then he set down his razor and indicated to his customer that his siesta was over.

'Come on, Uncle Jabori, time to get back to your goats.'

'Please . . .'

'Enough is enough, I said. I've better things to do with my time.'

The old man grudgingly got to his feet, peered at himself in the sliver of mirror, then pretended to rummage through his pockets.

'I think I must have left my money at home,' he said, trying to sound exasperated.

The barber smiled; he had seen this coming.

'Don't worry about it, Uncle Jabori.'

'I was sure I'd put it in my pocket this morning, I swear to you. Maybe I lost it on the way here.'

'It doesn't matter,' the barber said wearily. 'God will repay me.'

'I won't hear of it!' said the old man politely. 'I'll go and get it right this minute.'

'That's very touching. Just try not to get lost on the way.'

The old man twisted his turban round his head and hurried off. The barber watched him go, then squatted on his munitions box.

'It's always the same – do people think I do this for fun?' he muttered. 'This is my living, for God's sake! How am I supposed to eat tonight?'

He ranted on, trying to get Peg-Leg to respond.

Peg-Leg ignored him.

The barber went on for several minutes, and when the ex-soldier still did not react, he took a deep breath and, staring up into the sky, started to sing:

> I miss your eyes
> And I go blind
> Every time you look away
> I die a little every day
> Searching for you
> In vain among the living
> What does it mean to live this love
> When all the world proclaims
> That you are gone?
> What will I do now with my hands
> Now your body is not here . . .

'Use them to wipe your arse!' yelled Peg-Leg.

It was as if someone had thrown a bucket of cold water over the barber. He was sickened by the vulgar way the grocer had broken the spell, the beauty of his song. Looking on, I felt sad, as though I had been woken from a dream.

The barber tried to ignore Peg-Leg; he shook his head sadly, cleared his throat and tried to begin again, but there was a lump in his throat and his heart was not in it any more.

'You can be such a pain in the arse!'

'What about you, forever wailing those pathetic songs of yours?' Peg-Leg shifted lazily on his box.

'What if I am?' the barber said. 'Look around. There's no one here, there's nothing to do. The whole place is dying and there's not a soul around can even raise a smile. If a man can't sing, what's left?'

Peg-Leg jerked his thumb at the coils of rope on the hook above his head.

'There's always that. Take your pick, tie one end to the branch of a tree, wrap the other end around your neck, then bend your knees and you'll have peace; that's a sleep no one can disturb.'

'Why don't you go first? You're the one who hates life.'

'How am I supposed to go first? I've got a wooden leg – I can't bend my knees.'

Resigned, the barber sat back on his munitions box and put his head in his hands – probably so he could go on humming to himself. He knew there was no one to listen to his song. His only muse was one he conjured out of whispers and sighs, and he knew he would never be worthy of her. The sliver of mirror reflected the disparity between his lowly body and his grand desires: he was short, scrawny, and so stooped he was almost a hunch back, as ugly and as poor as Job himself; he had no house, no family and no prospect of making his pitiful life any better. And so he contented himself with living in a dream, an unattainable dream, a dream he could not admit to in public without seeming a fool, a dream that in private he gnawed on like a juicy bone.

It broke my heart.

'Come here, lad,' shouted Peg-Leg, unscrewing the top of the jar of sweets. He handed me a sweet, gestured for me to sit next to him. He stared at me for a long moment.

'Let me look at your face, son,' he said, lifting my chin with his finger. 'Well, now . . . The good Lord was particularly inspired when he made you, wasn't he. A face takes talent. How come you have blue eyes? Is your mother French?'

'No.'

'Your grandmother, then?'

'No.'

He tousled my hair with his calloused hand, then slowly stroked my cheek.

'You have the face of an angel, lad.'

'Leave the kid alone,' hissed Bliss the broker, appearing suddenly around the corner.

Peg-Leg jerked his hand away quickly.

'I didn't do nothing,' he whined.

'Don't give me that,' said Bliss. 'I'm warning you, the boy's father is a brute – he'll rip your other leg off as soon as look at you, and I won't have a legless cripple on *my* street. They bring bad luck.'

'Honestly, I don't know what you're talking about, Monsieur Bliss.'

'You know and everyone else round here knows what I'm talking about. If you're so keen on war, why don't you fuck off to Spain instead of hanging around here drooling over little boys? They're always fighting some war in Spain, they need cannon fodder.'

'How can he?' the barber interrupted. 'He's got a wooden leg that doesn't bend at the knee.'

'Shut up, you cockroach,' Peg-Leg roared, trying to save face, 'or I'll make you swallow your rusty razor blades one by one.'

'You'd have to catch me first.'

Bliss waved for me to clear off.

As I scrambled away, my father appeared from a narrow alleyway and I ran to meet him. He was home earlier than usual and I could tell from the parcel under his arm that he was in a good mood. He asked where I'd got the sweet I was eating, then marched over to Peg-Leg and tried to pay for it. At first the grocer refused to take the money – it was only a sweet, he said – but my father would have none of it and insisted he take it.

Then we went home.

My father unwrapped the brown paper package and gave each of us a present: there was a scarf for my mother, a dress for my little sister and a pair of brand-new rubber boots for me.

'You're mad,' my mother said.

'Why?'

'It's a lot of money, and you need the money, don't you?'

'This is just the start,' my father said, getting carried away. 'Soon, we'll have a new house, I promise. I'm working hard and I'm doing well. Things are looking up, so why not make the most of it? I have a meeting with a well-established merchant on Thursday, a serious businessman. He's going to take me on as his partner.'

'Please, Issa, don't say another word. You've never had much luck. Don't talk about your plans if you want them to come true.'

'Don't worry, I wasn't going to tell you the details, just that this man said that to make me a partner in his business, I would have to invest a certain sum of money. And . . . *I've got the money!*'

'Please, don't say any more,' my mother begged, spitting on the ground to ward off the evil eye. 'Say nothing, and let things take their course. The evil eye has no pity for blowhards.'

My father did not say any more, but his eyes shone with a joy I had never seen in him before. That night, he was determined to celebrate his reconciliation with Lady Luck. He had been to the butcher's, wrung the neck of a capon, plucked and cleaned it and brought it home – hidden at the bottom of a straw basket out of respect for our neighbours, who rarely had much to eat.

My father was suddenly happier than a gang of boys let loose at a carnival. He was counting off the days until he would be a partner in his own business. Five days, four, three . . .

He worked as hard as he ever had, but now he invariably came home earlier so he could have the pleasure of seeing me run to meet him. He needed me to be awake when he got home to reassure me that his luck had changed, that there were clear skies ahead, that he, *my father*, was strong as an oak, capable of moving mountains with his bare hands . . .

Then came the long-awaited Thursday.

There are some days the seasons shun, days that fate and demons spurn, days when our guardian angels desert us, when a man is left to his fate and is forever lost. That Thursday was such a day. My father realised it as soon as he woke; I could see it in his face. To the end of my days I will remember that day – an ugly, miserable, brutal day of torrential rain and thunderclaps that rang out like a curse. The sky brooded, the coppery clouds lowered.

'Surely you're not going out in weather like this?' my mother said.

My father was standing on the threshold of our room, staring at the dark, bruised sky as at some evil omen. He considered postponing his meeting, but fortune does not favour those who hesitate. He knew this and dismissed his feeling of foreboding as the Devil attempting to disconcert him. At the last minute, he turned and asked me to go with him. Maybe he thought that if he brought me along, fate might relent, might spare him any low blows.

I slipped on my hooded *gandurah*, my rubber boots, and hurried after him.

We were soaked to the skin by the time we arrived at the meeting place. My feet squelched in the rain-filled boots, the sodden hood of my *gandurah* weighed on my shoulders like a yoke. The street was deserted, except for an overturned cart; there was no one to be seen . . . or almost no one. Because El Moro was lying in wait, like a bird of prey perched over the fate of man. When he saw us arrive, he stepped from his hiding place, his eyes like the barrels of a gun, dark sockets in which death seemed to smoulder. My father was taken aback. Before he could react, El Moro lashed out with his head, his foot, his fist. My father fought back as best he could, determined not to give in, but El Moro was quick; he ducked and weaved and in the end this thug got the better of my father, who, though brave, was a quiet, unassuming farmer unaccustomed to fighting. El Moro tripped him, and as he fell, he pinned him to the ground and began pounding him, clearly intent on killing him. I was petrified. It was like a nightmare. I tried to scream, to rush to my father's aid, but not a nerve or a muscle in my body would respond. Blood and rainwater coursed into the gutter, yet still El Moro did not give up: he knew exactly what he was looking for. When at last my father stopped fighting back, the animal crouched over his prey and pushed up my father's *gandurah*. His face lit up like a lightning flash in the darkness when he saw the purse strapped beneath my father's armpit. He slashed the straps with a knife, smiled as he felt the weight of the purse, then disappeared without so much as a glance at me.

His face a bloody mess, his *gandurah* hiked up exposing his belly, my father lay where he had fallen. I could do nothing to help him. I was in some other world. I don't remember how we got home.

'I was sold out,' my father cursed. 'That thug was lying in wait for me. He knew I was carrying that money. He knew it . . . This was no stroke of bad luck, that bastard was waiting for me.'

Then he said nothing.

For days and days he did not say another word.

I have watched huge cacti split in a rainstorm, seen cliffs crumble; watching my father in the weeks and months after the attack was no different. He was slowly coming apart, unravelling thread by thread. He crouched in a corner, refusing to eat or drink, his head buried in his lap, his hands clasped behind his neck, silently brooding on his hatred, his fury.

He knew now that no matter what he did, what he said, he was doomed to disaster, and no oaths sworn on mountain-tops, no holy vows could change the course of his fate.

One night we heard the voice of the local drunk howling and raging along the street, his filthy tirade echoing across the courtyard like a baleful wind whistling through a tomb. It was a rasping voice, filled with bile and scorn, that called all men dogs, all women pigs, that predicted dark days for the wretched and the cowardly; a voice that dripped with self-righteous scorn, with bloated pride; a voice the people of Jenane Jato had learned to recognise amid the thousand apocalyptic rumblings – the voice of El Moro.

When he heard it, my father looked up so quickly he slammed his head against the wall. For a moment he stayed crouched in the corner, petrified. Then, like a ghost emerging from the gloom, he got to his feet, lit the oil lamp, rummaged through a pile of clothes, pulled out a battered leather case and opened it. His eyes shone in the lamplight. He held his breath, hesitated a moment, then plunged his hand into the bag and the blade of a butcher's knife flashed in his fist. He put on his *gandurah*, slipped the knife into the sleeve. I saw my mother stir. She knew what her husband was thinking, knew the madness of it, but she dared not say anything: this was not a woman's business.

My father stepped into the shadows and I heard his footsteps in the courtyard dying away like prayers carried on the wind. The door to the street creaked as it swung shut, then there was silence . . . a roaring silence that kept me awake, watching for my father until morning.

He crept back furtively at dawn, took off his *gandurah* and threw it on the floor, slipped the knife back into its case. Then he went back to the murky corner where he had been brooding since that fateful Thursday, curled up and did not move again.

The news spread like wildfire through Jenane Jato. Bliss, the broker, was overjoyed. He went from door to door shouting, 'El Moro is dead! He will never terrorise any of us again! Someone stabbed him through the heart!'

Two days later, my father took me to my uncle's pharmacy. His eyes were bloodshot, his beard dishevelled and he was trembling as though he had a fever.

My uncle did not come out from behind the counter, suspicious that we had shown up unexpectedly at a time when most shopkeepers were only rolling up their shutters. He assumed my father had come to take revenge for the insult some days earlier. When at last my father spoke, my uncle was visibly relieved.

'You were right, Mahi. My son has no future with me.'

My uncle stared at him open-mouthed.

My father crouched down beside me, digging his fingers into my shoulders so hard that it hurt. He looked me in the eye and said:

'It's for the best, son. I am not abandoning you, I am not disowning you; I simply want you to have a chance in life.'

He kissed me on the forehead – a gesture usually reserved for venerable elders. He tried to smile, and finding that he could not, he quickly got up and almost ran out of the shop to hide his tears.

5

MY UNCLE lived in the European part of the city, in a quiet cul-de-sac lined with neat brick houses with wrought-iron railings and shutters on the windows. It was a beautiful neighbourhood. The streets were bordered by neatly trimmed ficus trees; there were benches where old men could sit and watch the world go by and leafy squares where children could play. These children were not dressed in rags like the children in Jenane Jato, their rosy faces were not pitted with the marks of damnation; they took in life in great lungfuls and seemed to genuinely enjoy it. The neighbourhood seemed impossibly hushed, the only sounds the burbling of babies and the chirp of birdsong.

My uncle had a two-storey house with a small front garden and a lane running down the side. Bougainvillea spilled over the fence, its purple flowers tumbling into space, and a grapevine grew in a dense tangle over the veranda.

'In summer, there are grapes everywhere,' my uncle told me as he opened the gate. 'If you stand on tiptoe, you'll be able to pick them.'

His eyes were shining. He was in seventh heaven.

'You'll like it here, boy.'

The door was opened by a red-haired woman of about forty. She was beautiful, with an oval face and huge aqueous green eyes. Seeing me standing on the step, she clasped her hands to her heart and stood for a moment, speechless, then glanced at my uncle, who nodded.

'He's so handsome!' she cried, crouching down to study me more carefully.

She threw her arms around me so suddenly that I almost fell over backwards. She was a powerful woman, with quick, brusque, almost masculine gestures. She hugged me to her, and I could feel her heart beating. She smelled as wonderful as a field of lavender, and the welling tears simply accentuated the green of her eyes.

'Germaine, darling,' my uncle said, his voice tremulous, 'this is Younes. Yesterday he was my nephew, today he is *our* son.'

I felt the woman's body tremble, saw a glittering tear quiver on her lashes then roll down her cheek.

'Jonas,' she said, choking back a sob, 'Jonas, if you knew how happy this makes me.'

'You have to speak to him in Arabic, he's never been to school.'

'It doesn't matter, we'll soon fix that.'

Still trembling, she got to her feet, took me by the hand and led me into a room full of grand furniture that to my eyes looked bigger than a cowshed. Daylight streamed through the French windows that led on to the veranda, where two rocking chairs stood either side of a table.

'This is your new home, Jonas,' Germaine said to me.

My uncle followed, a parcel under one arm, smiling from ear to ear.

'I bought him some clothes. You can buy him some more tomorrow.'

'That's fine, I'll look after him. You'd better go back, your customers will be getting impatient.'

'Well, well . . . so you want him all to yourself?'

Germaine crouched down again and looked at me.

'I think we're going to get along just fine, aren't we, Jonas?' she said to me in Arabic.

My uncle put the parcel of clothes on a sideboard and settled himself on the sofa, hands in his lap, his fez pushed back from his forehead.

'You're not going to hang around here spying on us, are you?' said Germaine.

'Absolutely. Today is a holiday, my darling. I've just become a father.'

'You're not serious.'

'I've never been more serious in my life.'

'Very well then,' Germaine conceded. 'Jonas and I are going to take a nice bath.'

'My name is Younes,' I reminded her.

She gave me a tender smile, stroked my cheek and whispered:

'Not any more, my darling . . .'

Then, turning to my uncle:

'Since you're here, make yourself useful and go and heat some water.'

She led me into a little room where there was a sort of large cast-iron cauldron, turned on a tap and began to undress me.

'Let's get rid of these old rags, shall we, Jonas?'

I didn't know what to say. I watched her pale hands

working, removing my fez, my *gandurah*, my threadbare vest, my rubber boots. I felt like a bird plucked of its feathers.

My uncle came back with a bucket of scalding water. Out of decency, he stayed in the hall. Germaine helped me into the tub, soaped me from head to foot, rinsed me over and over then rubbed me energetically with some perfumed lotion and wrapped me in a huge towel while she went to get my new clothes. When I was dressed again, she stood me in front of a large mirror. I was a different person. I was wearing a sailor's pea jacket with a high collar and four brass buttons down the front, a pair of short trousers with pockets, and a beret like the one Ouari wore.

When I reappeared in the living room, my uncle got to his feet to greet me. He looked so happy it almost scared me.

'My little barefoot prince,' he said. 'Isn't he handsome?'

'Stop that, you'll draw the evil eye on him . . . And speaking of bare feet, you forgot to buy shoes.'

My uncle clapped his hand to his forehead. 'You're right,' he said. 'Where was my head?'

'In the clouds, probably.'

My uncle immediately went out again and a little later reappeared with three pairs of shoes of different sizes. The smallest pair – black leather lace-up shoes that scraped my heels – fitted me perfectly. He didn't take the other pairs back; he was keeping them, he said, for me to grow into.

Like two moths flickering around a flame, Germaine and my uncle flitted around me constantly. They took me on a tour of the house, any one of whose vast high-ceilinged rooms was large enough to accommodate all of Bliss's tenants. Each spotless window was adorned with heavy drapes and framed by green shutters. It was a beautiful, sunny house, though a little disorienting, with its hidden doors, its spiral staircases and the built-in wardrobes that at first I mistook for rooms. I thought about my father, about our shack and the farm we had lost, about our filthy hovel in Jenane Jato; the difference was so great that I felt dizzy.

Every time I looked up, I saw Germaine looking down. She was determined to spoil me. My uncle did not quite know how to behave, but he did not leave my side. They tried to explain everything at once, burst out laughing for no reason at all, or simply stood, holding hands, staring at me with tears in their eyes. Meanwhile, wide-eyed, I discovered the wonders of the modern world.

That evening, we ate in the living room and I discovered something else strange: my uncle had no need of an oil lamp, he simply pressed a button on the wall and a host of lights in the ceiling lit up. I felt terribly awkward at dinner. At home I had been used to eating from the same plate as my family. Now that I had a plate all to myself, I didn't know what to do. Ill at ease with the eyes watching my every move, the hands constantly stroking my hair, pinching my cheeks, I barely ate a thing.

'Don't rush him,' Germaine kept saying to my uncle. 'Give him some time to get used to things.'

My uncle would curb his excitement for a minute, only to get carried away again a moment later.

After dinner, they led me upstairs.

'This is your room, Jonas,' Germaine announced.

'My room' was twice as big as the room my family shared

in Jenane Jato. In the middle was a huge bed flanked by two night tables. On the walls were paintings, some dreamlike landscapes, others of people praying, their hands clasped under their chins, heads ringed with golden haloes. On the mantelpiece was a statue of a little boy with wings and above it was a crucifix. In one corner was a small writing desk and an overstuffed chair. The room was pervaded by a strange perfume, sweet and ephemeral. Through the window I could see trees and the roofs of the houses opposite.

'Do you like it?'

I didn't answer. The lavishness of my surroundings frightened me. Everything seemed to be perfectly, precariously balanced; I was terrified that with one false move I would bring it all crashing down.

Germaine asked my uncle to leave the two of us alone. She waited until he had left and then undressed me and put me into bed, as though I would be incapable of doing so myself. My head sank into the mountain of pillows.

'Sweet dreams, my son.'

She drew up the blankets, kissed my forehead, turned out the bedside lamp, then crept out on tiptoe, carefully closing the door behind her.

As a rule I was not scared of the dark – a solitary boy with little imagination, I usually found it easy to get to sleep – but now, in this opulent room, I felt strangely uneasy. I missed my parents. But this was not the reason I felt fearful. There was something ominous about the room, something I could sense but could not put my finger on. Was it the smell of the blankets, or the scent that hung in the air that made me feel light-headed? Was it the sound like breathing that echoed in the room and wailed in the chimney? I was convinced that I was not alone, that there was something crouched in the shadows watching me. The hair on the back of my neck stood up; I gasped for breath. I felt an icy hand over my face. Outside, the full moon lit the street. The wind whistled through the railings and whipped the trees. I forced myself to close my eyes, clutching the sheets. I could still feel the cold hand on my face, and the impression that there was something else here with me became unbearable. I could sense it standing by the end of the bed, ready to leap on me. The air felt thin, my heart felt as though it would explode. I opened my eyes again and saw the statue of the winged boy on the mantelpiece turn slowly and stare at me through vacant eyes, its mouth fixed in a sad smile.

Terrified, I leapt out of bed and crouched behind the headboard. The winged boy turned again to stare at me, its monstrous shadow splayed across the wall. I scuttled under the bed, dragging a blanket with me, curled up as small as I could and closed my eyes tight, convinced that if I opened them, I would find the statue on all fours, peering in at me.

I was so petrified, I'm not sure if I finally fell asleep or simply passed out.

'Mahi!'

The scream woke me with such a start, I hit my head against the slats of the bed frame.

'Jonas isn't in his room,' Germaine shouted.

'What do you mean, he isn't in his room?'

I heard running in the corridor, doors slamming, foot-steps on the stairs. *He can't have left the house . . . The door is double-locked.* My uncle's voice. *The veranda door is locked too . . . Did you look in the toilet? I just checked — he's not in there.* Germaine was panicking. *Are you sure he's not in his room? . . .*

I told you, his bed is empty . . . They searched downstairs, moving furniture, then came back upstairs and into my room.

'My God, Jonas,' Germaine cried when she saw me sitting on the edge of the bed, 'where did you get to?'

My right side was stiff and my joints hurt. My uncle examined the lump on my forehead.

'Did you fall out of bed?'

I pointed stiffly at the statue: 'It kept moving all night.'

Germaine put her arms around me.

'Jonas, my poor little Jonas, why didn't you wake us? You're so pale, I feel terrible.'

The following night, the statue of the winged boy was gone, and with it the crucifix and the holy pictures. Germaine sat beside my bed telling me stories in a jumble of Arabic and French, stroking my hair until I fell asleep.

As the weeks went by, I missed my parents terribly, though Germaine did everything she could to make my life happy. In the morning, when she went shopping, she would take me with her, and I never came home without a new toy or some sweets. The afternoons she spent teaching me to read and write. She was eager to enrol me in a school, but my uncle was determined not to rush things. Sometimes he let me come to work at the chemist shop with him, and sitting me at a little desk in the back office while he served customers, he had me copy out the alphabet in an exercise book. I was a fast learner, Germaine thought, and she didn't understand why my uncle was so hesitant to send me to school. After two months, I could read whole words without stumbling over the syllables, but still my uncle would not hear of sending me to school until he was sure my father would not change his mind and come looking for me.

One evening, as I was wandering around aimlessly upstairs, he called me into his office. It was a dark room, lit only by a small skylight. There were books everywhere. Every inch of wall was lined with bookcases and there were piles of books on the sideboard and on his desk. His glasses balanced on the bridge of his nose, my uncle looked up from the book he had been reading. He perched me on his lap and pointed to the portrait of a woman on the wall.

'You need to know something, my boy. You haven't fallen from a tree into a ditch . . . You see that woman in the picture there? Her name is Lalla Fatna. She was a woman of money and status, and as domineering as she was rich – one general used to call her Jeanne d'Arch. She owned land enough for a small country, with meadows teeming with livestock. Eminent people came for miles to visit her and she had them eating out of her hand. Even officers of the French army courted her. They say that if the emir Abd al-Qadir had met her, it would have changed the course of history. Look closely at her, boy, because this woman, this legendary figure, was your great-grandmother.'

The woman in the portrait was beautiful. She lay back against plush cushions, neck straight, head held high, wearing a kaftan embroidered with gold and precious stones. She looked as though she might rule over men and over their dreams.

My uncle pointed to another photograph, one of three men in opulent *burnouses* with carefully trimmed beards and eyes so piercing they all but leapt from the frame.

'The man in the middle is my father, your grandfather. The others are his brothers. Sidi Abbas, on the right, went to Syria and never came back. Abdelmoumène, on the left, was a brilliant student. A man so wise he might have been a scholar – one of the great *ulemas* – but as a young man, he gave in to temptation. He spent too much time with the European bourgeoisie; he neglected his lands and his livestock and squandered his money in brothels. He was found dead in an alley with a knife in his back.'

He turned and pointed to a third portrait, bigger than the other two.

'The man in the middle, that's your grandfather, with his five sons. He had three daughters by his first marriage but he never talked about them. On his right is Kaddour, the eldest of the brothers. He and his father did not get on well, and your grandfather disinherited him when he moved to the city to become a politician. On the left is Hassan, who liked to live like a lord. He kept company with women of easy virtue, showering them with jewels, while in secret he was brokering deals that would result in the family losing vast swaths of our lands and a large share in our stud. Your grandfather did not even realise how much damage he'd done until he was dragged before the courts. Your grandfather never really recovered. Next to Hassan is Abdessamad. He was a hard worker, but he left the family because your grandfather would not consent to him marrying a cousin whose family had sided with the French. Abdessamad died somewhere in Europe fighting in the Great War. And the two little boys sitting at your grandfather's feet, that's your father, Issa, the youngest, and me, I was two years older. As children we were very close, but then I got sick, very sick . . . I was about your age at the time. The doctors and the healers couldn't cure me. My father – your grandfather – was desperate, and someone suggested he take me to the Catholic nuns. At first he refused, but I got worse and worse, I was wasting away, and one morning your grandfather found himself knocking on the door of the convent . . .'

He showed me a photograph of a group of nuns.

'The nuns saved my life. It took years and years. By the time I was well again, I had already passed my *baccalauréat*. Although he was crippled with debts by then, your grandfather agreed to pay for me to study chemistry. Maybe he realised that I had a better chance of making a future with my books than with his creditors. Germaine and I met when we were at university. I was studying chemistry, she was studying biology. And even though your grandfather had probably planned for me to marry a cousin or one of his friends' daughters, he didn't oppose our marriage. When I graduated, he asked me what I planned to do with my life, and I told him I wanted to set up a chemist's shop in the city. He agreed. He made no conditions. That's how I came to buy my house here, and the shop . . . Your grandfather never came to the city – not even for our wedding – not because he disowned me, but because he wanted to *give me a chance in life*. Like your father did when he brought you here to live with me . . . Your father is a brave, honest, hard-working man. He did his best to save the family's lands, but he was the only one left. It wasn't his fault. He was simply the last wheel on a cart that was already falling apart. Your father still believes that if I had helped him, if there had been two of us, we might have saved the farm, but fate decided otherwise.'

He took my chin between finger and thumb and looked into my eyes.

'I'm sure you're wondering why I'm telling you all this, boy . . . I'm doing it so that you know who your family are. Lalla Fatna's blood flows in your veins. Where your father failed, you can succeed, and climb back to the lofty place from where you came.'

He kissed me on the forehead.

'Now, go and find Germaine. I'm sure she's missing you.'

I slipped off his lap and ran to the door.

When he saw me stop and turn, he raised his eyebrows.

'What is it, boy?'

In turn, I stared into his eyes and asked: 'When will you take me to see my little sister?'

He smiled.

'The day after tomorrow. I promise.'

My uncle came home early. Germaine and I were outside. She was sitting reading a book in the rocking chair on the veranda. I was looking for a tortoise I had seen in the garden the night before. Germaine set her book down on the table and frowned. My uncle went into the house without coming over to kiss her as he did every day. She waited for a moment, but when he did not come out, she went inside to find him.

My uncle was sitting on a chair in the kitchen, elbows propped on the table, his face buried in his hands. Germaine knew something terrible had happened. I watched as she sat opposite him and took his wrist.

'Problems with a customer?'

'Why would I have problems with my customers?' My

uncle was angry. 'I'm not the one who prescribes their medicine.'

'You're upset . . .'

'That's hardly surprising. I've just come back from Jenane Jato.'

Germaine started slightly.

'I thought you were taking the boy there tomorrow?'

'I wanted to get the lie of the land first.'

Germaine fetched a jug of water and poured a glass for her husband, who drank it, then, seeing me standing in the living room, she gestured upstairs.

'Wait for me up in your room, Jonas. We'll go over your lessons in a little while.'

I pretended to do as she asked. I waited on the landing for a minute, then crept down a few steps so I could listen. The mention of Jenane Jato had intrigued me. I wanted to know why my uncle suddenly looked so old. Had something happened to my parents? Had my father been arrested for murdering El Moro?

'So?' Germaine whispered.

'So, what?' my uncle said wearily.

'Did you see your brother?'

'He looks terrible, I mean really terrible.'

'Did you give him money?'

'You must be joking. The minute I reached for my pocket, he went rigid, like I was going to pull out a gun. "I didn't sell you my son" is what he said to me. "I left him in your care." I was really shaken, I can't tell you. Issa is going downhill, honestly. I'm starting to fear the worst.'

'What do you mean?'

'It's obvious – if you saw his eyes. He looks like a zombie.'

'What about Jonas? Are you going to take him to see his mother tomorrow?'

'No.'

'But you promised.'

'I've changed my mind. He's barely crawled out of the gutter; I'm not about to push him back into it.'

'Mahi . . .'

'Don't go on about it. I know what I'm doing. Our son has to look to the future. There's nothing back there but misery.'

I heard Germaine shift nervously in her chair.

'You can't give up so easily, Mahi. Your brother needs you.'

'Don't you think I've tried to help him? Issa is like a ticking time bomb – touch him and he's liable to explode. He won't give me a chance. If I offered him a hand, he'd cut my arm off. As far as he's concerned, anything he gets from other people is charity.'

'But you're not other people, you're his brother.'

'You think he doesn't know that? To him, it's all the same. His problem is that he won't admit how bad things are. He's a shadow of the man he was. Besides, he resents me. You can't imagine how much he resents me. He thinks that if I had stayed with him, we could have saved the farm, the family lands. He's convinced of it, now more than ever. He's obsessed with the idea, I know he is.'

'You're the one who blames himself . . .'

'Maybe, but he's obsessed. I know him. He's never said anything, but he nurses his anger. He hates me, he thinks I sold out, turned my back on my family, married a heathen. As far as he's concerned, I sold my birthright for a house

75

in the city, traded my *gandurah* for a European suit, and even though I wear the fez, he hates me for giving up the turban. We'll never get along.'

'You should have given the money to his wife.'

'She wouldn't take it. She knows Issa would kill her.'

I rushed upstairs and locked myself in my room.

The following day at noon, my uncle shut up the shop and came to fetch me. Having slept on it, he had changed his mind, or perhaps Germaine had persuaded him; whatever the reason, he was determined to set things straight. He was tired of living in fear. Tired of watching as my father became more and more withdrawn. Tired of worrying that my father might show up unannounced and take me away without so much as an explanation.

My uncle brought me back to Jenane Jato, and the place seemed more terrible than it ever had. Here, time stood still; nothing ever happened; the same weather-beaten faces stared into the sun, the same shadows melted into the darkness. When he saw me, Peg-Leg doffed his turban and the barber almost cut off the ear of the old man he was shaving. The street urchins stopped dead, then lined up to stare at us as we passed, their tattered rags hanging from their scrawny bodies.

My uncle did his best to ignore the abject poverty, walking straight ahead, head held high, his face expressionless. He did not come into the courtyard with me, but waited outside.

'Take all the time you need, son.'

I dashed inside. Two of Badra's kids were fighting near the edge of the well; the smaller boy seemed to be trying to dislocate his brother's elbow. In a corner, near the toilets, Hadda was bending over a pail doing her laundry. Her skirt, hiked up to her thighs, exposed her bare legs to the gentle sun. She had her back to me and didn't seem to notice the vicious brawl her neighbour's sons were having.

I lifted the curtain to our tiny room and it took a moment for my eyes to adjust to the darkness. I saw my mother lying on a pallet, blanket thrown over her, her face wrapped in a shawl.

'Is that you, Younes?' she whimpered.

I ran over and threw myself at her. She wrapped her arms around me and hugged me close. Her arms felt weak. She was burning with a fever.

Feebly she pushed me away; my weight was making it difficult for her to breathe.

'Why did you come back?' she asked.

My sister was sitting by the low table, so silent and meek that I hadn't noticed her at first. Her big vacant eyes were staring at me, wondering where they had seen me before. I had barely been gone two months and already she hardly remembered me. My sister had not yet started to talk. She was not like other children her age; she seemed determined not to grow up.

From my bag I took out the toy I had bought for her and put it on the table. My sister didn't take it; she simply glanced at it and then went back to staring at me. I picked up the toy – it was a little rag doll – and put it in her hands. She did not even notice.

'How did you manage to find the house?' my mother asked.

'My uncle is waiting outside.'

My mother gave a little cry as she sat up, then threw her arms around me again and hugged me.

'I'm so happy to see you again. What is it like in your uncle's house?'

'Germaine is very nice. She baths me every day and buys me anything I want. I've got lots of toys and shoes and I can have jam whenever I want . . . It's a big house, Maman, there's lots of rooms for everyone. Why don't you come and live with us?'

My mother smiled, and all the pain that lined her face disappeared as if by magic. She was beautiful, my mother, with long dark hair that fell to her hips, and eyes as big as saucers. Sometimes, back when we lived on the farm, and I saw her standing on a hill looking out over the fields, I thought she looked like a sultana. She was beautiful, graceful, and when she raced back down the little hill, the misfortune snapping at the hem of her dress could not catch up.

'It's true,' I insisted. 'Why don't you come and live with us in my uncle's house?'

'That's not how things work with grown-ups, son,' she said, wiping something from my cheek. 'Besides, your father would never agree to live in someone else's house. He wants to get back on his feet by himself, he doesn't want to be in anyone's debt . . . You're looking well,' she said. 'I think you've put on weight. And you're so handsome in your new clothes! You look like a little *roumi*.'

'Germaine calls me Jonas.'

'Who is Germaine?'

'My uncle's wife.'

'It doesn't matter. The French don't know how to pronounce our names. They don't do it to be hurtful.'

'I've learned how to read and write.'

She ruffled my hair.

'That's good. Your father would never have let your uncle take care of you if he didn't know that your uncle could give you things he cannot.'

'Where is he?'

'He's at work. He's always working . . . You'll see, one day he'll come and take you to the house of his dreams. Did you know you were born in a beautiful mansion? The shack you grew up in used to belong to one of the tenant farmers who worked for your father. When your father and I got married, he was rich. The whole village came to celebrate our wedding. We had a proper house with big gardens. Your three elder brothers were born like princes. They didn't survive. When you were little, you used to run around the gardens until you were exhausted. Then God decided that spring should turn to winter and the gardens died. Such is life, my son. It gives with one hand and takes with the other. But there is no reason why one day we might not get it back. And you – you will be a success. I asked Batoul, and she read it in the ripples of the water. She said you will be a great man. That's why, whenever I miss you, I know I'm being selfish and I say to myself, he's better off where he is. He's safe.'

6

I DID not stay long with my mother, or perhaps I stayed for an eternity, I couldn't tell. Time did not matter; there was something else, something more dense, more fundamental. Like prison visiting rooms, what matters is what you remember of the moment shared with the person you have missed so much. I was young, I had no idea of the pain my leaving had caused, of the wound I had become. When I left, my mother did not shed a single tear. She would find time to cry later. She took my hand, she talked to me and smiled. Her smile was like a benediction.

We said what we had to say to each other, which was not very much – nothing we did not already know.

'It's not good for you to be here,' she announced.

At the time, I did not understand what she was saying. I was a child; to me, words were simply sounds you made with your lips. Did I take them in, did I think about them? Besides, what difference did it make? I was already elsewhere.

It was my mother who reminded me that my uncle was waiting outside, that it was time for me to go, and the eternity we had shared winked out so quickly – like a light bulb when you flick the switch – that it caught me unawares.

Beyond the curtain, the courtyard was silent. There was no fighting, no screaming – had they been eavesdropping on our conversation? As I stepped out I saw most of our neighbours gathered around the edge of the well: Badra, Yezza, Batoul the clairvoyant, the beautiful Hadda, Mama and her children. They stood, staring at me from a safe distance, as though terrified that I would break if they came closer. Badra's boys hardly dared to breathe – these two little savages stood with their arms stiffly by their sides. All it had taken to confuse them was a change of clothes. Even now, I wonder if the world is nothing but appearances. A man with a face as grey as papier mâché wearing a crude jute tunic over his empty belly is a pauper, but wash his face, comb his hair, give him a pair of clean trousers and he is a different man. Everything is in the details. At the age of eleven, these are the things that puzzle you, and since you can find no answers, you settle on answers that are convenient. Poverty, I decided, had nothing to do with fate; it was simply a state of mind. We accept the world as we see it; we believe it to be immutable. But if we look away from the misery even for a moment, another path appears, bright as a new penny, and so mysterious that we begin to dream . . . The people of Jenane Jato did not dream; they had decided that their fate was sealed, that there was no way up, no way out. Years of poverty had left them blinkered.

My uncle held out his hand. I grabbed it. The moment his fingers closed around my wrist, I stopped looking behind me.

I was already elsewhere.

* * *

The first year I lived with my adoptive parents passed without incident. Relieved, my uncle enrolled me in a school two blocks from our house. It was an unremarkable building with bare corridors and tall plane trees in the playground. It seemed perpetually dark, as though the sunlight barely reached the roof of the building. Unlike the stern, austere man who taught us French (in a thick Auvergne accent some of the pupils could imitate perfectly), the other teacher was gentle and patient. A plump woman who always wore the same drab pinafore, she would walk up and down between the desks trailing a cloud of perfume behind her like a shadow.

The only two other Arab boys in my class, Abdelkader and Brahim, were both sons of diplomats and had servants who came and picked them up after school.

My uncle took a keen interest in my studies; I was the apple of his eye. His joy gave me confidence. From time to time he would invite me into his study and tell me stories whose meaning and import I did not understand.

Oran was a beautiful city. There was something unique about the place, a charm that was more than simply Mediterranean exuberance. It was brash and vital and alive. When evening came, the city was magical. The air was cool after the sweltering heat of the day, and people would set chairs out on the pavement and spend long hours chatting over a glass of *anisette*. From our veranda we could see the glow of their cigarettes, overhear their conversations; their scandalous stories streaked across the darkness like shooting stars, their throaty laughter crashed at our feet like waves on a beach.

Germaine was happy. Every time she looked at me she offered up a prayer of thanks. I could see how happy I made her and her husband, and I felt flattered.

Sometimes my uncle entertained guests from out of town, Arabs and Berbers, some in European suits, others in traditional dress. They were distinguished, eminent people who talked about some country called Algeria. This was not the same country they taught us about at school, nor the one people talked about in the posh neighbourhoods, but a country that had been ravaged, conquered, silenced; a country that gnawed on its anger like rotting meat. These men talked about the Algeria of Jenane Jato, about the yawning gulf between rich and poor, about whipping boys and scapegoats . . . they talked about a country that was yet to be redefined, a country in which every paradox seemed to live a life of ease.

I think I was happy at my uncle's house. I did not miss Jenane Jato. I had a friend who lived across the road. Her name was Lucette. We were in the same class and her father allowed her to play with me. She was nine; she was not pretty, but she was sweet and generous and I loved being with her.

At school, things settled down in my second year. I managed to blend in with everyone else. I still found *roumi* children to be strange creatures – they could be all smiles one minute and snub you the next. In the playground they would sometimes fall out with each other, declare themselves sworn enemies, but the moment an interloper appeared – usually an Arab or a 'poor relation' from their own community – they joined forces against him. They would ignore him, mock him, bully him. At first, they sent Maurice, a stupid, brutish boy, to bully me. Once they realised I was a 'sissy' who would not fight back and would not tell tales, they left me alone. They moved on, found another scapegoat, and now they would tolerate me on the periphery of their group. But I was not really one of them – a fact they were quick to remind me of. Strangely, my chief weapon if I wanted them to be my friends was my lunchbox. The moment I opened it, they would crowd round and treat me with disarming respect. But as soon as I had shared out my food and the last crumb had been eaten, they turned their backs so fast it made my head spin.

One afternoon, I arrived home from school in a rage, fuming at Maurice, at my teacher, at the whole class. I needed answers and I needed them now. Something had happened to undermine my self-assurance; for the first time I realised that my self-respect did not depend solely on those close to me, but on people whom I did not even know. It had happened during class. We had all handed in our homework, all except Abdelkader, who was embarrassed because he had forgotten to do it. The teacher dragged him to the front of the class by the ear and said: 'Would you like to tell us why, unlike your friends, you have no home-work to give me, Monsieur Abdelkader?' The boy kept his head down, flushed with humiliation. 'Why, Monsieur Abdelkader? Why have you failed to do your homework?' When he got no response, the teacher turned to the rest of us. 'Can anyone in the class enlighten me as to why Monsieur Abdelkader did not do his homework?' Without bothering to put his hand up, Maurice yelled: 'Because Arabs are lazy and shiftless, sir.' The whole class had erupted with laughter and this had set me brooding.

As soon as I got home, I went and found my uncle in his study.

'Is it true that Arabs are lazy and shiftless?'

My uncle was surprised by the anger in my voice. He set down the book he had been reading and turned to me. What he saw on my face moved him to pity.

'Come here a minute, son,' he said, opening his arms.

'No . . . I want to know if it's true. Are Arabs lazy?'

My uncle took his chin between thumb and forefinger and looked at me. He realised that I was serious, that he *owed* me an explanation.

He thought for a moment, then sat opposite me and said:

'No, Arabs are not lazy, but we take the time to live life to the full; it is something Europeans don't understand. To them, time is money. To us, time has no price. We can be happy simply taking the time to share a glass of mint tea, whereas nothing in the world is enough to make them happy. That is the difference between us, son.'

I never spoke to Maurice again, and I no longer feared him.

Then came a day when one of my dreams – for I was learning to dream now – was shattered.

I had walked Lucette to her aunt's house in Choupot, some distance north of where we lived, and was heading home. It was an October morning. The sun hung in the sky as big as a pumpkin, autumn was plucking the last tatters from the trees, while the wind whipped armfuls of the dead leaves into eddies. On a wide boulevard where Lucette and I liked to stare in the shop windows, there was a bar. I don't remember the sign that hung over the door, but I still remember the drunks who frequented the place – angry, foul-mouthed men given to brawling. The police often had to restore the peace with truncheons. That afternoon as I was walking past, a fight broke out. I heard shouting and swearing and tables crashing, then I watched as a furious barman grabbed a beggar by the collar and the seat of his pants and threw him down the steps. The poor fellow landed at my feet like a bale of hay. He was dead drunk.

'Don't let me see your face round here again, you lousy bastard,' the barman threatened from the top of the steps. 'We don't want the likes of you here.'

He stepped inside and reappeared with a pair of old slippers.

'Here! Take your slippers. You'll need to run if I set eyes on you again.'

The tramp tried to duck, but a slipper hit him on the head. He lay in front of me, splayed across the pavement, and not knowing whether to walk round him or cross the road, I stood rooted to the spot.

Face down on the ground, his turban unravelled, the tramp panted and gasped as he tried to get to his feet, but he was too drunk. After a couple of attempts he managed to sit up. He groped around for his slippers, put them on, then picked up his turban and would it crudely round his head.

The stench from him was terrible; I think he had wet himself.

Swaying as he sat, one hand pressed against the ground to steady himself, he looked round for his walking stick. Seeing it lying in the gutter, he crawled over to get it. Suddenly he became aware of my presence and froze. As he looked up at me, his face contorted.

It was my father.

My father . . . a man who had the power to move mountains with his bare hands, who could conquer all uncertainties, who could wring the neck of fate itself . . . was lying at my feet, dressed in filthy, stinking rags, his face swollen, his lips flecked with spittle, his blue eyes as pained as the bruises on his face. A wreck, a ruin, a tragedy.

He looked at me as though I had returned from the dead. His puffy eyes misted over and his face crumpled like old paper.

'Younes?' he said.

It was not a cry, but something between an exclamation and a sob.

I was dumbstruck.

Still staring at me, the strain showing in his face, he struggled to get to his feet. Leaning on his walking stick, he managed to haul himself upright, careful not to let out a groan, but his knees buckled and he fell back into the gutter. And as he fell, it was as though all the promises he had ever made, all my dreams and aspirations, were whipped away by a harsh gust of the sirocco. I was shocked. I wanted to lean down, to put my arm around his shoulders and help him to his feet. I wanted him to take my hand, to allow me to support him. I wanted so many things, but still my eyes refused to believe what they saw and my limbs refused to obey my commands. I loved my father too much to see him like this, sprawled at my feet in rags and tatters, his finger-nails black, his nostrils flaring . . .

In a last spasm of pride, my father took a deep breath and, leaning on his walking stick and drawing on his last reserves of dignity, hauled himself upright again. He swayed, stumbled backwards and collided with a wall. Though his legs threatened to give out under him, he marshalled every ounce of strength in his struggle to stay standing. He looked like an old nag ready for the knacker's yard. Then, carefully putting one foot before the other, shoulder still pressed to the wall, he stumbled away. As he went, he tried to step away from the wall, to show me he could walk unaided. In his piteous battle with himself I saw everything that was brave and grotesque about suffering. He was too drunk to walk far, and after a short distance he stopped, gasping for breath. He turned to see if I had gone, but I was still standing where he had left me, as helpless as he was. At that moment he gave me a look that was to haunt me for the rest of my life – a look of such despair that it choked the life out of a noble father's promises to his son. It was a look such as a man can give only once in his lifetime, since after it there is nothing. Seeing it, I realised that those eyes, which had fascinated and terrified me, which had watched over me, warned me, loved and pitied me, would never look upon me again.

'How long has he been like this?' the doctor asked, slipping his stethoscope back into his case.

'He seemed fine when he came home at lunchtime,' Germaine said. 'Then when we sat down to eat, he took a few bites then ran to the bathroom to be sick.'

The doctor was a strapping, big-boned man with a pale, thin face. The coal-black suit he wore made him look like a marabout. He fastened the straps of his briefcase as he stared at me.

'I don't know what's wrong with him,' he confessed. 'He has no fever, he's not sweating and he doesn't seem to be cold.'

My uncle, who was standing next to Germaine at the foot of my bed, said nothing. He had followed the examination carefully, glancing worriedly at the doctor from time to time. The doctor had looked in my mouth, shone a small torch in my eyes, run his fingers over my ears, listened to my breathing. As he straightened up, he looked circumspect.

'I'll give him something for the nausea,' he said. 'You need to keep him in bed for the rest of the day. These things usually settle down by themselves – it's probably something he ate. If he's not better by tomorrow, give me a call.'

After the doctor left, Germaine stayed with me. She was worried.

'Did you eat something while you were out?'

'No.'

'Have you got a pain in your stomach?'

'No.'

'What's the matter, then?'

I didn't know what the matter was. I felt as though I was falling apart. Whenever I lifted my head I felt dizzy, my insides felt twisted and tangled, my soul felt numb . . .

When I woke up, it was dark and there was no sound from the street outside. My room was lit by the glow of the full moon and a gentle breeze tugged at the trees. I knew it had to be late, since usually the neighbours did not go to bed until they'd counted every star. I had a bitter taste in my mouth, and my throat was burning. I pushed off the blankets and got up. My legs were shaking. I went over to the window and stood, my nose pressed to the glass, watching every shadow, hoping that in each of them I might see my father.

Germaine found me standing there, freezing cold, the

window misted with my breath. She put me back to bed and whispered to me, but I could not understand what she was saying. Her face would melt to become my mother's face and then my father's, then my stomach would clench and I would feel sick.

I don't know how many days I spent in this state, but when at last I was well enough to go back to school, Lucette told me I had changed. She said I was not the same person. Something inside me had broken.

Bliss the broker came to see my uncle at the pharmacy. I realised who it was as soon as I heard him clear his throat. I was in the back office doing my homework when he arrived. I peered through a gap in the curtain that separated the office from the shop. Bliss was soaked to the skin, wearing a second-hand *burnous* that was much too big for him, a mud-spattered baggy *sarouel* and rubber sandals that tracked dirt all over the floor.

My uncle looked up from his ledger, clearly none too pleased to see the broker. Bliss rarely ventured into the European part of town. From the look on the man's face, my uncle could tell that whatever had brought him here was not good news.

'Yes . . . ?'

Bliss pushed his fez back off his face and scratched his head furiously, obviously embarrassed.

'It's about your brother, Doctor,' he said.

My uncle slammed the cash register shut. Realising I had been watching, he came out from behind the counter, took Bliss by the elbow and led him to a corner of the shop. I climbed down off my stool and crept to the curtain to listen.

'What about my brother?'

'He's disappeared.'

'What? What do you mean, he's disappeared?'

'He hasn't been home . . .'

'Since when?'

'It's been three weeks now.'

'Three weeks? And you're only coming to tell me this now?'

'It's his wife's fault. You know what women are like when their husbands run off. They'd let their house catch fire rather than ask for help. I only found out this morning when Batoul the clairvoyant said that your brother's wife came to her last night and asked her to read her palm and tell her where her husband was. That was the first Batoul knew that the woman hadn't seen her husband for three weeks.'

'My God!'

I dashed back to my desk.

My uncle pulled back the curtain and found me poring over my poetry book.

'Go get Germaine and tell her to look after the shop. I have some urgent business I need to deal with.'

I picked up my book and left the shop. As I passed, I tried to see what Bliss was thinking, but he turned away. I tore through the streets like a child possessed.

Germaine couldn't sit still. As soon as she'd served each customer, she would come into the back office to check on me, worried by how calm I seemed. From time to time, unable to stop herself, she would tiptoe up behind me and lean over my shoulder as I learned my recitation pieces by heart. She stroked my hair, then let her hand slide down to my forehead to take my temperature.

'Are you sure you feel all right?'

I said nothing.

That last look on my father's face as he stood, reeling from drink and shame, gnawed at my insides again like a tapeworm.

Night had fallen hours ago and still my uncle was not back. Outside, in the driving rain, a horse had collapsed in the street, upending the cart it had been pulling and spilling a load of coal across the road. The driver, cursing his horse and the weather, tried in vain to get the animal to its feet.

Germaine and I watched from the window as the horse lay in the street, its neck twisted, its mane rising and falling on the rising river of rainwater.

The carter went to fetch help, and found a group of men prepared to brave the storm. One of them crouched next to the horse.

'The old nag is dead,' he said in Arabic.

'He can't be, he just slipped.'

'I'm telling you, he's stone dead.'

The carter refused to believe the man and crouched down next to the animal, though he did not dare touch it.

'I can't believe it, he was fine earlier.'

'Animals can't tell you when they're sick,' said the first man. 'You've probably been driving the horse too hard.'

Germaine took the crank handle to lower the security grille, handed me her umbrella, turned out the lights then urged me outside. She put the padlock on the shutter, took the umbrella from me and hugged me close to her as we dashed home.

My uncle did not arrive back until late that night. He was dripping wet. Germaine took his coat and his shoes in the hall.

'Why isn't he in bed?' he said, jerking his chin at me.

Germaine shrugged as she climbed the stairs to the first floor. My uncle looked at me carefully, his wet hair glistening in the light but his expression solemn.

'You should be in bed, you've got school tomorrow.'

Germaine reappeared with a dressing gown. My uncle put it on, slipped his feet into his slippers and came over to me.

'Go on, son, go up to your room . . . for me.'

'He knows about his father,' Germaine said.

'He knew before you did, but that's no reason.'

'He won't get a wink of sleep until you tell him what you found out. This is about his father.'

Germaine's remark irritated my uncle and he glared at her, but she did not turn away. She knew I was worried and felt that it was unfair to keep the truth from me.

My uncle put his hands on my shoulders.

'We looked everywhere,' he said. 'We checked all the places he usually goes, but no one has seen him for a long time. Your mother doesn't know where he is, she can't understand why he would leave . . . We'll keep looking for him. I've told Bliss to find three men I can trust to scour the city for him.'

'I know where he is,' I said. 'He's gone to make his fortune. He'll come back in a shiny new car.'

My uncle glanced anxiously at Germaine, clearly afraid I was delirious, but she shook her head.

Up in my bedroom, I stared at the white expanse of ceiling, imagining it was a cinema screen, and pictured my father somewhere making his fortune, like in the movies Lucette's father sometimes took us to see on Sunday afternoons. Germaine came up more than once to check on me and I pretended to be asleep. She came over to the bed, felt my forehead, adjusted my pillows, pulled the blankets up, then tiptoed out. The moment I heard the door shut, I threw off the covers and went back to staring at the ceiling. Spellbound as a little boy, I watched my father's adventures.

The men my uncle sent out to find my father came back empty-handed. They checked the police stations, the hospitals, the brothels; they checked the rubbish tips and the souks; they questioned gravediggers and gangsters, drunks and horse traders. There was no word of my father.

Several weeks after his disappearance, I went to Jenane Jato without telling anyone. I knew my way around the city by now, and I wanted to go and see my sister without having to ask Germaine's permission, without having my uncle take me there. When she saw me, my mother was angry. What I had done was stupid, she said, making me promise never to do it again. Jenane Jato was crawling with criminals. It was no place for a well-dressed boy; I might end up in a dark alley with my throat cut. I said I'd come to see if my father had come home. My mother told me I didn't need to worry about my father any more, that Batoul had told her he was fine and well on his way to making a fortune. 'When he comes back, he'll stop off and pick you up from your uncle's house and then come and collect your sister and me, and we'll all drive off to a big house with gardens and fruit trees.'

Then she sent Badra's eldest son to fetch Bliss so that he could walk me back to my uncle's house.

This brusque dismissal by my mother troubled me for a long time. I felt as though I were to blame for all the misfortunes on earth.

7

FOR A whole month, I couldn't fall asleep until I had watched my father's adventures play out on the bedroom ceiling. I lay on my back, propped up on my pillows, and watched as a disjointed movie unfolded above my head. I imagined my father as a sultan surrounded by courtesans, as an outlaw plundering far-off lands, as a prospector discovering the biggest gold nugget of the century or a gangster in a three-piece suit, a cigar in the corner of his mouth.

Some nights, seized by a nameless fear, I imagined him drunk and unkempt, wandering through some squalid neighbourhood pursued by a pack of street urchins. When the fear took hold of me, it was as though my wrists were trapped in a vice, a vice exactly like the one that had almost forced my coins into my flesh the night I tried to make my father proud of me by giving him the money I had made selling goldfinches.

My father's desertion stuck in my throat; I could neither swallow it nor spit it out. I felt I was to blame. My father would never have abandoned my mother and my sister if he hadn't run into me that night. He would have gone home, slept it off and none of the neighbours would have suspected a thing. My father was a man of principles. He used to tell me that if a man should lose his money, his land, his friends, his fortune, even his bearings, there was always a possibility, however small, for him to get back on his feet again, but that if a man lost face, then all the rest was futile.

My father had lost face. Because I had seen him that night, seen him at his lowest ebb. This was what he could not bear. He had been determined to prove to me that he would not allow misfortune to break him. But the look I had seen on his face as he struggled to stand outside the bar in Choupot told me something different. There is a despair from which there is no way back; that was what I had seen in my father's face.

I blamed myself for taking that particular street, for passing at precisely the moment when the barman tossed my father into the gutter and my world with him; I blamed myself for leaving Lucette so quickly, for spending too much time staring in shop windows . . .

At night, in the darkness, I brooded on my sadness, searching for something that might absolve me. I was so miserable that one night I went into the box room to look for the statue of the winged boy that had terrified me on my first night in my uncle's house. I found it at the bottom of a musty crate full of bric-a-brac, dusted it off and set it on the mantelpiece opposite my bed. I stared at it intently, convinced that I would see its wings flap, its head turn towards me . . . Nothing. The winged boy stood on its pedestal, mute, unknowable, and just before dawn I put it back in its crate.

*   *   *

'God is cruel!'

'It has nothing to do with God, son,' my uncle said. 'Your father decided to leave, that's all there is to it. The Devil didn't push him nor the Angel Gabriel lead him by the hand. Your father did everything he could, but after a while, he couldn't take it any more. It's as simple as that. Life is ups and downs – there is no middle ground. The important thing to remember is that you don't have to go through it alone. Misfortune is like lightning, it doesn't decide when or where to strike; it doesn't realise, doesn't suspect what tragedy it brings. If you want to cry, then cry; if you want to hope, then hope, pray, but there is no sense looking for something or someone to blame.'

And so I cried and I prayed, and as the months passed, the ceiling above my bed slowly went back to being just a ceiling. Taking Lucette by the hand, I went back to school. There were hundreds of other children like me, children who had done nothing wrong and who, like me, had suffered some tragedy and were patiently serving out their time, coping as best they could. If they did not ask questions it was because they knew they would not like the answers.

Mysterious guests continued to show up at my uncle's house in the dead of night. They would arrive one by one and sit for hours with my uncle in the living room, smoking like chimneys – the whole house reeked of cigarette smoke. Their meetings always followed the same course: at first their discussion was calm and full of thoughtful silences, then it would become loud and impassioned, threatening to wake the neighbours. My uncle would take advantage of his position as master of the house to pour oil on troubled waters. If they could not agree, they would go out to the garden for some air and I would watch the tips of their cigarettes glowing in the darkness. When the meeting was over, they would tiptoe out, one by one, carefully checking to make sure no one was watching, then disappear into the night.

The morning after these meetings, I would invariably find my uncle in his study, jotting notes in a large hardback notebook.

One night, my uncle asked me to come and join his guests in the living room. He proudly introduced me to them. I recognised some of the faces. The meeting that night was different, less strained, almost solemn. Only one man spoke, the others hanging on his words. He was a man of great charisma, and clearly an honoured guest; my uncle was obviously in awe of him. Only much later did I put a name to his face: it was Messali Hadj, the guiding light of the movement for Algerian independence.

In Europe, war exploded like a blister.

Poland fell to the Nazi jackboots with terrifying ease. Where everyone had predicted fierce resistance there were only a few pitiful skirmishes, quickly crushed by the advancing Panzer divisions. The stunning success of the Nazi forces provoked terror and fascination. People began to turn their attention northward and watch as events on the far side of the Mediterranean played out. The news was not good; the spectre of an all-consuming conflagration haunted them. On café terraces men sat poring over their fears in the newspapers. People stopped each other in the street, they argued, they gathered in bars or in parks and talked in hushed whispers about how Europe was on the road to ruin. At school, our teachers no longer paid us any attention. They would arrive every morning with more news, more questions, and leave every evening with the same fears, the same anxieties. The headmaster had gone so far as to install a wireless in his office, where he spent most of the day listening to the news, indifferent to the thugs and bullies who now ran amok in the playground.

Germaine no longer took me out on Sundays after mass, instead she disappeared, shutting herself away in her room, kneeling in front of the cross, intoning interminable litanies. She had no family in Europe, but still she prayed that reason would triumph over madness.

Since my uncle also began to disappear more and more often, going out with a briefcase full of tracts and pamphlets under his coat, I relied more and more on Lucette for company. We would lose ourselves in our games until we heard a voice telling us it was time for dinner or time to go to bed.

Lucette's father, Jérôme, was an engineer in a factory close to where we lived. At home, he spent much of his time with his nose in an engineering book or lying on the sofa listening to Schubert on the gramophone, and so no longer bothered to check to see what we were up to. Jérôme was tall and thin, his face half hidden behind thick round glasses, and he seemed to live in his own little world, careful to keep his distance from everyone and everything, including this war that seemed about to consume the whole planet. Summer and winter he wore the same khaki shirt with its breast pocket stuffed full of pens. He only ever spoke if we asked him a question, and even then he answered as though we were interrupting him. His wife had left him some years after Lucette was born and he had never quite got over it. Though he could not refuse Lucette anything, I never saw him hug her. At the cinema, where he always took us to see silent serials, I would have sworn that as soon as the lights went out, he disappeared. At times he frightened me, especially when he casually told my uncle he was an atheist. I had not realised before that moment that atheists existed. I was surrounded by believers: my uncle was Muslim, Germaine was Catholic, all our other neighbours were Jewish or Christian. At school and in the street, everyone talked about God, believed in God – I was shocked to discover Jérôme getting by without Him. Once, I overheard him tell an evangelist who called to his house: 'Every man is his own god. In choosing to follow another god he denies himself and in doing so becomes blind and unjust.' The evangelist looked at Jérôme as though he were the Devil incarnate.

On the Feast of the Ascension, Jérôme took Lucette and me to the top of Djebel Murdjadjo to see the city. We visited the medieval fortress on the mountaintop before joining the crowds of pilgrims flocking to the basilica of Our Lady of Santa Cruz. There were hundreds of them: women, old men and children, all milling around the base of the statue of the Virgin Mary. Some had come up the mountain barefoot, clutching at the broom and the bushes for support; others had climbed up on their knees, which were now scratched and bleeding. The pilgrims stood under the blazing sun as though in a trance, their eyes rolled back in their heads, their faces pale, imploring their guardian angels, beseeching the Almighty himself to spare their miserable lives. They were Spaniards, Lucette explained, and they made the pilgrimage every year to give thanks to the Virgin Mary for sparing Oran from the cholera epidemic of 1849 that had wiped out thousands of families.

'But look at them,' I said, shocked by the extent of their self-inflicted injuries.

'They do it for God,' Lucette said fervently.

'God never asked them to do this,' Jérôme interrupted, and his voice, like a whip crack, put paid to my curiosity. I no longer saw these people as pilgrims, but as cursed souls. If truth be told, Hell never seemed closer than it did to me on holy days. All my life I had been warned of the evils of blasphemy. Nor did you to have to utter a blasphemy to be damned; simply to overhear it was a sin. Lucette sensed that I was upset. I could see that she was angry with her father, but I couldn't bring myself to respond to her embarrassed smile. I wanted to go home.

We took the bus back to the city, but the twisting cliff roads to Vieil Oran simply made me feel worse. At every bend in the road I thought I might be sick. Whereas usually when we were in the old town, Lucette and I liked to wander around La Scalera, eat paella or a *caldero* in a cheap Spanish café or buy trinkets from the Sephardic craftsmen in the old Jewish quarter, that day my heart wasn't in it. What Jérôme had said had cast a pall over the day. I feared his blasphemy would bring about some catastrophe.

We took the tram back to the European sector of the city and then walked home. The weather was magnificent, and yet the sunlit streets felt strange and dreamlike. Lucette squeezed my hand, but I could not seem to wake up.

And then the catastrophe I had feared hit me like a

thunderbolt. Our street was teeming with crowds of people; all the neighbours had come out and were standing around, arms folded across their chests. Jérôme gave a puzzled look to a man in shorts standing at his gate, who had clearly been watering his garden. The man turned off the hose and set it down, wiped his hands on his shirt, then spread them wide to indicate his bafflement.

'There must be some mistake. The police have arrested Monsieur Mahi, the chemist. They've just taken him away in a police van. The cops didn't look too happy.'

My uncle spent a week in custody. When he was finally released, he waited until dark before he dared to come back to the house. His face was gaunt, his eyes lifeless, the few short days he had spent in jail had changed him completely. He was barely recognisable. An unkempt beard emphasised his pallor, making him look like a ghost. He looked as though he had not eaten or slept in prison.

Germaine's relief at her husband's return was short-lived when she realised that he had not been returned to her whole. My uncle seemed to be in a constant daze. He found it difficult to understand what was said to him; he jumped if Germaine asked whether she could get him; anything. At night I heard him pacing up and down, mumbling and cursing. Sometimes, when I looked up from the garden, I would see him standing at the window, framed behind the curtains, constantly scanning the street as though expecting the Devil himself to arrive.

Forced to take over the running of the business, Germaine now had little time to spend on me. She was terrified – her husband was having a breakdown and refused to see a doctor.

Sometimes she would stand, sobbing, in the middle of the living room.

Jérôme took over responsibility for taking me to school. Every morning, smiling and cheery, her hair in ribbons, Lucette would call for me. She would take my hand and we would run to catch up with her father at the end of the street.

I assumed that after a few weeks my uncle would be back to his old self. Instead, he got worse. He began to lock himself away in his study and would refuse to open the door when we knocked. It was as though there was an evil spirit in the house. Germaine was frantic. I was mystified. Why had my uncle been arrested? What had happened at the police station? Why would he not talk about what had happened in custody, even to Germaine? The secrets a house is desperate to conceal will, sooner or later, be shouted from the rooftops. A cultured, well-read man, aware of the upheavals in the Arab world, my uncle had been a supporter on an intellectual level of the nationalist cause spreading through educated Muslim circles. He had learned the speeches of Shakaib Arslan by heart, cut militant articles out of the newspapers that he catalogued, annotated and wrote dissertations on. Obsessed with the theoretical aspects of political upheaval, he had not realised the risks of his actions. All that he knew about political activism were his flights of rhetoric, the secret contributions he made to fund work-shops, the clandestine night-time meetings at our house. Though committed to the cause of Algerian nationalism, he was drawn to the principle rather than to the radical activism espoused by members of the *Parti du Peuple Algérien*. It would never have occurred to him that he would ever set foot inside a police station, let alone spend the night in a stinking cell with rats and thugs for company. My uncle was a pacifist, a hypothetical democrat, an intellectual who put his faith in words, in demonstrations, in slogans, with a visceral hatred of violence. He was a law-abiding citizen, keenly aware of the social standing conferred on him by his university education and his profession as a chemist. He could never have imagined that the police would come for him one night while he was sitting in his armchair, feet up on an ottoman, reading *El Ouma,* the party newsletter.

The gossips said that before the police even put him in the van my uncle was a broken man, that he had confessed everything he knew as soon as he was questioned. They said that it was only because he had been so cooperative that the police released him without charge – an allegation he would deny to his dying day. Unable to bear the gossip and the slander, he suffered several breakdowns.

When he recovered some measure of sanity, he told Germaine what he had planned: there could be no question of us going on living in Oran. We had to move.

'The police are trying to turn me against my own people,' he confided wearily. 'Can you imagine? How could they think that they could ever get me to do that? Do I look like a traitor, Germaine? For the love of heaven, how could I possibly inform on my friends, my colleagues . . . ?'

From now on, he told her, he would be under constant surveillance, something which in itself would put his friends in danger.

'Do you at least have somewhere in mind?' Germaine

asked, clearly devastated at the idea of having to leave her home town.

'We'll move to Río Salado.'

'Why Río Salado?'

'It's a quiet little town. I went there the other day to look into the possibility of opening a pharmacy. I found a place – the ground floor of a large house . . .'

'You want us to sell everything here in Oran: the shop, the house, everything?'

'We have no choice.'

'But if we do, then we can never come back, where we dreamed—'

'I'm sorry.'

'What if things don't work out in Río Salado?'

'Then we'll move to Tlemcen, or to Sidi Bel Abbès, or out into the Sahara. God's earth is vast, Germaine, or have you forgotten?'

Somewhere it was written that I was born to leave my home, to constantly leave, each time leaving a part of me behind.

Lucette stood in the doorway of her house, hands behind her back, leaning against the wall. She refused to believe me when I told her we were moving away. Now, seeing the truck arrive, she was upset with me. I couldn't bring myself to cross the street and tell her that I was upset too. I simply stood and watched the movers load our furniture and our trunks into the truck. It was as though they were taking my whole world to pieces.

Germaine helped me up into the cab. The truck roared. I leaned out to look back at Lucette, hoping she might wave; she kept her hands behind her back. It was as though she didn't believe I was really leaving, or perhaps she simply refused to accept it.

As the truck pulled away, the driver blocked my view of Lucette, so I craned my neck in the hope of taking with me the glimmer of a smile, some sign that she realised that this was not my fault, that I was as devastated as she was. But nothing . . . The street flashed by in a roar of metal and then disappeared.

Goodbye, Lucette.

For a long time I thought it had been her eyes that filled my soul with a gentle peace. Now I know that it was not simply her eyes, it was the way she looked at me – the gentle, caring, maternal expression of a girl not yet a woman . . .

Río Salado was only sixty kilometres west of Oran, but this journey was the longest I have ever known. The truck coughed and spluttered like a camel on its last legs, the engine stalling every time the driver changed gears. He wore trousers spattered with oil and grease, and his shirt had seen better days. He was a short, stocky man with broad shoulders and a face like a veteran boxer. He drove in silence, his hairy hands like tarantulas gripping the steering wheel. Her face pressed to the window, Germaine said nothing, but stared out at the orange groves that lined the road. Her hands were clasped, half hidden in her lap; I realised that she was praying.

We had to slow to a crawl as we drove through the village of Misserghin. It was market day and the road was lined with carts and stalls; housewives bustled about, and here and there were Bedouins – recognisable from their turbans

– offering their services as porters. A policeman strutted around the town square, twirling his truncheon lazily. His kepi pulled down over his eyes, he greeted the women respectfully as he passed, turning back afterwards to catch a glimpse of their behinds.

'My names is Costa.' The driver spoke suddenly. 'Coco to my friends.'

He shot Germaine a glance and, seeing her smile politely, went on:

'I'm Greek.'

He shifted in his seat.

'I own a half-share in this truck. I might not look like a rich man, but it's true. Soon I'll be my own boss and I will never have to leave my office. The men in the back, they are Italian. They can unload a steamship in half a day. They have been hauliers since they were in their mother's womb.'

His big eyes, set in rolls of fat, twinkled now.

'You know, madame, you look just like my cousin Mélina. When we arrived this morning, I thought I was seeing things. It's incredible how much you look like her. You have the same hair, the same eyes, you are the same height. I don't suppose you're Greek, madame?'

'No, monsieur.'

'Where are you from?'

'From Oran. Fourth generation.'

'Really? Perhaps one of your ancestors crossed swords with the patron saint of Arabs. Me, I have only been in Algeria fifteen years. I was a sailor, we put into port here, and it was here I met Berthe in a *funduq*. The moment I set eyes on her, I thought, this is where I will stay. I married Berthe and we settled in La Scalera. Oran is a beautiful city.'

'It is,' Germaine said sadly. 'A very beautiful city.'

The driver swerved to avoid two donkeys standing in the middle of the road. The furniture in the back of the truck groaned and the Italian movers swore loudly in their own language.

The driver straightened up the truck and accelerated hard enough to blow a gasket.

'Cut your chatter and keep your eyes on the road, Coco,' one of the Italians yelled.

The driver nodded and fell silent.

A lush landscape flashed past, orange groves and vineyards jostling for space across the plains and the hills. Here and there, on rocky outcrops overlooking the scrubland, were beautiful farmhouses, ringed by majestic trees and lavish gardens, the driveways leading to them lined with olive trees and willowy palms. Every now and then we would see a colonial farmer walking his fields, or on horseback, galloping flat out towards some unseen joy. Then, without warning, like a pockmark in this fairytale landscape, we would see some squalid shack, crushed by the weight of poverty and the evil eye. Some of these shacks, out of a sense of decency, were hidden behind screens of tall cacti – all we could see was the ramshackle roof, which looked about to collapse on the people below; others clung to the rocky hillsides, their doorways ugly as a toothless smile, their cob walls pale and pitted as a death mask.

The driver turned to Germaine again and said:

'It's incredible how much you look like my cousin Mélina.'

2. Río Salado

8

I LOVE Río Salado – the place the Romans called Fulmen Salsum and one we now call El Malah. I have loved this town all my life; I cannot imagine growing old beneath any other sky, cannot imagine dying far from these ghosts. It was a beautiful colonial village with leafy streets lined with magnificent houses. The main square, where dances were held and famous musical troupes came to play, unfurled its flagstone carpet a stone's throw from the steps of the town hall, flanked by tall palm trees strung together by garlands studded with Chinese lanterns. The great jazz musician Aimé Barelli performed here, and bandleader Xavier Cugat with his famous chihuahua, as well as Jacques Hélian and Pérez Prado. The town attracted artists and orchestras that even Oran, for all its charm and its standing as the capital of the West, could not afford. Río Salado liked to flaunt its wealth, to avenge itself on all those who for years had written it off. The ostentatious mansions that lined the main street were the town's way of telling passers-by that ostentation was a virtue if it meant refuting others' preconceptions, if it meant enduring every hardship in order to catch the moon. The land here had once been a stony wilderness left to lizards, the only human soul a shepherd passing, never to return; it was a landscape of scrubland and dry riverbeds, the domain of boars and hyenas – a land forgotten by men and angels. Those pilgrims who passed this way raced through like gusts of wind as though it were a cursed cemetery. Later, exiles and nomads, Spaniards mostly, laid claim to this desolate land, which mirrored their suffering. These men rolled up their sleeves and set about taming this savage landscape. They uprooted the mastic trees and replaced them with vineyards, ploughed and hoed the wasteland to create farms, and from their Herculean efforts Río Salado blossomed, as green shoots grew over mass graves.

Nestled amid hundreds of vineyards and wine cellars, Río Salado was a town to be savoured, like one of its own vintages. Though there were chill January days when the sky was streaked with snow, the town had an aura of perpetual summer about it. The contented inhabitants went joyfully about their business, coming together at sunset to share a drink or some piece of scandal or gossip. Their braying laughter or their righteous anger could be heard for miles around.

'You'll like it here,' my uncle promised as he greeted Germaine and me on the steps of our new home.

The majority of the inhabitants of Río Salado were Spaniards and Jews, who were fiercely proud of having built their houses with their bare hands, of having snatched from this dry, pitted land sweet grapes that would have delighted even the gods of Olympus. They were friendly, impulsive people who would shout across the street to one other, hands cupped like megaphones. They knew each other so well that it was as if they had all been cast from the same mould. It was utterly unlike Oran, where to go from one neighbourhood to another was like moving between centuries, between different planets. Río Salado was easy-going and broad-minded; even the church, which stood next to the town hall, was set back from the square so as not to disturb revellers.

My uncle was right. Río Salado was the perfect place to start afresh. We lived on a hill to the east of the village in a large, bright, airy house set in magnificent gardens and with a small balcony that overlooked a sea of vineyards. The ground floor had been converted into a pharmacy, with a small back office lined with shelves and compartments. A spiral staircase led to the first-floor living room, off which were three large bedrooms and a tiled bathroom with an iron bathtub with claw feet in the shape of lion's paws cast in bronze. I felt at home here from the moment I first stood on the sunlit balcony watching a partridge soar above the vineyards, and felt myself soar with it.

I was overjoyed. Having been born in the countryside, here in Río Salado I rediscovered the familiar sights and smells of my childhood, the smell of the newly ploughed earth, the silent hills. I was a farmer's son again, happy to discover that the city clothes I had been forced to wear for so long had not warped my soul. The city was an illusion, the countryside a joy that was constantly renewed, a place where day breaks like the dawn of the world, where night-fall brings with it perfect peace. From the first, I loved Río Salado. It was a blessed place and I could easily imagine gods and titans finding rest here. It was a place of serenity, undisturbed by primordial demons. Even when the jackals came at night to prowl the sleeping town, I felt like going with them, following them into deep forest. Sometimes I would go out on to the balcony to watch them, sly shadows slinking through the vineyards; I could stand there for hours listening for every hushed sound, gazing at the moon, which dipped and seemed to brush my eyelashes.

And then there was Émilie.

The first time I saw her, she was sitting on the porch outside the pharmacy, toying with the laces of her boots. She was a pretty girl with timorous coal-black eyes. I could have mistaken her for an angel were it not that her face, so white it looked like marble, bore the unmistakable sign of some terrible illness.

'Hello,' I said. 'Can I help you?'

'I'm waiting for my father,' she said, shifting to one side to let me pass.

'You can wait inside. It's freezing out here.'

She shook her head.

When I saw her some days later she was with her father, a hulking man who looked as though he had been carved from a menhir. He waited by the counter, silent and motion-less, as Germaine led the girl into the back office. When they reappeared some minutes later, the man set some money on the counter, took his daughter by the hand and left.

'What was she here for?' I asked Germaine.

'Her injection . . . I give it to her every Wednesday.'

'Is it serious . . . what she's got?'

'Only God can know that.'

The following Wednesday, I hurried home from school so I could see her. She was sitting on a bench opposite the counter, leafing through a book.

'What are you reading?'

'It's a book about Guadeloupe.'

'What's Guadeloupe?'

'It's a French island in the Caribbean.'

I tiptoed closer, afraid that I might startle her – she looked so fragile.

'My name is Younes.'

'Mine's Émilie.'

'I'll be thirteen in three weeks.'

'I was nine last November.'

'Are you in a lot of pain?'

'It's not too bad.'

'What's wrong with you?'

'I don't know. The doctors at the hospital couldn't work it out, and the medicine they're giving me doesn't seem to do any good.'

Germaine appeared and Émilie went with her, leaving the book on the bench. There was a rose bush in a pot on the sideboard. I picked a rose and slipped it between the pages of the book, then went up to my room.

When I came down again, Émilie was gone.

She did not come for her injection the following Wednesday, nor the Wednesday after that.

'She must be in hospital,' Germaine said.

After several weeks, I gave up all hope of seeing Émilie again.

Then I met Isabelle. She was the niece of Pépé Rucillio – the richest man in Río Salado. Isabelle was a pretty little girl with big periwinkle-blue eyes and long hair that cascaded down her back. She thought of herself as sophisticated. She looked down her nose at everything and everyone, but when she looked at me, she suddenly seemed thin and frail. Isabelle wanted me all to herself and woe betide anyone who came too close to me.

Isabelle's parents – successful wine merchants – worked for Pépé Rucillio, the patriarch of the village. They lived in a huge villa on a street cascading with bougainvilleas near the Jewish cemetery.

Isabelle's mother was a highly strung French woman whose family, people said, were penniless aristocrats (though she was quick to remind everyone that she had blue blood in her veins). Isabelle had inherited little from her mother except her obsession with order and discipline, but she owed much to her father, a handsome olive-skinned man from Catalonia. She had his face – the same high cheekbones, the chiselled mouth, the piercing eyes. Even at the tender age of thirteen, with her aristocratic nose and her regal manner, Isabelle knew what she wanted and how to get it. She was as careful about the company she kept and the image she projected of herself. In a previous life, she told me, she had been a chatelaine.

It was Isabelle who approached me. I was at some festival on the village square when she came over to me and asked: 'Are you Monsieur Jonas?' She addressed everyone, young and old, as *monsieur* or *madame*, and insisted they do the same to her. 'Thursday is my birthday,' she went on imperiously, not waiting for me to answer. 'You are cordially invited to attend.' I didn't know whether this was an invitation or a command. When I arrived at her party on Thursday, feeling somewhat lost in the confusion of her cousins and her friends, she grabbed me and introduced me to everyone: 'This is my best friend.'

My first kiss, I owe to Isabelle. We were in an alcove of the grand drawing room at her house. Isabelle, her back straight, her chin held high, was playing the piano. I was sitting next to her, watching her slender fingers flutter over the keys. Suddenly she stopped, closed the piano lid carefully and, after a moment's hesitation – or a moment's thought – turned to me, took my face in her hands and pressed her lips to mine, closing her eyes in mock passion.

The kiss seemed to go on for ever.

Isabelle opened her eyes again before she pulled away.

'Did you feel anything, Monsieur Jonas?'

'No,' I said.

'Me neither. It's strange, in the movies, it looks so sophisticated . . . Perhaps you have to be grown up to really feel these things.'

She looked deep into my eyes and announced:

'Never mind. We'll wait as long as it takes.'

Isabelle had the patience of those who believe that tomorrow belongs to them. I was the most handsome boy on earth, she told me, and in some previous life I must have been a prince. She informed me that she had chosen me to be her fiancé because I was 'worth the candle.'

After that first attempt, we didn't kiss, but we saw each other almost every day and dreamed up fantastical plans.

Then suddenly, abruptly, our 'engagement' came to an end. It was a Sunday morning. I had been skulking around the house – my uncle had shut himself in his room and Germaine had gone to church – half-heartedly trying to play or read. It was a glorious spring day; the swallows had come early, and Río Salado was scented with jasmine.

I went for a walk, my head in the clouds, and though I

had not planned to do so, I found myself standing outside the Rucillios' house. I called to Isabelle through the window. She did not come down to the door, but peered at me through the shutters for a moment before slamming them open and screaming:

'Liar!'

From her tone and the incandescent fury of her stare, I knew she hated me – it was the tone, the look that she invariably used when she had decided to declare war. I had no idea of the charges levelled against me; I was completely unprepared for the attack. I stood there speechless.

'I never want to see you again, *Jonas*!' she declared, and I realised this was the first time I had ever heard her address anyone without using *monsieur* or *madame*.

'Why did you lie to me?' she screamed, infuriated that I simply stood there looking confused. 'Why?'

'I've never lied to you . . .'

'Haven't you? Your name is *Younes*, isn't it? *You-nes*? So why do you go round calling yourself Jonas?'

'Everyone calls me Jonas . . . What difference does it make?'

'It makes all the difference!' she shouted breathlessly, her face flushed as she spat scornfully. 'It changes everything.'

'We are from different worlds, Monsieur Younes,' she said implacably when she had got her breath back. 'And the fact that you have blue eyes is not enough.' Then, before slamming the shutters closed, she spluttered contemptuously: 'I am a Rucillio, or had you forgotten? You surely don't think I could marry an Arab? I'd rather die!'

As a child, such a glimpse into the adult world can scar you for life. I was shell-shocked; I felt as though I had woken from a nightmare. I would never again look at things the same way. There are things that, though to a child's eye they seem so trivial as to be inconsequential, come back to haunt you; even when you close your eyes, you feel them drag you down, tenacious and cruel as the pangs of remorse.

Isabelle had ripped me from my safe little world and tossed me into the gutter. Adam cast out of Eden could not have felt more wretched, and the lump in my throat was harder to swallow than his apple.

After what Isabelle said, I began to be more circumspect, more attentive. I noticed that no one in Río Salado wore a billowing *haik*, and that the dishevelled wretches in turbans who haunted the vineyards from dawn to dusk did not dare come into Río Salado itself, and that my uncle – whom most of the villagers assumed was a Turk from Tlemcen – was the only Arab to have succeeded in putting down roots in this fiercely colonial village.

What Isabelle had said had shocked me.

After that, whenever we met, she would stalk past, head high as a butcher's hook, as though I had never existed. Nor did it stop there: she invariably imposed her prejudices on others. If she had decided to hate someone, she insisted all her friends do so too. I watched as a yawning gap opened up around me in the school playground, my classmates deliberately shunned me.

It was for Isabelle's sake, too, that Jean-Christophe Lamy picked a fight with me at school and beat me to a bloody pulp. Though he was a year my senior, Jean-Christophe had little to boast about, since his father was the son of a caretaker. But Jean-Christophe was hopelessly in love with Pépé

Rucillio's indomitable niece, and he hoped by beating me up to show her how much he loved her, how far he was prepared to go.

Shocked by the sight of my injuries, the teacher called me up before the whole class and demanded that I name the 'little savage' who had done this. When I refused, the teacher ordered me to hold out my hands and thrashed me with a ruler, then made me stand in the corner for the rest of the day. After class, he had me stay behind, thinking he could coerce me into giving him the name of the culprit. Still I refused, and eventually he let me go.

When she saw the state of me, Germaine was livid. She demanded to know who had done this to me, but again I stubbornly refused to answer. She insisted on taking me back to the school so she could find out what had happened, but my uncle, who was slumped in a corner, dissuaded her. 'You're not taking him anywhere,' he said. 'It's high time he learned to stand on his own two feet.'

Some days later, as I was wandering through the vineyards, I saw Jean-Christophe Lamy and his two henchmen, Simon Benyamin and Fabrice Scamaroni, coming across the fields towards me. Though their manner was not hostile, I was terrified. They did not usually play around here; they hung around the town square or played football together on a patch of waste ground. The very fact that they were in my neighbourhood was not good news. I didn't really know Fabrice. He was in the class above me: I often saw him reading comics in the playground. He seemed an unremarkable boy whose only talent was his ability to give Jean-Christophe an alibi when he needed it, but I suspected that he might wade into the fight if things turned nasty.

Not that Jean-Christophe needed any help; he knew how to throw a punch. Simon was a different matter. I did not trust him at all – he was wildly unpredictable, capable of head-butting a friend just to put an end to a boring conversation. He was in the same year as me, and was the class clown. He always sat at the back and constantly persecuted the clever students. He was a dunce who would complain when the teacher gave him a bad grade, and he hated girls – especially the pretty, clever ones. Simon and I had met on my first day at the school. He and his gang had crowded around me and jeered at me, at the scabs on my knees, at my delicate features, 'like a little girl', at my new shoes, which they said made me look like a frog. When I did not react, Simon called me a sissy. After that, he ignored me.

Jean-Christophe was carrying something under his arm. I watched carefully, waiting for him to signal to his friends. Strangely, I saw no sign of the malicious grin, the tenseness in his movements he usually exhibited when about to beat somebody up.

'We're not here to hurt you,' Fabrice said.

Jean-Christophe approached me warily, looking embarrassed, even apologetic. His shoulders sagged under the weight of some invisible burden.

He held out a package.

'I came to say sorry,' he said.

I did not take the package, suspecting some practical joke, so he placed it in my hands.

'It's a wooden horse. It means a lot to me, but I'd like you to have it. Take it, please, and forgive me.'

Fabrice stared at me, willing me to forgive him.

Once he felt that I had a grip on the package, Jean-Christophe took his hands away and whispered: 'And thanks for not telling on me.'

In that moment, the friendship between the four of us, one that was to prove among the most important in my life, was sealed. Later, I discovered that Isabelle, furious at Jean-Christophe's hapless attempt to impress her, had insisted he apologise to me in the presence of witnesses.

Our first summer in Río Salado began inauspiciously. On 3 July, Algeria was rocked by Operation Catapult, in which a British naval squadron bombed the French fleet at the Battle of Mers-el-Kébir. Three days later, before we had had time to weigh the extent of the disaster, His Majesty's Air Force returned to finish the job.

One of Germaine's nephews in Oran, a cook on the warship *Dunkerque*, was among the 1,297 sailors killed in the raid. My uncle, who was gradually, inexorably withdrawing into himself, refused to come to the funeral, so Germaine and I had to go without him.

The city of Oran was in a state of shock. The whole population had gathered on the docks and was staring aghast at the burning barracks. Many of the ships had been on fire since the first bombing raids, and thick clouds of black smoke now choked the city and veiled the mountains. What had happened was all the more shocking because the warships the British had bombed had been in the process of laying up, the French having signed an armistice with Germany two weeks earlier. This war that people had assumed posed no threat to this side of the Mediterranean was now on our doorstep. After the initial panic and confusion, there was mayhem. Half-truths and rumours were rife, and people seemed prepared to believe even the wildest and most terrifying stories. There was talk of a German invasion, of nightly parachute drops outside the city, of massive bombing raids targeting the civilian population and dragging Algeria into this savage war, which even now was returning all of Europe to the Stone Age.

I was desperate to get back to Río Salado.

After the funeral, Germaine gave me some money so that I could go to Jenane Jato, and asked her nephew Bertrand to go with me so he could bring me back safe and sound.

Jenane Jato looked different, larger. It sprawled now towards Petit Lac, towards the shanty towns and the camp grounds of the nomads. Scrubland was fast disappearing under the advancing concrete. Patches of waste ground and dark alleys were now building sites. The high walls of a barracks or a prison rose up where once the souk had been. Crowds milled outside employment 'offices' – most of which were no more than tables set up in front of vast mountains of scrap iron. Jenane Jato was different, yet poverty still clung tenaciously to the place, resistant to even the most fervent municipal projects. The same shambling shadows still hugged the walls, the same human wrecks still sprawled drunkenly in cardboard boxes; the destitute, faces ashen, shrouded like mummies in their *burnous*, still teemed around the filthy cafés, hoping to dip a dry crust into the smells of cooking. The poor, the drunken and the wretched stared at us as though we were time itself, as though we had appeared from some parallel universe. Whenever he heard some insult directed at us, or saw someone stare a little too long at our fine clothes, Bertrand, who had never seen a place like

Jenane Jato, walked a little faster. There were *roumis* here and there, and some Muslims who wore European suits, fezzes perched at rakish angles, but in the air there was still the stifling smell of a storm about to break. As we walked, we happened on squabbles, some of which degenerated into brawls while others simply petered out into uneasy silence. The sense of dread was overpowering. Even the jingling dance of the water sellers, whose leather harnesses were studded with tiny bells, could not ward off the unwholesome effects.

There was far too much suffering.

Jenane Jato was crumbling beneath the weight of broken dreams. Abandoned children stumbled in their parents' shadows, weak from starvation and sunstroke, fledgling tragedies set loose upon the world. Feral and brutish, they raced barefoot through the streets, hanging on to the backs of trucks, dashing between the carts, laughing, heedless, flirting with death. Gangs of boys fought, or played soccer with a ball of knotted rags. In their terrifying games, there was something exhilarating, something dizzyingly suicidal.

'Makes a change from Río Salado, doesn't it?' Bertrand tried to smile, but he was sweating and pale with fear. I was scared too, but my terror vanished when I saw Peg-Leg standing outside his stall. The poor devil had lost a lot of weight. He looked ten years older. He gave me the same puzzled frown he had the last time he had seen me – half surprise, half delight.

'Can you give me the address of your guardian angel, blue eyes?' he shouted. 'Because if there is a God, I want to know why he looks out for you and not for us lot here.'

'That's enough of your blasphemy,' called the barber.

'It's probably your ugly mug that made God turn his back on us.'

The barber had not changed, though he now had the scar of a razor slash across his face. Jenane Jato was clearly on the move, but where it was headed I could not tell. The shacks behind the jujube hedges had been cleared away to leave a vast expanse of red clay surrounded by a wire fence into which had been dug the foundations for a bridge that was to span the railway line. Where the old barracks had stood rose the towers of a huge new factory.

Peg-Leg jerked a thumb at his jar of sweets.

'You want one, kid?'

'No thanks.'

Crouched beneath a rotting lamp post, a waffle-seller clicked a pair of metal castanets. He offered us waffles in paper cornets and the gleam in his eyes sent shivers down our backs. Bertrand urged me on, clearly not prepared to trust a face or a shadow in this place.

When we came to the courtyard, he said, 'I'll wait for you outside. Take all the time you need.'

Opposite, where Ouari's chicken coop had once been, there was a new brick house with a low stone wall that ran along what had been the patch of waste ground where a gang of boys had once tried to lynch me. I thought about Ouari, remembered him teaching me to catch goldfinches; I wondered where he was now.

Badra peered at me when she saw me step into the court-yard. She was hanging out her washing, the hem of her dress tucked into the rainbow-coloured cord she used as a belt, revealing her bare legs. She stood, feet apart, hands on her broad hips, barring my way.

'So it's only now that you remember you have a family?'

Badra looked different. She had put on weight. Her strong face had slipped to join a double chin, her fearsome energy had waned and she now seemed flabby and listless.

I didn't know whether she was teasing or scolding me.

'Your mother and your sister are out.' She nodded to our curtained room. 'But they should be back soon.'

She pushed her laundry pail aside with her foot and shoved a stool towards me

'Sit down,' she said. 'Kids! You're all the same! You suckle till you've sucked us dry, and as soon as you learn to walk, you clear off and leave us to starve. You're just like your fathers; you creep out and you don't give a thought to what happens to us.'

She turned and went back to hanging out her laundry. I could see only her shoulders rising and falling. She stopped for a moment to wipe her nose or brush away a tear, shook her head then went back to hanging clothes on the old hemp washing line that bisected the courtyard.

'Your mother's not been well,' she said. 'Not well at all. I'm sure something terrible has happened to your father, but she won't believe it. Lots of men walk out on their families, they go away and start again somewhere. But that's not the only possibility . . . There's a lot of violence these days. I've got a bad feeling about your father. I think he was murdered and dumped in a ditch. He was a good man, not the kind of man who walks out on his kids. I'm sure he's dead. Like my poor husband. Cut down for three *soldies* – three lousy cents. In broad daylight they killed him – stabbed him in the middle of the street. A single stab and it was all over. How can it be so easy for a man to die when he has hungry mouths to feed? How could he let himself be stabbed in the back by a kid not much older than you are?'

Badra chattered on, never pausing for breath, as though someone had opened up a Pandora's box inside her. It was as though this was all there was left for her: to talk about her tragedies, a casual gesture here, a sudden silence there. Above the clothes she was hanging out I could see her shoulders; beneath them, her bare legs, and sometimes, in the gap between the clothes, a glimpse of her plump hips. She told me that Bliss had evicted the beautiful Hadda, with her two kids trailing after her and nothing but a bundle of clothes. She told me that one night, when her drunken husband beat her yet again, poor Yezza had thrown herself into the well and killed herself. She told me how Batoul, the psychic, who had managed to extort a tidy sum from the poor wretches who came to consult her, finally amassed enough to buy a house and a Turkish hammam in the Village Nègre, and she told me about the new tenant who had shown up from God knew where and, in the afternoon, when all the shutters were closed, admitted every kind of deviant into her room. Badra told me that Bliss, now there were no men living in the courtyard, had become a pimp.

When she had finished hanging out her washing, she tipped the dirty water into the drain, untucked the hem of her skirt from her belt, and went back into her dingy rat hole, where she continued to rail and curse until my mother came back.

My mother did not seem surprised to see me sitting there on a stool in the courtyard. She barely seemed to recognise me. When I went over to kiss her, she took a step back. It was only when I pressed myself to her that her arms – hesitating for an instant – finally wrapped themselves around me.

'Why did you come?' she asked me over and over.

I proffered the money Germaine had given me. Hardly had I held it out than, like lightning, my mother had whipped the few grubby banknotes from my hand and conjured them away like a magician. She pushed me into the poky little room where we had lived, and as soon as we were safe, took the money out and counted it over and over to assure herself she wasn't dreaming. I was ashamed by her greed, ashamed of the unkempt hair she had clearly not brushed for ages, ashamed of the tattered *haik* draped like an old curtain round her shoulders, ashamed of the hunger and the pain that distorted her face, this woman who, once, had been as beautiful as the dawn.

'It's a lot of money,' she said. 'Did your uncle tell you to give it to me?'

Fearing she might react the same way my father had, I lied:

'I saved it up.'

'Are you working?'

'Yes.'

'You've stopped going to school?'

'I still go to school.'

'I don't want you to leave school. I want you to be educated and get a good job so you can live happily for the rest of your life. Do you understand? I don't want your children to have to live like dogs.'

Her eyes burned as she grabbed me by the shoulders.

'Promise me, Younes, promise me that you'll go to university like your uncle, that you'll have a proper house and a proper job . . .'

Her fingers dug into my shoulders until I thought they might break.

'I promise . . . Where is Zahra?'

Warily she took a step back. Then, remembering that I was her son and not some envious evil neighbour, she whispered:

'She is learning a trade . . . She is going to be a seamstress. I got her a post as an apprentice in a dressmaker's shop in the New Town. I want her to make something of herself . . .'

'Is she better?'

'She was never sick and she wasn't mad; she's simply deaf and dumb. But she understands people and the senior dressmaker told me she's a quick learner. She's a good woman, the dressmaker. I work for her three days a week. I do the cleaning. Here or there, what's the difference? Besides, you do what you have to to survive.'

'Why don't you come and live with us in Río Salado?'

'No,' she shrieked as though I had uttered some obscenity. 'I can't leave this place until your father comes back. Imagine if he came back and we weren't here? How would he find us? We have no family, no friends in this terrible city. And besides, where is Río Salado? It would never occur to your father that we might leave Oran. No, I am staying right here until he comes.

'But what if he's dead?'

She grabbed me by the throat and slammed my head against the wall.

'You little fool! How dare you! Batoul the clairvoyant told me. She saw it in my palm and she saw signs on the water. Your father is safe and well. He's making his fortune; when he is rich, he will come home. We will all live in a beautiful house with a veranda and a vegetable garden, and there will be a garage for our new car, and all the troubles of the past will be forgotten. Who knows, maybe we might go back and buy back the lands we were forced to sell.'

All this she said quickly, very quickly, with a quaver in her voice and a curious gleam in her eye, as her hands sketched her impossible dreams on the air. Had I known that this was the last time we would ever speak, I might have believed her fantasies; might have stayed with her. But how could I have known?

Once again it was she who urged me to leave; to go back to my adoptive parents.

9

THEY CALLED us 'the pitchfork'. We were as inseparable as the tines of a fork.

There was Jean-Christophe Lamy, a hulking giant at the age of sixteen. As the eldest of the group, he was the leader. His hair as blonde as a hayrick, he had a permanent smile. Every girl in Río Salado swooned over him, but ever since Isabelle Rucillio had *provisionally* agreed to make him her 'fiancé', he watched his step.

Then there was Fabrice Scamaroni, two months younger than me, a boy who had his heart on his sleeve and his head in the clouds. His sole ambition was to be a writer. His mother, a young widow who was a little crazy, owned businesses in Río Salado and Oran. She lived by her own rules and was the only woman in the whole district to drive a car. The wagging tongues in Río Salado constantly gossiped about her, but Madame Scamaroni didn't care. She was beautiful, rich, independent. What more was there?

In the summer, we would pile into the back seat of her sturdy six-cylinder truck and she would drive us to the beach at Terga. After a swim, she would throw together a barbecue, stuffing us with black olives, lamb kebabs and sardines grilled over charcoal.

Then there was Simon Benyamin. Simon, like me, was fifteen. He was a short, fat Jewish boy who loved tricks and practical jokes. He was jolly, a little cynical because he had been unlucky in love, but he could be endearing when he wanted to. He dreamed of working in the theatre or the movies. His family was not exactly popular in Río Salado. His father trailed bad luck in his wake. Every time he set up a business it went bust, which meant that he owed money to everyone, even the seasonal workers.

Of the gang, Simon and I were closest. We lived a stone's throw from each other, and every day he called for me and we would go and meet Jean-Christophe on the hill. The hilltop was our fort. We would meet under an ancient olive tree and look down at Río Salado shimmering at our feet. Fabrice was always last to show up, and always with a basket full of kosher sausage sandwiches, pickled peppers and fresh fruit. Together we would hang out there until late into the night, dreaming up improbable schemes and listening to Jean-Christophe talking about the tribulations he suffered at the hands of Isabelle Rucillio. Fabrice, for his part, drove us insane reciting poems and dysenteric prose strung together with words he had found in the dictionary.

Sometimes we allowed other boys to join us. More often than not this meant the Sosa cousins: José, who shared a tiny garret with his mother and ate gazpacho for breakfast, lunch and dinner, and André – we called him Dédé – who was every inch the son of his father, the stern Jaime Jiménez Sosa, who owed one of the largest farms in the area. André was sometimes a bully, he could be brutal with the hired help but he was kind to his friends. Spoiled and precocious, he was capable of saying outrageous things, seemingly indifferent to who he hurt, but I could never stay angry with him for long. Despite the cruel, casual remarks he made about *the Arabs*, he was always considerate to me. He did not discriminate; I was invited to his house just as often as his other friends. Yet even in my presence he was capable of disparaging Muslims, as though this was simply how things were. His father ruled his estate like a feudal lord, keeping the countless Muslim families who worked for him packed in like cattle. Wearing a pith helmet and slapping at his boots with a riding crop, Jaime Jiménez Sosa IV was always up at first light and always last to bed. He worked his 'galley slaves' until they dropped, and God help the malingerers. He worshipped his vineyards, and any incursion on to his land he regarded as sacrilege. People said that he once killed a goat who dared to nibble on a vine leaf and shot at the flabbergasted shepherd for trying to save the animal.

These were strange times.

As for me, time marched on – I was becoming a man. I had grown almost twelve inches, and when I licked my lips, I could feel a little downy moustache.

It was the summer of 1942, and we were on the beach, sunning ourselves. The sea was crystalline and the horizon so clear that you could see all the way to the Habibas Islands. Fabrice and I were lounging under a sunshade while Simon, wearing a pair of revolting shorts, was entertaining the crowd doing ridiculous dives, hoping his antics might impress some girl, but his Apache war cries simply terrified the children and irritated the old ladies slumped in their deckchairs. Jean-Christophe was posing, holding his stomach in, hands on his hips, showing off the perfect V of his torso. Nearby, the Sosa boys had set up a tent. André loved to put on airs. Whereas other people brought deckchairs to the beach, he brought a tent; if they showed up with a tent, he would turn up with a whole caravanserai. At the age of eighteen, he already owned two cars, including a convertible. This he would drive lazily through the streets of Oran, except when it was time for siesta, when he would tear through Río Salado with an ear-splitting roar. Today, he could think of nothing better to do than mistreat his manservant Jelloul. He had already sent him back to the village three times in the blazing sun, the first time to get cigarettes, the second to get matches, and the third because Monsieur André had asked for Bastos cigarettes, not something that 'a navvy might smoke'. The village was a fair distance and poor Jelloul was melting like an ice cube.

Fabrice and I had watched the scene play out from the beginning. André knew that the way he treated his manservant annoyed us and took malicious pleasure in winding us up. As soon as Jelloul got back, he sent him off a fourth time to get a tin-opener. The servant, a timid boy, turned on his heel stoically and headed back up the embankment in the sweltering afternoon heat.

'Give him a break, Dédé,' José said.

'It's the only way to keep him on his toes,' said André, clasping his hands behind his neck. 'Give him a break, and next minute he'll be snoring.'

'It's a hundred degrees out there,' pleaded Fabrice. 'The poor guy is only flesh and blood, he'll get sunstroke.'

José got to his feet to call Jelloul back. André grabbed his wrist and forced him to sit down again.

'Leave it, José. You don't have servants, you don't know what it's like . . . Arabs are like dogs, you have to beat them to get them to behave.' Then, remembering that I was there, he corrected himself: 'Well, some Arabs . . .'

Suddenly realising just how offensive his remark had been, he leapt to his feet and raced down to the sea. We watched him dive in, throwing up great sheets of spray. There was an uncomfortable silence in the tent. José clenched his jaw, finding it difficult to contain himself. Fabrice closed the book he had been reading and glared at me.

'You need to give him a smack in the mouth, Jonas.'

'What for?' I asked wearily.

'For what he says about Arabs. What he said was outrageous, I expected you to put him in his place.'

'This is his place, Fabrice . . . *I'm* the one who doesn't know my place.'

With that I grabbed my towel and headed back towards the road to hitchhike back to Río Salado. Fabrice came after me, tried to persuade me not to go home so early, but I felt sick at heart and the beach now seemed as bleak as a desert island. It was at that moment that a four-engine plane shattered the silence, appearing over the headland trailing a ribbon of smoke.

'It's on fire,' José shouted, shocked. 'It's going to crash.'

The crippled plane disappeared beyond the ridge. Everyone on the beach was on their feet now, shading their eyes with their hands, waiting for an explosion or a cloud of smoke marking out the crash site. Nothing. The plane continued to coast, its engines stalled, but to the relief of everyone it did not crash.

Was this some terrible omen?

Some months later, on 7 November, as night fell over the deserted beach, monstrous shadows appeared on the horizon. The landings on the coast of Oran had begun.

'Three shots fired,' roared Pépé Rucillio. The man who rarely showed himself in public was standing on the village square. 'Where is our valiant army?'

In Río Salado, news of the landings had been greeted like hail at harvest time. The men of the town had convened a meeting on the steps of the town hall. Some glowered with fury and disbelief while others, panic-stricken, had slumped and were sitting on the pavement, drumming their fingers on their knees. The mayor had rushed back to his office, where, according to those close to him, he was in constant contact with the military authorities at the barracks in Oran.

'The Americans tricked us,' roared Pépé, the richest man in the district. 'While our soldiers were stationed in their bunkers, the enemy ships skirted the Montagne des Lions, bypassing our defences, and landed at Arzew without firing a shot. From there, they marched all the way to Tlélat without meeting a living soul, then advanced on Oran by the back door . . . While our troops were still keeping lookout on the clifftops, there were Americans strolling down the Boulevard Mascara. I'm telling you, there wasn't so much as a skirmish! The enemy marched into Oran and made themselves right at home. What's going to happen now?'

The day passed in a dizzying whirl of half-truths and wild rumours. Night fell, but no one seemed to notice – in fact most of the villagers did not go home until dawn. By now, they were disoriented. Some swore they could hear tanks roaring through the vineyards.

'What kept you out so late?' Germaine demanded, opening the door. 'You've had me worried sick. Where have you been? The whole country is at war and you're out wandering the streets . . .'

My uncle had emerged from his room. He was slumped in an armchair in the living room, unable to keep his hands still.

'Is it true the Germans have landed?' he asked me.

'Not the Germans, the Americans.'

'The Americans?' He looked puzzled. 'What the hell would the Americans be doing here?'

He jumped to his feet, looked about him contemptuously and announced: 'I'm going to my room. When they get here, tell them I don't have time to see them, tell them they can torch the house.'

No one came to torch our house, no air raid troubled the quiet of our fields. A couple of motorcyclists were spotted near Bouhadjar, the neighbouring village, but they turned out to be lost. They drove around for a while, then headed back the way they had come. Some said they were German soldiers, others said it was an American reconnaissance mission, but since no one had ever seen either army up close, we drew a line under the matter and went about our business.

André Sosa was the first of us to go to Oran.

He came back completely confused.

'The Americans are buying up everything,' he told us. 'War or no war, they're behaving like tourists. They're all over Oran – in the bars, in the whorehouses, in the Jewish Quarter, they've even gone into the Village Nègre, against the express orders of their commander. They want everything: carpets, rugs, fezzes, *burnous*, tapestries. And they don't even haggle! I saw one of them give a Moroccan veteran a wad of cash for just some rusty old bayonet from the Great War.'

He pulled a banknote from his back pocket and laid it on the table as though this were proof of what he had said.

'Just look at what they do with their money . . . This is a hundred-dollar bill. Have you ever seen a French banknote scribbled over like this? They're autographs. It's stupid, but it's the Yanks' favourite game. They call it 'Short Snorter'. You can do it with other notes too. Some of them have rolls of bills all like this. They're not trying to get rich, they're just collecting them. See those two autographs there, that's Laurel and Hardy, I swear it is. That one there is Errol Flynn, you know, the guy who plays Zorro . . . Joe gave it to me for a crate of wine . . .'

He picked up the note, stuffed it back in his pocket and, rubbing his hands together, told us he'd be going back to Oran within the week to do some deals with the GIs.

As the fear subsided and people realised the Americans had not come as conquerors but as saviours, others from Río Salado headed for Oran to see what was going on. Little by little, the last pockets of suspicion died away and people stopped posting guards over the farms and the houses.

André was keyed up. Every day, he jumped in his car and headed for Oran to barter, and after each sortie he would come back and try to impress us with his treasures. We had to go to Oran for ourselves to corroborate the wild stories circulating about the Yanks. Jean-Christophe pestered Fabrice, who pestered his mother to drive us there. Madame Scamaroni was reluctant, but eventually she relented.

We left at dawn. The sun had barely risen above the horizon when we reached Misserghin. Jeeps droned back and forth across the roads and the fields. In the streams, GIs, stripped to the waist, washed themselves, singing loudly. There were broken-down trucks along the verge, their hoods up, surrounded by listless mechanics. By the gates of the city, whole convoys waited. Oran had changed. The GIs teeming through the streets gave the place a carnival air. André had not been exaggerating – there were Americans everywhere: on the boulevards and the building sites, driving their half-tracks through the chaos of camels and tipcarts, dispatching units to the nomads' *douars*, filling the air with dust and noise. Officers in civvies honked their horns to cut a path through the mayhem. Others, dressed up to the nines, lounged on the terraces of cafés with lady friends while a gramophone played Dinah Shore. Oran was operating on American time. It was not only Uncle Sam's troops that had landed, they had brought his culture with them: their ration boxes were crammed with condensed milk, chocolate bars, corned beef, chewing gum, Coca-Cola, Twinkies, processed cheese, American cigarettes and white bread. Local bars were playing American music, and the *yaouleds* – the shoeshine boys – who had suddenly metamorphosed into newspaper sellers, dashed from the squares to the tram stops howling 'The Stars and Stripes' in some incomprehensible pidgin English. From the pavements came the rustle of magazines ruffled by the breeze: *Esquire*, *The New Yorker*, *Life*. Fans of Hollywood began to adopt the traits of their favourite actors: they swaggered as they walked and curled their lips into a sneer even as the merchants in the souks effortlessly learned to lie and haggle in English.

Río Salado suddenly seemed like a backwater. Oran had taken possession of our souls, its clamour pulsed through our veins, its audacity cheered us. We felt drunk, caught up in the commotion of gleaming avenues and teeming bars, made dizzy by the constant weaving of the carts, the cars, the trams, while the girls, insolent but not flighty, their hips swaying seductively, whirled around us like *houris*.

There could be no question of going back to Río Salado. Madame Scamaroni headed back alone, leaving us in a room over one of her shops on the Boulevard des Chasseurs and making us promise not to do anything foolish in her absence. Hardly had her car turned the corner than we began our invasion of the city. Oran was ours: the Place des Armes, with its rococo theatre; the town hall, flanked by its colossal bronze lions; the Promenade de l'Étang, the Place de la Bastille, the Passage Clauzel, where lovers met; the ice-cream stands that served the finest lemonade on earth, the lavish cinemas and Darmon's department stores . . . In its charm and its daring, Oran lacked nothing, every spark became a firework, every joke an uproar, every drink a celebration. Ever generous and impulsive, the city was determined to share every pleasure and despised anything it did not find entertaining. A sullen face could ruin its equanimity, a killjoy sour its mood; it could not bear to see the cloud darken its silver lining. Every street corner was a party, every square a carnival, and everywhere its voice proclaimed a hymn to life itself. In Oran, pleasure was not simply a state of mind; it was a cardinal rule: without it, the whole world was a mess. Beautiful, alluring and well aware of the spell she cast over strangers, Oran was bourgeois in an understated fashion. She needed no fanfare and was convinced that no storm – not even the war – could curb her flight. Oran was a city of airs and graces, people referred to her as *la ville américaine*, and every fantasy in the world was becoming real. Perched on a clifftop, she gazed out to sea, pretending to languish, a captive maiden watching from a tower for Prince Charming to arrive. She was pleasure itself, and everything suited her.

We were caught up in her spell.

'Hey, rednecks!' André Sosa yelled to us.

He was sitting on the terrace of an ice-cream parlour with an American soldier. From the way he waved, it was obvious he was trying to impress. He looked dashing: his hair was scraped back and plastered down with brilliantine, his shoes freshly polished, and his sunglasses hid half his face.

'Hey, come join us,' he called, getting up to fetch more chairs. 'They do the best double-chocolate malt here, and the best snails *piquant*.'

The soldier shifted over to make room, and watched confidently as we surrounded him.

'This is my friend Joe,' said André, delighted to be able to introduce the Yank he had been boasting about. 'Our American cousin. He comes from a godforsaken hole just like ours. He's from Salt Lake City and we're from Río Salado, which means Salt River.'

He threw his head back and gave a forced laugh, delighted by this notion.

'Does he speak French?' Jean-Christophe asked.

'Kind of. Joe says his great-grandmother was French, from Haut-Savoie, but he never really learned the language, he picked it up while he was stationed here in North Africa. Joe's a corporal. He fought on all the fronts.'

Joe punctuated André's comments by nodding vigorously, clearly amused to see us all raise our eyebrows in admiration. He shook hands with the four of us and André introduced us as his best friends and the finest stallions in Salt River. Although he was thirty and had been in the wars, Joe still had a boyish face, thin-lipped, with high cheekbones that seemed too delicate for a guy of his build. His keen eye lacked any real acuity and made him look a little simple when he grinned from ear to ear; and he grinned whenever anyone so much as looked at him.

'Joe's got a problem,' André told us.

'Is he a deserter?' asked Fabrice.

'No, Joe's no coward – he lives for fighting. The problem is, he hasn't had it off for six months and his balls are so full of spunk he can't put one foot in front of the other.'

'Why?' asked Simon. 'Don't they issue hand towels with the rations?'

'It's not that.' André patted the corporal's hand gently. 'Joe wants a real bed with red lampshades on the nightstands and a real flesh-and-blood woman who can whisper dirty things to him.'

We all burst out laughing and Joe joined us, nodding his head, his smile splitting his face.

'Anyway, I've decided to take him to a whorehouse,'

André announced, throwing his arms wide to indicate the extent of his generosity.

'They won't let you in,' said Jean-Christophe.

'They wouldn't dare refuse André Jiménez Sosa . . . They're more likely to roll out the red carpet for me. The madame at Camélia is a friend – I've put so much money her way, she melts like butter as soon as she sees me. So, anyway, I'm going to take my friend Joe over there and we're going to fuck their brains out, aren't we, Joe?'

'Oh, yeah.' Joe twisted his hat nervously in his hands.

'I wouldn't mind going with you,' Jean-Christophe ventured. 'I've never done anything serious with a woman. You think you could arrange it?'

'Are you crazy?' said Simon. 'You're not seriously thinking of going into a dive like that with all the diseases the whores have got?'

'I'm with Simon,' said Fabrice. 'I don't think we should go. Besides, we told my mother we'd behave ourselves.'

Jean-Christophe shrugged, leaned over to André and whispered something in his ear. André gave him a superior look and said, 'I can get you into Hell itself if you want.'

Relieved and excited, Jean-Christophe turned to me.

'What about you, Jonas, are you coming?'

'Absolutely . . .'

I was more shocked than anyone to hear myself say this.

The red-light district In Oran was behind the theatre on the Rue de l'Aqueduc, a squalid alleyway with stairs at either end that reeked of piss and teemed with drunks. Hardly had we set foot in the alley than I felt horribly uncomfortable, and it took every ounce of energy not to turn tail and run. Joe and André raced ahead, eager to get inside. Jean-Christophe followed close behind. He was clearly intimidated and his attempt at seeming offhand was unconvincing. He turned round from time to time and winked at me, to which I responded with a nervous smile, but the moment we passed anyone shifty we swerved out of the way and made as if to leave. The brothels were all lined up on the same part of the alley, their front doors painted in garish colours. The Rue de l'Aqueduc was heaving; there were soldiers, sailors, furtive Arab men terrified of being spotted by a neighbour, barefoot boys running errands, Senegalese pimps with flick knives tucked into their belts watching over their livestock, 'native' soldiers wearing tall red fezzes – a feverish yet somehow muted tumult.

The madame at the Camélia was a giant of a woman with a voice that could make the earth quake. She ruled her demesne with a rod of iron and was bawling out an ill-mannered customer on the steps as we arrived.

'You fucked up again, Gégé, and that's not good. You want to come back here and see my girls? Well, it's down to you. If you keep acting like a thug, you'll never set foot in my house again. You know me, Gégé, when I put that little red cross next to someone's name, I might just as well be digging his grave. You understand what I'm saying, or do I need to draw you a picture?'

'Don't act like you're doing me some big favour,' Gégé protested. 'I come here with my cash, all I'm asking is that your whore does what she's told.'

'You can stick your money up your arse, Gégé. This is a brothel, not a torture chamber. If you don't like the service, you can take your custom elsewhere. Because if you try something like that again, I'll rip your heart out with my bare hands.'

Gégé, who was almost a dwarf, rose up on the tips of his shoes and glared at the madame, purple with rage. Then he rocked back on to his heels and, livid at having been publicly ticked off by a woman, elbowed his way past us and disappeared into the crowd.

'Serves him right,' yelled a soldier. 'If he doesn't like it, he can take his business elsewhere.'

'That goes for you too, Sergeant,' the madame said. 'You're no saint yourself.'

The soldier shrank back. The madame was clearly in a bad mood, and André realised that things might not go his way. He managed to persuade her to let Jean-Christophe in, given his height, but could do nothing for me.

'He's just a kid, Dédé,' she said. 'He still smells of mother's milk. I can turn a blind eye to your blonde friend here, but this little cherub with his blue eyes, there's no way. He'd be raped in the corridor before he even got to a room.'

André made no attempt to insist. The madame was not the sort to go back on a decision. She told me I could wait for my friends behind the counter, instructing me not to touch anything or speak to anyone. I felt relieved. Now that I had seen the brothel, I didn't want to go any farther; the place turned my stomach.

In the waiting room, veiled by curtains of smoke, the hunters, looking shrunken and dazed, eyed their prey. Some of the men were drunk and they grumbled and jostled. The prostitutes were displayed on a long upholstered bench in an alcove carved into the wall of the corridor that led to the bedrooms. They sat facing the customers, some of them barely dressed, others squeezed into see-through corselets. It looked like a painting of ruined concubines by a despondent Delacroix. There were big girls rippling with rolls of fat, breasts stuffed into bras the size of hammocks; scrawny women with dark sunken eyes who looked as though they had been dragged from their deathbeds; brunettes in cheap blonde wigs; blondes wearing so much make-up they looked like clowns, one breast casually exposed. The women sat in silence, patiently scratching their crotches, smoking, eyeing the cattle opposite.

Sitting behind the counter, I contemplated this world and regretted ever having ventured inside. It smelled of adulterated wine and the stench of rutting flesh. A terrible tension hung in the room like some noxious gas. One spark, one misjudged comment, one wrong look and the whole place could go up . . . The decor, although contrived and naïve, did its best to be cheery: delicate wall hangings framed with velvet, gilded mirrors, cheap paintings of nymphs dressed as Eve, matching lamps and mosaic walls, empty love seats in the alcoves. But the customers seemed oblivious to all this; they could see only the half-naked girls on the long bench. Veins throbbing in their necks, all but pawing the ground, they were eager to get started.

I was beginning to get bored. Jean-Christophe disappeared with some fat old woman, followed by Joe leading two girls caked in make-up. André had vanished.

The owner offered me a bowl of toasted almonds and promised that when I came of age I could have her prettiest girl.

'No hard feelings, kid?'

'No hard feelings, Madame.'

'You're sweet . . . and for God's sake don't call me Madame, it gives me constipation.'

Calmer now, the woman was trying to make peace. I was terrified she might do me a 'favour' and allow me to choose from the sweaty flesh laid out on the bench.

'Sure you're not angry with me?'

'I'm not, honestly,' I yelped, now convinced she would overlook my age and pick out a girl for me. 'Actually,' I said quickly, to cover every eventuality, 'I didn't want to come in the first place. I'm not ready.'

'You're right, kid. When it comes to dealing with women, you're never ready . . . There's lemonade behind you if you're thirsty. It's on the house.'

She left me and disappeared into the corridor to make sure everything was okay.

It was then that I saw her. She had just finished with a client and gone back to sit with her co-workers on the bench. Her arrival created a ripple in the waiting room. One burly soldier loudly announced that he was first in the queue, causing a storm of protests. I paid no attention. Suddenly the noise in the room seemed to die away; even the room had vanished. There was only *her*. It was as if a shooting star had come from nowhere and traced a halo of light around her. I recognised her at once, though this was the last place I would have expected to see her. She did not seem to have aged at all. Her body, in a tight-fitting, low-cut dress, was still that of an adolescent girl, her hair spilled over her shoulders just as I remembered it, her cheekbones were as perfectly chiselled as ever. It was Hadda . . . Hadda the beautiful, the woman I had secretly loved, the object of my first boyish fantasies. How could Hadda, who simply by stepping into the courtyard of our house lit it up like the sun, have wound up in this seedy dive?

I was shocked, frozen with disbelief.

Seeing her, I was suddenly transported back to a morning several years before. I was sitting in the courtyard outside our tiny room in Jenane Jato, listening to the laughter and the chatter of our neighbours, the squealing of their children. Hadda was not laughing. She was sad. I remembered watching her place her hand on the low table, palm upwards, and say: 'Tell me what you see, Batoul, I need to know. I can't go on like this,' and Batoul saying, 'I see you surrounded by many men, Hadda. But there is little happiness . . . It looks like a dream, yet it is not a dream.'

Batoul had been right. Hadda was surrounded by many men, but there was little joy. This place where she had washed up, with its sequins and spangles, its subdued lighting and extravagant decor, was dream-like, yet it was not a dream. I stood behind the counter, open-mouthed, unable to give voice to the terrible feeling that crept over me like a fog and made me feel as though I might go mad.

The burly soldier with the shaven head grabbed two men and smashed their heads against the wall. After that, things calmed down somewhat. He glared around him, nostrils flaring, and when he realised that no one else was prepared to take him on, let go of the two men and strode over to Hadda, grabbed her by the elbow and pulled her to her feet. In the silence as they walked down the corridor, you could cut the atmosphere with a knife.

I rushed out into the street, choking for breath.

André, Jean-Christophe and Joe found me sitting, dumbstruck, on a step, and assuming it was because the madame had refused to let me in, they asked no questions. Jean-Christophe was crimson with embarrassment. Things, apparently, had not gone well. André had eyes only for his Yank, and seemed prepared to grant his every wish. He suggested to Jean-Christophe and me that we go and find Simon and Fabrice and meet up later at the Majestic, one of the most fashionable brasseries in the new town.

The six of us spent the rest of the evening in a high-class restaurant at André's expense. Joe could not hold his wine. After we had eaten, he started acting up. It started with him pestering a journalist who was quietly trying to put the finishing touches to a story. Joe wandered over to tell the man about his exploits – how he had fought at the front, how many times he had risked his life. The journalist, a patient, polite man, heard him out, clearly eager to get back to his work, irritated but too shy to say anything. He was visibly relieved when André went to collect his soldier friend. Joe came back and joined us, but he was restless and volatile. From time to time he turned back to the journalist and bellowed across the tables: 'I want a big headline, John, I want to see my face on the front page. You need a photo, it's no problem, okay, John? I'm counting on you.' Realising he had no hope of finishing his story with this lunatic nearby, the journalist picked up his rough draft, dropped some money on the table and left.

'You know who that is?' Joe said, jerking his thumb over his shoulder. 'That's John Steinbeck. He's a writer, a war correspondent with the *Herald Tribune*. He wrote a piece about my regiment.'

After the journalist had left, Joe looked for other prey. He went up to the bar and asked them to play some Glenn

Miller. Then he climbed on to his chair, stood at attention, and sang 'Home on the Range'. Later, egged on by a bunch of Americans having dinner on the terrace, he forced one of the waiters to repeat after him the lyrics to 'You'd Be So Nice To Come Home To'. Gradually, the laughter faded to smiles and the smiles to frowns and people began to ask André to take his Yank elsewhere. Joe was no longer the biddable young man he had been during the day. He was drunk now. His eyes bloodshot, his lips flecked with spittle, he clambered up on the table and began to tap-dance, sending cutlery and crockery flying and glasses and bottles crashing to the floor. The manager came over and politely asked him to stop, but Joe, who did not take kindly to the request, punched the man in the face. Two waiters rushed to help their boss and were immediately sent flying. Women started crying. André grabbed his protégé, begging him to calm down, but Joe was no longer listening. He lashed out in all directions and the brawl spread to other customers, then the soldiers on the terrace waded in and chairs started flying. It was chaos.

It took a number of officers from the military police to overpower Joe, and the restaurant did not begin to relax until the MP's jeep disappeared into the night with Joe inside.

Back in our room on the Boulevard des Chasseurs, I couldn't get to sleep. All night I tossed and turned, unable to get the image of Hadda the prostitute out of my mind. Batoul's voice echoed in my head, stirring up old fears, unearthing silences buried deep within me. It was as though I had seen a glimpse of some terrible catastrophe that would befall me. I buried my head under the pillow, trying to suffocate myself with it, but it was useless: the image of Hadda sitting half naked in that brothel turned and turned in my head like a dancer on a music box to the voice of Batoul the clairvoyant.

The following morning, I asked Fabrice to lend me some money, and I headed off on my own to Jenane Jato. This was the other side of Oran; no uniformed soldiers strutted about the streets here, and the air was filled with the stench of rotting prayers and hopes. I needed to see my mother and my sister, wanted to touch them with my own hands, hoping I might shake off the terrible sense of foreboding that had hounded me all night, that clung to me still . . .

But my terrible fears were proved right. Jenane Jato had changed since my last visit. The courtyard where we had lived stood empty; it looked as though a tornado had swept through and carried everyone off. There was barbed wire across the doorway, but someone had made a hole in it large enough for me to crawl through. The courtyard was filled with blackened rubble, rats' dropping and cat shit. The metal cover of the well was warped and twisted. The doors and windows were all gone. Fire had gutted the left-hand side of the building; the walls had collapsed. A few charred beams still hung from the roof. Above them there was only the pitiless blue of the sky. Our tiny room lay in ruins, and here and there amid the rubble were broken kitchen implements and half-charred bundles of clothes.

'There's no one there.' A voice rang out behind me.

It was Peg-Leg, propped against the doorway, wearing a *gandurah* that was too short for him. His face was gaunt, his toothless mouth gaped, a terrible maw his grey beard did little to hide. His arm was trembling and he was having trouble standing on his one good leg, which was pale now and covered with brownish pustules.

'What happened here?' I asked him.

'Terrible things . . .'

He hobbled over to me, picking up a can as he passed. He turned it over to see if there might be anything inside worth salvaging, then threw it over his shoulder.

'Look at this mess.' He flung his arm wide. 'It's a terrible shame.'

Seeing me standing there, waiting, he went on:

'I warned Bliss about it. This is a respectable house, I told him, you've no business putting that whore in with decent women; it'll end in tears. But he wouldn't listen to me. One night, a couple of drunks came round looking for her, but she already had a customer, so they tried their luck with Badra. You can imagine – they never knew what hit them. The widow's two sons butchered them. After that, it was the whore's turn. She defended herself better than her clients, but there were two of them. At some point, someone knocked over the oil lamp and the fire spread like lightning. It's lucky it didn't reach the other houses. The police arrested Badra and her sons and boarded up the house; it's been like this for two years now. Some people say it's haunted.'

'What happened my mother?'

'I've no idea. I do know that she survived the fire; I saw her with your little sister the next day on the corner of the street. They weren't injured.'

'What about Bliss?'

'He disappeared.'

'What about the other tenants? Maybe they know something . . .'

'I don't know where they went, sorry.'

I made my way back to the Boulevard des Chasseurs with a heavy heart. My friends pestered me to know where I'd been, but their questions simply infuriated me and I went out again and wandered the streets for hours. Again and again I found myself standing in the middle of a street, my head in my hands, trying to compose myself. My mother and my sister were safe, I told myself, and probably better off now than they had been. Batoul the psychic was never wrong – after all, she had predicted Hadda's fate. My father would come back – it was written on the ripples of the water. My mother would not have to worry any more.

This was what I was thinking when suddenly I saw him . . .
My father!

I was sure it was him – I could have recognised his shadow in the darkness among ten thousand, among a hundred thousand men. It was my father. He had come back. Bent beneath the weight of a thick green coat he was wearing in spite of the heat, he was crossing a crowded square in the Village Nègre. I rushed to catch up with him, pushing through the crowded square, but it seemed that for every step forward, I was pushed two steps back. Not for a moment did I take my eyes off the figure of my father as he shambled away, limping slightly, bowed beneath the weight of his green jacket. I was terrified that if I lost sight of him, I might never find him again. But by the time I finally struggled free of the crowd and made it to the far side of the square, he had vanished.

I looked for him in the local cafés, in the bars, in the hammams . . . but he was gone.

I never saw my mother or my sister again. I do not know what became of them, whether they are alive still or dust mingled with the dust of ages. My father I saw several times. About once every ten years I would spot him in a crowded souk or on a building site; sometimes standing alone on his own, or in the doorway of an abandoned warehouse. I never managed to speak to him. Once, I followed him into a blind alley, certain that at last I had tracked him down, and was shocked to discover that the alley was deserted, there was no one waiting at the foot of the crumbling wall. Only when I realised that he always wore the same green jacket, which seemed to be untouched by time and weather, did I finally understand that the man I saw was not flesh and blood.

Even now, in my declining years, I still see him in the distance sometimes, bowed beneath the weight of his old green jacket, limping slowly towards his doom.

10

THE SEA looked smooth enough to walk on; not a wave lapped at the beach, not a ripple disturbed the glassy surface. It was a weekday and the beach belonged to us. Next to me, Fabrice lay on his back dozing, a book open over his face. Jean-Christophe was strutting along the water's edge, showing off as always. The Sosa cousins, André and José, had set up a tent and a barbecue a hundred metres away and were waiting for the girls from Lourmel. Here and there a few families lay sunning themselves along the shore. Were it not for Simon's antics, we might have been on a desert island.

The sun poured down like molten lead, and seagulls darted across the flawless sky, drunk on space and freedom. From time to time they skimmed the waves, like planes chasing each other and hedge-hopping, only to soar again to melt into the blue. In the distance, a trawler heading for port trailed a cloud of birds in its wake; it had been a good day's fishing.

The weather was beautiful.

Sitting beneath a parasol, a woman gazed out at the horizon. She wore a broad-brimmed hat with a red ribbon, dark glasses and a white swimsuit that clung to her tanned body like a second skin.

And there would be no more to tell had it not been for a gust of wind.

Had I known that a gust of wind can change the course of a life, I might have been more wary, but at the age of seventeen, we all believe we are invulnerable . . .

The midday breeze had come up and the fateful gust of wind, waiting in ambush, raced along the beach stirring up eddies of sand, whipping the parasol into the air as the lady clutched her hat to stop it from flying away. The parasol pirouetted through the air, sailed along the sand, turned somersaults. Jean-Christophe tried but failed to catch it. If he had, my life would have gone on as before, but fate decreed otherwise. The parasol landed at my feet. I simply reached out and picked it up.

Smiling, the lady watched me as I made my way towards her with the parasol tucked under one arm. She got to her feet.

'Thank you,' she said.

'Don't mention it, madame.'

I knelt down beside her and began scooping out sand, making the hole where the parasol had been deeper and wider. Then I replanted the parasol, and trampled the sand to make sure it did not fly off again.

'You are very kind, Monsieur Jonas,' she said. 'I'm sorry . . .' she added quickly. 'I heard your friends call you that.'

She took off her dark glasses.

'Are you from Terga?'

'From Río Salado, madame.'

Her piercing eyes unsettled me. In the distance I could see my friends giggling and laughing at me. I quickly took my leave of the woman and went back to join them.

'You're red as a beetroot,' Jean-Christophe teased me.

'Leave me alone,' I said.

Simon, who had just come back from a swim, was rubbing himself vigorously with a towel, a mischievous smile on his lips. He dropped into my chair and said:

'So what did Madame Cazenave want with you?'

'You know her?'

'Of course I know her. Her husband was governor of a penal colony in Guyana. They say he disappeared in the jungle tracking a couple of escaped prisoners. When he didn't show up, she decided to come home. She's a good friend of my aunt. My aunt says she thinks Madame Cazenave's husband succumbed to the charms of some big-bottomed Amazonian beauty and ran off with her.'

'I'm glad your aunt's no friend of mine!'

Simon burst out laughing and threw the towel at my face, beat his chest like a gorilla and, with a shrill war cry, raced back down to the sea.

'Completely mad,' sighed Fabrice, propping himself up on one elbow to watch Simon perform some ridiculous dive.

The girls André had been waiting for arrived on the stroke of ten. The youngest was at least four or five years older than André and José. The girls kissed the Sosa cousins on both cheeks and settled themselves in canvas chairs. André's manservant, Jelloul, busied himself at the barbecue, fanning the coals and sending clouds of white smoke across the surrounding dunes. José pulled a hamper from under the piles of bags around the centre pole of the tent, took out a couple of strings of spicy *merguez* sausages and laid them on the grill. The smell of burning fat began to drift along the beach.

I don't remember why I decided to head over to André's tent. Perhaps I was deliberately trying to attract the attention of Madame Cazenave so that I could get another glimpse of her magnificent eyes. If so, she was reading my mind, because as I passed her, she took off her sunglasses, and as she did, I suddenly felt as though I was wading through quicksand.

I saw her again some days later on the main street in Río Salado. She was coming out of a shop, a white hat perched like a crown over her perfect face. People turned to look at her but she did not even notice. She had an aristocratic bearing and did not walk but strode along the avenue to the rhythm of time itself. She reminded me of the enigmatic heroines of the silver screen, who seemed so real that next to them our reality paled into insignificance.

She glided past as I sat with Simon Benyamin on the terrace of a café on the square. She did not even see me. My only consolation was the cloud of perfume that trailed in her wake.

'Easy does it,' whispered Simon.

'What?'

'Take a look in the mirror! You're red as a beetroot! Don't tell me you're in love with a respectable housewife and mother?'

'What are you saying?'

'I'm saying you look like you're about to have a heart attack.'

Simon was joking. What I felt for Madame Cazenave wasn't love but a profound admiration. My feelings towards her were entirely honourable.

At the end of the week, she came into the pharmacy. I was behind the counter helping Germaine fill a pile of prescriptions that had come in as the result of an epidemic of gastritis. When I looked up and saw her, I almost fainted.

I expected her to take off her sunglasses, but she kept them perched on her pretty nose, and I could not tell if she was staring at me or ignoring me.

She handed Germaine a prescription, proffering her hand as though to be kissed.

'It might take a little while . . .' Germaine said, struggling to decipher the doctor's scrawl. 'I'm a little busy at the moment.' She nodded to the packages on the counter.

'When do you think it might be ready?'

'This afternoon, hopefully, but it won't be before three.'

'That's all right . . . but I won't be able to come back to pick it up. I've been out of town for a while and my house needs some serious spring cleaning. Would you mind having a messenger bring it round? I'll happily pay.'

'It's not a question of money, Madame . . . ?'

'Cazenave, Madame Cazenave.'

'Pleased to meet you. Do you live far?'

'Just behind the Jewish cemetery. The house is set back from the marabout road.'

'Oh, I know where you mean . . . It's no problem, Madame Cazenave, I'll have the prescription delivered to you this afternoon sometime between three and four.'

'Perfect!'

As she left, she gave me an almost imperceptible nod.

I could barely sit still as I watched Germaine struggle to fill the orders in the back office. The hands of the clock hardly seemed to move; it felt as though night would come before the delivery was ready. At last came my hour of deliverance, like a great lungful of air after too long underwater. At exactly three p.m., Germaine emerged from the back office with a vial wrapped in brown paper. I did not even wait for her to give me directions, but tore it from her hands and leapt on my bicycle.

Gripping the handlebars, my shirt billowing in the wind, I was not pedalling, I was flying. I cycled around the Jewish cemetery, took a short cut through the fields and, weaving between the potholes, raced along the marabout road.

The Cazenaves lived in an imposing mansion perched on a hill some distance outside the village. It was a large whitewashed house that faced southward, overlooking the plains. There were stables, now derelict, but the house was still magnificent. A steep, narrow driveway lined with dwarf palms led up from the road. Wrought-iron gates leading to a courtyard hung from a low wall of finely chiselled stone on which a climbing vine vainly tried to get purchase. The pediment, supported by two marble columns, had the letter 'C' carved into the stone, and underneath, as though supporting the initial, was the date 1912, the year in which the house had been built.

I ditched my bicycle by the gates, which creaked loudly as I pushed them open, and stepped into the small courtyard with its fountain; there was no one there. The gardens had fallen into decline.

'Madame Cazenave?' I called out.

The shutters on the windows were closed; the wooden door leading inside was locked. I stood by the fountain in the shade of a stucco statue of Diana the Huntress, clutching the bottle of medicine. There was not a living soul in sight. I could hear the breeze rustle through the vine.

After having waited for a while, I decided to knock on the door. My knocking echoed through the house; it was clear there was no one home, but I refused to accept that fact.

I went back and sat on the edge of the fountain, listening for the rasp of footsteps on the gravel, eager to see her appear. Just as I was about to give up, I was startled to hear her cry, 'Bonjour!'

She was standing behind me wearing a white dress, her broad-brimmed hat with the red ribbon pushed back over the delicate nape of her neck.

'I was down in the orange grove. I like to walk there; it's so quiet, so peaceful . . . Have you been waiting long?'

'No,' I lied. 'I just got here.'

'I didn't see you as I was coming up the drive.'

'I've brought your medication, madame,' I said, handing her the package.

She hesitated before taking it, as though she had forgotten her visit to the pharmacy, then, gracefully, she slipped the bottle out of its wrapping paper, unscrewed the lid and delicately inhaled what appeared to be some cosmetic preparation.

'It smells wonderful, the salve. I just hope it eases my stiff joints. The house was in such a state when I got here that I've been spending all day every day trying to get it back to how it used to be.'

'If there's anything you need carried or repaired, I'd be happy to do it for you.'

'You're very sweet, Monsieur Jonas.'

She nodded to the wicker chair by the table on the

veranda, waited for me to sit down, then took the seat facing me.

'I expect you're thirsty, with all this heat,' she said, proffering a jug of lemonade. She poured a large glass and pushed it across the table towards me. The movement clearly hurt her, and she winced and bit her lower lip with exquisite grace.

'Are you in pain, madame?'

'I must have pulled a muscle lifting something.'

She took off her sunglasses, and I felt my insides turn to jelly.

'How old are you, Monsieur Jonas?' she asked, gazing deep into my very soul.

'I'm seventeen, madame.'

'I expect you're already engaged.'

'No, madame.'

'What do you mean, "No, madame"? With a pretty face like yours, and those eyes, I refuse to believe you don't have a whole harem of girls pining after you.'

Her perfume intoxicated me.

Once again she bit her lip, bringing a hand up to her neck.

'Is it very painful, madame?'

'It is painful.'

She took my hand in hers.

'You have beautiful hands.'

I was embarrassed that she might see the effect she was having on me.

'What do you plan to be when you grow up, Monsieur Jonas?'

'A chemist.'

She considered this for a moment, then nodded.

'It is a noble profession.'

A third twinge in her neck almost bent her double with pain.

'I think I need to try the balm right away.' With great dignity, she got to her feet.

'If you like madame, I can . . . I can massage your shoulder for you . . .'

'I'm counting on it, Monsieur Jonas.'

I don't know why, but for an instant, something broke the solemnity of this place. It lasted only a fraction of a second, for when she looked at me again, everything returned to how it had been.

My heart was beating so hard that I wondered whether she could hear it. She took off her hat and her hair tumbled on to her shoulders, and I was all but rooted to the spot.

'Follow me, young man.'

She pushed open the door and gestured for me to follow her inside. The hall was lit by a faint glow, and I had a sudden sense of déjà vu. I felt certain I had seen the corridor ahead somewhere before, or was I imagining things? Madame Cazenave walked on ahead of me. For one searing instant, I mistook her for my destiny.

We climbed the stairs, my feet stumbling on each step. I held on to the banister, seeing only her body swaying before me, magnificent, bewitching, almost dreamlike in its gracefulness. As we came to the landing, she stopped in the dazzling radiance of a skylight, and it was as though her dress disintegrated and I could see every detail of her perfect figure.

She turned suddenly and found me in a state of shock.

She quickly realised that I was incapable of following her much farther, that my legs were about to give out under me, that I was like goldfinch in a trap. Her smile was the *coup de grâce*. She came back towards me, her step light, floating, and said something I did not hear. Blood was pulsing in my temples, making it impossible for me to think. *What's the matter, Monsieur Jonas?* She placed her hand on my chin and lifted my head. *Are you all right?* The whisper of her voice was lost in the throbbing uproar of my temples. *Is it me that has you in this state?* Perhaps she was not saying these things, perhaps it was me, though it did not sound like my voice. Her fingers moved over my face, I felt the wall at my back like a barricade obstructing any attempt at retreat. *Monsieur Jonas?* Her gaze swept over me, conjuring me away as if by magic. I was dissolving in her eyes, her breath fluttered about my breathless panting. When her lips brushed against mine, I thought I would shatter into a thousand pieces; it was as though she had obliterated me, only to refashion me with her fingers. It was not a kiss, but a glancing, hesitant touch – was she testing the waters? She took a step back, and it felt like a wave rolling away, revealing my nakedness, my confusion. Her lips returned, more confident now, more assertive; a mountain stream could not have slaked my thirst as she did. My lips surrendered to hers, melted into hers to become a flowing stream, and Madame Cazenave drank me down to the last drop in a single, endless draught. My head was in the clouds, my feet on a magic carpet. Frightened by the intensity of this pleasure, I must have tried to draw away, because I felt her hand hold me hard. I let her pull me to her, offering no resistance, feverish, willing, astounded by my own

surrender, my body joined to hers by her invading tongue.
With infinite tenderness, she unbuttoned my shirt and let
it fall to the floor. My every breath now was her breath, my
heartbeat was her pulse. I had the vague sensation of being
undressed, being led into a bedroom, of being laid on a bed
deep as a river. A thousand fingers exploded against my skin
like fireworks; I was light and joy, I was pleasure at its most
intoxicated; I felt myself dying even as I was reborn.

'Could you come back down to earth a bit?' Germaine
scolded me. 'You've broken half the crockery in the house
in the past two days.'

I realised that the plate I had been rinsing had slipped
from my hands and shattered at my feet.

'Your mind is elsewhere . . .'

'I'm sorry . . .'

Germaine looked at me curiously, wiped her hands on
her apron and put them on my shoulders.

'What's the matter, Jonas?'

'Nothing, the plate just slipped.'

'I know . . . the problem is, it's not the first one.'

'Germaine!' My uncle called her from his room at the
far end of the corridor.

I hardly recognised myself. Since my encounter with
Madame Cazenave, my mind was elsewhere; it was sounding
the depths of a euphoria that seemed endless and eternal.
This was my first experience of being a man, my first taste
of sexual discovery, and I was intoxicated by it. My body
was tight as a bow; I could still feel Madame Cazenave's
fingers moving over my skin, her caresses like a thousand
tiny cuts gnawing at the fibre of my being, trilling through

my body, becoming the blood pulsing in my temples. When I closed my eyes, I could still feel her breathless gasps, and my whole being was flooded with her intoxicating breath. At night, I did not sleep a wink; the memory of our lovemaking kept me restless until dawn.

Simon found my change of mood infuriating, but though Jean-Christophe and Fabrice fell about laughing at his jokes, his jibes could not touch me. I was like marble. I watched them laugh, unable to understand what was funny. How many times did Simon wave a hand in front of my face to see if I was awake? At moments like this I would come alive for a moment, only to sink back into a sort of trance, the sounds of the world outside suddenly dying away.

On the hill, in the shade of the olive tree or on the beach, I was now an absence among my friends.

I waited for two weeks before summoning the courage to go back to the big white mansion on the road to the marabout's house. It was late; the light was failing. I left my bicycle by the gates and stepped into the courtyard . . . and there she was, crouched beneath a shrub with a pair of secateurs, tending to her garden.

'Monsieur Jonas,' she said, getting to her feet.

She set the secateurs down on a mound of pebbles and wiped the dust from her hands. She was wearing the same hat with the red ribbon, the same white dress, which, in the light of the setting sun, faithfully described the charming contours of her body.

We stared at each other, neither of us saying a word.

I found the silence oppressive; the drone of the cicadas seemed loud enough to split my eardrums.

'*Bonjour*, madame.'

She smiled, her eyes wider than the span of the horizon.

'What can I do for you, Monsieur Jonas?'

Something in her voice made me fear the worst.

'I was just passing,' I lied, 'so I came up to say hello.'

'How very sweet.'

Her brusqueness left me speechless. She stared at me as though waiting for me to justify my presence; she did not seem to appreciate my intrusion. It was as though I was disturbing her.

'You don't need to . . . I just thought . . . I mean, if you needed help with carrying things?'

'I have servants to do that.'

Having run out of excuses, I felt foolish, felt that I had ruined everything.

'Monsieur Jonas, you shouldn't turn up at someone's house unannounced.'

'I just thought—'

She brought a finger to my lips, interrupting me.

'You shouldn't think.'

My embarrassment turned to a sort of dull rage. Why was she treating me like this? How could she behave as though nothing had happened? Surely she knew why I had come to see her.

As though reading my mind, she said:

'If I need you, I will let you know. You must learn to let things happen, you understand. To rush things is to ruin them.'

Her finger gently traced the line of my lips, then parted them and slipped into my mouth, lingering for a moment on the tip of my tongue before returning to rest on my lips once more.

'There is something you need to understand, Jonas: with women, these things are all in the mind. They are only ready when their thoughts are in order. They control their emotions.'

Not for a moment did she take her resolute, regal eyes from mine. I felt as though I was a product of her imagination, a plaything in her hands, a puppy she might order to roll over so she could tickle its tummy. I had no intention of rushing things, of ruining any chance I might have. When she took her hand away, I realised it was time for me to leave . . . and to wait for a sign from her.

She did not walk me back to the gates.

I waited for weeks. The summer of 1944 was drawing to a close. Madame Cazenave no longer came down to the village. When Jean-Christophe called us all together and Fabrice read his poems, all I could do was stare out towards the white mansion on the hill. Sometimes I thought I could see her working in the courtyard, could make out her white dress through the heat haze on the plains. At night I would go out on to the balcony and listen to the howl of the jackals, hoping it might fill the yawning silence of her words.

Madame Scamaroni regularly took us to the apartment on the Boulevard des Chasseurs in Oran, but I have no memory of the movies we saw or the girls we met. Simon was getting tired of my distracted state. One day, on the beach, he tipped a bucket of water over me to get my attention. If Jean-Christophe had not been there, the joke would have turned into a brawl.

Worried by my sudden change of mood, Fabrice came to my house to ask me what was wrong. He got no answer.

Finally, tormented by the waiting, I jumped on my

bicycle one Sunday at midday and raced down to the white house. Madame Cazenave had hired an old gardener and a housekeeper, and I found them having lunch together in the shade of a carob tree. I waited in the courtyard, clutching my bicycle, trembling from head to foot. Madame Cazenave gave an imperceptible start when she saw me standing by the fountain. She glanced around for the servants, saw that they were at the far end of the garden, turned back to me. She stared at me in silence; behind her smile, I could tell she was furious.

'I couldn't wait,' I said.

She came down the small flight of steps and walked towards me.

'But you have to,' she said firmly.

She beckoned me to follow her back to the gates, and there, without worrying whether it was indiscreet, as though we were the only two people in the world, she slipped her arms around my neck and kissed me hard. The passion of her kiss was such that I knew that this was the end, that this was goodbye.

'You were dreaming, Jonas,' she said. 'It was just a young man's dream.'

She took her arms from round my neck and stepped back.

'Nothing ever happened between us, not even this kiss.'

Her eyes forced me to retreat.

'Do you understand?'

'Yes, madame,' I heard myself mumble.

'Good.'

She patted my cheek, a brisk, maternal gesture.

'I knew you were a sensible boy.'

I had to wait until it was dark before I went home.

11

I HOPED for a miracle; it never came.

Autumn arrived, stripping the trees of their leaves, and I realised I had to face facts. It had all been a dream. Nothing ever happened between Madame Cazenave and me.

I went back to my old life, to my friends, to Simon's antics and Fabrice's feverish idealism. Jean-Christophe had found a way of dealing with the demanding Isabelle Rucillio. With any compromise, he would say, the important thing was to make sure you got something out of it. Life was a long-term investment, he insisted, and fortune smiled on those who played the long game. He seemed to know what he wanted, and if his theories came unburdened with any actual proof, we were more than happy to take him at his word.

With 1945 came a stream of contradictory stories and rumours. Gossiping over a glass of *anisette* was the favoured pastime in Río Salado. The smallest rumour would be wildly exaggerated, embellished with daring feats attributed to people who for the most part had nothing to do with it. Everyone on the café terraces had a theory about the war. The names Stalin, Roosevelt, Churchill rang out like trumpets announcing the final assault. One joker, noting that General de Gaulle looked undernourished, suggested sending him a fine Algerian couscous to fatten him up, thereby making it easier for us to trust him, since Algerians invariably associate power with a pot belly. Everyone laughed and drank, then went on drinking until every passing donkey looked like a unicorn. The mood was optimistic. Jewish families who had left the town when news came of the mass deportations in France began to return home. Slowly, surely, things were getting back to normal. The grape harvest had been exceptional and the end-of-season ball was glorious. Pépé Rucillio married off his youngest son, and for seven days and seven nights the whole district rang to the sound of the guitars and castanets of a famous troupe of troubadours shipped in from Seville. We were even treated to an extravagant display in which the finest horsemen in the region were pitted against the greatest warriors of the Ouled N'har.

In Europe, the Third Reich was crumbling. Newsreels predicted that the war would soon be over, even as the bombing intensified: whole cities vanished in flames and ashes, the sky was black with the smoke of aerial battles, trenches collapsed beneath the caterpillar treads of advancing tanks. The cinema in Río Salado was constantly full of people who only came to watch the Pathé News they showed before the main feature. Allied troops had liberated great swaths of occupied territories and were now marching relentlessly on Germany. Italy was a shadow of its former self. The Resistance and the partisans were inflicting heavy losses on Nazi troops caught in a vice between the Red Army and the advancing American forces.

My uncle, wearing the thick jumper that hid his increasingly emaciated frame, sat glued to the wireless, never moving from his chair. From morning to night he sat turning the dial of the radio, trying to tune to some station without interference. Over the whine and static of the airwaves, the house hummed with news and speculation. Germaine had given up on her husband, allowing him to do exactly as he pleased. My uncle insisted on having his dinner served in the living room by the wireless, so that he didn't miss a scrap of news.

As 8 May 1945 dawned, and the whole world celebrated the end of their nightmare, in Algeria a new nightmare appeared, devastating as a plague, monstrous as the Apocalypse itself. Popular celebrations turned to tragedy. In Aïn Temouchent, near Río Salado, marches for Algerian independence were brutally suppressed by the police. In Mostaganem, riots spread to the surrounding villages. But the horror reached its height in the Aurès and in the Constantine province, where the police, aided and abetted by former colonists turned militiamen, massacred thousands of Muslims.

'I can't believe it.' My uncle's voice quavered as he sat trembling in his pyjamas. 'How could they? How could they murder people who are still mourning children who died fighting for the freedom of France? Why should we be slaughtered like cattle simply for demanding our own freedom?' Pale, distraught and haggard, he shambled up and down the living room in his slippers.

The Arabic radio station reported the bloody suppression of Muslims in Guelma, Kherrata and Sétif, the mass graves where thousands of corpses lay rotting, the Arabs hunted by packs of dogs through vineyards and orange groves, the lynchings in the village squares. What was happening was so horrific that my uncle and I did not even dare to join the peaceful demonstration down the main avenue of Río Salado.

This savage, bloody cataclysm left the Muslim population of Algeria in mourning and almost killed my uncle. One night as he listened, he suddenly brought his hand up, clutched at his chest and collapsed. Madame Scamaroni drove us to the hospital, where we left him in the care of a doctor he knew and trusted. Germaine was distraught, and Madame Scamaroni offered to stay with her. Jean-Christophe and Fabrice came round and waited with us late into the night. Simon borrowed his neighbour's motorbike so he could come too.

'Your husband has had a heart attack, madame,' the doctor explained to Germaine. 'He's still unconscious.'

'Is he going to pull through?'

'We've done everything we can; the rest is down to him.'

Germaine did not know what to say. She had barely uttered a word since we arrived at the hospital. Her face was pale, her eyes haunted; she clasped her hands and bowed her head in prayer.

At dawn the next day, my uncle regained consciousness, asked for a drink of water, and demanded he be discharged immediately, but the doctor insisted on keeping him under observation overnight. Madame Scamaroni offered to pay for a nurse so that my uncle would have full-time care, but Germaine politely declined. She thanked Madame Scamaroni for everything she had done, but insisted that she would look after her husband herself.

Two days later, as I sat by my uncle's bed, I heard a voice outside, calling me. I went to the window and saw a figure crouching in the shadows. It was Jelloul, André's manservant. I went outside, and as I crossed the path separating the house from the vineyard, Jelloul came out from his hiding place.

'My God!' I said.

Jelloul was limping. His face was swollen, his lip split; he had a black eye and his shirt was lashed with red stripes, clearly whip marks.

'Who did this to you?'

Jelloul glanced around, as though afraid someone would hear, then said:

'André.'

'Why? What did you do wrong?'

He smiled at what was clearly a preposterous question.

'I don't need to do anything wrong. André always finds some excuse. This time it was the Muslim unrest in the Aurès. André doesn't trust Arabs any more. When he got back from town drunk last night, he laid into me.'

He lifted his shirt and showed me the welts on his back. André had not pulled his punches. Jelloul turned back to face me, pushing his shirt tails back into his dusty trousers. He sniffed loudly and then said:

'He told me it was a warning, that he didn't want me getting any ideas. Said I needed to get it into my head that he was the boss, and he wasn't going to tolerate insubordination from the hired help.'

Jelloul was clearly waiting for something, but I did not know what. He took off his fez and began twisting it in his grubby hands.

'Jonas, I didn't come here to tell you my life story. André threw me out without a penny. I can't go back to my family with no money. If I don't earn, my family will starve.'

'How much do you need?'

'Just enough to feed us for a couple of days.'

'Give me two minutes.'

I went up to my room and came back with two fifty-franc notes. Jelloul reluctantly took them, turning them over in his hands.

'It's too much . . . I could never pay you back.'

'You don't need to pay me back.'

He looked at me and shook his head, thinking. Then, flushed and embarrassed, he said:

'In that case, fifty francs is enough.'

'Take the hundred francs, please,' I said. 'I'm only too happy to give it.'

'I believe you, but it's not necessary.'

'Have you got work lined up?'

'No.' Jelloul suddenly gave a mysterious smile. 'But André can't survive without me. He'll send for me before the end of the week. He won't find a better dog than me.'

'Why do you call yourself a dog?'

'You wouldn't understand . . . You're one of *us*, but you live like one of *them*. When your whole family depends on you for money, when you have to support a half-crazed mother, a father who had both arms amputated, six brothers and sisters, a grandmother, two aunts disowned by their families and a sickly uncle, you are no longer a human being. You are a dog or a jackal, and every dog seeks out a master.'

Jelloul's words unsettled me, and I realised that though he

was not yet twenty, he had an inner strength, a maturity. The young man who stood before me that morning was not the lackey we had long thought him. He even looked different: he had a quiet dignity I had not noticed, a handsome face, high cheekbones, and eyes that were perceptive and unnerving.

'Thank you, Jonas,' he said. 'I'll make it up to you some day.'

He turned and began to hobble away.

'Wait,' I called after him. 'You're not going to get far on that foot.'

'I got this far, didn't I?'

'Maybe, but you're only going to make it worse . . . Where do you live?'

'It's not far, honestly. It's just the other side of the marabout's hill. I'll manage.'

'I won't hear of it. Wait there, I'll get my bicycle and drop you off.'

'No, Jonas, it's all right. You have better things to do.'

'I insist.'

I thought that I had seen poverty in Jenane Jato; I was wrong. The shanty town where Jelloul and his family lived was beyond anything I had ever imagined. The *douar* was made up of a dozen squalid hovels on the banks of a dried-up riverbed. A few scrawny goats ambled around. The place smelled so foul I found it difficult to imagine how anyone could spend two days here. When the path petered out, I left the bike on the slopes and helped Jelloul down the hill. The marabout's hill was only a few kilometres from Río Salado, but I could not remember ever having passed this way. People shunned the place, as though it were cursed. Suddenly the simple fact that I was on the far side of the hill terrified me. I was scared something might happen to me, and I knew that if anything did, no one would think to come looking for me here. It was ridiculous, but the fear was all too real. I felt a mortal dread at being in this *douar* of ramshackle huts pervaded by the stench of rotting flesh.

'Come,' Jelloul said. 'Come in and meet my father.'

'No,' I almost screamed, petrified. 'I have to get back to my uncle. He's very ill.'

A group of naked children were playing in the dust, their bellies swollen, flies crawling on their faces. Then I realised that it was not simply the stench; it was the drone of the flies, incessant, voracious, filling the foul air like some baleful supplication, like the breath of some demon that lowered over human misery, a sound as old as time itself. At the foot of a low *toube* wall, a group of old men lay dozing, mouths open, huddled beside a sleeping donkey. A madman, arms raised to the heavens, stood babbling wildly beneath a marabout tree from which hung talismans, coloured ribbons and candle wax. There was no one else: it was as though the *douar* had been abandoned to feral children and dying men.

A pack of dogs ran towards me, growling. Jelloul picked up a stone and drove them off. There was silence again. He turned and gave me a strange smile.

'This is how our people live, Jonas; *my* people and *your* people too. Here, nothing ever changes, while you go on living like a prince . . . What's the matter? Why don't you say something? You're shocked; you can't believe it, can you? Maybe now you know why I call myself a dog. Even a dog would not live like this.'

I stood, speechless; the stench and filth turned my stomach, the piercing drone of the flies drilled into my brain. I wanted to vomit, but I was afraid that Jelloul would get the wrong impression.

He sniggered, amused by my awkwardness, then showed me around the *douar*.

'Look at this godforsaken slum. This is our place in this country, the country of our ancestors. Take a good look, Jonas. God himself would not set foot here.'

'Why are you saying these terrible things?'

'Because I believe them. Because they're true.'

Suddenly, I felt more afraid, but now it was Jelloul, his furious stare, his sardonic smile, that terrified me.

'That's right, *Younes*. Turn your back on the truth, on your people, run back to your friends . . . *Younes* . . . You do still remember your name? Hey, *Younes* . . . Thanks for the money. I'll pay you back some day soon, I promise. The world is changing, or hadn't you noticed?'

I rode away, pedalling like a madman, Jelloul's catcalls like rifle shots whistling past my ears.

Jelloul was right. Things were changing, but to me it was as though these changes were happening in some parallel world. I sat on the fence, torn between loyalty to my friends and solidarity with my people. After the massacre in the Constantine province, the dawning awareness of the Muslim majority, I knew that I had to choose, but still I refused to take sides. In the end, events would make my decision for me.

There was a fierce rage in the air; it bubbled up from the *maquis* in the scrubland where militants met in secret, it

spilled into the streets, seeped into the poor neighbourhoods, trickled out into the *villages nègres* and isolated *douars*.

The four of us who made up Jean-Christophe's gang
turned a blind eye to what was happening in these demonstrations. We were young men now, and if the down on our
upper lips was not yet thick enough to qualify as a moustache, it emphasised our desire to be men, to be masters
of our fate. The four of us, inseparable as the tines of a
pitchfork, lived for ourselves; we were our own little world.

Fabrice was awarded the National Poetry Prize, and
Madame Scamaroni drove all of us to Algiers for the ceremony. Fabrice was overjoyed. Aside from the prestige, the
winning collection of poems was to be published by Edmond
Charlot, an important Algerian publisher. Madame Scamaroni put us up in a charming little hotel not far from the
Rue d'Isly. After the ceremony, at which Fabrice received
his award from the great poet Max-Pol Fouchet, the prize-
winner's mother treated us to a lavish seafood dinner at a
magnificent restaurant in La Madrague. The next day, eager
to get back to Río Salado, where the mayor had organised
a lunch to honour the town's prodigy, we set off early, stopping at Orléansville for a snack and at Perrigault to stock
up on the finest oranges in the world.

Some months later, Fabrice invited us to a bookshop in
Lourmel, a small colonial town near Río Salado. His mother
was there, looking stunning in a burgundy trouser suit and
wearing a broad-brimmed feathered hat. Smiling benevo-
lently, the bookseller and a number of local dignitaries stood
around a large ebony table on which sat piles of books fresh
out of their boxes. On the cover, beneath the title, was the
name 'Fabrice Scamaroni'.

'Holy shit!' sputtered Simon, who could always be counted on to undermine any solemn occasion.

The moment the speeches were over, Simon, Jean-Christophe and I pounced on the books. We leafed through the pages, turning the books over in our hands, so reverential that Madame Scamaroni was surprised to find a tear that trickled mascara down her cheek.

'I read your work with great pleasure, Monsieur Scamaroni,' a man of about sixty said to Fabrice. 'You have considerable talent and, I think, every chance of reviving the noble art of poetry, which has always been the soul of Algeria.'

The bookseller handed Fabrice a letter of congratulations from Gabriel Audisio, founder of the magazine *Rivages*, in which the editor suggested that they might collaborate.

Back in Río Salado, the mayor promised to open a library on the main street, and Pépé Rucillio bought a hundred copies of Fabrice's poems to send to his acquaintances in Oran — who, he suspected, called him an upstart peasant behind his back — to prove to them that there was more to Río Salado than idiots, wine growers and drunks.

Winter tiptoed away one night, and by morning, swallows dotted the telegraph lines like ink blots and the streets of Río Salado were awash with the scents of spring. My uncle was slowly returning to life. He had recovered his health, his old habits, his passion for books; he devoured them, closing a novel only to open an essay. He read in both French and Arabic, moving from El Akkad to Flaubert. Though he still did not venture out of the house, he had begun to shave and dress every day. He now ate with us in the dining room and occasionally exchanged pleasantries with Germaine. As regular as clockwork, he would get up at dawn, perform his morning prayers and appear at the table for breakfast at seven o'clock sharp. After breakfast, he would retire to his study to wait for the newspaper to be delivered, and when he had read the paper, he would open his spiral notepad, dip his pen into the inkwell and write until noon. At one p.m. he would take a short nap, and then pick up a book and lose himself in its pages until sundown.

One day, he came to my bedroom.

'You need to read this. It was written by Malek Bennabi. The man himself seems a little suspicious, but he is a clear thinker.'

He set the book down on my night table and waited for me to pick it up. It was a slim volume, barely a hundred pages, entitled *The Conditions of the Algerian Renaissance*.

As he left the room, he said:

'Never forget what it says in the Qur'an: *Whosoever killeth a man, it shall be as if he had killed all mankind.*'

He never asked me whether I had read Malek Bennabi's book, still less what I thought of it. At dinner he only ever spoke to Germaine.

Our lives had recovered some semblance of stability. Things were far from being back to normal, but just seeing my uncle standing in front of the wardrobe mirror knotting his tie was wonderful. Germaine and I waited anxiously for him to cross the threshold, to step outside and rejoin the world of the living. Germaine would throw the French windows open so he could adjust to the sounds of the street again. She dreamed of seeing her husband adjust his fez, smooth his jacket, glance at his fob watch and hurry out to visit a café, to sit on a park bench, to be with friends. But my uncle dreaded the outside world, he had a morbid fear of crowds, he panicked if someone crossed his path. Only at home did he truly feel safe.

Germaine believed that her husband was capable of the superhuman effort it would take to rebuild his life.

Then, one Sunday as we were finishing lunch, my uncle suddenly banged his fists on the table, sending plates and glasses crashing to the floor. We thought it might be another heart attack, but it was not. He leapt to his feet, knocking over his chair, then shrank back to the wall, pointing at us, and thundered:

'You have no right to judge me!'

Germaine stared at me in astonishment.

'What did you say to him?'

'Nothing . . .'

She looked at her husband as though he were a stranger.

'No one is judging you, Mahi.'

But my uncle was not talking to us. Though he was staring straight at us, he could not see us. He frowned as though shaking off a bad dream, then he picked up his chair, sat down again, took his head in his hands and did not move.

That night, at about three a.m., Germaine and I were woken by the sound of raised voices. My uncle had locked himself in his study, where he was arguing violently with someone. I dashed downstairs to see if the front door was open, but it was locked and bolted. I went back upstairs. Germaine tried peering through the keyhole to see what was going on, but the key was in the lock.

'I am not a coward,' my uncle screamed hysterically. 'I

didn't betray anyone, do you hear? Don't look at me like that. How dare you sneer at me. I never informed on anyone . . .'

Then the study door flew open and my uncle emerged, raging, his lips flecked with foam, and pushed past without even seeing us.

Germaine was first to go into the study; I followed her. There was no one there.

Early in the autumn, I saw Madame Cazenave again. It was raining hard, Río Salado was gloomy and dismal, the café terraces were deserted. Seeing her come towards me, I realised that she still had the same ethereal beauty, but my heart did not leap in my chest. Did the rain temper my passion, the dreary weather blunt my memories? I did not care to wonder. I crossed the road to avoid her.

In Río Salado, which drew its vital force from the sun, autumn was always a dead season. In autumn, the masks that people wore in summer fell away like the leaves from the trees and, as Jean-Christophe Lamy discovered, deathless loves took on a sudden brittleness. One evening Jean-Christophe arrived at Fabrice's house, where we were waiting for Simon to come back from Oran. He did not say a word; he simply sat on the veranda and brooded.

Simon Benyamin had gone to Oran to try his luck as a comedian. He had seen an ad in the paper looking for talented young comedians and thought this was his chance. Stuffing the ad in his pocket, he hopped on the first bus, bound for glory. From his expression when he arrived back, it was clear things had not gone as he had hoped.

'So?' Fabrice asked.

Simon slumped into a wicker chair and folded his arms, clearly in a foul mood.

'What happened?'

'Nothing.' Simon cut him off. 'Nothing happened. The bastards didn't even give me a chance . . . I knew straight off that this wasn't going to be my day. I hung around backstage for hours before I got to go on. The theatre was completely empty; there was nobody there except an old guy in the front row and some dried-up old witch next to him with round glasses that made her look like a barn owl. They had a big spotlight pointed right on me. It was like I was being interrogated. Then the old guy says, "You may begin, Monsieur Benyamin." I swear it was like my great-grandfather's voice from beyond the grave. I couldn't make the guy out. He looked like he could watch a church burn down and not bat an eyelid. I've only just started when he interrupts me. "Do you know the difference between a clown and a fool, Monsieur Benyamin?" He's spitting the words. "No? Well let me enlighten you: a clown makes people laugh because he is both funny and sad; a fool makes people laugh because he is ridiculous." Then he waved me offstage and shouted, "Next!"'

Fabrice doubled up with laughter.

'I sat in the dressing room for two hours trying to calm down. If the guy had come in to apologise, I'd have eaten him alive. You should have seen the two of them, sitting in the empty theatre; they looked like a couple of undertakers.'

Seeing us all laughing, Jean-Christophe fumed silently.

'What's the matter?' asked Fabrice.

Jean-Christophe bowed his head and sighed.

'Isabelle is starting to get on my nerves.'

'Only starting?' said Simon. 'I told you at the beginning she wasn't right for you.'

'Love is blind,' Fabrice said philosophically.

'Love makes you blind,' Simon corrected him.

'Is it serious?' I asked Jean-Christophe.

'Why? Are you still interested in her?' He shot me a curious look, then added: 'You never did get over her, did you, Jonas? Well, I've had it with her, she's all yours.'

'Why would I be interested in her?'

'Because you're the one she's in love with,' he yelled, banging the table.

There was an uncomfortable silence. Fabrice and Simon looked from me to Jean-Christophe. He clearly hated me.

'What are you telling me?' I said.

'I'm telling you the truth. Whenever she knows you're around, she's impossible, she's always sneaking looks at you. If you'd seen her at the last dance, there she was on my arm and then you show up and she starts fooling around just to get your attention. I nearly slapped her.'

'Love might be blind, Chris, but I think jealousy has got you seeing things.'

'I am jealous, you're right. But I'm not seeing things.'

'Hang on a minute,' Fabrice interrupted, sensing there was trouble brewing. 'Isabelle manipulates people, Chris, it's what she always does. She's just testing you. If she didn't love you, she would have dumped you long ago.'

'It doesn't matter, I've had enough. If the girl I love spends her time looking over my shoulder, then maybe it's better if I walk away. To be honest, I don't know if I was ever really serious about her.'

I felt uncomfortable. This was the first time anything had

upset the friendship between the four of us. Then, to my relief, Jean-Christophe turned and pointed at me. 'Ha! Fooled you, didn't I? You fell for it hook, line and sinker!'

No one laughed. We all still believed Jean-Christophe had been serious.

The next day, as I wandered to the village square with Simon, we saw Isabelle and Jean-Christophe arm in arm, headed for the cinema. I don't know why, but I ducked into a doorway so they wouldn't see me. Simon was surprised by my reaction, but he understood.

3. Émilie

12

ANDRÉ INVITED everyone in Río Salado to the opening of his 'American Diner'. While it was easy to imagine André as a feudal lord, prowling his vineyards, slapping his riding crop against his boots, beating his workers and dreaming of Olympus, the idea of the son of Jaime J. Sosa running a bar, opening bottles of beer, left us speechless. André had changed since his trip to the United States, where his friend Joe had taken him on a dazzling odyssey. America had opened his eyes to a life we could not even begin to understand: something he referred to with mystical fervour as 'the American dream'. When asked what exactly he meant by it, he'd shift from one foot to the other, then frown and explain that it meant living however you pleased and to hell with taboos and propriety. André wanted to shake us out of our bourgeois provincial habits – he found it intolerable that young people in Algeria did as they were told, played only when they were permitted and did not go out unless they were invited. Society, he maintained, could be judged by the energy, the spirit, the passion of its youth. It was the arrogance of the young that revitalised each new generation. According to him, the youth of Río Salado were deferential, docile sheep, chained to the customs and ideas of a bygone era, completely out of touch with the brave new world in which young men should 'burn, burn, burn like fabulous yellow Roman candles exploding like spiders across the stars'. In Los Angeles, in San Francisco, in New York, he told us, young people were busy wringing the neck of filial pieties, shaking off the yoke of family to spread their wings, like Icarus.

The winds of fortune had shifted and now favoured the American way, André maintained. A country's fortunes could be judged by its thirst for change, for revolution, but in Río Salado generation followed generation and nothing ever changed. André had decided that urgent changes were needed, and could think of nothing better than a California-style diner, to shake us out of our obscene, provincial, antiquated sheep-like instincts; to turn us into rebels with a cause.

André's diner was outside the village, behind the R.C. Kraus vineyards, on a patch of waste ground where we had played football as children. For the opening night, some twenty tables, each with a huge parasol, had been set out on a gravel terrace. As soon as we saw the boxes of wine and lemonade, the crates of fruit, and the grills set up around the perimeter, we relaxed.

'We're going to eat till we throw up.' Simon sounded excited.

Jelloul and a handful of other workers moved between the tables, laying out napkins, setting out carafes and ashtrays. André and his cousin José, Stetson hats pushed back off their heads, legs apart, thumbs hooked into their belts, stood proudly on the steps leading up to the diner.

'You should buy a herd of cattle,' Simon said, nodding at André's ten-gallon hat.

'You don't like my diner?'

'As long as there's food and drink . . .'

'Well then, stuff your face and shut up.'

André came down the steps and hugged us all, groping Simon's crotch playfully.

'Hey! Hands off the family jewels!' Simon yelped, jumping back.

'Some jewels!' André quipped, herding us towards the bar. 'You'd be lucky to get two francs on a flea-market stall.'

'What are you betting?'

'Whatever you like . . . I'll tell you what, a number of beautiful young ladies will be joining us this evening. If you can manage to seduce one, I'll pay for a hotel room – and not just any hotel; I'm talking about the Martinez.'

'Deal!'

'Dédé is like a machine gun,' said José, who considered his cousin to be a paragon of rectitude and gallantry. 'When he goes off, there's no stopping him.'

André took us on a tour of his 'revolution'. The diner was nothing like any café we had ever seen. It was painted in bright, garish colours; behind the bar was a huge mirror with a silhouette of the Golden Gate Bridge etched into the glass. There were tall upholstered bar stools, brass shelves groaning beneath the weight of bottles and curios, bright neon signs and strange gadgets. The walls were plastered with huge photographs of Hollywood stars. The shutters were closed and the curtains drawn, so the ceiling lights gave off a warm muted glow while wall sconces cast blood-red shadows all around. The seats, bolted to the floor, were arranged in booths like the seats of a train around rect-angular tables on which were scenes of the American Wild West.

In the next room, a pool table took pride of place. No café in Río Salado or Lourmel had a pool table. The one André had imported for his guests was a work of art, beautifully lit by a hanging lamp that all but touched the table.

Picking up a pool cue, André chalked the tip, then leaned over the table and lined up his shot using his knuckles as a rest. The rack of coloured balls exploded across the table, ricocheting off the cushions.

'From now on,' he declared, 'people here won't go to a bar to get drunk. At my place, they'll come to play pool. And this is only stage one. I've got three more tables on order, which should be here by the end of the month. I'm planning to set up a regional tournament.'

José appeared with beers for the others and a soft drink for me, and suggested we go take a table on the terrace until the other guests arrived. It was about seven p.m. The sun was slipping slowly behind the hills, shooting its last glimmers through the vineyards. From the terrace, we had a perfect view of the surrounding plains and the road that wound its way to Lourmel. A bus dropped passengers just outside the village: people from Río Salado on their way back from Oran, and Arab labourers coming in from the building sites in the city. The labourers, clearly exhausted, cut across the fields with bundles under their arms, heading for the dirt track that led to their village of squalid shacks.

Jelloul watched me watching them, and as the last labourer disappeared around a bend in the dirt track, he turned and shot me an unsettling glance.

As the sun sank behind the hills, the Rucillio clan rolled up – Pépé's two youngest sons, some of their cousins and their brother-in-law, Antonio, who worked as a cabaret singer in Sidi Bel-Abbès – in a spanking new Citroën straight from the factory, which they parked near the entrance where everyone could see it.

André greeted them all with the back-slapping good humour of the rich, and then escorted them to the best seats.

'You can be rolling in it and still smell horse shit for miles around,' complained Simon, piqued that the Rucillio family had walked past without so much as a nod to us.

'You know what they're like,' I said.

'I don't care – they could at least have said hello. We're hardly the dregs of society: you're a chemist, Fabrice is a poet and a journalist, I'm a civil servant.'

It was not quite dark as the terrace began to fill with beautiful girls and young men dressed to the nines. Older couples arrived in gleaming cars, the ladies in evening gowns, their escorts wearing suits and bow ties. André had invited the cream of Río Salado society and every notable family for miles around. In the crowd we could make out the son of the richest man in Hammam Bouhadjar. His father owned a private plane and on his arm was one of Oran's rising singing stars, who was surrounded by eager fans showering her with compliments, eager to light her cigarette.

Chinese lanterns were lit and floated above the terrace. José clapped his hands for silence and the noise died away. André went up on to the stage and thanked his guests for coming to celebrate the opening of his diner. He began with a crude joke that made his guests, who were more used to refinement, somewhat uncomfortable, then, deploring the fact that his audience was not broad-minded enough to let him continue in a similar vein, he cut short his speech and left the stage to the musicians.

The evening began with music the like of which no one in Río Salado had ever heard, all trumpets and a double bass. The audience were left cold.

'It's jazz, for God's sake!' André cursed them. 'How can anyone not like jazz?'

The jazz band began to realise that if Río Salado was only sixty miles from Oran, its musical taste was a million miles away. Being professionals, they continued to play for a while, then, as an encore, they played something that sounded like a curse. The crowd barely noticed when they finally left the stage.

Though André had anticipated that this might happen, he had at least expected his guests to treat the finest jazz band in Algeria with some respect. We watched his grovelling apology to the furious trumpeter, who seemed to be saying that he would never again set foot in this godforsaken, culturally benighted hole.

As André and the bandleader argued, José introduced a second band – a group of locals this time. From the moment they took the stage, the whole audience heaved a sigh of relief, and the floor was suddenly filled with people dancing and swaying.

Fabrice Scamaroni invited the mayor's niece to dance and eagerly led her on to the floor. I asked a shy girl, who politely refused me, though I managed to convince her friend to take the floor. Simon did not dance, but sat in some strange state of rapture, his plump, childish face in his hands, gazing at what seemed to be an empty table at the far end of the terrace.

When the musicians took a break, I walked my dancing partner back to her seat, then went back out to where Simon, oblivious of my presence, sat smiling vaguely, still staring into the distance. I waved a hand in front of his eyes but he didn't react. I followed his gaze and I saw . . . *her*.

She was sitting alone at a table that had been hastily added and so had no tablecloth or napkins. I glimpsed her as she appeared and disappeared between the swaying dancers. Suddenly I knew why Simon – who could usually be relied on to turn any social event into a circus – seemed so serene. The mere sight of this girl had left him speechless.

She was wearing a pale, figure-hugging dress and elbow-length gloves; her black hair was pulled up into a chignon. With a smile as delicate as a wisp of smoke, she gazed out at the dancers without seeing them, her chin perched on her gloved fingertips, absorbed in her own thoughts. From time to time she vanished behind the shadows that whirled about her, only to re-emerge like a nymph appearing from a lake.

'Isn't she beautiful?' Simon gasped.

'She's magnificent.'

'Just look at those eyes. I'll bet they are as black as her hair. And her nose! Her nose, it's perfect . . .'

'Easy does it.'

'And her lips, Jonas, have you seen her tiny rosebud lips? How does she manage to eat?'

'Hey, Simon, come back down to earth!'

'What would I want to do that for?'

'Because it's a long drop from that cloud of yours.'

'I don't care . . . For a beauty like that, I'm happy to take a tumble.'

'And how exactly do you plan to win her over?'

At length he looked at me, and I saw a sad smile steal over his face.

'You know perfectly well I've got no chance,' he said. The sudden change of tone was heartbreaking, but he soon rallied. 'Do you think she's from Río Salado?'

'I don't think so. We would have seen her before now.'

'You're right.' Simon smiled. 'I could never have forgotten a face like that.'

We both held our breath as we watched a young man saunter over to the girl and ask her to dance, then both of us let it out in a sigh of relief when she politely declined.

Fabrice came back from the dance floor bathed in sweat, dabbing his face with a handkerchief. He leaned over to us and whispered:

'Have you seen the girl sitting on her own, at the far end of the terrace?'

'You bet we have,' Simon replied. 'I don't think there's a man here who can look at anyone else.'

'I've just been dumped because of her,' Fabrice explained. 'The girl I was dancing with nearly gouged my eyes out when she caught me looking at her. Have you any idea who she is?'

'She must be visiting family,' I said. 'From her dress and the way she acts, she looks like a city girl. I've never seen any girl around here who looks like that.'

Suddenly the girl turned and looked at the three of us, and we froze as though we'd been caught trying to steal her handbag. Her smile broadened a little and the brooch on the neckline of her dress seemed to flash like a lighthouse in the darkness.

'Isn't she stunning?' Jean-Christophe said, appearing from nowhere. He took the empty chair, spun it round and straddled it.

'There you are,' said Fabrice. 'Where did you get to?'

'Where do you think?'

'Have you and Isabelle been fighting again?'

'Let's just say that for once, I sent her packing. Can you believe it? She couldn't decide what jewellery to wear. I waited in the living room, I waited in the hall, I waited outside, and *mademoiselle* still couldn't decide which brooch to put on.'

'So you left her there?' Simon was incredulous.

'Why shouldn't I?'

'Congratulations!' Simon got to his feet, clicked his heels and saluted Jean-Christophe. 'It's about time someone told that priggish bitch where to go. I salute you!'

Jean-Christophe tugged Simon's arm and pulled him down. 'Sit down, you're blocking my view, you big lump.' He nodded to the girl at the table. 'Who is *she*?'

'Why don't you go over and ask her?'

'With the Rucillio clan over there in the corner? I might be stupid, but I'm not crazy!'

Fabrice crumpled his napkin, took a deep breath, pushed back his chair and announced:

'Well, I'm going.'

He didn't even have time to get up from the table before a car pulled up and the girl got to her feet and walked towards it. The four of us watched as she climbed into the passenger seat, and flinched when she slammed the door.

'I know I've got no chance,' said Simon, 'but I have to try. First thing tomorrow, I'm going to take my glass slipper and go round every girl in the village until I find one my size.'

We all burst out laughing.

Simon picked up a teaspoon and unthinkingly began stirring his coffee again. He had stirred it three times now and still had not taken a sip. We were sitting on a café terrace in the village square, making the most of the glorious weather. The sky was clear and the March sun spilled its silver light over the avenue. Not a breath of wind stirred the leaves. In the silence of the morning, broken only by the babble of the fountain, the village heard an echo of itself.

The mayor, shirtsleeves rolled up, stood watching a group of workers paint the curb of the pavements red and white. In front of the church, the priest was helping a carter unload sacks of coal, which a boy was stacking against the wall. On the far side of the square, housewives stood gossiping around the market stalls, watched over by Bruno, a policeman who was barely out of his teens.

Simon set the teaspoon down.

'I didn't sleep a wink at Dédé's last night,' he said.

'Is this about that girl?'

'You catch on fast . . . I've got a serious crush on her.'

'Really?'

'What can I say? I've never in my life felt the way I feel about this dark-haired girl with the mysterious eyes.'

'Did you find out who she is?'

'Of course! First thing I did the morning after the party

was track her down. The only problem is, I found out I'm not the only person interested. Even that brainless moron José is hanging around her. You can't have a fantasy in this godforsaken town without a bunch of cretins gatecrashing it.'

He swatted an imaginary fly with a brutal, angry gesture, then picked up the spoon and went back to stirring his coffee.

'I wish I had your blue eyes, Jonas, and your angelic face!'

'Why?'

'So I could try my luck. Just look at me: I've got an ugly mug, a pot belly, a pair of stumpy legs . . . I've even got flat feet.'

'Girls aren't just interested in looks . . .'

'Maybe, but as it happens, I don't have much else to offer them. I don't have a vineyard or a wine broker's or a fat bank account.'

'You've got other things – your sense of humour, for a start. Girls love guys who can make them laugh. And you're honest, you're sincere, you're not a drunk, you're not two-faced. That stuff means a lot.'

Simon batted away my compliments.

There was a long silence. He bit his lip and looked awkward.

'Jonas,' he asked, 'do you think love trumps friendship?'

'What do you mean?'

'Well . . . I saw Fabrice flirting with our vestal virgin the day before yesterday . . . It was down by Cordona's wine cellars. Fabrice was leaning on the hood of his mother's car, arms folded, looking cool . . . and she didn't look like she was in a hurry to go home.'

'It's only because Fabrice is everyone's favourite person

in Río Salado these days. Girls, guys, even old men stop him in the street – he's *our* poet.'

'I know, but I didn't get the impression they were talking about literature, and it didn't look like a one-off thing.'

'Hey, peasants!' André called to us, parking his car across the street. 'Why aren't you down at my diner initiating yourself into the glories of pool?'

'We're waiting for Fabrice.'

'You want me to go on ahead?'

'We'll come over in a little while.'

'I'm counting on you.'

'We'll be there.'

André brought two fingers to his temple in a salute and floored the accelerator, raising a growl from an old dog curled up in a doorway.

Simon grabbed my hand.

'I haven't forgotten how you and Chris fell out about Isabelle. I don't want that happening to me and Fabrice. His friendship means a lot to me.'

'Don't get ahead of yourself.'

'Even thinking about it, I feel ashamed of my feelings for this girl.'

'There's no reason to be ashamed of our feelings when they're positive – even if they seem unfair.'

'Do you really believe that?'

'Everyone has an equal chance in love; everyone has the right to try his luck.'

'Do you think I've got a chance? I mean, Fabrice is rich and he's famous.'

'Do I think, do I think . . . Every time you open your mouth these days you ask me that. Well, I'll tell you what I think

– I think you're a coward. I think you're going round in circles when you should be getting somewhere. Anyway, here's Fabrice – let's change the subject.'

André's diner was crowded and too noisy for us to really enjoy our *escargots à la sauce piquante*. Besides, Simon obviously felt awkward. More than once he seemed about to confess everything to Fabrice, only to change his mind as soon as he opened his mouth. For his part, Fabrice was oblivious to what was going on. He took out his notepad and began scribbling down a fragment of a poem, crossing out and rewriting as he went. His blond fringe fell over his eyes like a barrier between his thoughts and Simon's.

André came over to ask if we needed anything, leaning over the poet's shoulder to read what he was writing.

'Do you mind?' Fabrice said, irritated.

'A love poem! So, are you going to tell us who's making your heart beat faster?'

Fabrice snapped his notebook closed and looked André up and down.

'I guess I'm ruining your inspiration,' grumbled André.

'You're winding him up is what you're doing,' Simon barked. 'Just go away and leave us alone.'

André pushed his Stetson back off his head and put his hands on his hips.

'What the hell is up with you? Why are you so pissed off at me?'

'Can't you see he's in the middle of writing a poem?'

'It's just hot air . . . Pretty words are not the way to a girl's heart, take my word for it. All I have to do is click my fingers and I can have any girl I want.'

Disgusted by André's crassness, Fabrice picked up his notebook and stormed out of the diner. Stunned, André watched him leave, then turned back to us. 'What did I say? Has he lost his sense of humour or what?'

We were all slightly shocked by Fabrice's sudden departure. Ordinarily, he was the most considerate and polite of us and the least likely to take offence.

'Must be the side effects of being in love,' Simon said bitterly, realising that what he had seen between Fabrice and his fantasy girl with the mysterious eyes was not just an idle chat.

That night we went over to Jean-Christophe's house. He had something he wanted to talk to us about; he wanted our advice. He ushered us into his father's small study on the ground floor. He watched us sip fruit juice and eat crisps for a minute, then announced:

'It's all over . . . I've finally broken up with Isabelle.'

The rest of us expected Simon to be overjoyed at this news, but he said nothing.

'Do you think I made a mistake?'

Fabrice rested his chin in his hands and thought.

'What happened?' I found myself asking, though I had long sworn never to get involved in their affairs.

Jean-Christophe, who had been waiting for an excuse to tell all, gave a weary shrug and said: 'Isabelle's too complicated. She's always finding fault, always correcting me about stupid things, always reminding me that my family is poor and she's doing me a favour just by being with me . . . I've threatened to break up with her lots of times, and every time she says: "Go ahead!" This morning was the last straw. She nearly lynched me right in the street in front of everyone just because I looked at that girl we saw the other night at the party.'

A tremor ran around the room. The table seemed to shake. I saw Fabrice's Adam's apple bob and Simon's knuckles go white.

'What?' asked Jean-Christophe, astonished at the sudden silence. Simon glanced at Fabrice, who cleared his throat and stared at Jean-Christophe.

'Did Isabelle catch you with that girl?'

'No . . . I haven't even seen her since the party. I was just walking Isabelle to the dressmaker's and the girl was coming out of Benhamou's shop.'

Fabrice looked relieved; he relaxed a little and said:

'You know, Chris, none of us can tell you what you should do. We're your friends, but we don't really know what goes on between you and Isabelle. You're always saying you're going to dump her, then the next day we'll see the two of you walking hand in hand, so it's hard to believe you're really serious. In any case, it's your business. You need to decide what you want to do. You and Isabelle have been together ever since you were at school. You know better than we do where you stand.'

'But that's my point – we've been together since we were at school, and I still don't know where I stand. I don't know if I'm happy. It's like Isabelle owns my soul. Even though she can be difficult and she orders me around, sometimes I can't imagine my life without her. I swear that's the truth. There are times when all her faults just make me love her more . . .'

'Forget her!' said Simon, his eyes blazing. 'I always said she wasn't right for you. You can't go through life with her like some chronic illness. A handsome guy like you, you shouldn't give up on life. Besides, all this fighting and making up is getting boring.' As he said this, he got to his feet – just as Fabrice had done at the diner that morning – and stormed out.

'Did I say something stupid?' Jean-Christophe asked, astonished.

'He hasn't really been himself lately,' Fabrice said.

'What's the matter with him?' Jean-Christophe turned to me. 'You know him better than anyone; what's going on in his head?'

I shrugged. 'I don't know.'

Simon had got it bad, and his frustration was beginning to get the better of his natural good humour. All the insecurities he had spent a lifetime hiding from were finally coming to the surface. His clowning around and his self-deprecating jokes had been a way of hiding his faults – being fat, being short, being awkward with women. The sudden appearance of this dark-haired girl was forcing him to face up to the unspoken truths that were ruining his life.

Simon and I ran into each other by accident a week later. He was on his way to the post office and was happy for me to tag along.

His rage since the flare-up with Jean-Christophe had not abated. He looked as though he hated the whole world.

We walked though the village in silence, like shadow-graphs on a wall. Having collected his forms from the post office, Simon seemed lost. He did not know what to do. We met Fabrice as we were coming out of the post office. He wasn't alone. *She* was with him, and she had her arm through his. All we had to do was look at them – Fabrice in his tweed suit and her in a flowing pleated dress – and we knew. In an instant, all the bitterness drained from Simon's face. How could he not accept this when they looked so perfect together?

Fabrice quickly introduced us.

'This is Simon and Jonas, I told you about them, they're my best friends.'

Framed by the sun, the girl was even more beautiful now – she was not flesh and blood but a blaze of sunlight.

'Simon, Jonas, this is Émilie, Madame Cazenave's daughter.'

It was as if someone had thrown a bucket of cold water over me. Simon and I simply nodded and smiled – speechless, though for very different reasons. By the time we had regained our composure, they had left. We stood on the steps of the post office for a long time, unable to utter a word. How could we resent them? How could we question such loving completeness without appearing brutish?

Simon owed it to himself to concede defeat, and this, with considerable flair, he did.

13

SPRING WAS gaining ground. The dew on the hills shimmered in the dawn light like a sea so inviting you wanted
to strip off, dive in and swim until, exhausted, you found
a shady tree where you could lie and dream, one by one,
of the things the good Lord had made. Every intoxicating
morning was a miracle, every stolen moment a fragment
of eternity. In the sunshine, Río Salado was a marvel. Everything the sunlight touched turned to dream; nowhere in
the world had my soul ever found such peace. News of the
outside world filtered through as garbled rumours that
did nothing to disturb the pleasant rustle of the vines. We
knew Algeria was at war, that a seething anger festered
among the people, but the villagers in Río Salado seemed
to care little about this. They built high walls around their
happiness; walls with no windows on the outside world.
They were content to gaze at their handsome reflections
in the mirror, then head off into the vineyards to harvest
the sunshine.

Río Salado was unperturbed. The burgeoning harvest
promised good wines, a dazzling whirl of dances and fruitful
marriages; the ominous thunderclouds gathering elsewhere

could not be allowed to darken a sky of such pure, perfect blue.

Often, after lunch, I would sit in the rocking chair on the veranda for half an hour so I could gaze out over the dappled greens of the plains, the ravines of ochre clay and the many-coloured mirages rising in the distance. The view was almost otherworldly in its serenity. I would gaze out across the fields and doze. Sometimes Germaine would find me, head thrown back, mouth open, and would tiptoe away so as not to wake me.

Río Salado was waiting expectantly for summer. We knew time was on our side, that soon the beaches and the grape harvest would breathe new life into us the better to enjoy the feasting and the riotous bacchanalia. Already summer loves blossomed in the idle hours like flowers in the sunlight. Girls strolled down the main street, dazzling in their summer dresses, flaunting bare arms or a flash of tanned shoulder. The boys on the café terraces were wont to fly into a rage if someone began delving into their secret sighs and fantasies.

But the very things that made some hearts beat faster becalmed others. Jean-Christophe and Isabelle broke up. The whole village gossiped about their turbulent relationship. I watched as my friend shrivelled. Usually Jean-Christophe was always quick to call attention to himself; he loved to shout to people across the street, to stop traffic, to yell to a barman for a beer. He had always been self-centred and self-seeking, proud to be the centre of his own universe. Now he could not bring himself to look people in the eye, pretended not to hear when some called to him from across the road. He could be tortured by an innocent smile and would analyse the least comment for some malicious implication.

He became quick-tempered, distant, and half mad with heartache. I was worried about him. One evening, having spent the day roaming the hills far from wagging tongues, he went to André's diner, and after knocking back several bottles, was so drunk he could barely stand. José offered to give him a lift home, but Jean-Christophe punched him in the face, then picked up an iron bar and drove the rest of the customers out of the diner. Alone amidst the empty benches and tables, he clambered up on to the bar and, reeling and staggering, his nose streaming with blood, pissed copiously over the flower beds, roaring that he would do the same to the bastards talking about him behind his back. It took considerable skill to steal up on him, take the iron bar, tie him up and carry him home on a makeshift stretcher. The incident provoked a howl of indignation in Río Salado. They had never seen the like of it. This was *hchouma* – mortal shame – something no Algerian village could forgive. Anyone might stumble, fall and pick themselves up again, but having sunk so low, a man lost the respect of others and often their friendship. Jean-Christophe knew that he had overstepped the mark, and knew that he could not show his face in the village again. He set off for Oran, where he spent his days wandering aimlessly from bar to bar.

Simon, for his part, was pragmatic. He took his fate in his own hands. He had long been tired of being a factotum, frittering his life away in an office that smelled of mildew and interminable lawsuits. It was a job ill-suited to his sense of himself as the life and soul of the party. He had neither the temperament nor the forbearance for a career as a badly paid pen-pusher. The office walls were closing in; his world was reduced to a sheet of yellow paper. He was suffocating, waiting like a dumb animal for a bell to tell him he could go home. Worst of all, he realised, the worries and anxieties of his job were the only things that still reminded him that he was human. One morning after a blazing row with his boss he resigned, determined to set himself up in business and be his own boss.

I barely saw him any more.

Fabrice, too, had less and less time to spend with me, but I understood. His relationship with Émilie seemed serious. They met every day behind the church, and on Sundays I could see them from my balcony walking through the vineyards, or heading out of the village on their bicycles, his shirt billowing, her hair whipped back by the wind. It was a joy to watch them ride up the hill, out of the village, away from the gossips. Sometimes, in my mind, I would go with them.

Then, one morning, a miracle occurred. I was stocking the shelves in the pharmacy when I saw my uncle slowly come down the stairs in his dressing gown, cross the room and go outside. Germaine, who was two steps behind him, could hardly believe her eyes. My uncle had not set foot outside the house for years. That morning he stood on the steps of the shop, hands in the pockets of his dressing gown, looking around him, his gaze lingering on the orange groves and then flitting towards the distant hills on the horizon.

'It's a beautiful day,' he said, grinning, and so unaccustomed was he to smiling, I thought his lips might crack. Germaine and I watched as laughter lines spread across his face like the ripples from a pebble in a pond.

'Would you like me to bring out a chair?' Germaine asked with tears in her eyes.

'What for?'

'You can sit in the sun. I'll set it next to the window with a little table and make some fresh mint tea and you can watch the people go past.'

'No.' My uncle shook his head. 'No chair today. I think I'll take a little walk.'

'In your dressing gown?'

'If it were up to me, I'd walk around naked,' said my uncle, and he stepped off the porch.

A prophet walking on water would not have amazed us any more than the sight of my uncle stepping into the street, hands in his pockets, his back straight, walking with a slow, almost military gait. He headed towards a little orange grove and wandered among the trees. Then, catching sight of a partridge taking to the wing, he turned and, following the bird's flight, disappeared into the vineyards. Germaine and I sat on the veranda, holding each other's hand, until he came back.

A few weeks later, we bought a second-hand car. Germaine's nephew Bertrand – now a mechanic – delivered it in person. It was a tiny bottle-green car with hard seats and curved bodywork like a tortoise's shell. The steering wheel was so big it looked like it belonged in a truck. Bertrand told Germaine and me to climb in and he would put the engine through its paces. It felt like being in a tank. In time, everyone in Río Salado learned to recognise our car a mile off. Hearing the deafening roar of the engine, someone would shout: 'Attention, here comes the artillery!' and people would stand on the kerb and salute as we passed.

André offered to give me driving lessons. He took me out to a patch of waste ground, and every time I made a mistake he called me all the names under the sun. Once or twice I was so panicked by his swearing I nearly killed us both. As soon as he had taught me to drive around a tree without grazing it, and do a hill start without stalling, he went back to working at his diner, relieved to have come through the ordeal without a scratch.

One Sunday, after mass. Simon suggested we go down to the beach. He had had a tough week and needed some fresh air. Deciding to head for the port of Bouzedjar, we set off after lunch.

'Where did you buy that rust bucket? Army surplus?'

'Okay, maybe it doesn't look like much, but it gets me where I want to go, and so far it's never broken down.'

'I'm surprised you're not deaf . . . it's like listening to a steamboat on its last legs.'

'You get used to it.'

Rolling the window down, Simon stuck his head out, and as his hair was swept back by the wind, I noticed he was already going bald. Seeing my friend suddenly looking older, I glanced in the mirror to see if I did too. We drove through Lourmel and headed straight for the coast. Now and then, when the road crested the peak of a hill, it seemed as though we could almost touch the sky. It was a beautiful late-April morning; the sky was an immaculate blue, the horizon majestic and all around was a feeling of completeness. The last days of spring in Río Salado were often the most splendid. The orange groves thrummed with the sound of early cicadas, and clouds of gnats glittered over stagnant pools like fistfuls of gold dust. If it were not for the squalid shacks scattered here and there, you would have thought you were in paradise.

'Isn't that Fabrice's car?' Simon pointed to a car parked beneath a lone eucalyptus in the scrubland.

I pulled up on the hard shoulder and in the distance saw Fabrice with two girls having a picnic. Intrigued by the sudden appearance of the car, Fabrice got up and put his hands on his hips, clearly on the defensive.

'I always said he was short-sighted,' Simon whispered as he clambered out.

Fabrice walked a hundred metres before realising it was my car. Relieved, he stopped where he was and waved for us to join them.

'Did we give you a scare?' said Simon, hugging Fabrice. 'What are you guys doing out here?'

'We're just out for a drive. Are you sure we're not interrupting?'

'Well, we didn't bring enough cutlery, but if you can wait while we finish our apple tarts, it's no problem.'

The two girls readjusted blouses and tugged their skirts down past their knees to appear decent when they greeted us. Émilie Cazenave gave us a smile; the other girl simply looked quizzically at Fabrice, who quickly reassured her:

'Jonas and Simon, my best friends.'

Then, turning to us, he said, 'This is Hélène Lefèvre, a journalist with the *Écho d'Oran*. She's writing an article about the area.'

Madame Cazenave's daughter turned her deep, dark eyes on me and I had to look away.

Fabrice went back to his car and found a beach towel, and laid it out on a patch of grass so that Simon and I could sit down. Simon crouched down by the wicker basket, rummaged inside and found a piece of bread, then, taking a penknife from his pocket, cut slices of *saucisson*. The girls glanced at each other quickly, clearly amused by his nerve.

'Where were you headed?' Fabrice asked us.

'Down to the port to see the fishermen unload,' said Simon. 'What about you, what are you doing out here with these two charming girls?'

Émilie stared at me again. Could she read my thoughts? And if so, what did they say? Had her mother said something about me? Had Émilie detected some hint of me in her mother's bedroom, a scent I had been unable to erase, the trace of a kiss, the memory of an embrace? Why did I suddenly feel that she could read me like a book? And her eyes . . . They held me hypnotised. How could they plunge into mine, know my every thought, my every doubt? For an instant I saw her mother's eyes back in their vast house on the marabout road – eyes so radiant that one needed no other light to see into the deepest depths, discern the most secret weaknesses . . . I felt unsettled.

'I think we've met before. A long time ago.'

'I don't think so, mademoiselle. I'm sure I would remember.'

'It's strange, your face seems familiar,' she said, then added, 'What do you do for a living, Monsieur Jonas?'

Her voice had the gentle murmur of a mountain stream. She said 'Monsieur Jonas' just as her mother had, accentuating the 's', and it roused the same feelings in me, stirred the same emotions.

'Nothing much,' said Simon, jealous of the attention I was getting from his first real crush. 'Me, I'm a businessman. I'm setting up an import-export business. In two, three years, I'll be rich.'

Émilie ignored Simon's teasing. I could feel her eyes on

me, waiting for my answer. She was so beautiful I could not meet her gaze without blushing.

'I work in a pharmacy, mademoiselle.'

A lock of hair fell over her eyes and she swept it away with an elegant hand, as though lifting a veil to reveal her beauty.

'A pharmacy, where?'

'Río Salado, mademoiselle.'

Something flitted across her face, she arched her eyebrows and the piece of apple pie between her fingers crumbled. Fabrice noticed her confusion, and now, confused himself, quickly rushed to pour me a glass of wine.

'You know he doesn't drink,' Simon said.

'Oh, sorry . . .'

The journalist took the glass and brought it to her lips. Émilie did not take her eyes off me.

Twice, she came to visit me at the pharmacy. I made sure that Germaine was with me. What I saw in her face disconcerted me and I had no intention of hurting Fabrice.

I began to avoid her. I told Germaine that if Émilie phoned she should say I was out and she didn't know when I would be back. Émilie quickly realised that I found her attentions unsettling, that I could not deal with the friendship she was offering. She stopped trying to see me.

The summer of 1950 swaggered into Río Salado like a carnival strongman. The roads teemed with holidaymakers, the beaches were overrun. Simon's new business secured its first big contract and he took us all to dinner in one of the most fashionable restaurants in Oran. Simon – who had always been the life and soul of the party – surpassed himself.

His antics and his clowning had the whole restaurant in stitches; the priggish women at the adjoining tables giggled whenever he raised his glass and launched into some hilarious new tirade. It was a wonderful evening. Fabrice and Émilie had come, as had Jean-Christophe, who spent the whole evening asking Hélène to dance. Seeing Jean-Christophe enjoying himself after the months of black depression put the finishing touch to the celebrations. The four of us were together again, inseparable as the tines of a pitchfork, and all would have been for the best in the best of all possible worlds had it not been for that one awkward, inappropriate gesture. Under the table, I felt Émilie's hand slide along my thigh. My drink went down the wrong way and I almost passed out, gasping and choking as the others thumped me on the back. When I came to, it seemed that most of the restaurant was leaning over me. Simon heaved a sigh of relief when he saw me grab the table leg and hoist myself back on to my chair. Émilie's eyes had never seemed so dark, nor her face so pale.

The following day, when Germaine and my uncle had gone out – they were in the habit of walking in the vineyards every morning now – I was shocked to see Madame Cazenave come into the pharmacy. Although silhouetted against the sunlight, I recognised the curve of her figure, the singular way she held herself, shoulders back, head high.

She hesitated in the doorway for a moment, probably to be sure that I was alone, then strode into the shop, a rustle of shadows and light, her heady perfume pervading the space.

She was wearing a grey trouser suit and a hat adorned with cornflowers pulled down slightly over her turbulent face.

'Good morning, Monsieur Jonas.'

'Good morning, madame.'

She took off her dark glasses . . . but the magic did not work now. She was just another customer, and I was no longer the teenage boy who felt he might faint at the sight of her smile. This realisation disconcerted her somewhat, and she began drumming her fingers on the counter top.

'Madame . . . ?'

My innocent tone irritated her. Fire flickered in her eyes but she kept her composure; she could be uncompromising only if she was in control. Madame Cazenave was the sort of person who planned everything she did in meticulous detail; she chose the battleground and calculated her entrance to the last second. Knowing her as I did, I imagined she had spent the night plotting every move, every word of her performance. What she had not realised was that the boy she was expecting was no longer in the audience. My composure unsettled her; it was something she had not expected. She tried to adapt her plans, but the cards had already been dealt, and spontaneity had never been her strong suit.

She pressed the tip of her sunglasses to her lips to stop them quivering, but there was nothing she could do to hide her apprehension – her whole face was trembling; it seemed as though it might crumble like a piece of chalk.

'If you're busy, I can come back later,' she ventured.

Was she playing for time? Hoping to retreat so she might return better prepared?

'I am not particularly busy. How can I help you, madame?'

She grew more uneasy. What was she afraid of? I knew she had not come for a prescription, but I could not think why she should be so tense.

'Make no mistake, Monsieur Jonas,' she said, as though reading my mind, 'I am in full possession of my faculties. I simply do not know how to begin.'

'I'm listening . . .'

'I find your tone rather arrogant. Why do you think I am here?'

'I'm afraid you will have to tell me.'

'You haven't the slightest idea?'

'No.'

'Really?'

'Really.'

She took a deep breath, held it for a several seconds, then, taking her courage in both hands, in a rush of breath – as though afraid I might interrupt her – she said quickly:

'I've come about Émilie.'

It was like watching a balloon suddenly deflate. Her throat tightened, she swallowed hard, but she appeared relieved, as though a great weight had been lifted from her. But the battle was just beginning and she looked as though she had expended her last reserves of energy.

'My daughter, Émilie.'

'I know who you mean. But I don't see the connection.'

'Don't play the innocent with me, young man. You know exactly what I'm talking about. What is the nature of your relationship with my daughter?'

'I'm afraid you've got the wrong person, madame. I have no relationship with your daughter.'

She twisted the frame of her sunglasses, her eyes watching mine, waiting for some sign of weakness. I did not look away. She no longer scared me. Her suspicions had little effect on me, but they did make me curious. Río Salado was a small village, walls were thin and the best-kept secrets quickly became the source of idle gossip. What were people saying about me?

'She talks of nothing but you, Monsieur Jonas.'

'Of our gang . . .'

'I'm not talking about your *gang*. I am talking about you and my daughter. I want to know the precise nature of your relationship, and your intentions. I want to know whether you have made plans, whether your intentions are serious . . . I want to know whether anything has happened between you.'

'Nothing has happened, Madame Cazenave. Émilie is in love with my best friend Fabrice. I would never even think of doing anything that might ruin his happiness.'

'You are a sensible young man, Monsieur Jonas, as I believe I've told you before.'

She clasped her hands over the bridge of her nose, then, after a moment's thought, raised her head again.

'I shall get right to the point, Monsieur Jonas . . . You are a Muslim – a good Muslim from what I have heard – and I am a Catholic. A long time ago, in a moment of weakness, we gave in to temptation. May the Lord forgive us. It was a fleeting mistake. But there is one sin that He will never absolve or pardon – incest!'

She shot me a venomous look as she said the word.

'It is a terrible abomination.'

'I don't understand where you're going with this.'

'But we're already there, Monsieur Jonas. You know that to sleep with a mother and her daughter is an offence against God, against the saints, against angels and demons!'

Her face was flushed purple now and the whites of her

eyes curdled like milk. Her trembling finger was intended as the sword of justice as she thundered:

'I forbid you to go near my daughter.'

'The thought had not even crossed my mind.'

'I don't think you understand me, Monsieur Jonas, I don't care what goes on in that mind of yours. You can think whatever you want. What *I* want is for you to stay as far away from my daughter as possible, and I want you to swear you will respect my wishes.'

'Madame . . .'

'Swear it!' She screamed as though it were an order.

Madame Cazenave had intended to remain icily calm, to let me know that she was in control of the situation. From the moment she stepped into the shop she had carefully curbed her mounting anger, uttering a word only when she was sure that it would not rebound on her. Now, at the moment she most needed it, she had lost control. She tried to regain her composure but it was too late; tears were welling in her eyes.

She brought her hands up to her temples, focused on a single point, waited until her breathing was under control again, then, her voice almost inaudible, she said:

'I apologise. I am not in the habit of raising my voice to people. But this whole thing has shocked me deeply. To hell with hypocrisy. I'm completely at a loss. I can't sleep . . . I hoped to be firm, to be strong, but this concerns my family, my daughter, my faith, my conscience. It's too much . . . I never imagined such a yawning abyss might open up at my feet. If it were just that, just an abyss, I would throw myself in if it would save my soul. But that would not solve the problem.

'It must not happen, Monsieur Jonas; nothing good can come of your relationship with my daughter. It cannot happen, it must not happen, I need to be clear about that. I need to go home with a clear conscience. I need to be at peace. Émilie is just a child. She is fickle. She can fall for a boy because of his laugh, do you understand? And I do not want her to fall for you. So I am begging you, for the love of God and His prophets Jesus and Muhammad, promise me you will give her no encouragement. It would be appalling, immoral; it would be horribly obscene.'

She took my hands in hers and squeezed them. This was not the woman I had dreamed of long ago. Terrified at the thought of this abomination, frightened at the idea that she might live in infamy for all eternity, Madame Cazenave had renounced her charms, her spells, her lofty throne; the woman who stood before me was simply a mother. Her eyes sought mine; with a blink, I could have sent her straight to Hell. I felt ashamed to have the power to damn someone I had once loved, someone whose grace and generosity I had thought of as sin.

'Nothing will happen between me and your daughter, madame.'

'Promise me.'

'I promise.'

'Swear it.'

'I swear.'

She slumped on to the counter. A great weight had been lifted from her, yet she seemed crushed, and she took her head in her hands and sobbed.

14

'IT'S FOR you.' Germaine waved the phone at me.

'Are you angry with me?' It was Fabrice.

'No . . .'

'Has Simon done something to upset you?'

'No.'

'Have you and Jean-Christophe fallen out?'

'Of course not.'

'Then why have you been avoiding us? You've been sulking at home for ages. We waited for you all day yesterday. You said you'd come over, and by the time we ate, everything was cold.'

'I've been busy.'

'Come off it . . . it's not like there's an epidemic in the village, and don't tell me your uncle is sick, because I've seen him walking in the orange groves every morning. He's fit as a fiddle.'

He cleared his throat and his voice was calmer now.

'I've missed you, Jonas. You live down the road from me but it's like you've disappeared off the face of the earth.'

'I've been sorting out the shop. I have to get the accounts up to date, and there's an inventory to do.'

'Do you need a hand?'

'No . . . it's fine.'

'Okay, if everything's fine, I'll expect you at my house for dinner tonight.'

I didn't have time to say no; he had already hung up.

By the time he called for me at seven p.m., Simon was in a foul mood.

'Can you believe it? All that work I put in, for nothing. Like an idiot, I got my figures wrong. I'm the only one who lost out. The way they explained it, everyone stood to make a profit, but when the delivery showed up, I'm the one who has to pay the difference out of my own pocket. I can't believe I let myself get conned . . .'

'That's business, Simon.'

Jean-Christophe was waiting for us a couple of blocks away. Dressed in his Sunday best, he was freshly shaven, hair plastered down with a thick layer of Brylcreem, holding a big bunch of flowers and looking as nervous as an actor in his first role.

'I feel embarrassed now,' said Simon. 'What are me and Jonas going to look like, showing up empty-handed?'

'They're for Émilie,' Jean-Christophe admitted.

'Émilie's coming?' I said, disheartened.

'Of course she's coming,' said Simon. 'She and Fabrice hardly spend a minute apart. But what are you doing bringing her flowers, Chris? She's somebody else's girlfriend, and that somebody else happens to be Fabrice.'

'All's fair in love and war.'

Simon frowned, shocked by Jean-Christophe's comment. 'Are you serious?'

Jean-Christophe threw his head back and laughed.

'Of course I'm not serious, it was a joke.'

'Well it's not remotely funny,' said Simon, who was a stickler for points of principle.

Madame Scamaroni had set out a table on the veranda. She met us at the door. Fabrice and his beloved were lounging in a pair of wicker chairs under a small arbour in the garden. Émilie looked stunning. She was wearing a simple gipsy skirt, her hair hung loose down her back and her shoulders were bare. She looked good enough to eat. I immediately felt ashamed and put the thought out of my mind.

Jean-Christophe's Adam's apple was bobbing like a yo-yo, and his tie had almost come undone. He offered the flowers he was carrying to Madame Scamaroni.

'For you, madame.'

'Oh, thank you, Chris, you're an angel.'

'We all chipped in,' Simon said, feeling jealous.

'You did not,' Jean-Christophe shot back.

Everyone burst out laughing.

Fabrice set down the manuscript he had been reading to Émilie and came over to greet us. He put his arms around me and hugged me a little hard. Over his shoulder, I saw Émilie's eyes seeking mine. I heard Madame Cazenave's voice in my head. *Émilie is just a child. She is fickle. She can fall for a boy because of his laugh, do you understand? And I do not want her to fall for you.* A wave of shame, worse than the first, meant that I did not hear what Fabrice whispered in my ear.

All evening, while Simon told jokes and had everyone in stitches, in the face of Émilie's insistent offensive, I beat a retreat. Not that she put her hand on my thigh this time; in fact she did she not even speak to me. She simply sat opposite me, and in doing so obscured the whole world.

She was gracious. She pretended to be interested in the laughter and joking, but it was forced, she was just laughing to be polite. I watched as she fidgeted, plucked at her skirt, nervous and anxious like a frightened schoolgirl waiting to be called to the blackboard. Sometimes, when the others were falling about laughing, she would look over to see if I was laughing too. I only half heard the jokes. Like Émilie, I was only laughing to be polite; like her, my thoughts were on other things. I didn't like what was going on in my head; thoughts blossoming like poisonous flowers . . . I had *promised* . . . I had *sworn*. Strangely, though my scruples caught in my throat, they did not choke me – I took a certain perverse pleasure in allowing myself to be tempted. Why did my promises, my vows suddenly mean so little to me? Time and again I tried to concentrate on Simon's antics, but it was hopeless; I quickly found myself staring at Émilie again. I was enveloped in unearthly silence, which muffled the sounds of the night, the chatter on the veranda. I was suspended in a void and Émilie's eyes were my only beacon. I couldn't go on like this. What I was doing was treachery, it was a betrayal and I felt tainted. I had to leave, I had to go home as soon as possible. I was terrified Fabrice would realise what was happening. That was a thought I could not bear, any more than I could bear to look at Émilie. Every time her eyes met mine, they took away another fragment of my being; like ancient battlements worn by time, I was crumbling.

While the others were distracted, I went into the living room and phoned Germaine. I asked her to call me back; ten minutes later she did so.

'Who was that on the phone?' Simon asked, seeing the look on my face as I came back out on to the veranda.

'It was Germaine . . . my uncle isn't well.'

'Do you want me to drop you home?' Fabrice asked.

'No, it's okay.'

'Call me if it's something serious.'

I nodded and left as quickly as I could.

Summer that year was sweltering, and the grape harvest was superb. The usual round of lavish balls was in full swing. Every morning we headed for the beach, and every night, by the light of hundreds of Chinese lanterns, there was a party. A dizzying succession of bands and orchestras played in the marquees and we danced until we could barely put one foot in front of the other. There were weddings and birthdays, civic celebrations and engagement parties. In Río Salado, a banquet could be something as simple as a makeshift barbecue, and we could conjure an imperial ballet from a twist of the gramophone.

Half-heartedly I went to the parties and stayed for as short a time as possible. I was always the last to arrive, and often left so quickly no one realised I had come. Everyone was always there, and our gang would invariably be on the dance floor. I could not bring myself to interrupt Émilie and Fabrice during a slow dance; they looked so perfect together – although it seemed increasingly obvious that the relationship was one-sided. The eyes can lie, but the gaze cannot, and the glow in Émilie's was fading fast. Whenever I was around, she would look at me imploringly. It was pointless to turn away, since her distress signals reached me loud and clear. Why me? I racked the depths of my brain. Why does she look at me like this and never say anything? Émilie's beauty was matched only by the heartache that she tried to hide behind her radiant smile. She never betrayed what she was feeling, willed herself to be happy with Fabrice, but she was not happy. At night, when they huddled together in the sand dunes and Fabrice talked to her about the night sky, she did not see the stars. Twice I had almost stumbled on them in the darkness, wrapped in each other's arms on the beach, and though I could not see their faces, I knew that when Fabrice held her, Émilie was elsewhere.

And then there were Jean-Christophe's bouquets. He had never bought so many flowers. Every day he stopped by the florist on the village square and then went to the Scamaronis' house. Simon took a dim view of his gallantry, but Jean-Christophe did not seem to care; it was as though he had lost all sense of judgement, all notion of propriety. In time, Fabrice began to notice that his dates with Émilie were often interrupted as Jean-Christophe became more brazen, more intrusive. At first he thought there was nothing to it, but finding that he rarely had a moment alone with Émilie, he began to wonder. Jean-Christophe barely let them out of his sight; it was as though he was watching their every move.

Finally, the inevitable happened.

It was a Sunday afternoon and we were all at the beach in Terga. Holidaymakers skipped across the scorching sand like grasshoppers and dived into the cool water. Simon was having his usual afternoon nap, having just wolfed down a string of *merguez* sausages and drunk a whole bottle of wine. His fat hairy belly rose and fell like a blacksmith's bellows. Fabrice, however, was wide awake. A book lay at his feet, but he was not reading; he was watching Jean-Christophe and Émilie as they laughed and splashed in the waves, timing each other to see who could hold their breath longest, then swimming out to sea until they almost disappeared. As he watched them turn somersaults in the water, legs thrust above the waves, a sad smile played on Fabrice's lips and doubts shimmered in his dark eyes. When they emerged from the waves, Émilie and Jean-Christophe, in a gesture that seemed to surprise them both, grabbed each other around the waist, and Fabrice's face darkened as he watched his dreams and plans slip through his fingers.

I hated that summer; the long months of confusion and heartache and increasing isolation, of lies and half-truths. Later, I came to call it 'the dead season', the title of Fabrice's first novel, which began: *When love betrays you, it is proof that you were undeserving; to be noble one must set it free — only if you are prepared to pay this price can you say that you have truly loved.* Ever courageous, noble even in defeat, Fabrice kept on smiling, though his heart fluttered weakly in his chest like a caged bird.

Simon was sickened by what was happening, by the hypocrisy and the duplicity. To him, Émilie's betrayal was unforgivable. He could not understand how she could turn her back on Fabrice, who was gentle and unfailingly kind; who had given himself to her body and soul. But if Simon felt that Fabrice had been wronged, he did not blame Jean-Christophe — who was deeply depressed since his break-up with Isabelle, and seemingly unaware of how much he was hurting his best friend. To Simon, the blame clearly lay with Émilie, the 'preying mantis', an outsider who did not understand the ways or the principles of Río Salado.

I tried not to get involved. I found excuses not to be with my friends, to avoid the dinners and the parties.

Simon now despised Émilie and, like me, began to find excuses not to be with her. He and I would go to André's diner and play pool all night.

Fabrice left Río Salado for Oran, where he holed up in his mother's apartment on the Boulevard des Chasseurs, working on newspaper articles and sketching out his first novel. He rarely set foot in the village. On the one occasion I went to see him in the city, he seemed resigned to his fate.

Late that summer, Jean-Christophe invited Simon and me to his house, as he always did when he needed to make an important decision. He was hopelessly in love with Émilie, he told us, and intended to ask her to marry him. When he saw the look on Simon's face, he quickly went on, desperate to convince us:

'It's like I've been reborn . . . After what I've been through,' he said, referring to his break-up with Isabelle, 'I needed a miracle, and the miracle happened. I'm telling you, this girl was sent to me by God.'

Simon gave him a mocking smile.

'What? You don't believe me?'

'I don't have to believe you.'

'So why are you laughing?'

'I'm laughing because if I didn't laugh I'd cry.' Simon rose up in his seat, veins standing out on his neck. 'I'm laughing to keep myself from being sick.'

'Go on then,' Jean-Christophe said. 'Give me your two cents.'

'Two cents? More like two million. Okay, you're right, I don't believe you. What's more, I'm angry with you, I'm disgusted – the way you've treated Fabrice is despicable, it's unforgivable.'

Jean-Christophe accepted this; he knew he owed us an explanation. We were sitting in his living room. On the table stood a jug of lemonade and a jug of coconut water. The window to the street was open, the curtains billowed in the breeze and in the distance dogs barked, their yelps and growls echoing in the silent darkness.

Jean-Christophe waited until Simon had sat down again, then, his hands trembling, he brought his glass to his lips and took a long drink. He set down the glass, wiped his mouth with a napkin and, not daring to look at us, began to speak in a slow, deliberate voice.

'This isn't about Fabrice, it's about love. I didn't steal anything, didn't take anything from anyone. It was a thunderbolt – love at first sight – it happens all the time all over the world. That thunderbolt is a moment of grace, a blessing from the gods. I don't feel despicable, and I don't feel ashamed either. I've loved Émilie from the first time I saw her, and there's nothing shameful about that. Fabrice has always been my friend. I've never been one for talking. I take things as they come.

'I'm happy, for God's sake.' He banged his fists on the table. 'Is it a crime to be happy?' He turned angrily to Simon.

'What's wrong with loving someone and being loved? Émilie isn't a *thing* – she's not a painting you can buy in a gallery, she's not a deal to be haggled over. She's got the right to choose who she wants to be with . . . This is about two people sharing a life together, Simon! As it happens,

Émilie feels about me the way I do about her. Where's the shame in that?'

Simon was not about to back down. Hands balled into fists, nostrils flaring, he glared at Jean-Christophe and, stressing every syllable, said:

'If you're so sure of your decision, why did you invite us? Why force Jonas and me to listen to your speeches if you've got nothing to be ashamed of? Are you trying to ease your conscience? Or were you hoping we'd give your sordid little affair our blessing?'

'You're wrong, Simon, I didn't invite you here to ask for your blessing, or to try and convince you of anything. This is *my* life, and I'm old enough to know what I want . . . I plan to marry Émilie before Christmas. I don't need advice; what I need is money.'

Realising he had overstepped the mark, Simon leaned back in his chair and stared at the ceiling. Jean-Christophe was right, he had no business questioning his decision.

'Don't you think you're moving a bit fast?'

'Do you think I'm taking things too fast, Jonas?' Jean-Christophe turned to me.

I didn't answer.

'Are you sure she really loves you?' Simon asked.

'What makes you think that she doesn't?'

'She's a city girl, Chris, she's not like us. When I think of the way she dumped Fabrice—'

'She didn't dump Fabrice!' shouted Jean-Christophe, infuriated.

'Okay, I take it back . . . Have you talked to her about your plans?'

'Not yet, but I'll have to soon. The problem is, I'm broke.

What money I had, I frittered away in bars and brothels in Oran after I broke up with Isabelle.

'That's what I mean,' said Simon. 'You're only just over your break-up with Isabelle. You're still not your old self. I think this thing with Émilie is just an infatuation. I think you should wait a while, see how she feels. Don't go putting a rope around your neck. I have to say, I thought maybe you were just trying to make Isabelle jealous.'

'Isabelle is ancient history.'

'No she's not, Chris, you don't get over someone just by clicking your fingers.'

Offended by Simon's remarks and my refusal to say anything, Jean-Christophe got to his feet, walked over to the door and slammed it open.

'You're throwing us out?' said Simon indignantly.

'Let's just say I've heard enough. If you don't want to lend me the money, Simon, that's fine, but don't lecture me, and for God's sake don't talk about things you don't understand.'

Jean-Christophe knew that this was unfair. He knew Simon would give him anything he asked. He was deliberately trying to upset him, and he succeeded, because Simon stormed out of the room. I had to run to catch up with him on the street.

My uncle called me into his study and asked me to sit on the sofa where he liked to lie and read. He had regained much of his colour and put on some weight; he looked years younger. His fingers still trembled and his grip was weak, but there was a spark of life in his eyes again. I felt happy that the man I had so admired before the police raid in Oran was almost his old self again. He spent his time reading, writing; he smiled. I loved to see him walking arm in arm with Germaine, so intimate they barely registered the world around them. In the effortlessness of their relationship, the ease of their conversation, there was a tenderness and an honesty that was almost sacred. They were the most honourable couple I had ever known. Though they needed nothing and no one to complete them, still, when I watched them, I felt inspired and filled with a joy as beautiful as their modest happiness. Their love demanded no compromise, it was perfect. According to sharia law, a non-Muslim must convert to Islam before marrying a Muslim. My uncle had not seen things that way. It did not matter to him whether his wife was a Christian or a *kafir*. If two people love each other, he told me, they need not fear excommunication, for love appeases God – it cannot be negotiated or compromised, for to do so is to dishonour something sacred.

He set his pen back in the inkwell and looked at me pensively.

'What's the matter, son?'

'What do you mean?'

'Germaine thinks there is something bothering you.'

'I can't think of anything. I haven't said anything.'

'Sometimes, when we think our problems only concern ourselves, we don't talk about them . . . I just want you to know that you are not alone, Younes, that you can talk to me any time. Never think that you might be disturbing me. You are the person I love most in all the world. You are my future. You are at an age when young men have great concerns. You're thinking of marrying, of having a home of your own, of earning a living. That's normal. Every bird yearns to fly on his own wings.'

'Germaine is talking nonsense.'

'That's not a bad thing. You know how much she loves you. Her every prayer is for you. Don't hide things from her. If you need money, if you need anything at all, we are here for you.'

'I know, I know.'

'I'm glad.'

Before he let me go, he picked up his pen, scribbled something on a piece of paper and handed it to me.

'Could you go to the bookshop and pick this up for me?'

'Of course. I'll go now.'

I slipped the piece of paper into my pocket and headed out, wondering what could have made Germaine think that I was worried.

The sweltering heat of recent weeks had calmed somewhat. In a sky exhausted by the heatwave, a big cloud ravelled its wool, using the sun as its spinning wheel, its shadow gliding over the vineyards like a ghost ship. Old men began to emerge from their shacks, relieved to have survived the heat; they sat on their stools in shorts and sweat-soaked shirts, eating lunch, their red faces half hidden by their broad-brimmed hats. It was almost dark; the breeze from the coast was cool and gentle. I touched the scrap of paper in my pocket and headed for the bookshop. The shop window was groaning with books and crude watercolours by local amateurs. When I pushed open the door, I was shocked to see Émilie standing behind the counter.

'Hello,' she said, taken aback.

For several seconds I forgot why I had come. My heart hammered like a demented blacksmith on his anvil.

'Madame Lambert hasn't been well,' she explained. 'She asked me to fill in for her.'

My hand rummaged for a moment before finding the piece of paper at the bottom of my pocket.

'Can I help you?'

Speechless, I simply handed her the piece of paper.

'*The Plague*, by Albert Camus,' she read, 'published by Gallimard.'

She nodded and hurried off behind the bookshelves, while I tried to catch my breath. I could hear her pushing a stepladder, searching along the shelves, repeating: 'Camus . . . Camus . . .', climbing down from the stepladder, pushing it down the aisle, then crying:

'Ah, here it is . . .'

She reappeared, her eyes more vast than a prairie.

'It was right under my nose,' she said, increasingly bewildered.

As I took the book, my hand grazed hers and I felt a spark thrill through me just as I had in the restaurant in Oran when she made a pass at me under the table. I looked at her and her face was flushed, but I knew it was a mirror image of my own.

'How is your uncle?' she asked, still blushing.

I didn't understand what she meant.

'You seemed worried that night at Fabrice's house . . .'

'Oh . . . yes, yes . . . No, he's much better now.'

'I hope it wasn't serious.'

'No, it wasn't serious.'

'I was really worried when you left.'

'It was just a scare . . .'

'I was worried about you, Monsieur Jonas, you were so pale.'

'Oh me . . . you know . . .'

She was no longer blushing now, she was in control, and her eyes held mine, determined not to let go.

'It was a pity you had to leave. I've barely had a chance to talk to you. You don't say much.'

'I'm shy.'

'I'm shy too. It can be so exhausting. And we miss out on so much. After you left, I was bored.'

'Simon seemed to be having fun . . .'

'I wasn't.'

Her hand slipped from the book on to my wrist and I quickly jerked it away.

'What are you afraid of, Monsieur Jonas?'

Her voice! Now the quavering had stopped, it had gained in confidence; it was clear, powerful, as commanding as her mother's.

Her hand took mine again; I did nothing to stop her.

'I've wanted to talk to you for a while now, Monsieur Jonas, but you always seem to disappear. Why are you avoiding me?'

'I'm not avoiding you . . .'

'That's not true, I can tell. When people try to lie there are little things that betray the truth. I would so like us to spend some time together, Monsieur Jonas. I think we have a lot in common, don't you?

'I . . .'

'We could meet up, if you like.'

'I'm busy at the moment.'

'I need to speak to you in private.'

'What about?'

'This isn't the time or the place . . . Why don't you come

to my house. It's out on the marabout road. It won't take long, I promise.'

'But I don't know what we have to talk about. Besides, Jean-Christophe . . .'

'What about Jean-Christophe?'

'This is a small town, mademoiselle, people talk. Jean-Christophe might not appreciate . . .'

'Might not appreciate what? We're not doing anything wrong. Besides, what business is it of his? Jean-Christophe is a friend, there's nothing between us.'

'Don't say that, please. He is in love with you.'

'Jean-Christophe is a lovely person, I like him . . . but I don't intend to spend the rest of my life with him.'

I was shocked.

Her eyes glittered like the blade of a scimitar.

'Don't look at me like that, Monsieur Jonas. I'm telling the truth. There is nothing between us.'

'Everyone in the village thinks you're engaged.'

'Then they're mistaken . . . Jean-Christophe is a friend, nothing more. My heart belongs to someone else,' she said, and pressed my hand to her breast.

'Bravo!'

The voice was like an explosion. Émilie and I froze: in the doorway of the bookshop stood Jean-Christophe, holding a bouquet of flowers. I could feel his hatred like scalding lava. He stood, appalled, incredulous, trembling beneath the ruins of the sky that had fallen. Face distorted with rage, he struggled to express his fury.

'Bravo!' he said again, then threw the flowers on the floor and stamped on them. 'I bought these roses for the woman I love. It turns out they're a funeral wreath.

I've been so stupid . . . and you, Jonas, you are an utter bastard!'

He raced out, slamming the glass door so hard it cracked, and I rushed after him. He zigzagged wildly through the side streets, lashing out at everything in his path. Seeing me behind him, he turned and pointed an accusing finger.

'Stay where you are, Jonas, don't come near me or I swear I'll kill you.'

'You're making a mistake. There's nothing between me and Émilie, I swear.'

'Go to hell, and take her with you! You're a bastard, a fucking bastard!'

Furious, he rushed at me and slammed me against the wall, spraying spittle in my face as he screamed insults at me. He punched me hard in the stomach. I fell to my knees.

'Why do you have to ruin my happiness?' He was close to tears, his eyes bloodshot, his lips flecked with spittle. 'Why, for God's sake, why did you have to ruin everything?'

He kicked me in the side.

'Curse you, and curse the day I ever met you,' he shouted, running off. 'I never want to see you again, I never want to hear your name, you miserable two-faced bastard!'

I lay on the ground, unsure which was worse, the pain from the beating, or my heartache.

Jean-Christophe did not go home. André had spotted him running across the fields after our argument, but no one had seen him since. Days passed. Jean-Christophe's parents were sick with worry; their son had never disappeared without letting them know where he was. He had gone away after his break-up with Isabelle, but he had phoned his mother every night so that she would not worry. Simon came to see me to ask what had happened. He was clearly worried – Jean-Christophe had just recovered from a serious depression; he might not survive a relapse. I feared the worst too. I could not sleep for thinking about what might have happened. Sometimes I would get up, fetch a jug of water, and drink it as I paced up and down the balcony. I didn't want to talk about what had gone on in the bookshop. I felt ashamed; I tried to pretend it had never happened.

'I'm sure that bitch did something to upset him,' Simon growled. 'I'd swear to it. That little pricktease has something to do with this.'

I couldn't bring myself to look him in the eye.

After a week of phoning Jean-Christophe's friends in Oran and making discreet enquiries in Río Salado, his father finally called the police.

When he heard about Jean-Christophe's disappearance, Fabrice rushed back to Río Salado.

'What the hell happened?'

'I've no idea,' Simon told him.

The three of us set off for Oran and combed the brothels and the bars, the sordid *fondouks* in La Scalera where for a few francs you could hole up with the ageing whores, drinking cheap wine and smoking opium. There was no sign of Jean-Christophe. We showed his photograph to the brothel madams, the barmen and the bouncers at the cabarets, to the *moutchos* in the hammams, but no one had seen him. Nor was there any news of him at the hospitals and the police stations.

Émilie came to see me at the pharmacy. My first thought was to throw her out. Madame Cazenave had been right:

nothing good could come of my relationship with her daughter; when I looked into her eyes, a horde of demons was set loose. And yet when she stepped into the shop, all my anger drained away. I had felt she was to blame for Jean-Christophe's disappearance and for anything that might befall him; but in her face all I could see was an immense sadness, and I could not help but pity her. She stood at the counter, her fingers nervously twisting her handkerchief, pale, heartbroken, helpless.

'I'm so sorry.'

'How do you think I feel?'

'And I'm sorry I got you mixed up in all this.'

'What's done is done.'

'Every night I pray no harm has come to Jean-Christophe.'

'I just wish I knew where he was.'

'There's still no news?'

'Nothing.'

She stared at her hands.

'What do you think I should do, Jonas? I was completely honest with him from the beginning. I told him I was in love with someone else. But he didn't believe me, or maybe he thought he had a chance. Is it my fault that he never had a chance?'

'I don't know what you're talking about, mademoiselle. Besides, this is neither the time nor the place—'

She cut me off. 'You're wrong. This is the time and the place to tell the truth. It's because I didn't have the courage to tell the truth, to say what I really felt, that all this has happened. I'm not cruel, I never meant to hurt anyone.'

'I don't believe you.'

'You have to believe me, Jonas.'

'I can't. You showed no respect for Fabrice. You put your hand on my thigh while you sat in that restaurant smiling at him. But that wasn't enough. You had to break Jean-Christophe's heart. And now you've dragged me into your little game.'

'It's not a game.'

'What do you want from me?'

'I want you to know . . . that I love you.'

I felt the room crumble around me.

Émilie did not flinch. She stared at me with her big black eyes, her fingers still clutching her handkerchief.

'Please, mademoiselle, go home.'

'Don't you see? The only reason I flirted with other boys was so you would notice me; the only reason I laughed was so you would hear me. I didn't know what to do, how to say I love you.'

'Then don't say it.'

'Can a heart be silent?'

'I don't know, but I don't want to hear it.'

'Why not?'

'Please, don't say any more . . .'

'No, Jonas! I love you and I need you to know that. You don't know how hard this is for me, how humiliated I feel, baring my soul to you, telling you I love you when you don't seem to feel anything for me. But it would be much worse to go on saying nothing when everything inside me, every breath I take, is screaming "I love you". I loved you the first time I saw you . . . That was ten years ago, in this very pharmacy. I don't know if you remember, but I've never forgotten it. It was raining that morning, my gloves were soaking wet. I'd come for my injection; I used to come every Wednesday. You had just come home from school. I remember the colour of your school bag with the studded straps, the jacket you were wearing, the fact that the laces of your brown shoes were untied. You told me you were thirteen. We talked about the Caribbean. While your mother was giving me my injection in the back room, you pressed a rose between the pages of my geography book.'

I felt a spark, and suddenly memories whirled dizzyingly in my mind and it all came back to me: *Émilie* . . . a little girl with a hulking man who seemed to be carved from a standing stone. Suddenly I remembered her face at the picnic when I told her I worked in a pharmacy. She was right. We had met before, a long time ago.

'Do you remember?'

'Yes.'

'You asked me what Guadeloupe meant, and I told you it was a French island in the Caribbean . . . When I found the rose in my geography book, I was so touched and I hugged the book. There was a rose bush in a pot over there on the sideboard. And there used to be a statue of the Virgin Mary behind the counter, on that shelf . . .'

As she talked, the scene flooded back with extraordinary clarity and her soft voice held me spellbound; I felt as though I was being carried away by a great wave. Madame Cazenave's voice was ringing in my head, trying to drown out her daughter, pleading with me, imploring me, and yet I could still hear Émilie's voice over her mother's shrieking, clear and sharp as a needle.

'*Younes* . . .' she said. 'That's your name, isn't it? I remember everything.'

'I . . .'

'Please, don't say anything.' She pressed her finger to my lips. 'I'm afraid of what you might say. I need time to catch my breath.'

She took my hand and held it to her breast.

'Can you feel my heart beating, Jonas . . . Younes?'

'This is wrong,' I stammered, but I did not take my hand away.

'Why is it wrong?'

'Jean-Christophe loves you. He is madly in love with you,' I said, trying to drown out the voices of mother and daughter, locked in mortal combat in my head. 'He told us you were getting married.'

'Why are you talking about him? I was talking about us.'

'I'm sorry, but Jean-Christophe's friendship means more to me than some childhood memory.'

My words clearly shocked her, but she was graceful.

'I don't want to hurt you.' I tried to make up for my rudeness. 'I'm sorry.'

She pressed her finger to my lips again. 'You have nothing to apologise for, Younes. I understand. Maybe you were right, this isn't the time or the place. I just needed you to know how I feel. It's not just a childhood memory to me. I love you, and I have a perfect right to feel that way. There is no crime, no shame in love, except to sacrifice it, even for the best of reasons.'

She left the shop without another word, without turning back. Never in my life had I felt as alone as I did the moment she stepped out into the roar of the street.

15

JEAN-CHRISTOPHE was alive.

Río Salado heaved a sigh of relief.

One night, when she had almost given up hope, he phoned his mother to tell her he was all right. According to Madame Lamy, her son was rational. He spoke calmly, in simple phrases, and his breathing was normal. She asked why he had disappeared, where he was calling from, but Jean-Christophe answered with vague platitudes: there was more to the world than Río Salado, there were other places to explore. He was evasive about where he was living, how he was surviving, given that he had left with no money and no bags. Madame Lamy did not press him; she was happy simply to know her son was alive. She sensed there was something wrong, that Jean-Christophe was being rational as a means of hiding it; she was afraid that if she pushed him too hard, turned the knife in the wound, she might hurt him further.

Later, Jean-Christophe wrote a long letter to Isabelle telling her that he loved her, and regretting that he had not made things work. She thought the letter was a last testament of sorts; she cried her heart out, convinced that her spurned fiancé had thrown himself off a cliff or under a train after sending it. The postmark was illegible, so it was impossible to know where it had been posted.

Three months later, Fabrice received *his* letter, this one filled with apologies and regrets. Jean-Christophe admitted that he had been selfish, that, blinded by his passion, he had lost sight of what was important, had forgotten common decency and the loyalty he owed to Fabrice, whom he had known since primary school and whom he still thought of as his best friend . . . There was no return address.

Eight months later, Simon – who in the meantime had gone into partnership with Madame Cazenave to open a fashion house in Oran – received *his* letter. It included a recent photograph of Jean-Christophe in a soldier's uniform, head shaved, holding his rifle. On the back it read: *It's a great life, thank you, Sergeant.* The envelope had been postmarked somewhere in Khemis Miliana. Fabrice decided to go and find him, and Simon and I went with him to the local barracks, where we were told that for the past three or four years they had only been recruiting 'natives'. They suggested we ask in Cherchell, but no one at the military school there or the one in Kolea had heard of Jean-Christophe. We checked with the garrisons in Algiers and Blida, but we could not find him. We were chasing a ghost. We went back to Río Salado exhausted and empty-handed.

Fabrice and Simon still had no idea why Jean-Christophe had left. They suspected Émilie had been cheating on him, but they could not be sure. Émilie did not seem to think she had done anything wrong. We saw her from time to time, in the bookshop helping Madame Lambert, or window-shopping on the main street. Jean-Christophe's decision to join the army surprised a lot of people – it was something that would not have occurred to most boys in Río Salado. It was as though he was punishing himself. He had said nothing in his letters about the reason why he had turned his back on his freedom, his family, his village in favour of army regulations and a life of willing obedience.

Simon's was the last letter.

I never received mine.

Émilie still came by to see me. Sometimes we just stood and stared at each other, not saying a word, not even a greeting. Was there anything left to say? We had said all we had to say to one another. Émilie believed I needed time, and was prepared to be patient; I felt that there could never be anything between us, but how could I convince her of this without offending her or outraging the whole village? Her suggestion that we should be together was impossible, unnatural. I was distraught, I didn't know what to do, so I did nothing. Émilie did not try to rush me, but she did everything in her power to keep in touch. She thought I was feeling guilty about Jean-Christophe and that sooner or later I would get over it, that her great dark eyes would wear me down, would overcome my inhibitions. Now that we knew that Jean-Christophe was alive and well, things between us were less tense, but though he was not here, his absence was the gulf that separated us, cast a shadow over our thoughts, clouded our plans. Every time she came, Émilie would see it in my face. She would arrive with some speech she had spent the night preparing, but when the moment came, her courage failed her. She no longer dared to take my hand or place her finger on my lips.

She invented bizarre ailments so that she could come to the

pharmacy for some exotic medication. I would jot every-thing down on my notepad, call her when her prescription arrived. When she came to collect it, she would think for a moment, make some trivial comment, ask some anodyne question about how she should take the medication and then leave. She desperately hoped she could force me to react, trigger some realisation that would allow her to open her heart to me again. I did nothing to encourage her, pretended not to notice her mute insistence, struggled not to give in, convinced that if I showed any weakness she would redouble her efforts.

Though I reluctantly persevered in this crude strategy, I felt heartsick. Every time Émilie came into the shop – or rather every time she left – I realised that she occupied my every waking thought. At night, I could not sleep until I had summoned up her every gesture, her every silence. During the day as I worked behind the counter, waiting for her to appear, every customer who stepped through the door reminded me of her absence, and I found myself pining for her. I flinched every time I heard the door chime, became irritable when I realised it wasn't her. What was happening to me? Why did I hate myself for being a sensible young man? Should decency prevail over honesty? What was love if it could not triumph over blasphemy and sacrilege, if it bowed before taboos, if it did not stay true to its own wild obsession? Seeing Émilie heartbroken seemed to me to be worse than breaking my promise to her mother, worse than all the blasphemies in the world.

'How much longer is this going to go on?' she finally asked me.

'I don't know what you're talking about.'

'Of course you know. I'm talking about *us* . . . Why are you treating me like this? I come to this dingy little pharmacy to see you, and you pretend you can't see that I'm suffering, that I'm hanging on, that I'm waiting. It's as though you want to humiliate me. Why? What have you got against me?'

'I . . .'

'Is it because I'm a Christian and you're a Muslim?'

'No.'

'What, then? Don't tell me you don't care about me, that you don't feel anything. I'm a woman, I can sense these things. I don't understand what the problem is. I've told you how I feel about you; what more can I do?'

She was angry and tired, close to tears, her fists clenched as though she wanted to grab me by the throat and shake me until I came apart.

'I'm sorry.'

'What does that mean?'

'I can't.'

'You can't what?'

I felt embarrassed and miserable. Like Émilie, I was infuriated by my cowardice, my indecisiveness, my inability to give her back her freedom and her dignity, even if I knew that whatever was between us could not last. I felt that I was lying, that I was somehow testing myself even though there was nothing to prove, nothing to overcome. Was I trying to punish myself? How could I decide? Émilie was right, I did have feelings for her, but every time I tried to accept the fact, my heart rebelled. What would this love be that was built on sacrilege, with no blessing, no dignity? How could it survive the scorn and contempt that would rain down on it?

'I love you, Younes . . . Are you listening?'

I said nothing.

'I'm leaving now. This time I won't come back. If you feel the same way, you know where to find me.'

A tear trickled down her cheek, but she did not wipe it away. I was drowning in her great dark eyes. Slowly she drew herself up and left.

'Pity . . .'

My uncle was standing behind me. It took me a moment to realise what he was referring to. Had he heard what we were saying? He was not a man to eavesdrop. He and I had talked about everything – everything except women. The subject was taboo, and in spite of his wisdom, his liberal values, a sense of propriety prevented him from raising the subject with me. In our community, such things were traditionally only ever alluded to, or they were dealt with by proxy – by asking someone else to do so. My uncle would have asked Germaine to speak to me about it.

'I was in the back office, the door was open . . .'

'It doesn't matter.'

'Maybe it's for the best. An accidental indiscretion can be fortuitous. I overheard you talking to that girl, and I thought: close the door. But I didn't close it. Not out of misguided curiosity, but because I have always loved to hear one heart speak to another – to me it is the most glorious music in the world. May I?'

'Of course.'

'You can stop me whenever you want, son.'

He sat on the bench, studying his fingers, then, looking down, he said in a distant voice:

'For a man to think he can fulfil his destiny without a

woman is a misunderstanding, a miscalculation; it is reck-lessness and folly. Certainly a woman is not everything, but everything depends on her. Look around you, look at history, think about the whole world and tell me what man is without woman; what are his promises, his prayers when it is not her praise he sings? A man may be as rich as Croesus, as poor as Job, he may be a slave or a tyrant, but there is no horizon wide enough if woman turns her back.'

He smiled as though speaking to some distant memory.

'When woman is not the supreme ambition of man, when she is not the goal of all things in this world, then life holds no joys, no pains.'

He slapped his thigh and got to his feet.

'When I was young, I used to go out to the Great Rock and watch the sunset. It was magnificent. This, I thought, was true beauty. Later I saw plains and forests shrouded in a quiet mantle of snow, I saw palaces set in glorious gardens and many wonders, and I wondered if this was what paradise would be like.'

He laid a hand on my shoulder.

'Well, I can tell you now that without women – without the *houris* – paradise would be a still life.'

His trembling fingers dug into my flesh, shaking my whole being. Like a salamander, my uncle had been reborn from his ashes.

'Sunset, springtime, the blue of the sea, the stars in the sky, all the things that entrance us exert their magic only in the orbit of woman, my son . . . Because beauty, the one, true, unique beauty is woman. The rest, all the rest, exists simply to adorn her.'

His other hand seized my other shoulder. He stared into

my eyes, searching for something. Our noses were almost touching, our breath mingled. I had never seen him like this, except perhaps on the day he came to tell Germaine that his nephew had become their son.

'If a woman loves you, Younes, if she truly loves you, and if you have the wisdom to appreciate this great privilege, then there is no god to touch you.'

Before going back upstairs to his study, standing with one hand on the banister, he said:

'Run after her . . . One day, man will surely be able to catch a comet, but all the glories of this world will not console the man who allows the *real* opportunity in his life to slip away.'

I did not listen.

Fabrice Scamaroni married Hélène Lefèvre in July 1951. It was a beautiful wedding; there were so many guests that the marriage took place in two acts: one for the village, the other for colleagues – a contingent of journalists including the editorial team of *L'Écho d'Oran* – artists, athletes and much of the cream of Oran society, among them the celebrated writer Emmanuel Roblès. Act One took place in Aïn Turck, on the vast beachfront estate owned by a rich friend of Madame Scamaroni. I felt ill at ease at the reception. Émilie was there on Simon's arm. Madame Cazenave was there, looking a little lost. Her partnership with Simon was thriving; their fashion house already dressed the richest ladies in Río Salado and Hamman Bouhadjar, and in spite of tough competition was becoming the leading fashion house among well-to-do women in Oran. During the crush at the buffet table, Simon stepped on my foot. He didn't apologise. He looked for Émilie in the crowd and headed straight for her. What had she told him? Why was my oldest friend suddenly behaving as though I did not exist?

I was too tired to ask him.

Act Two was for the people of the village; Río Salado was determined to celebrate the marriage of its favoured son in privacy. Pépé Rucillio donated fifty sheep and paid for the finest *méchoui* specialists to come from Sebdou. André's father, Jaime Jiménez Sosa, offered the newly-weds a vast swathe of his estate for the occasion, which was bounded by palm trees hung with drapes and silks and garlands. Plush benches were set out among the trees, tables groaned under the weight of food and flowers. In the centre, a huge marquee had been erected, lavishly decorated with rugs and cushions. The servants, mostly Arab boys and beautiful young black men, were dressed as eunuchs in embroidered waistcoats, billowing calf-length breeches and yellow turbans studded with jewels – it looked like a scene from the *Thousand and One Nights*. Here, too, I felt awkward. Émilie did not leave Simon's side for a moment, while Madame Cazenave watched me like a hawk as though afraid of some jealous tantrum. In the evening, a famous orchestra of Arabo-Judaic music from Constantine, the mythical hanging city, thrilled the assembled company. I was barely listening, sitting on a crate at the far end of the festivities. Jelloul brought me a plate of food and whispered in my ear that the look on my face would curdle all the happiness on earth. I knew I looked miserable; I knew that instead of sitting sulking, spoiling everyone else's enjoyment, I should go home. But I couldn't. Fabrice would have been offended, and I was determined not to lose him too.

With Jean-Christophe gone, Fabrice married and Simon being elusive since starting up in business with Madame Cazenave, my world felt emptier. I got up early, spent my day in the pharmacy, but as soon as I pulled down the shutters in the evening, I had no idea what to do. At first I went to André's diner and played pool with José and then headed home; later I stopped going out at night altogether. I would go up to my room, pick up a book and read the same chapter over and over without making any sense of it. I could not seem to concentrate, even when serving customers in the pharmacy. More than once I misread a doctor's scrawl and handed over the wrong medicine. Sometimes I would stand in front of the shelves for minutes at a time, unable to remember where something was. At dinner, Germaine would have to pinch me under the table to wake me up. I barely ate. My uncle felt sorry for me, but he said nothing.

Events seemed to gather pace, but since I was too tired to keep up, they began to leave me behind. Fabrice and Hélène had their first child – a beautiful chubby-cheeked little boy – and moved to Oran. Shortly afterwards, Fabrice's mother sold her house in Río Salado and moved to Aïn Ture. Whenever I walked past their derelict, boarded house, I felt a lump in my throat. A part of my life had disappeared, an island had vanished from my archipelago. I began to avoid the street, to go around the block, to pretend that part of the village had never existed. André married a cousin three years older than him and took off for the United States. They went there for a month, but the honeymoon was indefinitely extended. He left José to run the diner, though it no longer drew the crowds it once had now that the novelty of playing pool had palled.

I was bored.

I didn't like to go to the beach. Now that all my friends had gone, I no longer wanted to laze idly in the sun. The breaking waves snuffed out my dreams; there was no one there to share them with me. When I did go to the beach, as often as not I didn't even get out of my car. I would park on a clifftop and sit behind the steering wheel, staring out at the rocks and the waves breaking against them in soaring sprays. I could lose myself for hours, parked in the shade of a tree, with my hands on the wheel or my arms behind my head. The cries of the seagulls and the children whirled around me, distracting me from my worries, bringing a sort of peace that I clung to until darkness came and the last glow of a cigarette had flickered out.

I thought about moving back to Oran. I was miserable in Río Salado. I no longer seemed to recognise the place. I was living in a parallel world. I recognised familiar faces, but I was afraid that if I should reach out to touch them, there would be nothing but the wind. It was the end of an era; a page had been turned, and the new page before me was blank, frustrating, unpleasant to the touch. I needed to take stock. I needed a change of scenery, a new horizon. And – why not? – to sever the ties that no longer bound me to anything.

I felt rootless.

I thought about trying to trace my mother and sister. I still missed them terribly. Without them I felt helpless and heartbroken. From time to time I would go back to Jenane Jato in the hope of gleaning some piece of information that might lead me to them. But here, too, I had misjudged things. Jenane Jato was a world of survival and of festering discontent – no one had time to worry about a woman and her deaf-mute child. Every day, thousands of people poured into Jenane Jato. What had once been a shanty town in the scrubland was now a teeming neighbourhood of noisy streets, angry carters, watchful stallholders, crowded hammams, asphalt roads and smoky workshops. Peg-Leg was still there, surrounded now by competition. The barber no longer sat on a munitions crate to shave old men; he had a proper salon now, with a swivel chair and a brass cabinet for his tools. The courtyard house we had once lived in had been completely rebuilt, and Bliss, the broker, was in charge again. He wouldn't recognise my mother, he told me, since he had never spoken to her. No one knew where my mother and sister were; no one had seen them since the fire. I managed to track down Batoul, who had traded tarot cards and crystal balls for ledgers and accounting books. She was better at business than she had been at dealing with other people's misfortune, and her Turkish baths were always full. She had promised to let me know if she heard anything about my mother. It had been two years since I had spoken to her.

I thought that looking for my mother again might take my mind off the misery I had felt since Jean-Christophe left, the absence that gnawed at my heart whenever I thought about Émilie. I couldn't bear to go on living in the same village as her, seeing her in the street, walking past as though I felt nothing when in fact my days and nights were haunted by the thought of her. Now that she no longer came to see me at the pharmacy, I felt the terrible scope of my loneliness. I knew that the wound would not quickly heal, but I could think of no cure. Émilie would never forgive me; she felt terribly bitter, perhaps she even hated me. Her anger was so palpable it burned into my brain. She did not even have to look at me – in fact these days she never looked at me – since even when she turned away I could feel the blaze in her eyes, like underwater volcanoes that a million tons of water and the darkness of the deep could not extinguish.

I was sitting having breakfast in a little café on the seafront in Oran when someone knocked on the window. It was Simon Benyamin. He was wearing a thick winter coat, and when he pushed his hood back, I saw he was almost entirely bald now.

He was surprised and delighted to see me. He pulled open the door and came inside, trailing an icy blast of wind.

'Come on,' he said. 'I'll take you to a real restaurant, where the fish is as tender as a teenage girl's buttocks.'

I told him I'd almost finished. He frowned, then took off his coat and scarf and sat opposite me.

'So, what's good in this greasy spoon?'

He waved to the waiter and ordered lamb kebabs, a green salad and a half-bottle of red wine; then, rubbing his hands excitedly, he said:

'So, are you playing hard to get, or are you just sulking? I waved at you the other day in Lourmel and you completely ignored me.'

'In Lourmel?'

'Yeah, last Thursday. You were coming out of the dry cleaner's.'

'There's a dry cleaner's in Lourmel?'

I couldn't remember. For some time now I would simply

jump into my car and drive wherever it took me. Twice I had found myself in the bustle of the souk in Tlemcen without knowing how I had got there. I was suffering from a waking form of sleepwalking that took me to places I barely knew. Germaine would ask me where I had been and I could not remember.

'You've lost a lot of weight. What's wrong with you?'

'I don't know, Simon. I ask myself the same question . . . What about you, what's wrong with you?'

'I'm fine.'

'Then why do you look the other way when you see me in the street?'

'Me? Why would I look away when I see my best friend?'

'People are fickle. It's been more than a year since you dropped by my house.'

'That's just the business. It's growing so fast and the competition is vicious. I spend more time in Oran than I do in Río Salado. Surely you don't think I was ignoring you?'

I wiped my mouth. I was finding the conversation irritating. There were too many false notes. The Simon who was sitting across the table was not the Simon I knew — the life and soul of the party, my confidant, my ally. In his meteoric rise, he had left me far behind. Maybe I was jealous of his success, of the new car he parked on the village square so the local kids could crowd around and gawp, of his radiant health, the fact that he had lost weight. Maybe I resented his partnership with Madame Cazenave. But I knew it was none of these things. The fact was that I was the one who had changed. Jonas was fading and Younes was coming to the fore. I was becoming bitter and mean, a latent spitefulness, never articulated, that welled in me like heartburn. I could no longer stomach the parties, the weddings and the balls, the people on café terraces. Their good humour irritated me. And I had learned to hate . . . I hated Madame Cazenave, hated her with every fibre of my being. Hatred is corrosive; it eats away at the soul, lives inside your head, takes possession of you like a djinn. How had I come to loathe and despise a woman who no longer meant anything to me? When you can find no reason for your misery, you look for someone to blame. Madame Cazenave was my scapegoat. Hadn't she seduced and abandoned me? Wasn't it because of that fleeting mistake that she had made me swear to give up Émilie?

Émilie!

Just thinking of her, I felt myself wasting away.

The waiter brought a basket of bread and a salad of black olives and cornichons. Simon thanked him and asked if he could have his kebabs as soon as possible, as he had a meeting. After two or three mouthfuls, he leaned over the table and whispered, as though afraid someone would overhear:

'I'm sure you're wondering what I'm so excited about . . . If I tell you something, can you keep it a secret? You know what people are like . . .'

In the face of my indifference, his excitement faded. He frowned.

'There's something you're not telling me, Jonas, something serious.'

'It's just my uncle . . .'

'Are you sure you're not pissed off with me?'

'What makes you think I'm pissed off with you?'

'Well, here I am about to tell you a wonderful piece of news and you have a face that could stop a clock.'

'Go on, then, tell me, maybe it'll cheer me up.'

'Oh, it will! Madame Cazenave offered me her daughter's hand in marriage, and I accepted. But don't say anything, it's not official yet.'

I was speechless.

In the restaurant window, my reflection was still sitting impassively, but inside I was falling apart.

Simon was trembling with excitement – the same Simon who had called Émilie a 'preying mantis' and a 'pricktease'! I could no longer take in what he was saying; all I could see was the jubilation in his eyes, his smile, his nervous fingers tearing a piece of bread, crumpling his napkin, hesitating between knife and fork, his whole body quivering with happiness . . . He wolfed down the kebabs, drank his coffee, smoked a cigarette, talking all the while. Then he got to his feet, and saying something that I couldn't hear for the shrieking in my head, put on his coat and left, waving to me through the window before he disappeared.

I sat glued to my chair, my mind a blank. I did not come to myself until the waiter came to tell me the restaurant was closing.

Simon's plan did not remain a secret for long. In a few short weeks his secret machinations were common knowledge. In Río Salado, when he drove past, people waved and shouted 'You lucky devil!'; girls stopped Émilie in the street to congratulate her. Malicious gossips said that Madame Cazenave had sold her daughter out. Everyone else simply looked forward to the celebrations.

Autumn tiptoed away and the winter that followed was particularly harsh. Spring arrived, and with it the promise of a glorious summer. The hills and plains were cloaked in deep lush green. The Cazenaves and the Benyamins planned to celebrate their children's engagement in May and their wedding with the first grape harvests.

A few days before the engagement party, just as I was bringing down the shutters, Émilie showed up. She pushed me back inside the pharmacy. She had crept through the village wearing a peasant shawl, a nondescript grey dress and flat shoes so that no one would recognise her.

She was so upset, she did not call me Monsieur Jonas.

'I suppose you've heard. My mother forced my hand. She wants me to marry Simon. I don't know how she got me to say yes, but nothing is sealed. *Everything* depends on you, Younes.'

She was ashen. She had lost weight and her eyes had lost their power to command. She seized my wrists and, trembling, pulled me to her.

'Say yes,' she said, choking. 'Just say yes and I'll call it all off.'

Fear blighted her beauty, she looked as though she had just recovered from some terrible illness. Wisps of tangled hair spilled out of the scarf, her lips trembled and her anxious eyes glanced from me to the street. Her shoes were white with chalk dust, her dress smelled of the vines, her throat glistened with sweat. She had clearly gone around the village and cut through the fields to get here without arousing curiosity.

'Say it, Younes. Tell me you love me like I love you, that I mean as much to you as you do to me. Take me in your arms and hold me . . . You're my destiny, Younes, the life I want to live, the risk I want to take. I will follow you to the ends of the earth. I love you . . . Nothing and no one is more important to me. For the love of God, say yes . . .'

I said nothing. I stood dazed. Frozen. Speechless. Agonisingly silent.

'Say something, for God's sake, say anything. Say yes, say no, but don't just stand there! What's the matter with you? Have you lost your voice? Don't torment me like this, just say something.'

She became more heated; she could not stand still, and her eyes blazed.

'What am I supposed to think, Younes? What does this silence mean? That I'm a fool? You're a monster . . . a monster!'

She beat her fists against my chest, piteous and angry.

'There's not a grain of humanity in you, Younes. You are the worst thing that has ever happened to me.'

She slapped my face, pounded on my chest again, screamed at me to drown out her sobs, and still I stood there speechless. I felt ashamed at what I was putting her through, ashamed that all I could do was stand there, mute and lifeless and a scarecrow.

'I hate you, Younes. I'll never forgive you for this, never . . .'

And she fled.

The following morning, a little boy brought me a package. He didn't tell me who had sent it. I removed the paper, carefully. I knew instinctively what I would find. Inside was a book about the French islands of the Caribbean, and when

I opened the cover, I found the remains of a rose as old as time itself; the rose I had slipped between the pages of this very book a million years before, while Germaine was treating Émilie in the back office.

The evening of their engagement party I spent in Oran with Germaine's family. I told Simon that there had been a death in the family.

The wedding was planned for the start of the grape harvest. This time, Simon insisted, I was not to leave Río Salado under any circumstances. He asked Fabrice to keep an eye on me. I had no intention of absconding. It would be ridiculous. What would my friends and everyone else in the village think? How could I not attend the wedding without arousing suspicion? Or was it more honest to arouse suspicion? None of this was Simon's fault. Simon would have done anything for me, just as he would for Fabrice. How would it look if I ruined the happiest day of his life?

I bought a suit and a pair of dress shoes for the ceremony.

As the wedding party drove through the village in a thunderous roar of car horns, I put on the suit and walked out to the big white house on the marabout road. A neighbour offered to give me a lift, but I said no. I needed to walk, to synchronise my footsteps to the rhythm of my thoughts, to deal with them rationally one by one.

The sky was cloudy and a fresh breeze whipped my face. Outside the village, I walked past the Jewish cemetery, and coming to the marabout road, I stopped and stood at the crossroads, looking up at the festive lights at Madame Cazenave's house.

A light drizzle had begun to fall, as if to rouse me from my thoughts.

Only after something is done do we truly realise it cannot be undone. Never had a night seemed to me so ill-omened; never had a celebration seemed to me so unjust, so cruel. The music drifting on the breeze sounded like an incantation that conjured me like a demon. I felt excluded from the joy of these people as they laughed and danced. I thought about the terrible waste my life had become . . . How? How could I have come so close to happiness and not had the courage to seize it with both hands? What terrible sin had I committed that I was forced to watch love seep though my fingers like blood from a wound? What is love when all it can do is survey the damage? What are its myths and legends, its victories and its miracles if a lover is not prepared to rise above, to brave the thunderbolt, to renounce eternal happiness for one kiss, one embrace, one moment with his beloved? Regret coursed through my veins like a poisonous sap, swelled my heart with loathsome fury. I hated myself, this useless burden abandoned by the roadside.

I went home, drunk on grief, leaning against walls so as not to fall. My bedroom seemed unwilling to accept me. I slumped against the door, eyes closed, and listened as every fibre of my being clanged. I got up and trudged to the window as though it was not my bedroom but a desert I was crossing.

A lightning flash lit up the shadows. Rain was falling gently. The window panes themselves were weeping. Be careful, Younes, I thought, you're wallowing in self-pity. But what did that matter? This was what I saw: the windows crying.

I *wanted* to see tears streak the window panes, I wanted to feel sorry for myself, I wanted to dissolve body and soul into my grief.

Maybe it's for the best, I thought, Émilie was not meant for me. It's as simple as that. You cannot change what is written in the stars. Lies! Later, much later, I would come to this realisation: *nothing is written*. If it were, there would be no need for trials, morality would be an ageing hag and shame would not blush in the presence of virtue. Though there are things beyond our understanding, for the most part we are the architects of our own unhappiness. We fashion our faults with our own hands, and no one can boast that he is less to be pitied than his neighbour. As for what we call fate, it is nothing but our own dogged refusal to accept the consequences of our weaknesses, great and small.

Germaine found me slumped by the window, face pressed against the glass. For once, she did not disturb me. She tiptoed out of the room and soundlessly closed the door.

16

I THOUGHT about jumping on a train and getting as far away from Río Salado as possible. I thought of Algiers. Of Bougie. Of Timimoun. But I could not picture myself strolling down a boulevard, or sitting on a rock staring out to sea, or meditating in a cave. I could not run away from myself. Whatever train or plane or boat I took, I would end up trailing this unshakeable thing that filled me with its bile. But I knew I could not go on brooding in my room. I had to go away. It did not matter whether I went a thousand miles or simply to the next village, I needed to be somewhere else. It was impossible for me to live in Río Salado now that Simon had married Émilie.

I remembered a deranged evangelist who used to preach on market days in Jenane Jato. He was a tall man, thin as a rake, who wore a threadbare cassock. Every week he would stand on a rock, ranting and raving: 'Misery is a dead end that stops at a brick wall. If you want to escape it, you must back out carefully, never taking your eyes off the wall. That way it looks as though the wall is receding.'

I had gone back to Oran, to the neighbourhood where I had lived with my uncle. Perhaps I was trying to go back in time to my schooldays so that, older, wiser, I might return to the present, a virgin in mind and body, with a thousand opportunities open to me and the wisdom not to waste them. Seeing my uncle's old house did nothing to ease my pain. I did not recognise the place – it had been repainted green, the bougainvillea had been ripped out, leaving the low wall bare, the shutters on the windows were closed. There was no echo of my childhood here.

I knocked on the door of the house across the street, but it was not Lucette who opened it. 'She's moved,' a strange woman said to me. 'She didn't leave a forwarding address.'

I wandered around the city, listening to the dull roar from the football stadium, but it could not drown out the roar within me. In Medina J'dida – the ghetto where Arabs and Kabyles lived – I sat on a café terrace and watched the crowds on the Tahtaha square, convinced that I would eventually spot the ghost of my father in his green coat. Men in starched white *burnous* moved among beggars in rags and tatters. An ancient world was being rebuilt here of bazaars and hammams, silversmiths, cobblers and tailors. Down the centuries, Medina J'dida had never given up hope. It had survived cholera, it had survived scorn and contempt. It was Muslim, Arabic and Berber to its fingertips. Cut off behind the Moorish walls of the mosques, it rose above the insults and the slander, considered itself dignified and noble, proud of its craftsmen, of folk heroes like S'hab el Baroud and his Raqba – respectable criminals who charmed children and women of easy virtue and made the locals feel secure. How had I managed to live without this part of my birthright? I should have come here regularly to fill the gaps in my identity. Río Salado and I no longer spoke the same language;

how should I speak now? When I lived in Río Salado, had I been Jonas or Younes? Why, when my friends laughed, did I hesitate a moment before laughing with them? Why had I always felt that I had to carve out a place for myself among my friends? Why did I feel guilty whenever I met Jelloul's eyes? Had I simply been tolerated, integrated, biddable? What had stopped me from being myself, forced me to identify with the society I was growing up in and turn my back on my own people? I was a shadow, indecisive, easily led. I was constantly listening for some slight, some insult, the way an adopted child is more aware of his parents' momentary indifference than he is of their love. But even now, as I tried to redeem myself in the eyes of Medina J'dida, I suspected I was still deluding myself, absolving myself and looking for someone else to blame. If Émilie had slipped through my fingers, who was to blame – Río Salado, Madame Cazenave, Jean-Christophe, Simon? The fault, I knew, was mine; I had not had the courage of my convictions. I could find excuses for myself, but the blame would still be mine. Now that I had lost face, I was looking for a place to hide.

Tahtaha loosened the vice-like grip of my fears and failings, and my pain subsided as I wandered through the crowds, watching the tireless dance of the water-sellers, bells on their ankles, water skins slung across their chests, coloured hats whipping in the wind as they pirouetted in a whirl of frills and flounces, pouring cool water flavoured with oil of cade into copper goblets, which passers-by drank down like magical elixirs. I imagined myself slaking my thirst with the crowd, smiling as the water-seller performed a quick dance, frowning as someone ran off without paying, ruining his good humour . . .

'Are you sure you're all right?' The waiter roused me from my thoughts.

I wasn't sure of anything . . .

And why wouldn't people leave me in peace?

The waiter stared at me, puzzled, when I got up to leave, and it wasn't until I got back to the European part of the city that I realised I had left without paying.

In a smoky bar where discarded cigarette butts lay smouldering in the ashtray, I stared at the glass in front of me, which seemed to be mocking me. I wanted to drink myself senseless – I felt myself unworthy to resist temptation – but though I tried to pick the glass up a hundred times, my arm refused to bring it to my lips. 'Got a cigarette?' asked the woman sitting next to me. 'Pardon?' 'Guy with a handsome face like yours has no business being miserable.' Her breath stank of alcohol. I was exhausted. I could barely see clearly. She was so caked in make-up that she barely had a face. Her eyes were invisible behind grotesque false eyelashes, her large mouth was flaming red, her teeth stained from smoking. 'You got troubles, pretty boy? Well don't worry, I'm here to sort them out . . . The good Lord sent me to find you.' She slipped her arm through mine and, with a jerk, pulled me away from the bar. 'Come on . . . there's nothing for you here . . .'

For seven days and seven nights she kept me in a squalid little room on the top floor of a *fondouk* that stank of hashish and beer. I can't say whether she was blonde or brunette, young or old, fat or thin. I remember only her big lips and her voice, ruined by cigarettes and cheap booze. Then one night, she told me I'd had my money's worth and pushed me towards the door, kissing me on the mouth – 'That one's on the house.' Before I left she said, 'Get a grip on yourself.

There's only one god here on earth, and that's you. If you don't like the world, make one you like better. Fortune smiles on those who smile on her.'

Strange how sometimes we find the wisdom we lack in the most unlikely places. My life had been turned upside down, and it was a drunken whore who set me on my feet again with a few choice words in a sordid room in a dark, dingy hotel that reeled and swayed with the sound of sex and fighting. By the time I reached the door of the *fondouk*, I was feeling better and the evening breeze cleared my head completely. I walked from one end of the seafront to the other, looking out at the boats in the port, the cranes on the quays, and deep in the night, the trawlers moving over the silent waters like fireflies mirroring the stars. Then I went to a Turkish bath, where I scrubbed myself clean and slept the sleep of the just. The next morning at dawn, I caught the bus back to Río Salado, determined that if I caught myself wallowing in self-pity for even a moment, I would rip my heart out with my bare hands.

I went back to work in the pharmacy. I was a little different, but I tried to remain clear-headed. At times I lost my patience trying to decipher some doctor's scrawled prescription, or snapped at Germaine, who constantly fussed and worried over me, but then I would sigh, pull myself together and apologise. In the evenings, after we closed up, I would go out for a walk. I would go to the village square and watch Bruno, the young policeman, strutting about, twirling his police whistle round his finger. I liked his calm enthusiasm, the way he wore his kepi at a rakish angle, the exaggerated politeness he lavished on the pretty girls. I would sit on the terrace of a café, sipping my lemonade, and wait until it was dark before heading home. Sometimes I would lose myself, rambling through the orange groves. I was not lonely, but I missed having company. André had come back from America and business at the diner had picked up, but I was bored of playing pool, and José always beat me. Germaine thought about marrying me off. She invited a number of nieces to Río Salado in the hope that I might fall for one of them; I barely even noticed when they left.

I saw Simon from time to time; we would say hello or wave to each other. Sometimes we'd sit together for a few minutes in a café and make small talk. At first he ticked me off for 'skipping' his wedding like some boring class at school, but he forgave me. I suppose he had more important things to think about. He was living at Émilie's place, in the big house on the marabout road. Madame Cazenave had been insistent. Besides, there were no houses available in the village, and the Benyamins' family home was small and unattractive.

Fabrice had a second child and everyone got together to celebrate – everyone except Jean-Christophe, of whom we had had no news since his letter to Simon – in a beautiful villa on the cliff road outside Oran. It was here that André introduced us to his cousin, now his wife, a strapping Andalusian girl from Granada, tall and broad-shouldered with a powerful face and extraordinary green eyes. She was funny, but strict when it came to her husband's manners. It was during the celebrations that I noticed that Émilie, too, was expecting a child.

Some months later, Madame Cazenave went to French Guyana. The body of her husband, who had been prison governor at Saint-Laurent-du-Maroni and had disappeared in the jungle during a manhunt, had been discovered by smugglers and identified from his personal effects. She never returned to Río Salado, not even to celebrate the birth of her grandson, Michel.

In the summer of 1953, I met Jamila, the daughter of a Muslim lawyer my uncle had known since university. We met by accident in a restaurant in Nemours. Jamila was not particularly beautiful, but she reminded me of Lucette; I loved her serene face, the pale, delicate hands that cradled everything they touched – a napkin, a spoon, a bag, an apple – as delicately as though they were sacred relics. She had dark, intelligent eyes, a small round mouth and a seriousness that betrayed a strict but modern education that had prepared her for life and its challenges. Jamila was studying law, and hoped to be a barrister like her father. She wrote to me first, a few anodyne lines on the back of a postcard depicting the oasis at Bou Saada, where her father worked. It was some months before I wrote back. We exchanged letters and cards for many years, neither of us straying beyond polite formalities; both of us too shy and too reserved to make any declarations.

On the first spring morning in 1954, my uncle asked me to take the car out of the garage. He was wearing the green suit he had not put on since the dinner in honour of Messali Hadj in Oran thirteen years earlier, a white shirt with a bow tie, a gold fob watch in the pocket of his waistcoat, black dress shoes and a fez he had bought recently in an old Turkish shop in Tlemcen.

'I want to go and visit the grave of the patriarch,' he informed me.

Since I did not know where the tomb of the patriarch was, my uncle had to direct me through the villages and the hamlets. We drove all morning without stopping for lunch or even to rest. Germaine, who could not stand the smell of petrol, felt ill, and the road, twisting steeply up and down, almost finished her off. In the late afternoon we came to the summit of a rocky peak. Below, on the plains, a patchwork of olive groves struggled to maintain their lushness. Here and there the ground was cracked and eroded and the scrubland turned to desert. A few small reservoirs tried to keep up appearances, but it was clear that before long the drought would drain them dry. Several flocks of sheep grazed at the foot of the hills, as far from each other as the dusty hamlets. My uncle brought a hand up to shield his eyes and looked out towards the horizon. Apparently he could not see what he had come to find. He climbed a steep stony path to a copse, in the midst of which stood a crumbling ruin. It was the remains of a marabout, a shrine to a Muslim holy man, or a sepulchre from another age that harsh winters and sweltering summers had worn away to rubble. In the shade of a low wall, half-buried beneath a pile of stones, was a faded, broken headstone. This was the tomb of the patriarch. My uncle was heartbroken to find it in such a state. He picked up a beam, leaned it against the dirt wall and considered it sadly, then he reverently opened a worm-eaten door and stepped inside the crypt. Germaine and I waited in silence in the small courtyard overgrown with thick brambles. My uncle stayed in the tomb of the patriarch for a long time. Germaine went and sat on a rock and held her head in her hands. She had not said a word since we left Río Salado. When she was silent like this, I always feared the worst.

My uncle rejoined us just as the sun was setting. The shadow of the sepulchre was now long and misshapen, and a cool breeze began to whistle through the brambles.

'Let's go home,' he said, heading towards the car.

I waited for him to talk to me about the patriarch, about our clan, about Lalla Fatna, about what had suddenly brought him here to this rocky peak fashioned by the wind; he said nothing. He sat next to me and did not take his eyes off the road even for a moment. We drove late into the night. Germaine fell asleep on the back seat. My uncle did not complain; he was lost in his thoughts. We had not eaten since morning, but he did not seem to notice. Looking at him, I saw his face was pale, his cheeks sunken; the look in his eyes reminded me of the look he used to have before he slipped into the nether world that had been his prison and his refuge for many years.

'I'm worried about your uncle,' Germaine told me some weeks later. I too was worried, though my uncle showed no real signs of having relapsed. He continued to read and write, to eat with us, to go out every morning and stroll through the vineyards; but he no longer spoke to us. He would nod, sometimes he would smile at Germaine to thank her when she brought him tea or smoothed his jacket, but he did not utter a word. Sometimes he would sit in the rocking chair on the balcony, staring out at the hills, then, when it grew dark, he would go back to his room, put on his slippers, and lock himself in his study.

One night, he took to his bed and asked for me. His pallor was worse now and his hand, as he gripped my wrist, was cold, almost icy.

'I would have liked to have lived to see your children, Jonas. I know they would have gladdened my heart. I've never bounced a baby on my knee.'

His eyes glistened with tears.

'Take a wife, Younes. Only love can make good the misfortunes and the evils of this world. And remember this: if a woman loves you, no star is beyond your grasp, no god can touch you.'

I felt the cold coursing through him begin to flood through me with every shudder of his hand on my arm, seeping into my very being. My uncle went on talking to me for a long time; with every phrase he withdrew a little further from this world. He was slipping away. Germaine was weeping, slumped at the foot of the bed. Her sobs drowned out my uncle's words. It was a strange night, profound and yet unreal. Outside, a jackal howled as I had never heard a beast howl. My uncle's fingers, tight as a tourniquet, cut off the circulation to my fingers, leaving a purple bruise; my arm went numb. It was only when I saw Germaine cross herself and close her husband's eyes that I accepted that someone I loved had the right to depart this life like the sun at dusk, like a candle with a breath of wind, and that the pain we suffered at his passing was simply a part of life.

My uncle would not see his country take up arms. Destiny had judged him unworthy. How, otherwise, to explain the fact that he passed away five months before the long-awaited, oft-postponed firestorm erupted for independence? All Saints' Day 1954 caught us unawares. The café owner stood behind the counter, cursing, reading his newspaper. The war of independence had begun, but ordinary mortals, after a brief outburst of indignation quickly forgotten, were not about to lose sleep over the burning of a handful of farms in Mitidja. There were a number of deaths in Mostaganem: policemen surprised by armed assailants. So what? they said. More people die in road accidents. What they did not know was that this time war had truly begun and there was no possible way back. A handful of revolutionaries had decided to take action, to shake up a population stupefied by a hundred years of colonisation, sorely tested by the various uprisings by isolated tribes that the colonial army, mythic and omnipotent, invariably quickly crushed after a few skirmishes, a few punitive raids, a war of attrition lasting several years. Even the famous Organisation Secrète, which become famous in the 1940s, had simply been a source of entertainment for a handful of bellicose Muslims. Surely the attacks that took place at midnight precisely on 1 November 1954 all over northern Algeria would turn out to be a flash in the pan, a fleeting spark of discontent by disorganised natives incapable of rallying to a cause?

Not this time. The 'acts of vandalism' spread across the country, at first sporadically, then with increasing violence, and with terrifying audacity. The newspapers spoke of 'terrorists', of 'rebels', of 'outlaws'. There were skirmishes here and there, notably in the *djebels*, and sometimes soldiers killed in the fighting were relieved of their weapons and their ammunition. In Algiers, a police station was razed to the ground, policemen and civil servants were murdered on street corners, traitors had their throats cut. In Kabylia, there was talk of suspect groups, even groups in full battledress with old guns, laying ambushes for the police and then vanishing into the scrubland. In the Aurès mountains, there were rumours of colonels leading whole squadrons, of elusive guerrilla armies and no-go areas. Not far from Río Salado, in the Felaoucene district, men began to leave the villages in droves for the hills, where nightly they would set up underground units. Closer still, barely a few kilometres away, Aïn Témouchent posted news of rebel attacks in the town square. Everywhere graffiti appeared, always the same three letters: FLN – *Front de Libération Nationale* – a vast organisation. The FLN had its own laws, its own directives. It made calls for a general uprising, decreed curfews and embargoes. It had its own tribunals, an administrative wing, well-organised, labyrinthine networks, an army and a clandestine radio station that streamed into every house at night, when the shutters were closed . . .

In Río Salado, we were on another planet. News from elsewhere came to us tempered by an endless series of filters. True, there was a strange gleam now in the eyes of the Arabs working in the vineyards, but they still arrived at dawn and worked without let-up until sunset. In the cafés, people continued to gossip over a glass of *anisette*. Even Bruno, the policeman, did not think it necessary to take the safety catch off his gun; it was nothing, he said, a passing storm, everything would go back to the way it had been. It was several months before the 'rebellion' disturbed the tranquillity of Río Salado. Strangers burned an isolated farm; three times they burned vineyards and then blew up a wine cellar. This was too much. Jaime J. Sosa set up a private militia and set up a cordon around his vineyards. The police tried to reassure him, explaining that they were taking all necessary measures, but it was futile. By day, the farmers combed the area carrying their hunting rifles; by night, there were full military patrols complete with passwords and warning shots.

Apart from a few dead boars, shot by trigger-happy militiamen, not a single suspect was arrested.

In time, vigilance was relaxed and people once again began to walk the streets at night without fear.

The grape harvests were celebrated in traditional style. Three big orchestras were brought in to play at the ball, and Río Salado danced until it was exhausted. Pépé Rucillio made the most of the season to marry a singer from Nemours forty years his junior. At first his sons protested, but given that their father's fortune was incalculable, they went to the wedding, ate like pigs and dreamed of other banquets. It was during the wedding ceremony that I came face to face with Émilie. She was getting out of a car with her husband, cradling her child; I was coming out of the ballroom with Germaine on my arm. For a split second Émilie turned pale, but then she quickly turned to Simon and smiled and the two of them went in to join the festivities. I walked home, leaving my car parked next to my friend's.

Then tragedy struck.

No one was expecting it. The war was now in its second year, and with the exception of the early acts of sabotage, Río Salado remained untouched. People went about their business as though nothing had happened, until one morning in February 1956. There was an atmosphere of fear in the village, the people seemed petrified, literally overtaken by events: when I saw the mob around André's diner, I realised why.

The body was lying on the ground, half inside and half outside the bar. One of the shoes was missing; lost as the man tried to fend off his attackers, or tried to run away. There was a gash that ran from the man's heel to his calf . . . José had crawled some twenty metres before he died, as was obvious from the marks in the dust. His left hand was still clutching the door jamb. He had been stabbed over and over; his shirt had been ripped from top to bottom and there were a number of stab wounds visible on his bare back. He lay in a thick, dark pool of blood that dripped over the threshold of the diner. A shaft of sunlight lit up part of his face, and it was as though he had his ear pressed to the ground listening for something, the way, as kids, we'd pressed our ears to the railway track to see if a train was coming. His expression was like that of an opium addict; eyes wide but unseeing.

'He used to say he was dung the Lord had stepped in,' André said quietly. He was sitting slumped on the floor beside the bar, chin resting on his knees, hugging himself.

He was barely visible in the half-light.

He was crying.

'I wanted him to live the good life, like the rest of my cousins, but he would never take anything from me. He was afraid I'd think he was taking advantage.'

Simon was there, propped on the bar, his head in his hands. Bruno, the policeman, was sitting on a chair at the far end of the room, trying to recover from the shock. Two other men stood next to the pool table, dumbstruck.

'Why him?' André was overcome with grief. 'José would have given anyone the shirt off his back if they'd asked.'

'It's not fair,' I heard someone behind me say.

The mayor arrived and, seeing José's body, clapped his hand over his mouth to stifle a scream. Cars began to pull into the diner's car park. I heard doors slam. 'What happened?' someone asked. No one answered. In a few scant minutes, the whole village was there. José's body was covered with a blanket. Outside, a woman began to wail. It was José's mother. Her family stopped her from coming near the body. There was a stir when André stepped out of the diner. He was livid, his eyes flashing with fury.

'Where's Jelloul?' he roared, his whole body shaking with rage. 'Where's that idiot Jelloul?'

Jelloul made his way through the crowd and stood before André. He was dazed; he didn't know what to do with himself.

'What the fuck were you doing while José was being stabbed?'

Jelloul stared down at his shoes. André lifted the servant's head with the tip of his riding crop.

'Where the hell were you, you bastard? I told you not to leave the diner.'

'My father was sick.'

'Your father's always sick. Why didn't you tell me you were going back to your shack? José wouldn't have come to take over from you and he'd still be alive now. And how come this happens the one night you're not here?'

Jelloul bowed his head, and André forced it up again with his riding crop.

'Look at me when I'm talking to you . . . What cowardly bastard did this to José? You know who, don't you? You were in it together, weren't you? You went back to your shack so your accomplice could murder José; that way you'd have an alibi, you son of a bitch . . . Look at me, I said. Maybe it was you . . . You've been bitter and resentful for years, haven't you, you fucker? What are you looking at the ground for? José is there!' André screamed, pointing to the doorway. 'I'm sure it was you. José would never have let himself be caught unawares by a stranger. It had to be someone he trusted. Show me your hands.'

André checked Jelloul's hands, his clothes, looking for some trace of blood, and finding nothing, started to whip him with his crop.

'I suppose you think you're clever? You murder José, then go home and change and come back here. That's what happened, I'd stake my life on it. I know you.'

Enraged by his own words, blinded by grief, he knocked Jelloul to the ground and began laying into him. No one in the crowd lifted a finger. André's grief was too deep, it seemed, to be challenged. I went home, torn between anger and indignation, ashamed and degraded, pained by both José's death and Jelloul's suffering. That's how it's always been, I said to myself. When you can't find a remedy for your pain, you look for someone to blame, and there was no better scapegoat at the scene of the crime than Jelloul.

Jelloul was arrested, handcuffed and taken to the police station. There were rumours that he had confessed, that the murder had little to do with the upheavals festering all over the country. Even so, death had struck the village and no one could be sure that there might not be something to these ideas. The farmers redoubled their patrols, and from time to time, gunfire punctuated the howls of the jackals in the night. The following morning there would be talk of fending off suspected intruders, of undesirables taken out like vermin, of arson attempts foiled. One morning, heading towards Lourmel, I saw a crowd of excited farmers with guns by the roadside. Lying at their feet was the bloody body of a young Muslim dressed in rags, displayed like a hunting trophy. Next to him was a battered old gun, the damning evidence against him.

A few weeks later, a puny, sickly boy came to see me at the pharmacy. He asked me to go with him. A weeping woman was sitting on the pavement on the opposite side of the street, surrounded by a brood of children.

'That's Jelloul's mother,' the little boy told me.

She threw herself at my feet. I couldn't understand what she was trying to say; her words were drowned out by her sobbing, her frantic pleading panicked me. I led her into the back office of the pharmacy and tried to calm her down so that I could work out what she was saying. She was talking quickly, getting the sequence of events mixed up, every sentence trailing off into trancelike silence. Her cheeks were covered in scratches. She had clearly been clawing at her face in grief. Finally, exhausted, she accepted a glass of water and collapsed on to a bench. She told me of the problems her family had been having, her husband who had had both arms amputated, the prayers she had said at every marabout in the area, before throwing herself at my feet again and begging me to save Jelloul.

'He's innocent, everyone in the *douar* will tell you. Jelloul was with us the whole night the *roumi* was killed, I swear. I went to the mayor, to the police, to the *kaids*, but no one will listen. You're our last hope. Monsieur André is your friend, he'll listen to you. Jelloul is not a murderer. His father took a turn that night and I sent my nephew to fetch him. It's not fair. They're going to execute him for no reason at all.' The little boy was the nephew she had mentioned. He confirmed what she had said, that Jelloul had never raised a hand to José, that he was very fond of him.

I did not see what I could do, but I promised to talk to André. After they left, I lost my nerve and decided to do nothing. I knew that the decision of the court would be final and that André would not listen to me. Since José's death, he had been in a state of constant fury, beating the Arabs working in his fields for minor infractions. I spent a restless night, my sleep filled with nightmares so terrifying that more than once I had to turn on the lamp on my bedside table. The grief of this half-mad woman and her brood filled me with a petrifying unease. My head was filled with wailing and inchoate lamentations. The following morning, I did not have the energy to work in the pharmacy. I thought about what I should do and decided it was best to stay out of things. I couldn't imagine pleading Jelloul's case with André, who was almost unrecognisable he was so filled with hate and anger. He was quite capable of treating my intervention as a Muslim siding with a murderer from his own community. Hadn't he brushed me off when I tried to offer my condolences at José's funeral; hadn't he said that *all* Arabs were ungrateful cowards? Why would he say such a thing in the Christian cemetery where I was the only Muslim if not to hurt me?

Two days later, I was surprised to find myself pulling up outside Jaime Jiménez Sosa's farm. André was not at home. I asked to see his father. A servant told me to wait in my car while he went to find out whether the master was prepared to see me. He reappeared a moment later and led me to a hill overlooking the plains. Jaime Jiménez Sosa had just come back from a ride and was entrusting his horse to his groom. He stared at me for a moment, puzzled by my visit, and then, having slapped the horse's rump, he walked towards me.

'What can I do for you, Jonas?' he said brusquely as he approached. 'You don't drink wine and it's not grape-picking season.'

A servant rushed over to take his pith helmet and his riding crop; Jaime waved him away contemptuously, then walked straight past me without stopping to shake my hand.

I followed him.

'What's the problem, Jonas?'

'It's a bit complicated.'

'Then get to the point.'

'You're not exactly making it easy, rushing off like that.'

He slowed a little, then, pushing his helmet off his face, he looked at me.

'I'm listening . . .'

'It's about Jelloul.'

He flinched and clenched his jaw, and taking off his helmet, mopped his face with a handkerchief.

'You disappoint me, young man,' he said. 'You're not cut from the same cloth, and you're better off where you are.'

'There's been some misunderstanding.'

'Really? And what might that be?'

'Jelloul might be innocent.'

'Don't be ridiculous. I've been employing Arabs for generations, I know what they're like . . . Vipers, the lot of them. And that vermin confessed. He's been found guilty and I'll personally see to it that he goes to the guillotine.'

He came over to me, took me by the arm and suggested I walk with him a while.

'This is serious, Jonas. This isn't some hothead making speeches; this is war. The country is crumbling; this is no time to sit on the fence. We have to strike hard, we cannot tolerate any laxness. These crazy murderers need to know that we are not going to give in. Every bastard we get our hands on has to pay for the others.'

'His family came to see me—'

'Jonas, poor little Jonas.' He cut me off. 'You don't have the first idea what you're talking about. You are an honest, sincere, well-brought-up young man. You need to steer clear of these thugs. It will only confuse you.'

He was furious at my insistence and outraged at having to lower himself to speak about the fate of a manservant. He let go of my arm, forced a wry smile, put his handkerchief back in his pocket and nodded for me to follow him.

'Come with me, Jonas . . .'

He walked on ahead, grabbing a glass of orange juice held out to him by a servant who had appeared from nowhere. Jaime Jiménez Sosa was a stocky man, but he seemed to have grown several inches. A large sweat stain blossomed on his shirt as it billowed in the wind. Wearing jodhpurs, with his pith helmet slung around his neck, he looked as though with every step he was conquering the world.

When we got to the top of the hill, he stood, legs apart, his hand describing a large arc, holding his glass like a sceptre. Down below, vineyards stretched away across the plains as far as the eye could see. In the misty grey distance, the mountains seemed like sleeping prehistoric monsters. Jaime surveyed the landscape, nodding as he did so: a god contemplating his universe could not have been as inspiring.

'Look, Jonas . . . isn't it magnificent?'

His glass trembled in his hand.

'It is the most wonderful sight in the world.'

When I said nothing, he shook his head slowly and went back to surveying his vineyards, which stretched all the way to the horizon.

'Sometimes . . .' he said, 'sometimes when I come here to look at it, I think of the men who, long ago, did just as I am doing, and I wonder what they saw. I try to picture this landscape through the ages, to stand in the shoes of the Berber nomad, the Phoenician explorer, the Christian evangelist, the Roman centurion, the Vandal chief, the Muslim conqueror – all the men whom destiny brought this way and who stopped on the brow of this hill exactly where I'm standing now.'

He turned and glared at me.

'What did they see when they looked out here down through the centuries?' he asked me. 'I'll tell you. Nothing. There was nothing to see, nothing but a wilderness of rats and snakes and a few hills covered with weeds; maybe a pond that's dried up since, and a path leading nowhere . . .'

As he threw his arms wide to encompass the whole plain, drops of orange juice glittered in the air. He came back and stood next to me and went on:

'When my great-grandfather set his sight on this godforsaken hole, he believed he would go to his grave without ever making a profit from it. I've got photos back at the house. There wasn't a shack for miles, not a tree, not so much as a skeleton blanched by the sun. But my great-grandfather did not move on; he rolled up his sleeves, he made the tools he needed with his bare hands, and he hoed and weeded and tilled this land until his hands could barely hold his knife to cut bread. It was hard labour; he worked day and night, and the seasons were hellish. But my family did not give up, not once, not even for a second. Some died from exhaustion, others from disease, but not one of them had any doubts about what they were building here. And thanks to *my* family, Jonas, thanks to its sacrifices and its faith, this land was tamed. Generation after generation it was transformed into vineyards and orange groves. Every tree you see around you is a chapter in the history of my ancestors. Every orange you pick contains a drop of their sweat, every mouthful of juice the taste of their dedication.'

He gestured theatrically, his hand sweeping over the farm.

'That mansion I think of as my castle, the huge white house where I was born, where I played as a child, my father built it with his own hands like a monument to the glory of his ancestors. This country owes everything to us . . . We built the roads, we laid the railway lines that run to the edge of the Sahara, we threw bridges across the rivers, built towns and cities each more beautiful than the last and idyllic villages in the depths of the scrubland. From a thousand-year-old waste-land we built a great and thriving country; from barren rock we created the Garden of Eden . . . And now they expect us to believe that we did all this for nothing?'

His roar was such that I felt his spittle on my face.

His eyes grew dark and he waved his finger pompously beneath my nose.

'Well I don't believe it, Jonas. We didn't wear out our bodies and our hearts for a puff of smoke. This land knows its people, and *we* are that people, we have served it as few sons have served their mother. This land is generous because she knows we love her. The grapes she gives us, she drinks with us. Listen to her, and she will tell you that we have earned every plot of land we hold. We came here to a dead place and we breathed life into it. It is our blood, our sweat that feeds its rivers. No one, Monsieur Jonas, no one on this planet or any other can take from us the right to go on serving her until the end of time. Especially not the idle vermin who think that by shooting a few farmers they can cut the ground out from under us.'

The glass in his hand was shaking. He stared at me, his eye attempting to bore straight through me.

'These lands do not belong to them. If the land could

speak, she would curse these criminals just as I curse them whenever I see them burn down another farm. If they think they can frighten us, they are wasting their time and ours. We will never give up. We created Algeria, it is our finest creation, and we will not let some unclean hand despoil our crops, our harvests.'

From a dim corner of my memory where I had thought him buried came an image of Abdelkader, red with shame, standing at the front of my primary school class. I could picture him squirming in pain as the teacher twisted his ear, and hear Maurice's voice explode in my head: 'Because Arabs are lazy and shiftless, sir.' A wave of shock ran though my body like an underground explosion rippling through a castle moat. The same blind fury I had felt that day at school surged through me like a stream of lava coursing from deep in my belly. Suddenly I forgot why I had come, forgot the consequences for Jelloul, his mother's worry, and could see only Monsieur Sosa in all his arrogance, the repulsive glare of his overweening pride, which seemed to give a purulent tinge to the sunlight.

Unconsciously, unable to stop myself, I drew myself up to my full height and in a voice clear and sharp as the blade of a scimitar, I said:

'A long, long time ago, Monsieur Sosa, long before you and your great-grandfather, a man stood where you are standing now. When he looked out over the plains, he could feel at one with it. There were no roads, no railroad tracks and the mastic trees and the brambles did not bother him. Every river, dead or alive, every shadow, every pebble reflected the image of his own humility. This man was self-possessed, because he was free. He had nothing, nothing but a flute to calm his flock of goats and a club to ward off the jackals.

When he lay down in the shade of this tree here, he had only to close his eyes and he could hear himself live. The crust of bread and the slice of onion he ate tasted better than a thousand banquets. He was lucky enough to find abundance even in frugality. He lived to the rhythm of the seasons, believing that peace of mind lies in the simplicity of things. It is because he meant no ill to anyone that he felt safe from aggression until the day that, on the horizon he furnished with his dreams, he saw the approaching storm. They took away his flute and his club, took away his lands and his flock, took away everything that comforted his soul. And now they expect him to believe that he was here merely by accident; they are amazed and angry when he demands a little respect. Well, I disagree, monsieur. This land does not belong to you. It belongs to that ancient shepherd whose ghost is standing next to you, though you refuse to see it. Since you do not know how to share, take your vineyards and your bridges, your paved roads and your railway tracks, your cities and your gardens and give back what remains to its rightful owners.'

'You are an intelligent boy, Jonas,' he retorted, unmoved. 'You were brought up in the right place. Stay here. The *fellagas* do not know how to build; if they were given paradise they would reduce it to rubble. All they can bring to your people is misfortune and disappointment.'

'You should take a look at the villages around you, Monsieur Sosa. Misfortune holds sway here since *you* reduced free men to the rank of beasts of burden.'

With that, I left him standing there and walked back to my car, my head whistling like a desert wind.

17

JEAN-CHRISTOPHE showed up unexpectedly in the spring of 1957. It was Bruno the policeman who gave me the news as I came out of the post office.

'So, how was the reunion?'

'What reunion?'

'You mean you don't know? Chris is home, he got back two days ago . . .'

Two days ago? Jean-Christophe had been back in Río Salado for two days and no one had told me? I had seen Simon the night before; we had even talked a little. Why hadn't he told me?

Back at the pharmacy, I phoned Simon at his office, though it was only a stone's throw from the post office – I don't know why I decided to phone him rather than call and see him. Maybe I was afraid of making him feel embarrassed, or afraid of seeing in his eyes what I already suspected: that Jean-Christophe still bore a grudge against me and did not want to see me.

Simon's voice quavered on the other end of the line:

'I thought you knew.'

'Really?'

'I swear, I thought you knew.'

'Did he say anything to you?'

Simon cleared his throat. He was embarrassed.

'I don't follow you.'

'It's okay, I understand.'

I hung up.

Germaine, who had just come back from the market, set her basket down on the floor and gave me a lopsided look.

'Who was that on the phone?'

'Just some customer complaining,' I reassured her.

She picked up her basket and went upstairs to the apartment. When she got to the landing, she stopped for a second, then came down a few steps and looked at me.

'Is there something you're not telling me?'

'No.'

'You would say that, wouldn't you . . . Oh, by the way, I've invited Bernadette to come down for the end-of-season ball. I hope you're not going to let her down too. She's a fine girl; she might not look it, but she's clever. Not educated, I'll grant you, but you won't find a better match than her. And she's pretty, too . . .'

I had met Bernadette when she was a little girl, at the funeral of her father, who had been killed in the attack on the naval base at Mers-el-Kébir in 1940 – a skinny child who'd stood a little apart while her cousins played with a hoop.

'You know perfectly well that I don't go to balls any more.'

'Precisely . . .'

And she went upstairs.

Simon called me back, having had time to think.

'What did you mean, you understand, Jonas?'

'I find it strange that you didn't tell me that Chris was back. I thought we were still friends.'

'Nothing about our friendship has changed; I'm still as fond of you as ever. I know my job hasn't left me much time off, but you're always in my thoughts. You're the one who's been distant. You've never come to visit us at the new house, not once. Every time we run into each other in the street, you're always in a hurry to get off somewhere. I don't know what's got into you, but it's not me who's changed. And I swear I thought you knew Chris was back. Actually, I haven't seen much of him, I left him to his family. If it makes you feel any better, I haven't even phoned Fabrice to tell him the good news. I'll do it now. The four of us can get together, just like the good old days. I know a great bistro in Aïn Truck. What do you say?'

I knew he was lying. He was talking too quickly, as though rattling off something he'd learned by heart, but I gave him the benefit of the doubt. He promised to pick me up after work so we could go to Jean-Christophe's house together.

I waited, but he didn't come. I closed up the shop and waited a little longer. When it got dark, I sat out on the steps of the shop, watching shadows moving in the streets, trying to pick out Simon's. He didn't come. I decided to go to Jean-Christophe's house on my own . . . Which was a mistake. Simon's car was parked outside the front door, beneath an avalanche of mimosa; next to it was André's car and the mayor's car and the grocer's car for all I knew. I was furious. Something told me to turn around and go home, but I didn't listen. I rang the doorbell. Somewhere a shutter creaked then slammed shut. It was a long time before someone opened the door. A woman I didn't know, probably a visiting relative, asked what I wanted.

'I'm Jonas, I'm a friend of Chris.'

'I'm sorry, he's asleep.'

I felt like barging past her, storming straight into the living room where everyone was holding their breath and surprising Jean-Christophe there with his friends and relatives. But I did nothing. There was nothing to be done. Everything was crystal clear. I nodded, took a step back, waited for the woman to close the door, then drove home. Germaine did not ask me where I'd been; it was kind of her.

The following day, Simon showed up looking tight-lipped.

'I swear I don't understand what's going on,' he stammered.

'There's nothing to understand. He doesn't want to see me, that's all. And you've known that from the beginning. That's why you didn't say anything when I ran into you two days ago.'

'Okay. You're right, I did know. In fact it was the first thing he said to me, that I wasn't allowed to mention your name. He actually insisted I tell you that he didn't want you to come by and see him. I refused, obviously.'

He lifted the hatch and came behind the counter, wringing his hands. His forehead was slick with sweat; his receding hairline glistened in the light.

'Don't hate him. He's had it rough. He fought on the front line in Indochina. He was captured and wounded twice. He was demobbed when he got out of hospital. You have to give him some time.'

'It doesn't matter, Simon.'

'I was going to come by and pick you up yesterday, like I promised.'

'I waited . . .'

'I know. I went round to see Jean-Christophe first, to try to persuade him to see you. I could hardly just bring you round; he would have been furious, and that would just have made matters worse.'

'You're right, there's no point forcing his hand.'

'That's not what I mean. He's unpredictable. He's not the same. Even with me. When I invited him round to meet Émilie and the kid, he flew into a rage. *Never!* he screamed at me. *Never!* You'd think I'd suggested taking him to hell. I don't understand. Maybe it's because of what he went through in the war. Sometimes I look at him and it's like he's a little crazy. If you saw his eyes – empty as the twin barrels of a rifle. I pity him. Don't hate him, Jonas. We have to be patient.'

When I did not reply, he tried another tack:

'I called Fabrice. Hélène told me he's in Algiers on account of what's happening in the Casbah. She doesn't know when he'll be back. Maybe by the time he gets home, Chris will have come round.'

Resentment prickled in me, insistent and biting, and I lashed out.

'You were *all* there last night.'

'Yes,' he admitted with a tired smile.

He leaned towards me, watching every twitch of my face.

'What happened between the two of you?'

'I don't know.'

'Come on, you can't expect me to believe that. You had something to do with him leaving in the first place, didn't you? It was because of you that he signed up and allowed himself to be torn to pieces by those slitty-eyed bastards. What the hell happened? I didn't sleep a wink for thinking about it. I thought of every possible scenario, but it doesn't make sense.'

'You're right, Simon. Let's give it time – time can't keep a secret, it's bound to tell us some day.'

'Is it something to do with Isabelle?'

'Simon, please, just drop it.'

That weekend I saw Jean-Christophe, from afar. I was coming out of the shoemaker's and he was coming out of the town hall. He was so thin he looked six inches taller. His hair was shaved, with a single blonde lock that fell over his forehead. He wore a thick coat in spite of the weather and limped slightly, leaning on a walking stick. Isabelle was with him, holding his arm. I had never seen her so beautiful, so down-to-earth. Her humility was almost admirable. They were walking slowly and chatting. It was Isabelle who did the talking; Jean-Christophe just nodded from time to time. They seemed to glow with a sort of serene happiness, some-thing ageless and enduring. I could not help but feel a pang of affection for them, this couple who could grow and mellow in silence and in questioning, made stronger by the tribulations they had come through together. I felt my heart go out to them, like a prayer that their reunion might last for ever. Perhaps because seeing them reminded me of my uncle and Germaine strolling through the orange groves. Seeing them together again, it was as though nothing had ever happened. I realised that I could not but go on being fond of one and loving the other. And yet I felt overwhelmed by a grief as terrible as I had felt when my uncle had died.

I felt tears prick my eyes, and I cursed Jean-Christophe for moving on with his life and leaving me stranded on the platform. I felt as though he had dismissed me on the basis of one snap judgement. I wasn't sure I wanted him to forgive me. Forgive me for what? What had I done? I felt I had more than paid for my loyalty; that my misdeed had hurt me first and foremost, hurt me much more than it had hurt others. It was strange. I was love and hate tied up in a single package, imprisoned in a straitjacket. I felt myself slipping towards something I could not quite define that was pulling me in all directions, distorting my perceptions, my thoughts, the very fibres of my being, like a werewolf transforming in all his monstrosity under cover of darkness. I was consumed by an inner fury that was insidious, corrosive. I was jealous when I saw others find their place in the world even as mine was crumbling around me. I was jealous when I saw Simon and Émilie walking together on the avenue, their little boy running on ahead; jealous of the intimacy they shared, an intimacy that excluded me; jealous of the aura that surrounded Jean-Christophe and Isabelle; jealous of every couple I met in Río Salado, in Lourmel, in Oran, of the couples I stumbled on by accident, as I roamed restlessly like the god of a shattered universe who realises that he does not have the energy to re-create a new one. I found myself spending the empty days wandering through the Muslim neighbourhoods of Oran, sitting at tables with people I didn't know, whose very presence deepened my loneliness. I found myself back in Medina J'dida, drinking water flavoured with oil of cade, getting to know an ageing Mozabite bookseller in a baggy *sarouel,* learning from a young imam of staggering erudition, listening to the ragged shoeshine boys – the *yaouleds* – talking about the war that was ripping Algeria apart. They knew much more about it than did I, the educated, intelligent pharmacist. I began to memorise names hitherto unknown to me, names that sounded in my mouth like the call of the muezzin: Ben M'hidi, Zabana, Boudiaf, Abane Ramdane, Hamou Boutlilis, the Soummam, the Ouarsenis, Djebel Llouh, Ali la Pointe, the names of places and of heroes of a populist movement that I had never for a moment suspected was so sincere, so committed.

Was I trying to compensate for the defection of my friends . . . ?

I went to Fabrice's house up on the cliff road. He seemed happy to see me, but I could not bear Hélène's aloofness. I never set foot in their house again. Whenever I ran into him, we would go to a café or a restaurant, but I politely declined any invitations to their house. I had no intention of putting up with his wife's snobbishness. I once said as much to him. 'You're imagining things, Jonas,' Fabrice said, piqued. 'What made you think Hélène doesn't like you? She's a city girl, that's all, she's not like the girls round here. Oh, I admit she's got some strange ideas, but that's just the city in her . . .' Even so, I did not go back to their house. I preferred to lose myself in the old quarters of Oran, in La Calère, around the Pasha Mosque and especially the Bey's Palace, watching the boys squabbling at Raz-el-Ain. After a life of crippling shyness, I suddenly found myself shouting at referees at football matches, buying black-market tickets to bullfights to watch Luis Miguel Dominquin deal the death blow to a bull at Eckmühl arena. Suddenly I liked nothing better than the roar of the crowd; it kept me from brooding over things

I did not want to think about. I became a keen fan of USMO, the Muslim football team. I went to boxing matches, and when a young Muslim boxer floored his opponent, I felt within myself a murderous rage I had never suspected. Their names were as intoxicating as a whiff of opium: Goudihb, Khalfi, Cherraka, the Sabbane brothers, Abdeslam, the extraordinary Moroccan. I barely recognised myself. Like a moth to a candle flame I was drawn to violence and to crowds. There could be no doubt: I was at war with myself.

Jean-Christophe married Isabelle at the end of the year. I found out the day after the wedding. No one had deigned to mention it to me, not even Simon, who – to his annoyance – had not been invited. Nor Fabrice, who had gone home at dawn so as not to have to apologise for I don't know what. All this simply served to push me even further away from their world. It was appalling.

Jean-Christophe decided they should settle somewhere far from Río Salado. The village was not enough to satisfy his desire to make up for lost time; to atone for certain memories. Pépé Rucillio gave them a beautiful house in one of the most fashionable areas of Oran. I was on the village square when the newly-weds left. André drove them to the city in his car, with a huge truck filled with furniture and wedding gifts following behind. Even today, though I am an old man now, I can still hear the horns blaring as the car moved off; still feel the pain I felt that day. And yet, strangely, I was relieved to see them go; it was as though some major artery in my body, long blocked, was suddenly clear again.

People were leaving Río Salado in droves. I felt like a

castaway adrift on an empty ocean. The streets, the vine-yards and the orange groves, the gossip in the cafés, the farmers' jokes, none of it meant anything to me now. Every morning I woke up eager for night to come so that I could retreat from the chaos of the day; every night I went to bed dreading the fact that I would wake again to this terrible emptiness. I began to leave Germaine to run the pharmacy and spent my time in the brothels of Oran. I never touched the prostitutes; I just listened to them recount their turbu-lent lives and pour scorn on their shattered dreams. I was comforted by their contempt for illusion. To tell the truth, I was looking for Hadda. Suddenly, for some reason, she mattered to me. I wanted to find her again, to find out if she still remembered me, to see if she knew anything that might help me find my mother. But even in this, I was lying to myself: Hadda had left Jenane Jato before the fire that had destroyed our old house. She could not possibly help me find my mother. But that was what I had planned to say to her to win her sympathy. I needed a friend, a confidant, someone I had known long ago, anyone who could offer me a feeling of closeness now that my friends in Río Salado had vanished.

The madame who ran the Camélia told me that Hadda had gone off with a pimp one night and never come back. I managed to track down the pimp – a hulking thug with hairy arms covered with tattoos of pierced hearts and pro-fanities. He warned me not to get involved unless I wanted to end up in the obituary column of the local paper. That same day, stepping off a tram, I thought I saw my childhood friend Lucette walking with a baby in a pram – a chubby young woman in a trouser suit and a white canvas hat. But it could not have been Lucette – she would have seen my smile, recognised something in the blue of my eyes. In spite of her eloquent indifference, I followed this woman along the boulevard, then, realising that what I was doing was somehow indecent, I turned back.

It was then that I came face to face with war . . . with the terrible reality of war, the succubus of Death, the fertile concubine of Disaster, this truth I had not wanted to face. I had read the newspaper reports of bombings in towns and villages, of police raids on *douars* suspected of harbouring FLN supporters, of the thousands of people displaced, the deadly clashes, the manhunts, the massacres, but to me it had been like a fiction that never seemed to end. Then, one day, as I was sitting on the seafront sipping an orange juice, a large black car pulled up, machine guns bristling from the windows. The gunfire lasted only a few seconds before it was drowned out by the squeal of tyres, but the shots kept ringing in my head for a long time. Bodies lay sprawled on the pavement opposite, while onlookers ran for safety. The silence was so total that the cries of the seagulls drilled into my temples. It was like I was dreaming. I stared at the broken bodies and I started to tremble. My hand juddered like a shutter in the wind, splashing me with orange juice; the glass fell and shattered at my feet and someone at the next table screamed. People stumbled from shops and offices, from their cars, shocked and dazed. A woman fainted in her friend's arms. I didn't dare to move. I sat, open-mouthed, heart hammering in my chest, frozen in my chair. The police arrived in a blast of whistles. Soon, a crowd had gathered around the victims: three people were dead – among them a young girl – and five more gravely wounded.

I went back to Río Salado, locked myself in my room and did not come out for two days.

For months, I couldn't sleep. From the moment I got into bed, I felt a terrible dread pulling me under, it was like tumbling into an abyss. I dared not let myself fall asleep: my dreams were grotesque and bloody nightmares. When I could no longer bear to stare at the ceiling, I sat up, put my head in my hands and stared at the floor. My feet left bloody prints, gunshots ricocheted through my head – it was useless to stop my ears, because I could still hear them, deadly, deafening, my body jolting with each shot. I left my bedside light on until morning to try to keep these ghosts at bay. The slightest rustle, the smallest sound, every creak of the woodwork, seemed loud enough to split my skull.

'You're in shock,' the doctor told me. This was some-thing I already knew. What I needed to know was how to get over it, but he had no magic cure to offer. He prescribed tranquillisers and sleeping pills, but they did not help. I was depressed. I knew I was lost, but I had no idea how to find myself again. It was as though I was a different person, an infuriating, disappointing yet indispensable person whose body was my only home.

I constantly felt claustrophobic and would go out and stand on the balcony. Sometimes Germaine would come and keep me company. She tried to talk to me but I didn't listen. Listening to her exhausted me and aggravated my anxiety. I needed to be alone. So I went out – night after night, week after week. The silence in the village did me good. I liked to stroll through the deserted square, wander up and down the main street, sit on a bench and think about nothing.

One moonless night as I stood thinking on the pavement, I saw a bicycle lamp weaving in the distance, the rattle of the bicycle chain echoing from the walls in a thousand high-pitched whimpers. It was Madame Cazenave's gardener. When he saw me, he braked hard, almost sending himself over the handlebars. Pale and dishevelled, he kept pointing back the way he had come, unable to speak. Then he climbed back on to his bike and, in his hurry to ride off, hit the kerb and fell backwards.

'What is it?' I asked. 'You look like you've seen a ghost.'

Shaking, he got to his feet, climbed back on his bicycle and managed to stammer:

'I'm going to the police . . . something terrible has happened at the Cazenave house.'

It was then that I noticed the huge reddish glow behind the Jewish cemetery. 'Oh my God,' I screamed, and started to run.

The house was on fire, great flames lighting up the surrounding orchards. I cut through the cemetery, and as I came closer to the house, I realised the scale of the catastrophe. Fire was raging though the ground floor and was already threatening the first floor. Simon's car stood burning in the driveway, but I could see no sign of him or of Émilie. The gates were open. The climbing vine on the trellis crackled and blazed. I had to shield my face to breach the wall of fire and get to the fountain. In the courtyard, two dogs lay dead. It was impossible to reach the house, which was now an inferno. Flames licked the walls, shooting out like tentacles. I tried to call to Simon, but no sound came from my parched throat. A woman sat huddled under a tree. It was the gardener's wife. Hands clapped to her face, she stared trancelike at the house as it burned.

'Where's Simon?'

She turned and pointed up the hill to the old stables. I plunged into the blaze, deafened by the crack of burning wood and shattering windows. The hill was cloaked in thick, acrid smoke; the old stables were shrouded in a silence even more terrifying than the cataclysm behind me. In the distance I saw a body lying face down on the grass, arms crossed, illuminated by the distant flickering flames. My knees locked. I realised I was utterly alone, and I did not feel I could face this thing without someone to help me. I waited, hoping the gardener's wife would follow me, but she did not move. I could hear only the roar of the fire, see only the body lying before me. Motionless and naked but for a pair of underpants, it lay in a pool of blood so black it looked like pitch. I recognised the bald head: it was Simon! This surely was some nightmare; I was at home, asleep . . . But a graze on my arm throbbed, reminding me that I was awake. The body gleamed in the glow of the fire. The face looked as though it had been carved from a block of chalk; there was no light in the eyes. Simon was dead.

I crouched down next to the body of my friend. I was in a daze. I no longer knew what I was doing, what I was thinking. Automatically, I reached out to the body as if to wake him.

'Don't touch him!' a voice screamed out of the darkness.

Émilie was crouched by a corner of the stable. Her face was so pale it seemed luminous. Her eyes burned with a fire as vast as the flames behind me. Her hair spilled down her back. She was barefoot and wearing only a silk night-dress, which somehow made her seem more naked. Her son Michel huddled against her.

'I forbid you to touch him,' she shouted in an unearthly voice.

A man appeared behind her holding a rifle: it was Krimo, Simon's chauffeur. Krimo was an Arab from Oran who had worked in a restaurant on the corniche until Simon hired him just before he got married. He stepped away from the wall and moved cautiously towards me.

'I've already shot one of them,' he yelled.

'Who did this?'

'*Fellagas*. They slit Simon's throat and torched the place. By the time I got here, they'd gone – I saw them running through the valley and I fired. The cowards didn't even fire back, but I heard one of them scream.'

He stood in front of me, the glow from the flames accentuating the contempt on his face.

'Why Simon?' he asked me. 'What did he ever do to them?'

'Go away,' Émilie screamed. 'Go away and leave us in peace. Make him go away, Krimo!'

'You heard her.' Krimo raised his rifle. 'Fuck off out of here.'

I nodded and turned away. It felt as though my feet did not touch the ground, as though I were gliding through a void. I went back past the burning house, cut through the orange groves and headed back to the village. Headlights swept around the cemetery and headed up the marabout road. Behind the cars, I could see the shadows of people running. Their breathless voices came to me in snatches, but their shouting was drowned out by Émilie's words, a maelstrom that was swallowing me up.

Simon was buried in the Jewish cemetery. The whole village was in attendance, crowded around Émilie and her son. Émilie wore black and her face was hidden by a veil. She was determined to be dignified in her grief. She was flanked on either side by members of the Benyamin family from Río Salado and elsewhere. Simon's mother sat on a chair, devastated, weeping, deaf to the whispers of her husband, an ageing, sickly man. Some rows back, Fabrice and his wife stood holding hands. Jean-Christophe was with the Rucillio clan, with Isabelle invisible in his shadow. I stood at the far end of the cemetery, behind everyone, as though I had already been banished.

After the ceremony was over, the crowd silently dispersed. Krimo helped Émilie and her son into a small car that the mayor had lent. The Rucillio family left. Jean-Christophe exchanged a brief word with Fabrice, then rushed off to join the rest of the family. Car doors slammed, engines droned, the cemetery slowly emptied. Only a group of militiamen and a few policemen remained around the grave, clearly devastated that they had let the tragedy occur. From a distance, Fabrice gave me a little wave. I had thought he might come over and comfort me; but he helped his wife into their car and without turning back, climbed in and drove off. When the car disappeared behind the cemetery wall, I realised that I was alone among the dead.

Émilie left Río Salado for Oran, but she never left my thoughts. I felt sad for her. Since no one had heard anything from Madame Cazenave, I could only guess at the depths of Émilie's loneliness, of her grief. What would become of her? How would she start again in a city like Oran, surrounded by thousands of people she didn't know? In the city, she would not find the compassion and the sympathy she had known in the village. There, relationships were based on self-interest, and a newcomer had to negotiate difficult hurdles in order to be accepted. Especially while a war was raging, one that grew more bitter with every passing day. The streets of Oran were dangerous; there were attacks, violent reprisals and kidnappings; every morning the citizens awoke to some fresh horror. I could not imagine how she would survive in the madness of that city, that war zone drenched in blood and tears, with a son to provide for, far from everything she knew.

In the village, everything had changed. The end-of-season ball was cancelled for fear that a bomb might turn the event into a tragedy. Muslims were no longer tolerated in the streets. They no longer had the right to leave the fields and the vineyards without permission. The day after Simon's murder, the army launched a wide-ranging manhunt, combing Dhar el Menjel and the surrounding scrubland. Helicopters and planes shelled any suspect village. After four days and three nights, the soldiers returned to their barracks exhausted and empty-handed. Jaime Jiménez Sosa's militia set up ambushes throughout the area, a tactic that eventually paid off. In their first ambush, they intercepted a group of *fidayin* on a supply mission for the rebels. They slaughtered the mules on the spot, burned the provisions, then drove the bullet-riddled bodies of the *fidayin* through the streets of Río Salado on a cart. Krimo enlisted with the *harkis*

– the Algerian soldiers loyal to the French – came upon eleven rebels hiding out in a cave, lit a fire and asphyxiated them with the smoke. Emboldened by his feat, he later lured a whole squad of *mujahideen* into an ambush in which he killed seven and dragged two, badly wounded, back to the village square, where the crowd all but lynched them.

I did not dare go out any more.

There followed a period of calm.

I thought of Émilie constantly. I missed her. Sometimes I would imagine she was there with me and talk to her for hours. Not knowing where she was, what had become of her, tormented me. When I could bear it no longer, I went to see Krimo to ask if he could help me find her. He gave me a chilly reception. He was sitting in a rocking chair outside his shack, an ammunition belt strung across one shoulder, his rifle between his legs.

'Vulture!' he said. 'She hasn't even grieved for her husband and you're already thinking about how to win her round.'

'I have to talk to her.'

'About what? She was pretty clear the other night. She doesn't want anything to do with you.'

'This is none of your business.'

'Oh, but that's where you're wrong. Émilie is my business, and if you ever try to contact her, I'll rip your throat out with my teeth.'

'What did she tell you about me?'

'She didn't need to tell me anything. I was there when she told you to go to hell, and that's enough for me.'

I had no hope of getting any information from the man.

For months I wandered the districts of Oran hoping to

run into Émilie. I haunted the schools when class let out, but saw no sign of Michel or his mother among the parents. I hung around the stalls and the supermarkets, the gardens and the souk, but there was no sign of her.

A year to the day after Simon's murder, when I was finally about to give up, I saw her. She was working in a bookshop. I could barely breathe. I went to the café across the road, took a table half hidden by a pillar and waited. At closing time, she left the bookshop and caught a tram from the stop at the end of the street. I didn't dare get on the tram with her. I had seen her on a Saturday, so the whole of Sunday I was forced to kill time. Early on Monday morning, I went back to the café opposite the bookshop and sat at the same table. At nine a.m. Émilie arrived wearing a black trouser suit, her head covered with a scarf. My heart shrivelled in my chest like a sponge being wrung out. A thousand times I took my courage in both hands and set off to cross the road, but every time, the very thought of speaking to her seemed somehow indecent.

I don't know how many times I walked past the bookshop and watched her serve a customer, climb a stepladder to get a book, ring something up on the till, rearrange the shelves, and still I did not dare push the door open. The simple fact that she was alive, that she seemed well, filled me with a vague but tangible joy. I was happy just to watch her live her life. I was afraid that if I came too close, she might disappear like a mirage. This went on for over a month. I spent little time at the pharmacy, leaving Germaine to cope as best she could. Often I would forget to phone to tell her I would not be home. I slept in a dingy *fondouk* so that I could be there, every day, watching Émilie from the café.

One evening, as the bookshop was about to close, I ventured from my hiding place, and, like a sleepwalker, crossed the road and found myself stepping through the door of the shop.

There were no customers, and the bookshop was almost in darkness. A fragile silence hovered over the shelves. My heart was beating fit to burst and I was sweating. The unlit lamp above my head was like a sword that might fall at any moment. I was seized by doubt: what was I doing here? Why was I determined to reopen old wounds? I gritted my teeth: I had to do this, I could not go on constantly brooding over the same questions, the same fears. A cold sweat clawed at my back like nails. I took a deep breath to try to expel the poison I could feel inside. Outside on the street, cars and pedestrians moved in a strange and intricate dance. The blare of car horns slashed at me like steel blades. I waited. Inside me, I heard a voice say: leave . . . I shook my head and the voice was still. Darkness unfurled, filling the shop, delicately silhouetting the towering piles of books . . .

'Can I help you, monsieur?'

She was behind me. Fragile, ghostly, she had appeared out of the half-light just as she had on the night of the fire. A night she still wore about her, her black dress, black hair, black eyes bearing mute witness to a grief a year had done nothing to diminish. In the darkness, I had to peer to make her out. She was standing three feet away and I saw that she had changed, that her beauty had withered. She was a shadow of the woman she had been, a heartbroken widow who paid no attention to her appearance. Life had taken from her more than it could ever repay. I immediately realised my mistake. I was not welcome here. I was a knife in a wound. Her icy aloofness bewildered me and made me realise just how wrong I had been to think I could come here and make right something that I myself had shattered. And then there had been the word *monsieur*, peremptory, disarming, unendurable, hurling me into an abyss, wiping me from the face of the earth. I truly believed that she had survived that tragedy only so that she might hate me. She did not need to say it; I could read it in the blank, expressionless eyes, which repelled me, dared me to try to hold her gaze.

'What do you want?'

'Me?' I said stupidly.

'Who else? You came by last week and the week before and almost every day in between. What are you playing at?'

I felt my throat tighten. I couldn't swallow.

'I was just passing . . . I thought I saw you through the window . . . I wasn't sure . . . I wanted to say hello . . . to talk to you . . . but I didn't dare . . .'

'Have you ever dared, Younes? Even once in your life?'

She realised she had hurt me. Something stirred in those dark eyes filled with night. Something like a shooting star that flickered out as soon as it appeared.

'So you found your tongue. All the time I've known you, you've had nothing to say. What did you want to talk to me about?'

Only her lips moved; her face, her pale, slender hands, her body remained motionless. Nor were they really words, just a rush of breath, like a spell, like a curse . . .

'Maybe I've come at a bad time.'

'I hope there'll never be another time. I want this over with. What did you want to talk to me about?'

'About us.' My words seemed to come by themselves.

A faint smile played on her lips.

'About *us*? Was there ever an us?'

'I don't know where to begin.'

'I can imagine.'

'You don't know how sorry I am. I'm so, so . . . Do you think you can ever forgive me?'

'What difference would it make?'

'Émilie . . . I'm so sorry.'

'They're just words, Younes. Oh, there was a time when one word from you would have changed everything, but you couldn't bring yourself to say it. You need to understand that it's over.'

'What's over, Émilie?'

'Something that never really began.'

I was shattered. My head was exploding, I couldn't hear my heartbeat, couldn't feel a pulse in my temples. I could hardly believe I was still standing.

She stepped towards me as though emerging from the wall behind her.

'What did you think, Younes? Did you think I'd rush into your arms? Why? Was I expecting you to come? Of course not. You never allowed me to expect anything from you. You took my love for you and strangled it before it could take flight. Just like that . . . My love for you was dead before it even hit the ground.'

I said nothing. I was afraid that if I opened my mouth I might burst into tears. I realised now the pain I had put her through, realised that I had crushed her hopes, her dreams, trampled her wholesome, innocent joy, the artless confidence that had once set her eyes ablaze.

'Can I ask you something, Younes?'

There was a lump in my throat, all I could do was nod.

'Why? Why did you turn me away? If there was someone else, I might have understood. But you never married . . .'

Taking advantage of a moment's inattention, a tear slipped through my lashes and trickled down my cheek; I did not have the courage or the strength to stop it. Not a single muscle in my body responded.

'It tormented me night and day,' she went on, her voice lifeless. 'What was it about me that made you reject me? What did I do wrong? He doesn't love you, I told myself, it's as simple as that. There's nothing wrong with you, he just doesn't love you. But I didn't believe it. You were devastated after I got married. It was then I realised there was something you weren't telling me . . . What are you hiding, Younes? What is it that you can't bring yourself to tell me?'

The dam burst; tears spilled out, coursing down my face, my neck, and as I wept, I felt everything drain away: the pain, the remorse, the deceit. I cried and cried and never wanted to stop.

'You see,' she said. 'You still can't bring yourself to talk to me.'

By the time I looked up, Émilie had vanished as though she had been swallowed up by the wall behind her, by the encroaching darkness. The bookshop was deserted but for a trace of her perfume drifting between the shelves, and in another aisle, two old ladies who stared at me pityingly. I wiped my tears away and walked out of the bookshop feeling as though a fog from nowhere was enveloping the last rays of sunlight.

18

IT WAS seven p.m. on a spring day in late April 1959, the sky licked by the last rays of sunset as a lone cloud, straying from the flock, hung suspended over the village waiting for a gust of wind to carry it away. I was stacking boxes in the back office and getting ready to close. When I came back into the shop, I found a young man standing in the doorway to the street. He was nervous, and clutched at his jacket as though hiding something.

'I'm not here to hurt you . . .' he stammered in Arabic.

He was sixteen, perhaps seventeen; his face was pale and I could clearly see a fine down on his upper lip. He looked like a runaway. He was skinny as a rail and wore trousers ripped at the knees, muddy boots, and a scarf around his throat.

'It is closing time, isn't it?'

'What do you want?'

He opened his jacket to reveal a pistol tucked into his belt. My blood ran cold.

'I was sent by El-Jabha – the FLN. Close up the shop. Nothing's going to happen to you if you do what you're told.'

YASMINA KHADRA

'What the hell is this about?'

'It's about your country.'

When I hesitated, he drew the gun though he did not aim it at me. He repeated his orders. I pulled down the shutters, my eyes fixed on the barrel of the gun.

'Now go back inside.'

He was almost as scared as I was. Terrified that his fear might get the better of his sense, I put my hands up to reassure him.

'Turn on the lights, then close the shutter on the window.'

I did as he said. In the silence of the back room, my heart hammered like the piston of a runaway train.

'I know your mother is upstairs. Is there anyone else in the house?'

'I'm expecting friends,' I lied.

'Then we'll wait for them together.'

He wiped his nose on his sleeve and jerked his head for me to go upstairs. As I climbed the stairs, I felt him push the barrel of the gun into my side.

'Like I said, nothing will happen to you if you do what you're told.'

'Put the gun away, I promise I'll—'

'You don't give the orders here, and don't go by how old I look – there's more than one who didn't live to regret it. I'm an agent of the Front de Libération Nationale. They think you can be trusted; don't disappoint them.'

'Can I ask what they want with me?'

'Do I have to remind you we're at war?'

On the landing, he pushed me against a wall, listening to the clatter of dishes being washed in the kitchen. A muscle in his cheek twitched.

'Call her.'

'She's old, she's not well . . . Why don't you put the gun away?'

'Call her.'

I called to Germaine. I expected her to scream when she saw the gun and was bewildered to find her perfectly calm. The sight of the pistol barely raised an eyebrow.

'I saw him coming through the fields,' she said.

'I'm with the *Maquis*,' the boy said in an arrogant tone he hoped was commanding. 'Both of you, sit in there in that big room. If the phone rings or there's someone at the door, don't answer. You've got nothing to worry about.'

He jerked the gun towards the sofa. Germaine sat down, crossing her arms over her chest. Her coolness made me feel more calm. She tried not to look at me, probably hoping I would do the same. The boy crouched down in front of us, staring at us as though we were just two more pieces of furniture. He seemed to be holding his breath. I couldn't work out what was going on in his head, but I was relieved to see he was less nervous than when he first arrived.

The living room was utterly dark. His gun pressed against his thigh, the boy crouched in the darkness; there was no movement but for the glitter of his eyes in the darkness. I suggested turning on the lights. He didn't respond. After several hours, Germaine started to fidget. She was not nervous or even tired – she obviously needed to go to the toilet and, out of a sense of propriety, could not bring herself to ask this strange boy for permission. I did it for her. The boy clicked his tongue.

'What are we waiting for?' I asked.

Germaine nudged me to signal me to stay calm. A flash

of lightning lit up the room, and the darkness afterwards seemed more opaque. I could feel the sweat on my back grow cold; I had a fierce urge to pull my shirt away from where it clung to my skin, but the boy's stillness persuaded me otherwise.

The sounds of the village grew less frequent. A car engine roared somewhere in the distance, then faded, and a deafening silence fell over the streets and the fields. Towards midnight, a stone rapped against the shutter. The boy ran and peered into the shadows below, then turned to Germaine and ordered her to go downstairs and open up. While she was going down, he pressed the barrel of the gun to the back of my neck and forced me to walk to the head of the stairs.

'If you try to scream, madame, I'll kill him.'

'I understand,' Germaine said simply.

She shot back the bolt and suddenly there was the sound of a scuffle downstairs. I wanted to know what was happening, but the gun kept my face pressed against the wall.

Germaine reappeared; I could just make out her shadow faltering on the staircase. 'Turn the light on, you idiot!' growled a hoarse voice. Germaine flicked the switch and the landing light revealed four armed men clumsily attempting to carry a body on a makeshift stretcher. I recognised Jelloul, André's former manservant. He had a machine gun slung over one shoulder and was wearing a tattered combat uniform and muddy boots. He pushed me aside and helped the other three lug their burden up the stairs and set it down in the living room. He paid no attention to us, but told his cohorts to be careful laying the patient out on the dining table.

'Dismissed,' he barked. 'Return to your units. Laoufi, you stay with me. There's no need to come back for us. If there are any problems, I'll manage.'

Two of the men went back downstairs and disappeared silently into the night. Not once had they acknowledged our presence. The boy took the barrel of his gun from my neck and pushed me into the living room.

'Thanks, kid,' Jelloul said. 'You were great. Now get going.'

'You want me to wait outside?'

'No, go back to you know where.'

The boy gave a military salute and disappeared.

Jelloul winked at me.

'How are things?'

I didn't know how to answer this.

'Do something useful, go lock the door.'

Germaine looked at me imploringly. She was pale, her whole face a mask of fear. I went downstairs. When I got back, Jelloul was removing a bloody commando jacket from the man on the table.

'If he dies, you'll be going to the next world with him.' His voice was menacing but calm. 'This man is more important to me than my life. He took a bullet during a clash with the police. It wasn't around here, don't worry. I brought him here so you can get that lump of lead out of him.'

'What with? I'm not a surgeon.'

'You're a doctor, aren't you?'

'A pharmacist.'

'I don't care. Your life depends on saving his. I haven't come all this way for him to die now.'

Germaine pulled my arm.

'Let me examine him.'

'That's better . . .'

Germaine bent over the wounded man, carefully pulling aside his bloodstained shirt; the entry wound, just above his left nipple, was hidden by a thick layer of congealed blood. It was an ugly wound and would be difficult to treat.

'He's lost a lot of blood—'

'Well then, let's not waste any time.' Jelloul cut her off. 'Laoufi,' he said to his colleague, 'you help the lady. Laoufi here is our nurse. Go down to the pharmacy with him and get whatever you need to operate on the captain. Do you have everything you need to sterilise the wound and extract the bullet?'

'I'll deal with it,' Germaine said. 'Jonas wouldn't be any help. And if you don't mind, I won't have guns in my living room. I need to be able to work in peace. Your nurse can stay, but you and my son . . .'

'That's exactly what I planned to do, madame.'

Germaine was trying to protect me; she was doing her utmost to stay calm but having me there made her anxious. I couldn't see how she could possibly deal with this. She had never held a scalpel in her life. What was she thinking? What if the man died? She glanced at me, urging me to leave the room, wanting me as far away as possible. She was trying to tell me something, but I could not understand her. She was obviously afraid for me and trying to shield me. Later she told me she would have brought the dead back to life if it would have saved me.

'Go into the kitchen and get yourself something to eat. I'll be more comfortable without you breathing down my neck.'

Jelloul nodded. I led him into the kitchen. He opened the fridge, took out a plate of boiled potatoes, cheese, slices of cured meat, some fruit and a bottle of milk and set them on the table next to his machine gun.

'Have you got any bread?'

'In the larder, on your right.'

He took out a large baguette and bit into it as he sank into a chair; he ate with astonishing voracity, picking at random a piece of fruit, a piece of cheese, a potato, a slice of meat . . .

'I'm starving,' he said, burping loudly. 'You've got it easy here, haven't you? The war doesn't affect you; you go on living the good life while we're out breaking our balls in the bush. Some day you're going to have to pick a side, you know.'

'I don't like war.'

'It's not a question of liking or not liking. Our people have had enough of suffering in silence; they've revolted. Of course, being caught between two stools, you can do what you like, you can side with whoever suits you.'

He took a penknife from his pocket and cut a slice of cheese.

'Do you see much of André?'

'Not these days.'

'They say he and his father have set up a militia.'

'That's true.'

'I can't wait to come face to face with him . . . He does know I escaped?'

'I've no idea.'

'Nobody in Río Salado said anything about me escaping from prison?'

'I didn't hear anything.'

'It was a miracle. They sent me to the guillotine but my head grew back. Do you believe in destiny, Jonas?'

'I don't feel as though I have one.'

'I do. I was being transferred from Orléansville prison when one of the tyres blew and the van went head first into a ditch. When I came to, I was lying in a bush. I got up and walked away, and when no one came after me, I kept on walking. I had to pinch myself to make sure I wasn't dreaming. You don't think that's a sign from heaven?'

He pushed his plate away and went to see what was happening in the living room, deliberately leaving his machine gun on the table. When he came back he said:

'He's in a bad way, but he's strong . . . he'll pull through. He has to pull through, otherwise . . .' He did not finish the sentence, but looked me up and down and changed his tone. 'I keep the faith. After our clash with the police when my senior officer was injured, I didn't know what to do. That's when your name popped into my head. I swear I heard it. I even turned around, but there was no one there. I didn't try to understand, I just set off. Two nights we spent, cutting through the woods; even the dogs didn't bark when we went past. Isn't that amazing?'

He pushed the machine gun to one side, pretending to be distracted.

'I've run into dozens of ambushes, but they never caught me, never hit me; eventually I became fatalistic. My time will come when God decides. I'm not afraid of men or thunderbolts any more . . . But what are you afraid of? The revolution is going well, we're winning on all fronts, even abroad; we have the support of our own people and the international community. The great day is coming soon. What are you waiting for? Why don't you join us?'

'Are you going to kill us?'

'I'm not a killer, Jonas, I'm a soldier. I am prepared to lay down my life for my country – what are you prepared to do for it?'

'My mother doesn't know much about surgery.'

'Neither do I, but someone's got to do it. You know who my commander is? It's Sy Rachid – "the elusive Sy Rachid" they talk about in the newspapers. I've seen a lot of firebrands, but no one with the personality of this man. A lot of times we've been cornered and he's managed to get us out just by clicking his fingers. He's extraordinary. I won't let him die. The revolution needs him.'

'Okay, but what happens if he does die? What are you going to do to us?'

'Coward – all you can think about is saving your own skin. There's a war on out there – hundreds, thousands of people are dying every day, but you don't care. I'd kill you like a dog if I didn't owe you . . . By the way, why is it that I still can't bring myself to call you Younes?'

He didn't shout, he didn't thump the table; he spoke quietly, reluctantly, scornfully. He was too tired to exert himself. But the contempt he felt for me was infinite, and it reawakened in me a fury I had not felt since Jean-Christophe rejected me.

The nurse knocked at the kitchen door before coming in; he was sweating.

'She did it.'

'God be praised,' Jelloul said with an air of detachment. He nodded at me. 'You see? Even fate is on our side.'

He ordered the nurse to guard me and hurried off to see his commander. The nurse asked if there was anything to eat. I pointed him to the fridge and the larder. He told me to move back to the window and not to try anything clever. He was a scrawny kid, still in his teens, his face pink and downy. He was wearing a thick sweater much too big for him, baggy trousers held up by a length of rope, and a pair of grotesquely large boots that made him look ridiculous. He ignored the fridge and the larder and ate what was left on the table.

Jelloul called me. The nurse nodded for me to leave the kitchen and watched me as I walked down the hall. Slumped in a chair, Germaine was trying to regain her composure. I could see her heart beating; she was bathed in sweat. The wounded man still lay on the table, his bare chest wrapped in bandages. The sound of his rasping breath filled the room. Jelloul dipped a compress in a bowl of water and mopped his commander's face, his every movement charged with reverence.

'We're going to stay here for a few days while the captain builds up his strength,' he announced. 'Tomorrow morning you'll open the pharmacy just like any other day. Madame will stay up here with us. If there are any messages to be done, you'll do them. You can come and go as you please, but if I notice anything out of the ordinary – well, I don't need to paint a picture. All we're asking for is a little hospitality. I'm offering you the opportunity to serve your people. Try not to let me down.

'I'll look after the pharmacy and do the shopping,' Germaine interrupted.

'I'd prefer him to do it . . . is that all right, Jonas?'

'How do I know you won't kill us before you leave?'

'You're pathetic, Jonas.'

'I trust you,' Germaine said.

Jelloul smiled. It was the same smile he had once given me in that little *douar* of squalid shacks behind the marabout's hill, a mixture of scorn and pity. He took a small revolver from the pocket of his trousers and handed it to me.

'It's loaded. All you have to do is press the trigger.'

The feel of cold metal made my hair stand on end.

Germaine turned pale, her hands, white-knuckled, clutching her dress.

'You want me to tell you something, Jonas? You break my heart. What kind of pathetic loser turns away from a chance to fulfil his destiny?'

He took the gun back and slipped it into his pocket.

The wounded man groaned and began to stir. He was about my age, perhaps a year or two older. He was tall, blonde, with well-defined muscles. A reddish beard hid much of his face, he had bushy eyebrows and his nose, slightly curved, was thin and sharp as a razor blade. He stirred again, reached out and tried to turn on to his side, but the movement sent a shooting pain through him that brought him round. It was then that I recognised him, in spite of what the years had taken out of him. It was Ouari, my partner in crime years ago in Jenane Jato, the boy who had taught me the art of camouflage and how to trap goldfinches. He looked prematurely old, but the eyes were still the same: dark, metallic, impenetrable – I would never forget those eyes.

Ouari was clearly coming out of a deep coma, because, not recognising me, his first reaction was one of self-defence.

He grabbed me by the throat and hauled himself to his feet.

'It's all right, Sy Rachid,' Jelloul whispered. 'You're safe here.'

Ouari did not seem to understand. He stared vacantly at his fellow soldier and went on choking me. Germaine rushed to try and help me, but Jelloul ordered her to go back and in a soft voice tried to explain the situation to his commanding officer. The hands around my throat still did not relax. I was having trouble breathing but had to wait until the wounded man came to his senses. By the time he let me go, my face was numb. Ouari collapsed on to the table, arms hanging limply by his sides; he shuddered for a moment and then lay still.

'Step back,' barked the nurse, who had come back into the room to see what the noise was.

He examined the injured man, took his pulse.

'It's all right, he just fainted. We have to get him into bed; he needs rest.'

The rebels stayed with us for almost two weeks. I went about my daily business as though nothing had happened. Worried that someone might show up unexpectedly, Germaine phoned her family in Oran and told them she was going out into the desert, to Colo-Béchar, and would call them when she got back. Laoufi, the nurse, put the captain in my room and sat by his bed day and night. I slept on the old sofa in my uncle's study. Jelloul constantly came in to lecture me. He was angry and disgusted at my indifference to our people's war of independence. I knew if I said anything it would simply make him angrier, so I said nothing. One evening, having tried to engage me in conversation while I sat reading a book, he said:

'Life is like a movie: there are actors who move the story forward and bit players who fade into the background. The bit players are part of the film, but no one cares about them. You're a bit player, Jonas. I don't hate you, I pity you.'

My continued silence infuriated him. He roared:

'How can you just look the other way when the whole world is right there in front of you?'

I looked up at him, then went back to my reading. He ripped the book from my hands and hurled it against the wall.

'I'm talking to you!'

I went over, picked up the book and went back to the sofa. He tried to snatch it away again, but this time I grabbed him by the wrist and pushed him away. Surprised by my reaction, Jelloul looked at me, amazed, and muttered:

'You're nothing but a coward. Don't you see that our villages are being napalmed, our heroes guillotined in the prisons, soldiers lying dead in the scrubland, rebels languishing in prison camps? Can't you see what's happening? What sort of madman are you, Jonas? Can't you understand that a whole nation is fighting for *your* salvation?'

I didn't say anything.

He slapped me across the face.

'Don't you touch me,' I said.

'You think I'm scared? . . . You're a coward, nothing but a coward. I don't know why I don't just cut your throat.'

I set down my book, got to my feet and stood in front of him.

'What do you know about cowardice, Jelloul? Who do

you think is the coward, the man with a gun to his head or the one holding the gun?'

He looked at me in disgust.

'I'm not a coward, Jelloul, I'm not deaf, I'm not blind and I'm not made of stone. If you really want to know, I don't much care about anything in this world now. Not even the gun that allows people like you to treat people like me with contempt. Wasn't it humiliation that first led you to pick up a gun? So why do you go around humiliating other people?'

He was trembling with rage, struggling to stop himself from grabbing me by the throat. He spat on the ground and went out, slamming the door behind him.

After that, he did not bother me. If we passed each other in the hall, he stepped out of my way with distaste.

All the time they stayed with us, Jelloul forbade me from going near the captain. If I needed something from my room, I would tell the nurse where it was and he would go and get it for me. Only once, as I came out of the bathroom, did I see the patient through the open door. He was sitting on the bed, a clean bandage around his chest, his back to me. I thought back to Jenane Jato, to the time when he was my protector, my friend, I remembered his bird coop filthy with droppings, our trips into the scrubland behind the souk to catch goldfinches. Then suddenly my heart contracted as I remembered the vacant look in his eyes as he watched Daho torment me with the snake. At that moment, the burning need I had felt since he arrived to tell him who I was suddenly vanished.

On the last day, the three *maquisards* bathed, shaved, put their clean clothes and boots into a bag, dressed in some of my clothes and gathered in the living room. My suit was too big for the nurse, who kept looking at himself in the mirror. All three of them tried to hide their nervousness. Jelloul was wearing the suit I had bought for Simon's wedding, and the captain one Germaine had given me some months earlier. At noon, after they'd had lunch, Jelloul told me to hang white sheets over the balcony. When it got dark, he went into the room that overlooked the vineyards and turned the light on and off three times. When he saw a light flash in the distance beyond the sea of vines, he ordered me to take the nurse into the back office and give him all the drugs and supplies he would need. We packed three boxes full and put them in the boot of the car, then went back upstairs, where the captain, still pale, was pacing up and down the hallway.

'What time is it?' Jelloul asked.

'A quarter to ten,' I said.

'It's time. You can drive, I'll tell you where to go.'

Germaine, who was standing off to one side, clasped her hands in silent prayer. She was shaking. The nurse went over to her. 'Everything will be all right, madame.' He patted her shoulder. 'Don't worry.' Germaine hid her face in her hands.

The captain and the nurse took the back seat of the car, their guns at their feet. Jelloul climbed into the passenger seat, tugging at his tie. I opened the garage door and Germaine closed it after we left. I drove with the headlights off until we reached Kraus's wine cellar, opposite André's diner. There were people in the bar and out on the terrace; we could hear shouting and laughter. Suddenly I was afraid that Jelloul had come to settle old scores with his former employer. But he simply gave a bitter smile and jerked his chin towards the road that lead out of Río Salado. I turned on the headlights and drove into the darkness.

We took the road towards Lourmel, turning off before we reached the village and taking the dirt road towards Terga. A motorcycle was waiting for us at a railway crossing. I recognised the rider as the boy with the gun who had showed up at the pharmacy that first day. He turned the motorcycle around and rode on ahead of us.

'Drive slowly,' Jelloul ordered. 'Don't try to catch up with him. If you see him coming back, switch off your headlights and turn the car round.'

The motorcycle did not come back.

After about twenty kilometres, I saw him waiting by the side of the road. Jelloul told me to pull up next to him and turn off the engine. Shadows appeared from the bushes carrying rifles, with knapsacks on their backs. One of them was leading a donkey that was just skin and bone. The three men got out of my car and went over to greet them. The nurse came back to me, told me to stay in the car, and opened the boot. The boxes of drugs and supplies were loaded on to the mule. After that, Jelloul waved for me to go. I didn't move. Surely they weren't just going to let me leave? I could easily turn them in as soon as I got to the first roadblock. I tried to look into Jelloul's eyes, but he had already turned away and was walking off with his captain, whom I had not heard speak a word since that first night when he had tried to strangle me. The mule stumbled up the steep path, staggered around a rocky outcrop and disappeared. The shadows of the others moved through the scrubland, helping each other up the hill, then disappeared into the darkness. Soon, all I could hear was the breeze rustling the leaves.

My hand refused to turn the key in the ignition. I was convinced that Jelloul was hiding somewhere nearby, rifle aimed at me, waiting for the sound of the engine to drown out the shot.

It took me an hour before I really believed that they had gone.

Months later, I found a letter with no stamp and no address among the post. Inside was a scrap of paper torn from an exercise book and on it a scribbled list of medications. There were no instructions. I bought the medicines on the list and packed them into a cardboard box. A week later, Laoufi came and picked them up. It was three o'clock in the morning when I heard the pebble hit the shutters. Germaine heard it too; I found her in the hall, wrapped in a dressing gown. She didn't say anything, she simply watched as I went downstairs to the back office. I gave the box to Laoufi, locked the door and went back up to my room. I was waiting for Germaine to come in and ask me questions, but she simply went back to her room and locked herself in.

Laoufi came to pick up supplies five more times. It was always the same: an envelope would be slipped through the letter box with a list of medicines. Sometimes it listed other supplies: syringes, bandages, scissors, a stethoscope, some tourniquets. Then a pebble would be thrown up at the window. The nurse would be waiting outside. Germaine would be standing in the doorway to her bedroom.

One night, I got a phone call. Jelloul asked me to meet him at the spot where I had dropped them off. Seeing me take the car from the garage early the next morning, Germaine made the sign of the cross. It was then that I realised that we no longer spoke to each other. When I arrived at the place, Jelloul wasn't there. He called me as soon as I got back to the pharmacy and told me to drive back to the spot again. This time there was a shepherd waiting for me with a briefcase full of banknotes. He told me to hide the money until someone came to fetch it. I kept the briefcase for two weeks, until Jelloul phoned one Sunday and told me to take the 'package' to Oran and wait in the car outside a small cabinetmaker's shop behind the BAO Brasserie. I did as I was told. The shop was closed. A man walked past the car, then walked back again and stopped when he came to the car. Flashing the butt of the gun under his jacket, he told me to get out. 'I'll be back in fifteen minutes,' he said as he drove off. The car was brought back to me a quarter of an hour later.

This other life went on all through the summer and into autumn.

The last time Laoufi came to the pharmacy, he was more nervous than usual. Glancing around suspiciously, he emptied the contents of the box I handed him into a backpack, threw it over his shoulder and gave me a look I had never seen before. He wanted to say something, but the words would not come. Standing on tiptoe, he kissed the top of my head – a mark of great respect. His body trembled as I hugged him. It was four a.m. and the sky was beginning to brighten. Was it the dawn that bothered him? He was clearly worried about something. He said goodbye and hurried into the vineyards. I saw him disappear into the darkness; listened for the dying rustle of the leaves as he moved away. The moon in the sky looked like a bitten fingernail. A faltering wind gave a brief gust and then died away.

Leaving the light in my bedroom off, I sat on the edge of the bed, alert, watchful. Suddenly gunfire ripped through the silent darkness and dogs began to bark.

At dawn there was a knock on my door. It was Krimo, Simon's former chauffeur. He was standing on the pavement, feet apart, hands on his hips, his rifle tucked under his arm. The expression on his face was one of vicious triumph. Six armed men, auxiliaries, were standing in the street around a wheelbarrow in which lay a bloody corpse. It was Laoufi. I recognised the oversized boots and the torn backpack.

'A *fellaga*,' said Krimo. 'A dirty stinking *fellaga* . . . It was the stink that led us to him.'

He took a step forward.

'I was wondering what this fucking *fellaga* was doing in my village. Who did he come to see? Where did he come from?'

He pushed the wheelbarrow towards me. The nurse's head lolled against the ground. Part of his skull had been blown off. Krimo picked up the backpack and threw it at my feet; the medications spilled out on to the pavement.

'There's only one pharmacy in Río Salado, Jonas, and that's yours . . . And then I understood.'

He slammed the butt of his rifle into my jaw. I heard the bone crack and Germaine scream, then everything went dark.

I woke up in a filthy cell surrounded by rats and cockroaches. Krimo wanted to know who the *fellaga* was, how long I had been supplying him with drugs. I said I had never seen him before. He forced my head into a bucket of cheap wine and whipped me with a riding crop, but I kept telling him I had never seen the *fellaga*. Krimo swore, he spat at me, he kicked me as I lay on the ground. I didn't tell him anything. He handed me over to an emaciated old man with a long grey face and piercing eyes. The old man began by telling me that he understood, that no one in the village believed I had anything to do with these 'terrorists', that *they* had forced me to help them. I continued to deny everything. I was passed from one interrogator to another; some tried to outwit me, others tried to beat the truth out of me. Krimo waited until nightfall to come back and torture me again. I held out.

In the morning, the door opened, and there stood Pépé Rucillio.

Next to him was an officer in combat uniform.

'We haven't finished with him, Monsieur Rucillio.'

'You're wasting your time, Lieutenant. This has been a terrible misunderstanding. The boy was simply in the wrong place at the wrong time. Your colonel agrees with me on this. You hardly think I'd try to protect a criminal?'

'That's not the problem . . .'

'There is no problem, and there won't be any problem,' Pépé Rucillio assured him.

They gave me back my clothes.

Outside, in the gravel-strewn courtyard of what seemed to be a barracks, Krimo and his fellow officers watched, angry and outraged, as I slipped through their fingers. They knew that Río Salado's most respected figure had pleaded my case to the highest authorities and had personally vouched for me.

Pépé Rucillio helped me into his car and got behind the wheel. He saluted the soldier at the gate, then drove off.

'I hope I'm not making the biggest mistake of my life,' he said.

I didn't answer. My mouth was bleeding and my eyes were so swollen I could barely keep them open.

Pépé did not say another word. I sensed him wavering between his doubt and a moral dilemma, between the efforts he had made on my behalf and the inconsistencies in what he had told the colonel to clear me of suspicion and have me released. Pépé Rucillio was more than simply a respected local figure, he was a legend, a moral compass, a man as towering as his fortune, but like many prominent people who put honour before all other considerations, he was as fragile as a porcelain monument. He could get people to do whatever he wished, and his integrity was worth more than any official document. Influential people of his stature, the mention of whose name could settle the stormiest argument, could be magnanimous, even extravagant, and they were granted a certain impunity, but in matters of honour – when they gave their word – no laxity was tolerated. If they gave their word on something that proved to be unfounded, there was no way back. Having personally vouched for me, Pépé Rucillio was wondering whether he had made a serious mistake; it was a possibility that clearly worried him deeply.

He drove me back to the village and dropped me outside my house. He didn't help me out of the car, leaving me to cope as best I could.

'My reputation is at stake here, Jonas,' he muttered. 'If I

ever find out that you're a liar, I'll personally see to it that they execute you.'

I don't know where I found the strength to ask him:

'Jean-Christophe?'

He shook his head. 'No . . . Isabelle. I never could refuse her anything. But if she's wrong about you, I'll disown her on the spot.'

Germaine came out to help me inside. She was so relieved to have me back alive that she did not reproach me; she simply ran a bath for me and made me something to eat. Afterwards, she cleaned my wounds, bandaged the most serious ones and put me to bed.

'Did you phone Isabelle?'

'No . . . she phoned me.'

'But she's in Oran . . . how could she possibly know?'

'Everyone in Río Salado knows.'

'What did you say to her?'

'I told her you were innocent, that you had nothing to do with this business.'

'And she believed you?'

'I didn't ask.'

My questions hurt her, more especially the way I had asked them. The half-heartedness of my tone, the implicit criticism of what I was asking turned her joy at having me back safe and sound into a vague feeling of irritation and later mute anger. She looked at me and there was a bitterness in her eyes I had never seen before. I realised that the ties that had bound me to her had finally sundered. This woman, who had been everything to me – mother, fairy godmother, sister, confidante, friend – now saw me simply as a stranger.

19

THE WINTER of 1960 was so harsh that even our prayers froze; we could almost hear them dropping from heaven and shattering on the hard ground. As if the overcast sky was not enough, dark clouds flocked like falcons over the sun, cutting off what little light might have warmed our numbed souls. Storms were brewing everywhere and no one now was under any illusions: war had found its calling and the cemeteries were answering.

At home, things were becoming complicated. Germaine's silence saddened me. It upset me that she would walk past me without a word, sit silently with me at dinner staring at her plate, clear the table as soon as I had finished and immediately go upstairs to her room without saying good night. I felt heartsick, and yet I could not find it in me to make peace with her. I didn't have the strength. Everything exhausted me, everything disgusted me. I would not see reason; I didn't care I was in the wrong: all I wanted was a dark corner where I refused to let myself wonder what I should do, think about what I had done, decide whether or not I had acted for the best. I was bitter as rose-laurel root, sullen and angry as something I dared not name. At times

I heard Krimo's insults exploding in my head. I would find myself imagining him suffering horribly, then I would shake off these thoughts and clear my mind. I felt no hatred; I had no more rage; my whole being felt so bloated that a breath of air might cause it to explode.

In calmer moments, I thought about my uncle. I did not miss him, but the gaping void he had left reminded me of those who had cut me off. I felt as though I had nowhere to turn for support, that I was floating in a suffocating bubble, a bubble that could be burst by the smallest twig. I had to do something, I felt myself slipping away, slowly disintegrating. So I summoned my dead. My uncle's memory supplanted mine; his ghost kept at bay all the horrors I had suffered. Perhaps, after all, I did miss him. I felt so alone that I almost faded away myself, like a shadow consumed by darkness. While I waited for my bruises to become less noticeable, I shut myself away in my uncle's study and pored over his note-books – a dozen exercise books filled with comments, remarks and quotes from writers and philosophers from all over the world. He also kept a diary, which I found by accident in the bottom drawer of his desk, under a vast swath of newspaper cuttings. He wrote about the dispossessed of Algeria, about the nationalist movement, about the absurdity of the human species that reduces everything in life to a vulgar power struggle, to the deplorable and mindless need of one group to enslave another. My uncle was a supremely cultivated man, both educated and wise. I could still remember his expression when he closed his notebook and looked up at me; an expression that radiated compassionate intelligence.

'I hope my writings will prove useful to future generations,' he had said.

'They will be your gift to posterity,' I replied, thinking it best to flatter him.

His features tensed. 'Posterity has never made the grave's embrace less cruel,' he said. 'It simply assuages our fear of death, because there is no better cure for our inevitable mortality than the illusion of a beautiful eternity. But there is one illusion I still hold dear: that is the thought of an enlightened nation. That is the only future I still dream of.'

When I looked out into the distance from my balcony and saw nothing looming on the horizon, I wondered if there was life after war.

A week after Pépé Rucillio's speech, André Sosa came to see me. He parked his car opposite the vineyards, leaned out of the window and waved for me to come down. I shook my head. He opened the car door and stepped out. He was wearing a large beige coat, unbuttoned to reveal his pot belly, and a pair of leather boots that came up to his knees. From his broad smile, I knew he had come in peace.

'Fancy coming out for the day in the old banger?'

'I'm fine where I am.'

'Okay, then, I'll come up.'

I heard him say hello to Germaine in the hallway, climb the stairs, then open the door to my room. Before he stepped out on to the balcony to join me, he glanced around at the unmade bed, then crossed the room to the mantelpiece on which sat the wooden horse Jean-Christophe had given me a lifetime ago, after he beat me up at school.

'Those were the good old days, weren't they, Jonas?'

'Days don't get old, Dédé, we're the ones who get old.'

'You're right. It's just a pity we don't improve with the years, like our wine.'

He came outside, propped his elbows on the balcony and surveyed the vineyards.

'No one in the village thinks you had anything to do with the *fellagas*. Krimo was completely out of order. I saw him yesterday and told him to his face.'

He turned to me, trying not to look at my bruises.

'I feel bad that I didn't come sooner.'

'What good would it have done?'

'I don't know . . . You don't fancy coming with me to Tlemcen? Oran is impossible now, people are being murdered every day, but I need a change of scenery. Río Salado depresses me.'

'I can't.'

'We won't stay long. I know a little restaurant . . .'

'Don't, Dédé.'

He shook his head slowly.

'I understand – not that I approve. It's not good to hole up here, brooding over your bitterness.'

'I'm not bitter. I just need to be on my own.'

'Am I bothering you?'

I stared off into the distance so I would not have to answer.

'It's insane, this thing that's happening,' he sighed, leaning on the balcony again. 'Who would have thought our country would be brought so low?'

'It was obvious, Dédé. A whole nation lay down while we walked all over them. Sooner or later they were bound to get up. That's when we lost our footing.'

'Do you really believe that?'

This time I turned to him and said:

'Dédé, how much longer can we go on lying to ourselves?'

He brought his fist up to his mouth and blew on it, measuring his words carefully.

'It's true, there was a lot wrong with how things were, but to go from there to waging a vicious, all-out war? It's not right. There are hundreds of thousands dead, Jonas; that's too many people, isn't it?'

'Are you asking me?'

'I'm lost . . . I honestly don't understand what's happening to Algeria. And the French obviously don't either. They're talking about self-determination. What exactly do they mean by that? Does it mean we wipe the slate clean and start again with everyone equal, or . . .'

He did not finish the sentence. His disquiet turned to anger; his knuckles were white.

'De Gaulle doesn't understand a fucking thing about our suffering,' he said, referring to the General's famous statement to the Algerians on 4 June 1958 – 'I have understood you' – which had stirred up the crowds and given their illusions a stay of execution.

A week later, on 9 December 1960, the whole population of Río Salado went to the neighbouring village of Aïn Trémouchent, where the General was holding a meeting that the parish priest called the 'last prayer mass'. The rumours circulating had prepared people for the worst, but they were not to be persuaded. They were united by fear and so blinkered they would not see the harsh truths bearing down on them. I had heard them, at dawn, taking their cars out of the garages, forming a convoy, joking and laughing to each other, shouting to drown out the insistent voice that would not let them sleep, the voice that said endlessly, relentlessly, that the die was cast. They laughed, they argued, they pretended they still had some say in the matter. But they no longer believed it; their brash self-assurance was belied by their bewildered faces. They hoped that by keeping their spirits up, by keeping up appearances, they might compel destiny to see reason, force its hand, produce a miracle. They had forgotten that the countdown had already begun, that there was nothing left to salvage. Only a blind man would have carried on walking through their dark Utopia, waiting for a day that had already dawned on a new era; an era in which they were to play no part.

I went out and wandered the deserted streets. Then I headed out past the Jewish cemetery to see the charred ruins of the house where, in a fleeting moment, I had had my first sexual experience. A horse stood grazing next to the old stables, indifferent to the shifting fortunes of men. I sat on a low wall; sat there until noon, trying to picture Madame Cazenave. All I could see was Simon's car in flames, and Émilie, half naked, clutching her child.

The cars came back from Aïn Trémouchent. They had left Río Salado that morning in a fanfare of horns, waving the tricolour; they returned like a funeral cortège, their flags at half-mast. A pall fell over the village. Every face bore the signs of mourning for a hope long since doomed, a dream they had tried to keep alive with prayers and incense. Algeria was to be *Algerian*.

The following morning, on the front of one of the wine-maker's cellars, someone had had daubed in red paint the letters FLN.

In the spring of 1962, Oran held its breath. I was looking for Émilie. I feared for her. I needed her. I loved her and

had come back to tell her so. I felt ready to brave hurri-
canes and thunderbolts, to flout every sacrilege, every
blasphemy. I could not bear to go on longing for her, reaching
out to touch her only to feel her absence in my fingertips.
I told myself, she will turn you away, she will say terrible
things, she will bring your world crashing down around
you, but still I went. I was no longer afraid of breaking the
oath I had made, of crushing my soul in my fist; I was no
longer afraid of offending the gods, of living in infamy to
the end of my days. At the bookshop, someone told me that
Émilie had left work as usual one night and that they had
not heard a word from her since. I remembered the number
of the tram she had taken the last time I had come here.
At every stop I got off and scoured the nearby streets. I
thought I recognised her in every woman I passed on the
street, in every shadow disappearing round a corner or into
a doorway. I asked for her in grocers' shops and police
stations; I asked the postmen and although I came back
empty-handed every night, never for a moment did I feel I
was wasting my time. How could I hope to find her in a
city under siege, in this midst of the chaos, the fury of men?
Algerian Algeria was being delivered by forceps in a torrent
of tears and blood as French Algeria lay bleeding to death.
And even after seven years of war and horror, though both
were on the brink of exhaustion, they still found the strength
to go on slaughtering one other.

The week in January 1960 in which *pieds-noirs* erected
barricades and seized government buildings in Algiers had
done nothing to stop the inexorable march of history. The
putsch in April 1961, a failed *coup d'état* instigated by a
quartet of generals intent on forming a breakaway republic,

served only to propel the people into even greater torment. The military were overtaken by events; they fired indiscriminately on civilians, fighting off one community only to be attacked by another. Those who felt they had been sold out by the machinations in Paris – that is, those who supported a complete break from the mother country – took up arms and vowed to reclaim the Algeria being taken from them piece by piece. Towns and villages where plunged into a horrifying nightmare. There were attacks and counterattacks, executions and reprisals, kidnappings and military raids. A European seen fraternising with a Muslim or any Muslim seen with a European risked his life. Demarcation lines divided towns and villages into isolated communities who banded together, anxiously policed their borders and did not hesitate to lynch an unwary passer-by who got the wrong address. Every morning there were broken bodies in the street; every night ghosts fought pitched battles. The graffiti on the walls was like epitaphs – amid the scrawls that read 'Vote Yes', 'FLN' and 'Long Live French Algeria', suddenly the three letters that signalled the apocalypse began to appear: OAS. The Organisation Armée Secrète, born of the anguish of the colonists, of their refusal to face facts, was determined to go on digging its own grave until it reached the pit of hell.

Émilie had disappeared, but I was prepared to bring her back from the underworld itself. I sensed that she was close by, almost within reach; I truly believed that I had only to pull back a screen, open a door, push past a bystander and I would find her. It was as if I were mad. I didn't notice the pools of blood on the pavements, the pockmarks left by bullets on the walls. I was indifferent to the suspicion of others: their hostility, their contempt, their insults went over my head and never for a moment slowed my search. I could think only of her; had eyes only for her; Émilie was the destiny I had chosen and I cared nothing about anything else.

Fabrice Scamaroni came upon me stumbling around this city that reeked of hate and death. He stopped his car, shouted for me to get in, then drove off at top speed. 'Are you insane?' he said. 'You could get your throat cut round here.' 'I'm looking for Émilie.' 'And how exactly do you plan to find her when you don't even know what sort of shithole you're in – I swear this area is worse than a minefield.'

Fabrice had no idea where Émilie was. She had never come to see him at the newspaper. He had run into her once in Choupot, but that had been months ago. He promised he would see what he could find out.

In Choupot I was directed to a building on the Boulevard Laurent-Guerrero. The concierge informed me that the lady in question had indeed been staying in an apartment on the second floor, but had moved out after an attack in the neighbourhood.

'Did she leave a forwarding address?'

'No . . . But if I remember rightly, I think she told the movers to take her to Saint-Hubert.'

I knocked on every door in Saint-Hubert without success. The city was in chaos. The ceasefire declared on 19 March 1962 had sparked off the last pockets of resistance. Knives were pitted against machine guns, grenades against bombs, bystanders were killed by stray bullets. And as I advanced through the horror and the stench of death, Émilie seemed to move farther away. Had she been killed in a bomb blast, by a stray bullet; had she been stabbed and left to bleed to death in a deserted stairwell? Oran spared no one: not the young or the old, not women or the simple-minded who stumbled through these horrors. I was in Tahtaha when two car bombs went off leaving a hundred dead and dozens of the Muslim population of Medina J'dida injured; I was at Petit Lac when the bodies of a dozen Europeans were fished from the polluted waters; I was at the city prison when an OAS unit stormed the building, dragged FLN prisoners into the street and executed them as crowds of people watched; I was on the seafront when saboteurs blew up the fuel depots on the port, cloaking the area in clouds of thick, oily smoke for days. Émilie heard the same explosions I did, I told myself, witnessed the same havoc, suffered the same terrors. I could not understand why our paths had not crossed, why chance, why fate, why providence did not bring us together in this seething mass of evil. I was furious as the days slipped away and brought me no closer to finding her; furious as I stumbled through firing squads, no-go areas, scenes of slaughter and carnage, finding no trace nor even the illusion of a trace that might lead me to her; furious to think she was still in this world as panic gripped every European in the country. A parcel in their letter box could send a family into paroxysms of fear. This was the season of '*the suitcase or the coffin*'. The first waves of emigration were anarchy. Cars laden with suitcases and sobbing people besieged the ports and the airports, while others headed for Morocco. Latecomers sold everything they possessed — shops, houses, cars, factories, concessions — for next to nothing; some did not wait to find buyers. They barely had time to pack their cases.

In Río Salado, houses stood empty, shutters banging, windows dark, and great piles of clothes and chattels lay piled up in the street. Most of the villagers had left; those who stayed behind did not know which way to turn. An old man, crippled by arthritis, keeled over on the porch of his house. A young man helped him to his feet and tried to get him to walk, while the rest of his family waited impatiently by a van filled to bursting. 'They could have waited until I died,' the old man whimpered. 'Where am I going to die now?' On the main street, trucks, cars, carts stood lined up waiting to take people into exile. At the train station, a bewildered crowd waited for a late train, agonising as the minutes passed. People ran about, confused, their eyes glazed, forsaken by their saints, their guardian angels. Madness, fear, grief, ruin, tragedy had but one face: it was theirs.

Germaine was sitting on the steps of the pharmacy, her head in her hands. Our neighbours had all left; in the gardens abandoned dogs paced and whined.

'What should I do?' she asked me.

'You should stay here,' I said. 'No one will raise a hand to you.'

I took her in my arms. She seemed so small it felt as though I could have held her in the hollow of my hand. She was distraught and confused, baffled and exhausted, beaten and uncertain. Her eyes were red from crying. I kissed the cheeks streaked with tears, the forehead lined with wrinkles; my hands cradled her head, troubled with all the worries of the world. I led her upstairs to her room, then went outside again. 'Where can I go?' Madame Lambert stood ranting in the street, hands raised to heaven. 'Where

am I supposed to go? I have no children, no family anywhere.'
I told her to go home. She did not hear me; she went on
raving. At the far end of the street, the Ravirez family were
racing around carrying suitcases. On the square outside the
town hall, families stood surrounded by their luggage,
begging for cars so they could leave. The mayor tried in
vain to calm them. Pépé Rucillio told them to go back to
their houses and wait for things to settle down. 'This is our
home,' he said. 'We're not going anywhere.' No one was
listening.

André Sosa was alone in the diner amid the broken tables,
the ruined bar, the shattered mirrors. The floor glittered
with broken glass and crockery. The lamps still dangled
forlornly over the devastation, their bulbs shattered. André
was playing pool. He did not seen to notice me; he didn't
seem to notice anything. He chalked his cue, leaned over
the table and took aim. There were no balls on the table;
the baize had been ripped away. André didn't care. He aimed
at a ball that he alone could see, took his shot and watched
and waited. Then he raised a triumphant fist, and moved to
the other side of the table to line up his next shot. From
time to time he went over to the bar, took a drag of his
cigarette, then went back to his game.

'Dédé,' I said. 'You can't stay here.'

'This is my home,' he grumbled, lining up another shot.

'I saw farms burning when I was coming back from Oran
just now.'

'I'm not leaving. I'm waiting for them.'

'That's madness and you know it.'

'I told you, I'm not going anywhere.'

He went on playing, ignoring me. He stubbed out his cigarette, lit another and another and another, until finally he crumpled the empty pack. The sun was setting, and darkness began to steal into the diner. André played another game, and another, before finally setting down the cue and going to sit at the bar. He drew his knees up, buried his face between them, clasped his hands behind his neck and sat like that for a long time, until finally there was a wail. André cried until he could cry no more. Then he wiped his face with his shirt tail and got to his feet. He went out into the courtyard and found a couple of jerry cans of petrol, doused the bar, the tables, the walls, the floor, then struck a match and watched as flames engulfed the room. I grabbed his elbow and dragged him outside. He stood on the terrace, watching spellbound as the diner burned.

When the flames began to lick at the roof, André went back to his car. Without a word, without even looking at me, he turned the ignition, released the handbrake and drove slowly back towards the village.

On 4 July 1962, a Peugeot 203 stopped in front of the pharmacy. Two men in suits and dark glasses ordered me to come with them. 'It's just a formality,' one of them said in Arabic, with a strong Kabylia accent. Germaine was ill and in bed. 'It won't take long,' the driver promised me. I climbed into the back seat, the car made a U-turn and I let my head fall back against the seat. I had spent the whole night at Germaine's bedside, and I was exhausted.

Río Salado looked like the end of an era, drained of its essence, delivered up to some new destiny. The French tricolour that had flown outside the town hall had been taken down. On the village square, a crowd of people in turbans stood listening to a speaker perched on the coping of the fountain. He was addressing them in Arabic and they were hanging on his every word. A few Europeans moved through the shadows, those who had been unable to leave behind their lands, their cemeteries, their houses, the cafés where their friendships had been forged, their projects; in sum, the small piece of their homeland that was their reason for living.

It was a beautiful day, the sun as big as the sadness of those leaving, as vast as the joy of those returning. The vines seemed to ripple in the sun and the heat haze in the distance looked like the ocean. Here and there, farms were burning. The silence that weighed heavy on the street seemed to be brooding. The men in front of me did not say a word. I could see nothing but the backs of their necks, the driver's hands on the steering wheel and the watch glittering on the wrist of the man next to him. We drove through Lourmel as though through some strange dream. Here, too, crowds were gathered about inspired orators. Green and white flags with a red crescent and a star bore witness to the birth of the new republic, to an Algeria that had been returned to its own.

As we approached Oran, abandoned cars lined the sides of the road, some burned out, others looted, the doors ripped off and the boot open. Bags and trunks and suitcases were strewn everywhere, torn open; clothes hung in the bushes, belongings lay on the road. There were signs of violence too: blood in the dust, windscreens shattered by iron bars. Many fleeing families were captured and butchered; others escaped through the orange groves and tried to reach the city on foot.

Oran was in turmoil. Thousands of children ran through the patches of waste ground, hurling stones at passing cars, shouting and singing. The streets were teeming with joyful crowds. The buildings shook to the screams of women wearing their veils like banners, rang with the sound of *bendirs*, drums, *darboukas*, the blare of car horns and patriotic songs.

The Peugeot drove into the barracks at Magent, where the National Liberation Army, who had recently taken the city, had set up its headquarters. It parked in front of a building. The driver leaned out and asked the guard to tell the lieutenant that his 'guest' had arrived.

The parade ground was teeming with men in combat uniform, old men wearing djellabas, and civilians.

'Jonas, my old friend Jonas, it's so good to see you again.'

Standing at the top of the steps, Jelloul spread his arms wide. He was the lieutenant. He was wearing a paratrooper's uniform, a safari hat, a pair of sunglasses but no stripes.

He hugged me hard enough to choke me, then held me at arm's length and looked me up and down.

'You've got thin,' he said. 'What have you been up to? I've been thinking about you a lot recently. You're an educated man, you responded when your country called, and I wondered whether you might like to put your education and your diplomas at the service of the new republic. You don't have to give me an answer right away. In fact, that's not why I had you brought here. I owe you something, and I want to repay you today, because tomorrow is another day and I intend to begin my new life with all my debts washed away. How can I enjoy untrammelled freedom if I've got debtors on my heels?'

'You don't owe me anything, Jelloul.'

'That's kind of you, but I want to be in your debt. I've never forgotten the day you gave me money and took me back to my village on your bicycle. For you, I suppose, it meant nothing; for me it was a revelation: I discovered that the Arab, the good Arab, the noble, generous Arab was not a mythical figure, nor was he what the colonist had made him . . . I'm not educated, I don't have the words to explain what I felt, but it changed my life.'

He caught me by the arm.

'Come with me.'

He led me to a building lined with metal doors, which I realised were jail cells. He slipped a key into one of the doors, shot back the lock and said:

'He was a ferocious militant in the OAS and implicated in dozens of terrorist attacks. I had to move heaven and earth to stop him being executed. I leave him to you. This way I will have paid my debt . . . Go on, open the door and tell him he's a free man, that he can go anywhere he likes, anywhere but *my* country, he's not welcome here.'

He saluted me, turned on his heel and went back to his office.

I didn't know what he was referring to. I reached out my hand, turned the handle and slowly opened the door. The hinges creaked. Daylight streamed into the windowless cell and a wave of heat flooded out. There was a shadow huddled in a corner; dazzled at first, he brought his hand up to shield his eyes.

'Get out of here,' roared a guard I had not noticed standing next to me.

The prisoner moved with difficulty, leaning against the

wall to get to his feet. He had trouble standing. As he walked towards the door, my heart leapt in my chest. It was Chris – Jean-Christophe Lamy, or what was left of him. He was a broken man, scrawny and shivering, wearing a filthy torn shirt, a tattered pair of trousers with the fly undone and shoes with no laces. His face was pale, gaunt and unshaven, he smelled of sweat and urine, his lips were hidden by a crust of dried spittle. He gave me a black look, surprised to see me here to witness the state to which he had been reduced. He tried to lift his head but was too exhausted. The guard grabbed him by the scruff of the neck and dragged him from the cell.

'Leave him alone,' I told him.

Jean-Christophe looked me up and down.

'I didn't ask you for anything,' he said.

As he limped away towards the exit of the barracks, I couldn't help but remember all the things we had shared, the memories of our youthful innocence, and a sudden wave of sadness came over me. I watched him shamble away, stooped and stumbling, and as he went, a whole life went with him. I realised that the reason the stories my mother had told me long ago had seemed unsatisfying was because they ended with the era Jean-Christophe had chosen to ally himself to – an era that now shuffled away with him towards some uncertain destiny.

I walked through the teeming streets, through the singing and the shouting, beneath the fluttering green and white flags as the trams clanged and clattered past. The next day, 5 July, Algeria would have an identity card, a symbol, a national anthem and a thousand other things still to devise. On the balconies, women whooped and wept tears of joy.

Children danced in the squares, climbing over monuments and fountains, up lamp posts and on to car roofs. Their cries drowned out the fanfares and the tumult, the sirens and the chatter; they were already tomorrow.

I went down to the port to watch the exodus. The quays were crowded with passengers, luggage and waving handkerchiefs. Steamers waiting to lift anchor groaned beneath the weight of the sorrow of those leaving. Families searched for each other in the crowds, children wept, old men slept on their suitcases, praying in their sleep that they might never wake. Leaning on a railing overlooking the port, I thought of Émilie, who might well be here in this crowd of helpless souls jostling before the door to the unknown. She might already have left; she might be dead; she might still be packing her cases in one of the buildings I could see around me. I stayed at the port until the dawn broke, leaning over the railing, unable to reconcile myself to the idea that something that had never really begun was truly over.

4. Aix-en-Provence (Present Day)

'MONSIEUR . . .'

The angelic face of the air hostess smiles at me. Why is she smiling at me? Where am I? I must have dozed off. After a moment of hesitation I realise I am on a plane, white as an operating theatre, and the clouds I can see flashing past the window are not some glimpse of the hereafter. And it all comes back to me: *Émilie is dead. She passed away on Monday in Aix-en-Provence hospital.* Fabrice Scamaroni had phoned a week ago to let me know.

'Could you bring your seat back up, monsieur, we're about to land . . .'

The gentle voice of the flight attendant echoes dully in my mind. What seat? My neighbour, a teenage boy in a hooded top emblazoned with the colours of the Algerian football team, points to a button on the armrest and helps me adjust my seat.

'Thank you,' I say.

'No problem, Grandad. You live in Marseille?'

'No.'

'My cousin's picking me up at the airport. We can give you a lift somewhere If you like.'

'That's very kind, but there's no need. There's someone meeting me.'

I look at his head, bizarrely shaved to conform to some curious fashion, with a single tuft of hair at the front held upright by a thick layer of gel.

'You scared of flying?' he asks me.

'Not particularly.'

'My dad can't even watch a plane land; he puts his hands over his eyes.'

'That bad, really?'

'You don't know my dad. We live on the ninth floor of Jean de la Fontaine, the housing estate in Gambetta in Oran, you know it? Those huge tower blocks facing away from the sea. Anyway, nine times out of ten my dad won't even take the lift – even though he's pretty old, he's, like, fifty-eight and he's had prostate surgery.'

'Fifty-eight isn't all that old.'

'Yeah, I know, but where I come from we don't say dad, we say the old man . . . How old are you, Grandad?'

'I was born so long ago I've forgotten.'

The plane is swallowed up by thick cloud, there is a flurry of turbulence and it goes into a nosedive. The boy next to me pats the back of my hand, which is clutching the armrest:

'Don't worry, Grandad, it's like we've come off the motorway on to a back road. It'll be fine in a minute. Flying is the safest way to travel.'

I look out of the window, watch the fleecy clouds become an avalanche, then mist, thinning out only to reappear thicker than ever, then disappear again. The blue sky returns, scuffed with frayed streaks of white. Why have I come here? I hear my uncle's voice above the roar of the engines: *If you want your life to be a small part of eternity, to be lucid even in the heart of madness, love . . . Love with all your strength, love as though it is all you know how to do, love enough to make the gods themselves jealous . . . for it is in love that all ugliness reveals its beauty.* These were my uncle's last words, the words he said to me on his deathbed in Río Salado. Even now, half a century later, his cracked voice still rings in my head like a prophecy: *A man who passes over the great love of his life will only be as old as his regrets, and all the sighing in the world will not be enough to soothe his soul.* Is it to disprove this truth or to face it that I have come so far? The plane wheels and turns and suddenly, out of nowhere, I see France. My heart stutters, and an invisible hand closes around my throat. It is so intense that I can feel my fingers ripping through the fabric of the armrest. Now I see rocky mountain peaks reflecting the sunlight, perpetual, implacable sentinels that keep watch over the shore, indifferent to the raging sea that dashes itself against the cliffs at their feet. Then, as the plane wheels, Marseille . . . like a vestal virgin lazing in the sun. Sprawled over the hillsides, radiant, dazzling, her navel bared, hip exposed to the four winds, she pretends to sleep, pretends not to notice the murmur of the waves and the whispers that drift in from the hinterland. Marseille, the legendary city, the land of titans, the landing place of the gods of Olympus, the crossroads of lost horizons, manifold because she is boundless in her generosity; Marseille, my last battlefield, where I finally had to lay down my arms, crushed by my inability to accept a challenge, to be worthy of my own happiness.

Here, in this city, the miraculous is a state of mind, the sun illuminates all consciences willing to take the trouble to unbolt their hidden trapdoors. It was here that I realised the extent of the pain I had caused, pain I have never forgiven myself. Forty-five years ago I came to this city to find the broken shards of my destiny, to try to put them back together, fill in the missing pieces, tend to the cracks, to make amends to fortune for failing to seize my chance when I had it, for having doubted, for having chosen to be prudent when it was offering me her heart; to beg for forgiveness in the name of that which God places above all accomplishments and all misfortunes: love. I came here distraught, uncertain but sincere, in search of redemption, mine first and foremost, but also that of those I still loved, despite the hatred that had come between us, the greyness that had clouded our summers. I still remember this port, its flickering lights welcoming steamships from Oran, the darkness that shrouded the quays, the shadows on the gangways. I can still see clearly the face of the customs officer with his curly moustache who asked me to empty my pockets and stand with my hands up like a criminal; the policeman who obviously disapproved of his colleague's zeal; the taxi driver who drove me to my hotel and swore at me because I slammed the car door too hard; the woman at the reception desk who had me wait half the night while she checked to see if there was a room available somewhere nearby, because I had failed to confirm my reservation . . . It was a terrible night in March 1964. The mistral howled and a coppery sky growled thunderously. My room had no heating. Though I rolled myself up in the blankets in search of a glimmer of warmth, I was freezing. The window creaked with every gust of wind. On the bedside table, faintly lit by an anaemic lamp, was my leather bag. Inside it was a letter from André Sosa:

Dear Jonas,

I've done what you asked and found Émilie. It took a long time, but I'm glad I've found her. Glad for you. She works as a secretary to a lawyer in Marseille. I tried to call her, but she refused to speak to me!! I'm not sure why. We were never really close, or at least not close enough to have fallen out. Maybe she mistook me for someone else. The war swept away so many of the country's points of reference that I sometimes wonder if what we went through was not just some group hallucination. But let's leave time to do its mourning. The wounds are still too fresh to insist that those who survived show restraint . . . Émilie's address is: 143, Rue des Frères-Julien. It's not far from La Canebière, you'll find it easily. Her building is opposite a café called Le Palmier, which is pretty well known. It's where all the pieds-noirs go now. Can you imagine, that's what they call us these days — 'pieds-noirs' — as though we've spent our whole lives trudging through mud . . .

Call me when you get to Marseille. It would be wonderful to see you and give you a kick up the backside.

Much love, Dédé.

The Rue des Frères-Julien was five blocks from my hotel. The taxi driver took me on a scenic trip for half an hour before dropping me off outside Le Palmier. The café was heaving. After the storm the previous night, Marseille glittered in the sunshine, light dappling the faces of the people. Wedged between two modern structures, number 143 was an old building of faded green with ramshackle windows and rickety shutters; a few flower pots bravely attempted to liven up the balconies shaded by drooping awnings. It had a curious effect on me. It was as drab and gloomy as though it repelled the sunlight, despised the exuberance of the street. I found it difficult to imagine Émilie laughing, smiling behind those dreary windows.

I took a table by the window in the café so that I could watch the coming and going opposite. It was a glorious Sunday – the rain had scoured the pavements clean and the streets were steaming. Around me, people with nothing better to do than set the world to rights over glasses of red wine; their accents were those of the Algerian suburbs, their faces were weathered still by the southern sun, they rolled their Rs with relish like stirring couscous. Though the conversations ranged across the planet, they invariably circled back to Algeria. It was all they could talk about.

'You know what I keep thinking, Juan? I keep thinking about the omelette I forgot on the cooker while I was rushing to pack my suitcase and get out of there. I'm wondering whether the house burned to the ground after.'

'Are you serious, Roger?'

'Of course I'm serious. You're always banging on about all the things you had to leave back in the *bled*. You never talk about anything else.'

'What do you want me to talk about? Algeria is my whole life.'

'In that case, why don't you drop dead and give me a bit of fucking peace? I've got other things to think about.'

At the bar, three drunks in Basque berets were drinking to their wild life as young men in Bab el-Oued. They were doing their best to be quiet, but people could hear them on the far side of the street. Next to me, twin brothers talked in thick, slurred voice over a table covered with empty beer bottles and full ashtrays. Their swarthy faces reminded me of the fishermen in Algiers in their faded sweaters, unlit cigarette butts dangling from their lips.

'I told you she was just using you, little brother. The girls here aren't like they are back home. Back home women respect men, they won't let you down. Anyway, I can't think what you saw in that frigid bitch. I feel cold just thinking about you with her. And she couldn't cook . . .'

I drank three or four cups of coffee, never taking my eyes from the door of 143. Then I had lunch. No sign of Émilie. The drunks at the bar had left; so had the twins. The chatter and the noise died away a little, only to pick up again when a group of half-drunk friends piled in. The waiter broke a couple of glasses, then spilled a carafe of water over a customer who took this as an opportunity to tell anyone who would listen exactly what he thought of Le Palmier, of *pieds-noirs*, of Marseille, of France, of Europe, of Arabs, of Jews, of the Portuguese and of his own family, 'a bunch of selfish hypocrites', who hadn't been able to find a wife for him even though he was about to turn forty. Everyone waited until he had spewed all the bile he had to spew, then he was politely asked to leave.

The day was drawing in; night was preparing to besiege the city. Every bone in my body was starting to ache from sitting waiting in the corner, when finally she appeared from the door of 143. She had no hat, her hair was piled into a chignon, she wore a raincoat with a flared collar and boots that came up to her thighs. Hands in her pockets, clearly in a hurry to be somewhere, she looked like a schoolgirl off to play with her friends.

I left all the change I had in the bread basket the waiter had forgotten to clear away and rushed to catch her up.

Suddenly I felt scared. Did I have the right to intrude in her life? Had she forgiven me?

Desperate to drown out the questions in my head, I heard myself call out: 'Émilie!'

She stopped abruptly, as though she had met an invisible wall. She must have recognised my voice, because her shoulders tensed and she drew her head in. She did not turn. She listened for a moment and then walked on.

'Émilie!'

This time she turned so quickly that she almost fell. Her eyes shimmered, her face was pale, but she quickly composed herself, choking back her tears. I smiled stupidly at her, having no idea what else to do. What would I say to her? Where could I begin? I had been in such a hurry to see her again that I not thought what I might do when I found her.

Émilie stared at me, wondering if I were really flesh and blood.

'It's me.'

'And . . . ?'

Her face was a mask of bronze, a cloudy mirror; I could never have believed she could react to my presence with such indifference.

'I've looked for you everywhere.'

'Why?'

The question caught me unawares. I lost the power of speech. How could she not see what was staring her in the face? I was reeling, like a punch-drunk boxer. I was dumb-struck. I did not know what to do now.

'What do you mean, why?' I heard myself stammer. 'The only reason I am here is because of you.'

'We said everything we had to say back in Oran.'

She was perfectly still, only her lips moved.

'Things were different in Oran.'

'Oran, Marseille, it's all the same.'

'You know that's not true, Émilie. The war is over, life goes on.'

'For you, maybe . . .'

I was sweating now.

'I really thought that—'

'Then you were wrong.' She cut me off.

Her coldness froze my thoughts, my words, my soul.

'Émilie . . . tell me what I have to do, but please, don't look at me like that. I'd give anything to—'

'You can only give what you have. Sometimes not even that, and you don't have *anything* . . . Besides, what good would it do? We can't solve the problems of the world, and it has taken much more from me than it can ever repay.'

'I'm so sorry.'

'They're just words. I think I told you that before.'

My grief was such that it filled my whole being; there was no room left for anger or resentment.

Against all expectations, her dark look softened and her features relaxed. She stared at me for a long time as though she were going far back into the past to find me. Finally she came towards me, her perfume hanging heavy in the air. She took my face in her hands the way my mother used to do to kiss me on the forehead. Émilie did not kiss me on the forehead, or on the cheek; she simply stared at me. Her breath mingled with mine. I wanted her to hold my face like this until the Last Judgement.

'Nobody is to blame, Younes. You don't owe me anything. It's just the way the world is, and I don't want that any more.'

She turned and walked away.

I stood on the pavement, speechless, frozen, and watched her walk out of my life.

It was the last time I ever saw her.

That night I took the boat back to Algeria, and not until today did I set foot in France again.

I wrote letters to her, sent her cards for her birthday and every holiday . . . Not once did she reply. I told myself she had moved, that she had gone away, as far away as she could from her memories of me, and that perhaps it was for the best. I missed her terribly, thought about the life we might have made together, the wounds we might have healed and those that would have healed themselves in time, the old demons we would have exorcised. Émilie had nothing she wanted to save, no page to turn, no pain she needed to grieve over. The few moments she had granted me on that pavement beneath the blazing sun had been enough for me to realise that there are doors that, once they close upon some sorrow, become an abyss that even the light of heaven cannot penetrate. For a long time I suffered over Émilie; I felt her pain, her self-denial, her decision to live shut up in her own tragedy. Later I tried to forget her, hoping to temper the pain in both of us. I had to accept it, had to confront what my heart stubbornly refused to face. Life is a train that stops at no stations; you either jump aboard or stand on the platform and watch as it passes, and there is nothing sadder than an abandoned station. Was I happy after that? I think so. I experienced moments of pleasure, moments of unforgettable joy; I loved again and dreamed again like a wide-eyed boy. And yet I always felt that there was something missing, something that left me somehow crippled, in short that I only ever hovered on the fringes of happiness.

The plane lands on the tarmac in a roar of the reverse thrust of the engines. The boy next to me points to the planes waiting to take off. Over the speakers, a flight attendant's voice tells us the temperature outside, the local time, and thanks us for choosing Air Algérie, before insisting that we remain seated with our seat belts fastened until the plane comes to a complete stop.

The teenager carries my hand luggage and gives it back to me when we reach immigration. After the official formalities, he points me to the exit, apologising that he has to wait for his luggage.

The frosted glass door into the arrivals hall slides back. Behind the yellow line, people are waiting impatiently to recognise a familiar face among the stream of arriving passengers. A little girl lets go her of father's hand, runs up and throws herself into the arms of a granny wearing a djellaba. A young woman is plucked from the crowd by her husband, who kisses her chastely on both cheeks, but there is passion in their eyes.

A man of about fifty stands off to one side holding a sign marked 'Río Salado'. For a second it is like seeing a ghost. He is the image of Simon: short, stocky, pot-bellied and bow-legged, his hair already receding. And his eyes are Simon's eyes; those eyes that immediately recognise me — how can he spot me in this crowd when we have never met before? The man gives me a little smile, comes over and holds out a chubby hand exactly like his father's.

'Michel?'

'That's me, Monsieur Jonas. Pleased to meet you. Did you have a good flight?'

'I slept for a bit.'

'Have you got any luggage?'

'Just this bag.'

'Okay. My car is in the car park.' He takes the bag and gestures for me to follow him.

Slip roads branch out dizzyingly ahead of us. Michel drives fast, eyes fixed on the road ahead. I don't dare to turn and look at him; I simply see his face in profile. It is astonishing how much he looks like Simon, my old friend, his father. My chest tightens at the fleeting memory. I take a deep breath to expel the poison suddenly seeping through me. Focus on the road as it whips past, on the shimmering sunlight of the cars as they weave, on the road signs flashing past above our heads: Salon de Provence, straight ahead, Marseille, bear right at next exit; Vitrolles, next exit . . .

'I expect you're hungry, Monsieur Jonas. I know a nice little bistro . . .'

'That's all right, they served us dinner on the plane.'

'I've booked you into the 4 Dauphins, not far from the Cours Mirabeau. You're lucky, apparently it's going to be sunny all week.'

'I'll only be staying for a couple of days.'

'Everybody's waiting to see you. Two days will never be enough.'

'I have to get back to Río Salado. My grandson is getting married . . . I wanted to come earlier, to be at the funeral, but getting a visa in Algiers is a devil of a job. I had to get friends in high places to put in a word . . .'

The car hurtles into a tunnel beneath a vast fortress of glass and steel that seems to surge from nowhere.

'It's the Aix-en-Provence TGV station,' Michel explains.

'But we're not in the city.'

'The station is on the outskirts. It's only been open five or six years. The town is about fifteen minutes away. Have you ever been to Aix, Monsieur Jonas?'

'No . . . In fact I've only ever been to France once. To Marseille in March 1964. I arrived at night and left the following night.'

'Just a flying visit?'

'You could say that.'

'Deported?'

'Rejected.'

Michel looks at me, puzzled.

'It's a long story,' I say, to change the subject.

We drive through a commercial district full of hypermarkets, shopping centres and underground car parks. Huge neon signs vie with billboards and a sea of people streams around the shops and the markets. There is a traffic jam at the exit and the tailback is half a mile long.

'The consumer society,' Michel says. 'People seem to spend their weekends shopping these days. It's terrible, isn't it? My wife and I come every other Saturday. If we miss a Saturday, we find we start arguing over nothing at all.'

'Every generation has its own drugs.'

'You're very right, Monsieur Jonas, every generation has its drugs.'

We are now coming in to Aix-en-Provence, twenty minutes late because of an accident at the Pont de l'Arc. The weather is beautiful and the whole town seems to have shut up shop and headed for the centre. The pavements are teeming with pedestrians and the atmosphere is festive. The stone lions are standing guard around the fountain in the middle of the roundabout on La Rotonde. A Japanese man is taking his girlfriend's photograph through the whirl of traffic. A small fairground has a flock of children crowding around a handful of attractions; children attached to bungee cords are making death-defying leaps as their terrified parents watch. The sunlit café terraces are full to overflowing, there is not a single free table; the waiters race around, trays balanced precariously. Michel lets a minibus full of tourists pass and drives slowly up the Cours Mirabeau, turning near the top on the Rue du 4 Septembre. My hotel is next to the Fountain of the Four Dolphins. A young blonde girl greets us at the reception desk and has me fill out a form, then directs me to a room on the third floor. A bellhop takes us upstairs, sets my bag down on a table, opens a window, checks that everything is in order and, wishing me a pleasant stay, disappears again.

'I'll leave you to take a nap,' says Michel. 'I'll come back and pick you up in a couple of hours.'

'I'd like to go to the cemetery.'

'We're doing that tomorrow. Today, you're coming over to my house.'

'I have to go to the cemetery now, while it's still light. Honestly, I need to.'

'Okay. I'll call our friends and ask them to put things back an hour.'

'Thank you. I don't need to freshen up and I certainly don't need a nap. We can go now if that's all right with you.'

'I've got something I need to do. Can we go in about an hour?'

'That would be fine, I'll be waiting downstairs at reception.'

Michel takes out his mobile phone and heads out, closing the door behind him.

He comes back an hour later and picks me up on the steps outside the hotel. I get into the car and he asks if I managed to get any rest; I tell him I lay down for a bit and feel much better now. We head down the Cours Mirabeau, still humming in the shade of the plane trees.

'What are they celebrating?' I ask.

'Life, Monsieur Jonas. Aix celebrates life every day.'

'It's always like this here?'

'Pretty much.'

'You're very lucky to live here.'

'I wouldn't live anywhere else. My mother used to say that the sun here almost makes up for missing Río Salado.'

Saint-Pierre cemetery, where Paul Cézanne among others is buried, is deserted. At the gates, a stone monument commemorating the French of Algeria and others who were repatriated greets me. The inscription reads: *The true resting place of the dead is the hearts of the living.* Tarmac pathways lead between grassy areas and ancient chapels. There are photos on some of the tombs as reminders of those who have passed away: a mother, a husband, a brother who died before their time. There are flowers on the graves and the shimmer of marble softens the harsh sunlight and fills the silence with an almost rural tranquillity. Michel leads me through the carefully laid-out paths, shoes crunching on the gravel. Grief is closing in. He stops before a grave with a black granite headstone heaped with mounds of wreaths and dazzling flowers. An inscription reads: *Émilie Benyamin, née Cazenave, 1931–2008*.

There is nothing more.

'I expect you'd like to be alone for a minute?' Michel says.

'Please.'

'I'll take a little walk.'

'That's very kind.'

Michel nods his head gently, biting his lower lip. His grief is overwhelming. He walks away, chin pressed against his chest, hands clasped behind his back. When he disappears behind a row of red limestone crypts, I crouch down next to Émilie's grave, clasp my hands next to my lips and recite a verse from the Qur'an. It is not Sunni tradition, but I do it all the same. In the eyes of popes and imams we are Us and Them, but in the eyes of the Lord we are one. I recite the Sura Al-Fatiha and two passages from the Sura Ya-Seen.

Then, from my pocket, I take out a small cotton purse. I untie the string and open it, slip my shivering fingers inside, take out a pinch of dried petals and scatter them over the grave; this dust is all that remains of a flower picked from a rose bush in a pot almost seventy years ago; the remains of the rose I slipped between the pages of Émilie's geography book while Germaine was giving her her injection in the pharmacy in Río Salado.

I put the empty purse back in my pocket and get to my feet. My legs are trembling; I have to lean against the headstone. It is my own footsteps I hear on the gravel now. My head is filled with fragments of voices and fleeting images. Émilie sitting in the doorway of our pharmacy, the hood of her coat pulled up, fingers playing with the laces of her boots. *I could have mistaken her for an angel come down from heaven.* Émilie absently leafing through a large hardback book. *What are you reading? A book about Guadeloupe. What's Guadeloupe? It's a French island in the Caribbean.* Émilie the day before her engagement party *Say yes — just say yes and I'll call it all off*. Ahead of me the path is reeling. I feel ill. I try to walk faster but I can't. Like in a dream, my legs refuse to move; they are rooted to the spot.

There is an old man standing at the gates of the cemetery wearing a uniform decked out with medals from the war. He leans on a walking stick, dark eyes staring out of his crumpled face, and watches me stagger towards him. He does not step aside to let me pass; he waits until I come alongside him and says to me:

'The French have left. The Jews and the Gypsies have left. There's just you lot left in Algeria, so why are you still slaughtering one other?'

I don't know what he is referring to or why he is talking to me like this. I can glean nothing from his face. I have a sudden flash of memory: this is Krimo. Krimo who swore he would kill me back in Río Salado. Just as I remember who he is, a searing pain shoots through my jaw; the same pain I once felt long ago when he hit me with his rifle butt.

'Remember me now? I can tell from your face that you remember me.'

I gently push him aside and walk on.

'It's true, though, isn't it? What is it with the massacres, the bombings that go on and on? You wanted independence – you've got it. You wanted to decide your own fate? Fine! And what have you got? Civil war, terrorists, the Armed Islamic Group. Isn't that proof enough that all you people are good at is wrecking and killing?'

'Please, I came to visit a grave, not to dig up the past.'

'How touching.'

'What do you want, Krimo?'

'Me? Nothing . . . Just to get a good look at you. When Michel phoned to tell us the reunion had been pushed back an hour, it was like they'd postponed the Last Judgement.'

'I don't know what you mean.'

'That doesn't surprise me, Younes. Have you ever stopped to think what a tragedy your life is?'

'I don't want to have to listen to you, Krimo. I didn't come here to see you.'

'But I came to see you – came all the way from Alicante to tell you that I haven't forgotten, and I haven't forgiven.'

'That's why you dragged your old uniform and your medals out of some cardboard box rotting away in your cellar?'

'Got it in one.'

'I'm not God, and I'm not the republic. I don't have the authority to recognise your people or to sympathise with your grief. I'm just a survivor who doesn't know how he came through without a scratch when he was no better and no worse than those who died . . . If it's any comfort, we're all in the same boat. *We* betrayed our martyrs, *you* betrayed your ancestors, only to be betrayed in turn.'

'I never betrayed anyone.'

'You poor fool. Don't you realise that one way or another, everyone who survives a war is a traitor?'

Krimo wants to wade in again, his mouth is twisted with rage, but Michel's sudden reappearance stops him in his tracks. He looks me up and down, then steps aside to let me pass, and I walk down to where the car is parked next to a fairground.

'Are you coming with us, Krimo?' Michel asks him, opening the car door.

'No, I'll take a taxi.'

Michel does not insist.

'Sorry about Krimo,' Michel says as he starts the car.

'Don't worry about it. Am I going to get the same kind of welcome wherever we're going?'

'We're going to my house. This might surprise you, but a couple of hours ago Krimo was jumping up and down he was so excited about seeing you again. He didn't seem angry or upset. He flew in last night from Spain and spent all night laughing and joking about the good old days in Río Salado. I don't know what got into him.'

'He'll get over it, and so will I.'

'Probably for the best. My mother used to say that sensible people always make up in the end.'

'Émilie used to say that?'

'Yeah, why?'

I don't answer.

'How many children have you got, Monsieur Jonas?'

'Two, a boy and a girl.'

'Grandchildren?'

'Five . . . the youngest – he's getting married next week

— was the champion diver in Algeria four years running. But my pride and joy is Norah, my granddaughter. She's twenty-five and she runs one of the most important publishing houses in the country.'

Michel accelerates. We drive along the Route d'Avignon and stop at a red light; a sign points to Chemin Brunet and Michel takes it. The road winds steeply upwards, lined on either side by walls behind which are beautiful villas, glorious houses protected by high gates. The neighbour-hood is tranquil, radiant and burgeoning with flowers. In the street there is not a single child playing, only a handful of old people waiting in the shade of climbing vines for their bus.

The Benyamin house is on the brow of the hill, nestled in a grove of trees. It is a small white villa surrounded by ivy-covered walls. Michel presses a remote control and the gate opens automatically to reveal a large garden and, in the distance, three men sitting at a patio table.

I clamber out. Two of the three old men get up. We stare at each other in silence. I recognise the taller man, one of my neighbours back in Río Salado, a little stooped now and bald, but I cannot remember his name. We were never very close; we'd say hello when we passed each other in the street, then promptly forget about each other. His father was station-master at the local train station. Next to him I recognise a man of about seventy — well preserved, with a determined chin and a high forehead — as Bruno, the young policeman who loved to strut about the village square, twirling his whistle around one finger. I am surprised to see him here; I'd heard he'd been killed in an OAS attack in Oran. He comes up to me and holds out his left hand – his right hand is a prosthesis.

'Jonas . . . it's a pleasure to see you again.'

'It's lovely to see you too, Bruno.'

The tall man also greets me, limply shaking my hand; he clearly feels self-conscious. I suppose we all do. In the car, I had been imagining a joyful reunion, wholehearted embraces, throaty laughs counterpointed by loud claps on the backs. I imagined myself hugging some, holding others at arm's length so that I could look at them, hearing old nicknames, old jokes; slipping back into childhood as someone told a story, finally exorcising fears that had haunted us for years, keeping only those memories we cherished. But now that we are finally together, all in one place, a strange awkwardness drains all our enthusiasm and we stand, speechless, like children meeting for the first time who do not know how to start the conversation.

'You don't remember me, Jonas?' the tall man asks.

'Your name is on the tip of my tongue, but I remember you – you lived at number six, behind Madame Lambert. I can still see you climbing over her wall to pilfer from her orchard.'

'It was hardly an orchard . . . just one big fig tree.'

'It was an orchard. I live at number thirteen, and I still hear Madame Lambert yelling at kids scrumping fruit from her orchard.'

'My God . . . all I remember is that big fig tree.'

'Gustave!' I shout, clicking my fingers. 'Now I remember – Gustave Cusset, the class clown. Always showing off.'

Gustave bursts out laughing, pulls me to him and hugs me hard.

'What about me?' the third man asks, not getting up from the table. 'Do you remember me? I never went out scrumping apples, and in class I was as obedient as a puppy.'

He has really aged – André J. Sosa, the braggart, the big shot of Río Salado, who used to fritter money away as fast as his father earned it. He is huge, obese even, his paunch hanging down to his knees; his braces barely hold it up. He's bald now, his face barely recognisable through the creases and the wrinkles. He smiles, showing a perfect set of false teeth.

'Dédé!'

'That's me,' he says. 'An immortal, like they say about those old codgers in the Académie Française.'

He pushes his wheelchair towards me.

'I can walk,' he insists. 'I'm just a little heavy . . .'

We throw our arms around each other and the tears that were misting our eyes begin to trickle down; we do not even try to stop them. We cry, we laugh, we slap each other on the back.

Evening surprises us, still sitting at the table, laughing and hacking hard enough to cough up our lungs. Krimo, who arrived an hour ago, is no longer angry with me. He said all he had to say at the cemetery; he is sitting facing me, feeling guilty about the things we said to each other, but he has the tranquil air of someone who has come to terms with things. It was a long time before he dared to look up at me. That done, he joins in our tales of Río Salado, about the end-of-season balls, the grape harvests, camping out in the moonlight, the drinking sessions and getting our leg over afterwards, about Pépé Rucillio and his secret escapades; not once does he recall anything unpleasant, any painful memory.

Michel's wife Martine, a strapping woman from Aoulef, half Berber, half Breton, whips up a bouillabaisse of gargantuan proportions. The *rouille* is delicious and the fish tender.

'You still don't drink?' Dédé asks me.

'Not a drop.'

'You don't know what you're missing.'

'If only that was *all* I was missing.'

He pours himself a glass, looks at it, and knocks it back in one.

'Is it true there's no wine-making in Río Salado any more?'

'It's true.'

'Fuck . . . what a waste. I swear there are times when I can still taste that glorious wine we used to make, Alicante d'El Maleh; it made us want to drink and drink until we couldn't tell a pumpkin from an old woman's arse.'

'The agricultural revolution ripped out all the vineyards in the area.'

'What did they plant instead?' Gustave asked indignantly. 'Potatoes?'

André moves the bottle standing on the table between us.

'What about Jelloul? What's happened to him? I know he was a captain in the Algerian army and that he was in charge of a military sector in the Sahara, but I haven't had any news of him for a couple of years now.'

'By the time he retired in 1990 he was a colonel. He never did live in Río Salado; he bought a little villa in Oran where he planned to live out his days. But then the riots started. A terrorist from the Armed Islamic Group gunned him down outside his own house, shot him with a single bullet while he was sitting daydreaming on his porch.'

André started, suddenly sober.

'Jelloul is dead?'

'Yes.'

'Killed by a terrorist?'

'By an *emir* in the AIG. And wait till you hear this, Dédé: it was his own nephew.'

'Jelloul was killed by his own nephew?'

'You heard what I said.'

'My God, there's a terrible irony there.'

Fabrice Scamaroni doesn't arrive until late in the evening because of the railway strike. The round of hugs and handshakes strikes up again. Fabrice and I have never lost touch. He is an important journalist and a successful writer. I often see him on television. He regularly comes back to Algeria on assignments for his paper and always makes the most of it and comes down to Río Salado. He stays at my house. Every time he visits, rain or snow, he and I get up early in the morning and go to the Christian cemetery to visit his father's grave. His mother died during the 1970s when a cruise ship sank off the coast of Sardinia.

The table by now is strewn with wine bottles. We have resurrected our dead and drunk to their memory; asked after the living: what became of so-and-so, why did he decide to go and live in Argentina, why did so-and-so move to Morocco? André is drunk as a lord, but he's holding up well. Bruno and Gustave keep running from the garden to the bathroom. I keep glancing towards the gate.

One person is still missing: Jean-Christophe Lamy.

I know that he's still alive, that he and Isabelle have been running a thriving business on the Côte d'Azur. Why isn't he here? Nice is barely a couple of hours by car from Aix. André made it here from Bastia, Bruno from Perpignan, Krimo from Spain, Fabrice from Paris, Gustave from Saône-et-Loire. Is Jean-Christophe still angry with me? What did I do to him? In retrospect, nothing . . . I didn't do anything. I loved him like a brother, and like a brother I wept for him when he left, trailing the dust of a generation on his heels.

'Earth to Jonas!' Bruno shakes my shoulder.

'What?'

'What are you dreaming about? I've been talking to you for five minutes.'

'I'm sorry . . . you were saying?'

'I was talking about the old country. I was saying that we were orphaned by our country.'

'And I was orphaned by my friends – I don't know which of us lost more, but it doesn't matter, it takes the same toll on the heart.'

'I don't really think you lost more than we did on the deal, Jonas.'

'C'est la vie,' André says philosophically. 'Life gives with one hand and takes away with the other. But it's not the same, it's not the same thing at all . . . losing your friends or losing your country. It eats me up inside just thinking about it. If you want proof, round here we don't talk about *nostalgia*, we say *nost-algeria*.'

He takes a deep breath, his eyes glittering in the lamp-light.

'Algeria still clings to me,' he confesses. 'Sometimes it burns like the Tunic of Nessus, sometimes it envelops me like a delicate perfume. I've tried to shake it off, but I can't.

How can I forget it? I've tried to stop thinking about my youth, to move on, to start with a clean slate. I can't. I've tried to summon all the horrors, to spew them out, to be rid of them once and for all, but it's no use . . . The memories of the sun, the beaches, the streets, the food we ate, the glorious drunken nights we spent together, the happy times always overshadow the rage, and though I start out snarling I find myself smiling. I've never forgotten Río Salado, Jonas. Not for a day, not for a second. I remember every tuft of grass on our hill, every witty remark on the café terraces, and Simon's jokes and antics even overshadow his death, as though he was determined not to let us associate his tragic death with our dreams of Algeria. I swear, I've tried to forget them. More than anything, I have wanted to rip out every memory with a pair of pliers, like pulling out a rotten tooth. I've been all over the world, to Latin America, to Asia, to try to get some distance, to reinvent myself somewhere else. I needed to prove to myself that there were other countries, that a homeland can be rebuilt like a new family; but it's not true. I only have to stop for a second and the *bled* seeps back into me; I only have to turn around to see it, there where my shadow should be.'

'If we'd left of our own free will that would be one thing,' protests Gustave, who is two sips from alcoholic poisoning. 'But we were forced to leave everything, to run away, our suitcases filled with ghosts and grief. Everything was taken from us, even our souls. We were left with nothing, with less than nothing, not even eyes to weep with. It wasn't fair, Jonas. Not everyone was a colonist, not everyone went round slapping a riding crop against their aristocratic boots; some of us didn't have any boots at all. We had our own poor, our own poor neighbourhoods, our own dispossessed, our own good Samaritans, we had small craftsmen who were smaller than yours, and more often than not we prayed the same prayers. Why were we all treated as an indiscriminate mass? Why did we have to be lumped together with a handful of feudal lords? Why were we made to feel like outsiders in a country where our fathers and our grandfathers and our great-grandfathers were born? Why were we made to feel like usurpers in a country we built with our own hands and watered with our sweat, our blood? For as long as we don't know the answer, the wound will never heal . . .'

The direction the conversation is taking unsettles me. Krimo is already knocking back one glass after another; I'm worried that he will start in on the exchange we had in the graveyard.

'You know, Jonas . . .' he says suddenly; it is the first thing he has said to me since our encounter in the graveyard. 'I really want Algeria to come through this all right.'

'It'll come through,' says Fabrice. 'Algeria is dormant El Dorado. All it needs is a soul. Right now, it's searching for that soul in all the wrong places, so it's hardly surprising that it's a tragedy. But it's a young country, it has time to grow.'

Bruno grasps my hand and squeezes it hard.

'I'd like to go back to Río Salado, even if only for a couple of days.'

'Who's stopping you?' says André. 'There are flights to Oran and Tlemcen every day. In an hour and a half you can be up to your neck in shit.'

We laugh loud enough to wake the whole neighbour-hood.

'Seriously,' says Bruno.

'Seriously what?' I say. 'Dédé's right. You can jump on a plane and in less than two hours you can be home, for a day or for ever. Río Salado hasn't changed much. Oh, it's a bit more depressing than it was: the flowers have withered, the wine cellars are gone and the vineyards have all disappeared, but the people there are wonderful and charming. If you come to visit me, you'll have to visit everyone else, and eternity will not be long enough.'

Michel drives me back to my hotel shortly after midnight and walks me up to my room, where he gives me a small metal case locked with a padlock.

'A few days before she died, my mother asked me to give this to you personally. If you hadn't come, I would have had to make a trip to Río Salado.'

I take the case, stare at the flaking design on the lid. It is an antique candy box with engravings of scenes from aristocratic life, noblemen in their gardens, princes flirting with beautiful girls in the shade of a fountain; from the weight, there cannot be much inside it.

'I'll come by and pick you up tomorrow at ten a.m. We'll have lunch at the house of André Sosa's niece in Manosque.'

'I'll see you at ten o'clock. And thank you.'

'You're welcome, Monsieur Jonas. Good night.'

He leaves.

I sit on the edge of the bed, holding the box in my hands. What postscript has Émilie left me, what message from beyond the grave? I picture again the Rue des Frères-Julien in Marseille, that day in March 1964; I can see her face, like a mask of bronze, her bloodless lips crushing my last hope of making up for lost time. My hand is trembling; the cold metal chills me to the bone. I have to open it. What difference does it make whether it is a music box or Pandora's box? At eighty, the future is behind us; all that lies ahead is the past.

I open the tiny padlock, lift the lid: letters . . . There is nothing inside but letters. Dozens of envelopes yellowed by time and blistered by damp; others look as though they have been crumpled up and smoothed again. I recognise my handwriting on the envelopes, stamps from my own country . . . and I realise why Émilie never wrote back to me: she never opened my letters, never opened my cards.

I tip the envelopes on to the bed, check every one of them, hoping to come upon a letter from her. There is one, a recent one, still firm to the touch, with no stamp and no address, only my name written on the front, the envelope sealed with a piece of sellotape.

I cannot bring myself to open it.

Perhaps tomorrow . . .

We have lunch in Manosque, at the house of André's niece. Here again we trot out old stories, but we are beginning to run out of steam. Another *pied-noir* comes to see us. When I hear his voice, I think Jean-Christophe Lamy has finally arrived and the thought breathes new life into me, only to fade just as quickly when I realise it isn't him. The stranger stays for about an hour and then leaves. He listens to our stories but cannot make head or tail of them, and he realises that though he comes from the outskirts of Oran – from Lamorcière, near Tlemcen – he is intruding on a private conversation, disturbing something he does not understand. Bruno and Krimo are the next to go, first to Perpignan, where Krimo will spend the night at his friend's house before crossing the border into Spain. At about four o'clock, we leave and drop Fabrice at the TGV station outside Aix-en-Provence.

'Do you really have to go back tomorrow?' Fabrice asks. 'Hélène would love to see you. Paris is only three hours by train; you could fly back to Algeria from Orly. I live near the airport.'

'Some other time, Fabrice. Give Hélène my love. Is she still writing?'

'She retired a long time ago.'

The train pulls in, a magnificent beast. Fabrice hops up on to the step, hugs me one last time, and goes to find his seat. The train pulls off, moving away slowly. I crane my neck to see Fabrice through the carriage windows, and there he is, standing, one hand raised in a salute. Then the train sweeps him away.

Back in Aix, Gustave offers to take us to Les Deux Garçons. After dinner, we stroll up the Cours Mirabeau. The weather is mild, the café terraces are still full, young people are queuing outside the cinemas. A dishevelled musician is sitting in the middle of the esplanade retuning his violin, his dog curled up next to him.

Outside my hotel, two pedestrians and a driver are yelling at each other. Having run out of arguments, the driver climbs back into his car, slamming the door behind him.

My friends leave me in the capable hands of the receptionist and promise to pick me up at seven a.m. to drop me at the airport.

I take a hot shower and slip into bed.

On the nightstand is Émilie's box, as immutable as a funerary urn. My hand automatically reaches out and unfastens the padlock, but does not dare lift the lid.

I can't get to sleep. I try to clear my mind. I hug the pillows, turn on to my left side, on to my back. I feel miserable. Sleep isolates me and I don't want to be alone in the dark. A private conversation with myself does not appeal. I need to be surrounded by courtiers, to share my frustrations, to designate scapegoats. When you can't find a remedy for your pain, you look for someone to blame. My pain is nebulous. I feel a sadness, but I can't put my finger on the cause. Émilie? Jean-Christophe? Old age? The letter waiting for me in the box? Why didn't Jean-Christophe come? Does he still bear me that ancient grudge?

Through the window, which is open on to the deep blue sky where the moon glitters like a medal, I prepare myself to watch, in slow motion, the parade of my misdeeds, my joys, the familiar faces. I hear them arrive, a thunderous roar like a rockslide. How should I sort them? How should I behave? I am going round in circles on the edge of an abyss, an acrobat on a razor's edge, a mesmerised volcanologist on the edge of a bubbling crater; I am at the gates of memory, the endless reels of film we all file away, the great dark drawers stocked with the ordinary heroes we once were, the Camusian myths we never could embody, the actors and the roles we played, genius and grotesque, beautiful and monstrous, bowed beneath the weight of our small acts of cowardice, our feats of arms, our lies, our confessions, our oaths and recantations, our gallantry and desertion, our certainties and doubts; in short, our indomitable illusions.

What to keep of all these reels of film, what to throw away? If we could take only one memory on our journey, what would we choose? At the expense of what or whom? And most importantly, how to choose among all these shadows, all these spectres, all these titans? Who are we, when all is said and done? Are we the people we once were or the people we wish we had been? Are we the pain we caused others or the pain we suffered at the hands of others? The encounters we missed or those fortuitous meetings that changed the course of our destiny? Our time behind the scenes that saved us from our vanity or the moment in the limelight that warmed us? We are all of these things, we are the whole life that we have lived, its highs and lows, its fortunes and its hardships; we are the sum of the ghosts that haunt us . . . we are a host of characters in one, so convincing in every role we played that it is impossible for us to tell who we really were, who we have become, who we will be.

I listen to the voices of the past; I am no longer alone. Whispers whirl in these splinters of memory like fragments of a vast sound: cryptic phrases, strangled cries, laughter and sobbing impossible to tell apart . . . I can hear Isabelle playing the piano – Chopin – see her slender fingers moving nimbly over the keyboard; I seek out her face, which I imagine tense with blissful concentration; but the image does not change, it remains fixed on the piano keys as the notes explode in a ballet of fireworks . . . My dog appears from behind a hill, eyebrows like circumflexes, a mournful expression. I reach out to stroke him; the gesture is absurd, yet I do it nonetheless. My fingers slip over the bedspread as over fur. I allow these memories to take possession of my breathing, my insomnia, my whole being. I see our shack again, on the side of a dirt track that is fading away . . . I am the child I once was. We do not have a second childhood – we never truly emerge from the first. Am I old? What is an old man but a child who has amassed time and flab? My mother is running down the little hill, her feet raising dust into a thousand constellations. *Maman, my darling Maman* . . . A mother is not merely a person, nor a unique being, nor even an epoch; a mother is a presence that neither time nor failing of memory can alter. I am the proof; every day God sends, every night when I crawl under the sheets, I *know* that she is here, that she has been here beside me through the years, the fruitless prayers, the unfulfilled promises, the unbearable absences, all this futility . . . Farther off, crouched by a mound of stones, a straw hat pushed down on his head, my father watches the breeze caress the slender stalks of wheat on the blade . . . then everything spins out of control: the fire raging through our fields, the *kaid* arriving in his barouche, the cart that brought us to a place where there was no room for my dog . . . Jenane Jato . . . the barber singing, Peg-Leg, El Moro, Ouari and his goldfinches . . . Germaine opening her arms wide as my uncle watched tenderly . . . then Río Salado, always, forever, Río Salado . . .

I close my eyes to put an end to something, to put a stop to this story I have summoned a thousand times, and a thousand times revised. Eyelids are like secret doors; closed they tell us stories, open they look out on to ourselves. We are prisoners of our memories. Our eyes no longer belong to us . . . I look for Émilie in these endless reels of film but cannot find her. It is too late to go back to the cemetery and reclaim the dust of the rose petals; too late to go back to number 143 Rue des Frères-Julien, to become the sensible people who always make up in the end. I struggle through the crowds flooding the port of Oran in the summer of 1962; I see the terrified families on the quays sitting on what little luggage they managed to salvage, the children exhausted, sleeping on the ground, the steamships readying themselves to take the dispossessed into exile. I pan around, now a face, now a cry, an embrace, a fluttering handker-chief. I can see no sign of Émilie . . . And where am I in all this? I am simply a disembodied gaze moving over the crowd, moving between the blankness of absence and the nakedness of silence . . .

What am I to do with the night?

Who can I confide in?

In truth, I do not want to do anything with this night; I do not want to confide in anyone. One truth compensates for every other: all things come to an end, even grief is not eternal.

I take my courage in both hands, open the metal box and then the letter. It is dated one week before Émilie died. I take a deep breath and I read:

Dear Younes,

I waited for you the day after our meeting in Marseille. Waited in the same spot. I waited for you the next day and all the days that followed, but you never came back. Fate — mektoub, *as we say in our country. A tiny detail can change everything, for better or for worse. We learn to accept it. In time we become calmer, wiser. I regret all the terrible things I said to you. Perhaps that is why I never dared open your*

letters. There are silences that should not be broken. Like still
waters, they restore our soul.

Forgive me as I have forgiven you.

Here, where I am now, with Simon and all those I loved
and lost, I will always think of you.

Émilie.

Suddenly, it is as though all the stars in the heavens meld
into a single star, as though the night, the whole of the night,
has come into my hotel room to watch over me. Now I
know that wherever I go, I will sleep peacefully.

Marignane airport is quiet, there are no crowds, and the
queues for check-in gradually peter out. The Air Algérie
wing of the terminal is almost deserted. A couple of men
with vast suitcases – *trabendistes* to the initiated, indefatig-
able traffickers in contraband, the natural result of chronic
shortages and survival instinct – use every trick in the book
to negotiate their excess baggage, but the person at the
check-in desk is unimpressed. Behind them a couple of
pensioners with overloaded baggage trolleys patiently wait
their turn.

'Any luggage, sir?' the girl behind the counter asks me.

'Just this bag.'

'You want to take it as cabin baggage?'

'It would save me having to hang around when I arrive.'

'That's very true,' she says, handing back my passport.
'This is your boarding pass; boarding is at nine fifteen through
gate fourteen.'

My watch reads 8.22 a.m. I ask Gustave and Michel if
they would like to join me for a cup of coffee. We find a

table. Gustave tries to think of an interesting subject for conversation, without success. We drink our coffee in silence, staring into the middle distance. I think about Jean-Christophe Lamy. Yesterday I was on the point of asking Fabrice why our elder and better had not come, but my tongue shrivelled in my mouth and I said nothing. I found out from André that Jean-Christophe had attended Émilie's funeral, that Isabelle, who had come with him, was in fine form and that he had told both of them that I was coming to Aix . . . I'm sad about him.

There is a boarding call for flight AH 1069 to Oran, my flight. Gustave gives me a hug. Michel kisses me on both cheeks and says something I do not quite catch. I thank him for his hospitality and then take my leave of them.

I do not go to the boarding gate.

I order another coffee.

I wait.

My intuition tells me something is going to happen, that I have to be patient and stay here in my seat.

Last call for passengers on flight AH 1069 to Oran. A woman's voice comes over the loudspeakers. *Final boarding call for passengers travelling on flight AH 1069.*

My coffee cup is empty, my mind is empty. I am floating in empty space. The minutes tramp across my shoulders like elephants. My back hurts, my knees hurt, my stomach hurts. The voice from the loudspeaker is drilling into my brain. Now I am personally being summoned to gate 14. *Would Monsieur Mahieddine Younes please come to gate 14, the flight is now closing . . .*

My intuition is none too good in its old age, I say to myself. Time to go; there's no point waiting any longer. Get a move on or you'll miss your flight, and you've got a grandson to marry three days from now . . .

I pick up my bag and head towards the boarding gate. Hardly have I reached it when I hear a voice call me from the depths of I don't know what:

'Jonas!'

It's Jean-Christophe.

There he is, standing behind the yellow line, wrapped up in a thick coat, his hair snow-white, his shoulders bowed, as old as the world.

'I was starting to give up hope,' I said, coming back towards him.

'God knows, I tried to stay away.'

'It's good to see you're still the same stubborn bastard. But don't you think at our age we're past all this foolish pride? We're already living on borrowed time. There aren't many pleasures left in our twilight years, and there is no greater pleasure than seeing the face of a friend you lost forty-five years ago.'

We throw our arms around each other, drawn by a powerful magnet, like two rivers coursing from opposite extremes bearing all the emotions in the world, which, having rushed past hill and valley, come together suddenly to form a single raging torrent of spume and eddies. I can hear our two old bodies collide, the dry rustle of our suits impossible to distinguish from the dry rustle of our skin. Time marks a pause. There is no one in the world but us. We hug each other hard as once we used to hug our dreams to us, convinced that if we were to relax our grip, even a fraction, they would slip away. We hold each other up with these ancient bodies worn to the marrow in a storm of creaks and groans. We are no more than two frayed nerves, two exposed wires that might short-circuit at any moment, two ancient children sobbing uncontrollably as strangers stand and watch.

Would Monsieur Mahieddine Younes please come immediately to gate 14, your flight is closing . . . The woman's voice roars over the loudspeakers.

'Where have you been?' I ask, holding him at arm's length so I can look at him.

'I'm here now, that's all that matters.'

'It is.'

We hug each other again.

'I'm so happy.'

'So am I, Jonas.'

'Were you around yesterday and the day before?'

'No, I was in Nice. Fabrice phoned and called me every name under the sun, then Dédé called. I told them I wasn't coming. Then, this morning, Isabelle practically kicked me out at five o'clock in the morning. I drove like a maniac. At my age.'

'How is Isabelle?'

'Exactly the same as when you knew her. Indestructible and impossible . . . What about you?'

'I can't complain.'

'You look good . . . Have you seen Dédé? You know he's really ill. He only made the trip for your sake. How was the reunion?'

'We laughed until we cried, and then we just cried . . .'

'I can imagine.'

Would Monsieur Mahieddine Younes please come immediately to gate 14, your flight is closing.

'What about Río Salado, how are things in Río?'

'Why don't you come and see for yourself?'

'Have I been forgiven?'

'What about you, have you forgiven?'

'I'm too old, Jonas, I don't have the energy to bear a grudge any more; just getting annoyed wears me out.'

'You see? I still live in the same house, right opposite the vineyards. It's just me, these days; my wife died ten years ago. I have one son who's married and living in Tamarasset and a daughter who's a professor at Concordia University in Montreal. It's not like I don't have the space. You can have your pick of bedrooms, they're all empty. The wooden horse you gave me to apologise for beating me up over Isabelle is right where you last saw it, on the mantelpiece.'

An Air Algérie employee comes up to me.

'Are you flying to Oran?'

'Yes.'

'Mahieddine Younes?'

'That's me.'

'If you wouldn't mind, the plane is waiting to leave. You need to board now.'

Jean-Christophe gives me a wink.

'*Tabqa 'ala kher*, Jonas. Go in peace.'

He hugs me again, and I can feel his body trembling in my arms. Our embrace lasts for an eternity – to the irritation of the Air Algérie attendant. Jean-Christophe is the first to break away. His voice choked, his eyes red, he says in a small voice:

'Go on, get going . . .'

'I'll be waiting for you,' I say.

'I'll come, I promise.'

He smiles.

I hurry to make my flight, the Air Algérie attendant in front, clearing a path through the queues, through the baggage scanner, through immigration. As I arrive airside, I turn around one last time to see what I am leaving behind, and I see them *all*, the living and the dead, standing at the window waving me goodbye.

www.vintage-books.co.uk